CAST OF CH

Archy Mitfold. A clever young man German with the idea of joining the Foreign Office.

Tony Wynkerrell. An old school chum of Archy's from St. Crispin's, now a prosperous junior partner in a very peculiar bookshop.

Philip Beltane. A levelheaded junior schoolmaster, also an old boy from St. Crispin's.

Marian Leaf. Archy's sensible aunt, with whom he lives.

Agatha Pell. An ill-tempered octogenarian, a former suffragette who is now a Fascist. Marian's godmother, Mrs. Pell lives with her daughter **Kathleen Byron**, who's twice widowed, at least once suspiciously.

Professor August Speyer. A German national who is tutoring Archy in his native language. He's a member of the Nordic Bond.

Rod and Frances Beaton. A young doctor and his wife, still newlyweds, who live next door to Marian Leaf.

Netta Traill. Their calm, observant maid.

Vera Moffat. Marian Leaf's equally helpful maid.

Sampson Vick. A missing millionaire/philanthropist, one of England's richest men, whose disappearance is of great interest to Archy.

Beatrice Vick. Sampson's wife.

Humphrey Vick. His brother, a notorious Chicago gangster.

Leofric Williams. Wynkerrell's senior partner in the bookshop.

Mr. Caffey. An irascible old man who belongs to the Nordic Bond.

Bianca Tommaseo. Formerly Bianca Vick, widow of Humphrey Vick.

Chief Inspector Dan Pardoe. The youngest chief inspector at Scotland Yard, a lean, pleasant man of forty with prematurely white hair.

Detective Sergeant Tommy Salt. Pardoe's loyal sidekick.

Plus assorted police officers, friends, servants, students, schoolmasters, secretaries, and family members.

Books by Dorothy Bowers

Postscript to Poison (1938)
Shadows Before (1939)
Deed Without a Name (1940)
Fear and Miss Betony (1941)
The Bells of Old Bailey (1947)

DEED WITHOUT
A NAME

Dorothy Bowers

What is't you do?
A deed without a name.
　　　　—MACBETH

Rue Morgue Press
Lyons / Boulder

TO MAY

The author's grateful acknowledgments are due to Messrs. J. M. Dent &
Sons, Ltd. for their kind permission to name in Chapter XXIII a bird book
published by them, and for allowing Inspector Pardoe a quotation from it.

The reader's indulgence is begged for the fanciful play made with the to-
pography of Chelsea. Needless to say, Pentagon Square, Rossetti Terrace,
Hammer Street and Mulberry Fountain are not, nor ever were, part and parcel
of that district's charm. What is more, neither the murders, the murderer, his
victims nor any of the other characters, incidents, houses, shops, clubs and
cinemas influencing and circumscribing the action have the slightest founda-
tion in fact. In short, places, people and plot have their being only in the
imagination of the writer.

Deed Without a Name
Copyright © 1940, 1968 by Dorothy Bowers
and Evelyn M. Bowers
New Material Copyright © 2005
The Rue Morgue Press

For information on our titles see
www.ruemorguepress.com
or call
800-699-6214
or write
The Rue Morgue Press
P.O. Box 4119
Boulder, CO 80306

ISBN: 0-915230-82-8

Printed by
Johnson Printing

PRINTED IN THE UNITED STATES OF AMERICA

About the author

Dorothy Bowers (1902-1948) was well on her way to establishing herself as one of Britain's leading mystery writers when she succumbed to tuberculosis at the age of 46. Her first Inspector Dan Pardoe novel, *Postscript to Poison*, was published in England in 1938 to enthusiastic reviews ("She ranks with the best."—*The London Times*). Three more Pardoe books followed, one a year until 1941, when Bowers left her longtime home in Monmouth for London, to do war work for the European News Service of the BBC. Her fifth and final novel was published in 1947, and she was elected to the prestigious Detection Club in 1948, shortly before her untimely death.

She was born on June 11, 1902, in Leonminster, Herefordshire, the second daughter of Albert Edwards Bowers, a confectioner who moved his family to Monmouth in 1903. He operated his own bakery on Agincourt Square in that city until he retired in 1936. Dorothy's early education was at the Monmouth School for Girls. She went up to Oxford on October 13, 1923, when she was twenty-one, a somewhat advanced age for a first-year student, though one should also remember that Oxford only started awarding degrees to women in 1920. She took a third honors in Modern History in 1926 from The Society of Oxford Home Students (now St. Anne's College) and returned to Monmouth to pursue a reluctant career as a history mistress, although her first love was writing. Her happiest memories during that time were of her days at Oxford.

In addition to her writing and substitute teaching duties, Dorothy compiled crossword puzzles for *John O'London Weekly* from 1936 to 1943 and for *Country Life* from 1940 to 1946. Like her sister and many of her Oxford friends, she never married. She died at Tupsley, Hereford, on Sunday, Aug. 29, 1948, at the age of 46, with her sister May at her bedside, and was buried near her mother.

For more information on Bowers see the introduction by Tom & Enid Schantz to The Rue Morgue Press edition of *Postscript to Poison*.

CHAPTER I: RIDDLE-ME-REE

Mischief, thou art afoot.
JULIUS CAESAR.

"YOU CAN HARDLY put it down to coincidence," Beltane protested. "Two perhaps, but not three." It was characteristic of him to register formal dissent from an opinion nobody had voiced.

Tony Wynkerrell gave a sly smile. He was finding it agreeable after four cups of tea to lounge by a good fire in another man's rooms on an October afternoon, listening to the rumble of Victoria Street below, and reflect how well Beltane did himself wartime weekends on a junior schoolmaster's salary.

"Our good Philip is revolted at the mere idea," he said in his languid voice, a lazily roving eye taking in both young men, "though actually it's the alternative should revolt him more. But it's the academic mind that does it. Catch a schoolmaster countenancing such frivolous tampering with logic as coincidence implies. He's all for cause and effect, not a bit of byplay against the rules. So—Archy's accidents can't be accidental. So—"

"So you're a confounded ass, Winkle." Beltane took him up hastily in a tone less good-tempered than the words. "Blow your blinking cause and effect. You're simply talking for the one without the other. It isn't a question of what I or you—"

"Oh, shut up, both," said Archy Mitfold, wriggling further back on the rug as the fire spouted fresh heat. He hugged his knees more tightly, with a sideways glance to the left at Tony's elegant legs slung across the arm of his chair, then to the right where Philip lolled, pulling at his pipe in short vexed puffs. He was feeling for both an unflattering distaste he did not experience on those occasions when he had each alone. The St. Crispin's Old Boys' lunch, attended annually by an ill-assorted gathering of Crispians, where one looked hopefully for one's contemporaries and then wished one hadn't found them, was as liable to prod ancient antagonisms as fail to fan the spark of some deathless friendship, and he half regretted the impulse which had made him wind up a disappointing afternoon at Philip's hotel with an account of his own misadventures.

Not that he had told them everything. Not by a long chalk. It would not do at this stage. But these two would make even a synopsis an excuse for the bickering which, because it had persisted since schooldays, seemed to him merely puerile.

He drew a quick breath and said with a rush before either could speak: "I know what you mean. I'm beginning to think the same thing. My accidents can't be accidental. Very well, there's only one thing they can be—and that's attempted murder."

"Rubbish," Beltane said briefly in his best housemaster manner, detecting the shrill note that sharpened the last word. "You've no proof even that the chocolates were tampered with since you've not had them analyzed."

"All right," Archy said. "But if you deny coincidence I don't see, like Winkle, what else you've got to admit but murder. Anyway, if there is a yearning to bump me off it won't stop at this. There will be another go soon."

A faint excitement behind the unemphatic words communicated itself to the other two.

"Look here, old man," Beltane urged, "forget what I said about coincidence. I know—everybody knows—it plays some damned odd tricks. You had a beastly tummy-ache, p'raps from a chill or something you'd eaten, and you immediately put it down to an anonymous gift of chocolates—*because* they were anonymous, I've no doubt. As for—"

"Yes. As for being nearly pushed under a train and all but run down by a car driven by a maniac—how do you square that with nerves and imagination?"

"I don't. People are always falling under trains or being sent to kingdom come by somebody's bus, more's the pity. But it's seldom with malice aforethought, I believe."

Wynkerrell laughed. "Excuse my vulgar hoots, old man. But it is rather funny listening to your earnest repudiation of the murder theory. Actually you were all for it just now. Nice of you, of course, to try cheering the poor patient. Oh, keep your hair on—you'll want a bit for Smith Minor on Monday. And I'm probably as averse as you are to having our little Archy murdered. There's no reason why he shouldn't bear his burden awhile longer in this vale of tears, apart from what the Foreign Office is going to miss if his diplomatic career's over before it begins. But facts are facts—and you've missed one or two of them, my good Bel. Of course you get a poor ass now and again with a weakness for falling on the electric line, and if it's not suicidal it's at a moment when the platform's jammed to the brim. *But*—I understand from Archy that his particular weakness overcame him at Sloane Square in what was definitely not the rush hour, and that he felt a smart push in the back as he moved toward the incoming train. Right, Mitfold?"

"Precisely," Archy agreed, his face oddly flushed. "There certainly wasn't a jam, and nobody, I thought, really close to me. I slipped on my knees, anyway, and grazed both hands clutching futilely at the edge of the platform, and somebody shouted, and somebody else squealed and the next thing I knew a woman had me by the arm and was dragging me back."

"You see. And while Archy was being patted and brushed and squeaked over the gentleman we should all like to know something about was probably showing the station a clean pair of heels."

"You know it was a man who pushed you then?" Beltane asked.

"Of course not," said Archy with a touch of impatience. "Haven't I said I didn't see anybody, only felt a shove? But naturally one doesn't first take for granted it's a woman doing that sort of thing."

"Not exactly a flattering assumption," Wynkerrell conceded.

"Matter of fact it was a woman nearest me. The one who yelped and grabbed me. But—"

Wynkerrell's feet described a parabola and came to rest by Archy. "Did you see her properly?"

"If you mean should I know her again, well—it was the wrong time to be very receptive. But, yes, I think I might."

"That's all right then. You can keep your eyes skinned for her at any rate. She'll know you saw her, and if she was up to anything she'll probably lie low."

"Hence an attempt through the post, I suppose," Archy said. He got up and began a restless perambulation of the room, fingering objects aimlessly, his usual supercilious expression replaced by one of barely suppressed excitement.

"By Jove, yes," Wynkerrell exclaimed. "The chocolates—she could be at the bottom of that too! One attempt in person, another—"

"Meantime," Beltane interrupted smoothly, "aren't you overlooking an important thing? The shilling shocker you're spinning won't get far without it. And that's motive. If we're determined to think somebody's trying to kill Mitfold we shall have to go further and consider why. The motive found, you're leagues nearer tracing the man."

"That's right," Wynkerrell said. "Providing there *is* a motive. Suppose it's a case of homicidal mania?"

Beltane was politely startled. "My dear Winkle, you have still the goriest mind of any man of my acquaintance. Not content with getting Archy murdered, you'd like to expose the lot of us to the tender mercies of a madman. Well, happily, I don't think that suggestion will hold water. A murderer of those unbridled tastes would hardly concentrate his attacks on a single victim."

"How the deuce d'you know he has?" was the shrewd retort. "We're not in a position to say he's confined his attentions to Archy."

"Perhaps not. But though I'm no authority on criminal mentality, I must say these attacks—if they are attacks—don't bear the peculiar monomark of the maniac. Not like Neill Cream and Jack the Ripper, for instance, whose methods, I believe, never varied."

This was firmer ground, and Wynkerrell admitted it.

"But I don't know if the Ripper's a sound example, all the same," he said. "It's thought he had a motive of sorts—mind you, it probably drove him crazy. Question is, should madness born of motive as well as motive born of madness constitute homicidal mania? I don't think so."

The knotty problem went unargued. Beltane had become too conscious of Archy's tour of the furniture to be sidetracked to anything so entirely academic. This purposeless padding about made him think of the zoo; it was unpleasantly infectious, and in another minute he felt he, too, would be on the prowl.

"Dammit, Mitfold," he burst out savagely, "can't you keep still? You're fretting your nerves to rags—mine too. If you feel as bad about it as all that why don't you go to the police?"

It was Wynkerrell who looked surprised. Archy stood still between them, his arms tightly folded, a smile for the temper he had provoked.

"Your mistake, Bel," he said. "My nerves are O.K. I think better when I'm on the move, that's all. As for the police, give me the chance. I came here prepared to believe I might only have run into a patch of bad luck. But now I've aired the whole thing you've convinced me that's unlikely. And I think I won't ask a policeman—yet. I'll handle this job myself."

He spoke with a mixture of defiance and vanity, spiced perhaps with the malice that comes from a superior knowledge there is no intention to disclose.

Beltane shrugged. "Please yourself. It's for you to decide, of course. I don't share your enthusiasm for amateur snooping—even in self-defense."

"Particularly in self-defense," Wynkerrell amended. "Must you look so Napoleonic, Archy? I don't wonder people want to murder you. Bel's right for once—if you muff it, and it is a murderer you're up against, you're pretty well done. Besides, that's what the Yard's for, to look into your sort of hoodoo. What does Miss Leaf say?"

"My aunt? Oh, she'd agree with you. But she doesn't know much about it."

"Why not?" asked Beltane.

"Oh, well—I don't know." Archy seemed embarrassed. "It's not the sort of thing to drag her into. And my own suspicions weren't properly formed. She knew how groggy I was, of course, soon after the chocolates came, but I hid the things away without saying what I thought."

"But didn't she eat any of 'em herself?" Wynkerrell broke in. "Greedy, greedy, Archy."

"Not at all. She's on a diet."

"Oh. One ought to commiserate with her then, but it seems congratulations are more the thing now."

"But what about motive?" Beltane insisted. "You're giving no attention to the very root of the matter. We've got the smoke—we ought to look for the fire. What've you been up to lately?"

"To inspire some manly—or womanly—breast with homicidal yearnings?" Wynkerrell finished. "What indeed? Stealing some other bloke's purse, honor, wife or mother-in-law? Or p'raps you're somebody's heir and the next of kin or what-d'ye-call-'em thinks you a bit superfluous? Which is it? Cough it up, my lad."

"That's just it," said Archy cautiously, using the phrase that invariably precedes an indecisive statement. "Exactly what I'm wondering myself. I don't honestly know. I mean, how it is I've got in the way. In fact I'm working— I mean, I'm going to work—along those lines. That's why I don't want to make it a police affair. Not immediately, anyway. If they've got to be brought in I've a fancy to have—well, something more complete to offer them."

"So's they can pat the brilliant tyro on the back and offer him a job in the force," Wynkerrell said lightly, glancing at his watch. As junior partner in a peculiarly selective bookshop in Hobby Court off Conduit Street he was prone to spasms of energy his friends found amusing. "I say, I've got to be rolling along—fellow to ring up about viewing a library. And I think it might be tactful to leave Bel to grapple with those acres of corrections which, of course, he never forgets to bring up with him on Saturdays. Drop you at the Fountain, Archy? There's still a drop of juice in the old bus so we needn't hoof it yet."

"I'm not there this weekend. Aunt's gone country visiting till Monday night, and the Pells are giving me a shakedown." He gave an address in Old Brompton. "Out of your way, I'm afraid."

"Not a bit. I'd like a run while it's still light."

Beltane came down, too, and waited with Archy on the pavement outside while Wynkerrell brought the car round. Their talk ranged idly over the Old Boys' reunion and the possibility that it might be the last for a year or two. But Philip's remarks were absent and a little curt. It struck Archy all at once that he had shown a bored indifference since they had failed to supply a motive for the alleged attacks upon himself. He flushed hotly as it occurred to him for the first time that Philip did not believe his story.

A passerby, crossing the street with an evening paper, paused near them a moment to read the headlines. They caught the staring words:

SAMPSON VICK: IS HE DEAD?
NINETEENTH DAY: NO NEWS

"Funny thing," Beltane said abruptly, "for a millionaire in this country to vanish like a wisp of smoke. Nearly three weeks now, and they're no forrader."

CHAPTER II: A VISIT AND A VISITOR

Enter first Murderer to the door.
STAGE DIRECTION, MACBETH.

DINNER WAS OVER at the Pells', and old Mrs. Pell had brought out her patience cards. She was an octogenarian of forcible character whose post-prandial sympathies did not embrace the young, guest or no guest. Games on a competitive basis she abhorred; there was always the chance that her opponent might win. So her fumbling old fingers started to arrange the soiled little cards as prescribed for the solitary and satisfying pastime known as Miss Milligan.

A widow herself, she lived with her widowed daughter in an expensively furnished, frowsty old house five minutes' walk from Queen's Gate. Its dining-room windows looked out upon the Square garden, pleasant enough in summer, but just now the repository of decaying Michaelmas daisies which by daylight looked like the less agreeable relics of a bygone time.

Their qualities were shared by the old lady herself. Age which had withered had never humanized her. For Agatha Pell there had been no mellowing process, for, without reconciling herself to the times she had lived through, she had always contrived to adopt their more militant virtues. In a day when the appearance of women on public platforms was still thought worth an argument she had succeeded in rousing to a frenzy of anti-Boer sentiment scores of bewildered matrons who had felt constrained to go home and consult at-lases before they could be sure of Cape Colony's whereabouts; in her sixtieth year she had repeatedly attached herself to the railings of Downing Street, stuck hatpins in policemen and lain down in front of ministerial cars for the sake of a vote which could not have given her a jot more power than she already wielded; and in the war of 1914 she had made it her business to see that, however strict an economy might be practiced in other directions, a liberal supply of white feathers was always at hand for distribution.

Such exertions had at least expressed her sense of masculine inferiority. It was twenty-five years since Brigadier General Pell, who had struggled unsuccessfully against this conviction throughout their married life, had abandoned for good a domestic career incomparably more lively than his professional, and nobody would have been more astonished than he to learn that Time's blurry spectacles had by now obliterated most of his defects. In other respects, however, his widow remained unsoftened and, though it had seemed as if the effete period following Versailles would offer no scope for her enthusiasms, the totalitarian states soon obliged with an ideal. She had become an avowed Fascist, black and brown, too little hampered by consistency to remark that the position to which women were relegated under the new regimes clashed with her own feminist outlook. Nor at the beginning of a new war had she found it more difficult to unite her approval of the Nazis to an uncomfortable display of patriotism than had Herr Hitler to persuade Russia into the Anti-Comintern Pact. Both had found easy of adjustment inconsiderable trifles like those.

As godmother to Marian Leaf she had invited Archy Mitfold to stay at her house from Friday evening till Monday while his aunt was away.

Not that she liked the young man. Apart from her contempt for men in general, she despised anybody over twenty who had not firmly wedged himself in a permanent and, preferably, violent career. That the physical disability of a maimed hand was keeping her guest out of khaki was neither here nor there. The world (on this side of the Channel at any rate) had grown soft. People were even silly enough to respect other people's consciences. But if white feathers were a little *démodé* nowadays there might be further ways, still more potent perhaps, of expressing disapproval.

Meantime, it was some consolation to know that pretty soon now the army would have drawn into its fold Archy's lounge-lizard friend who had brought him home this evening. Beneath the deference these young men were careful to pay her she was quick to detect a mockery that stung by its very tolerance. They laughed at her, she was sure. Their youth, too, made her acutely conscious of age. It brought to the surface the thoughts of mortality she was at pains to keep in the background.

What was worse, Archy himself was secretive. Agatha Pell was an aggressively inquisitive old woman, and reticence, especially when coupled with the sort of excitement which had been growing on the boy since his arrival yesterday, she regarded as a personal affront.

"Where's he got to now?" she demanded, a knave of clubs poised in her knuckly fingers, shooting a glance at her daughter who stood on the hearth turning over the pages of the morning paper.

"Going out," said Mrs. Byron laconically, and added, "to a tutorial—he says."

Her tone was dreamy, but when she folded the newspaper with a sudden discordant crackle there was nothing absentminded in the look she directed at her mother.

Kathleen Byron was a large woman of deceptively benign appearance. Her smooth white forehead, ample though controlled curves and warm brown hair unstreaked with gray suggested comfortable maternal instincts and drew men's eyes and women's hearts—but only temporarily. At a pinch, and pinches were frequent, the domestic staff preferred dealing with Mrs. Pell. Kathleen's large, full eyes had the amber clarity of a goat's, and something, too, perhaps, of that animal's innocent unchastity. Between her mother and herself there was seldom any verbal conflict. Mrs. Pell recognized a quality bluster could not dominate, Mrs. Byron a stupidity unamenable to correction. But the old lady was not so insensitive as to be wholly unsuspicious of her daughter's opinion of her. Behind those clear, gentle eyes who knew what thoughts ranged?

There was a sound on the stairs. The third tread from the bottom always creaked. The front door banged quickly.

"Without so much as a good evening," said Agatha Pell, who herself had no manners to speak of.

The two women exchanged a long look. Then the old one went back to her play with a vicious resolve to cheat if the aces lagged behind any longer, while her daughter slowly left the room.

It was nearly half past eight when Archy Mitfold came out into Old Brompton Road.

Though cold, the air had a clear buoyancy that did not chill. The fogs through which London might be groping and coughing its way in a month or so had not yet arrived. Only a finespun mist, too delicate to be more than sensed, blurred the unlit streets. On nights before the city had withdrawn into the shadows it had been a veil for the meanest design to shine through, blue and mysterious. Then the lamps might prick it, the sky signs burn it with rivulets of fire, every garish light prewar London could produce rip and splash and violate it, it still hung there, the indefinable beauty a great artist had once recognized and recorded.

But the second month of the blackout, with a moon-clouded night thrown in, was no time for appreciation. Archy pulled the collar of his coat up round his ears and the brim of his hat down over his nose, felt in his pocket for the key he knew was there and stepped out with confidence in the direction of Onslow Gardens. But the Gardens were not his objective. In Selwood Terrace he had the luck to pick up a taxi which had just disgorged. He asked, cautiously, to be put down in King's Road at the corner of Markham Street, and had covered the bulk of his journey in a few minutes.

Mulberry Fountain, where Miss Leaf lived when she was at home, is the smallest square in Chelsea. Bounded northwest by King's Road and southeast by Burton's Court and the Hospital, its forgotten charm encloses less than a dozen houses tucked away somewhere behind Wellington Square. The most sensible approach to it for anyone alighting at Markham Street is direct from King's Road. But, Archy reflected, sensible was only a relative term when you were stuck in the sort of bog which had fastened upon him lately. He wanted at all costs to be inconspicuous, a desire which in the circumstances should have been easy of realization. But Archy did not think his particular nemesis likely to be deterred by a blackness obliterating known landmarks.

So he paid his fare, tipping the gratified driver injudiciously, then dived into Smith Street, round into St. Leonard's Terrace and, after one or two more dodges, came out into a little cul-de-sac forming an outlet for the backs of houses in a road east of Mulberry Fountain. It yawned silent, deserted, almost invisible. Its mouth might be discerned as a thinning of the blackness that stretched unbroken on either side, but at the blocked end where Miss Leaf's garden ran down to meet the wall darkness was velvety and complete.

Archy glanced behind him. There was nobody about. The few windows that looked now only by day on the cul-de-sac turned blind eyes to the night. A small shadow close to the ground suddenly detached itself from the greater shadow as from a vast curtain and streaked from gutter to gutter with feline self-effacement. The place preserved a bleak stillness.

Archy gave a second glance over his shoulder. Then he took from his pocket a torch and switched it on, directing toward his feet the wan light penetrating its folds of paper. In a moment he was at the end of the alley and feeling for foothold in the aged brick wall; the next he was over, the damp grass of the garden under his feet and to his left a dark, writhing shape like a Rackham monstrosity that was only the old apple tree struggling to become visible.

Switching off his light as a preliminary measure he stood quite still for a few seconds, every sense alert, hearing strained for the distant swell and ebb of traffic. Its mumble reached him as a kind of accompaniment to the small sounds close at hand, the drowsy twitter of a bird in the laurels, a blown leaf's quick crackle on the path, the sudden cool, rounded notes of an owl in a neighbor's garden. As he moved forward the sharp split and squash of an apple crushed underfoot momentarily disturbed his balance and set his heart absurdly thumping. It was nothing. There was nobody near. But for all that he steered a course to the back of the house without the aid of the torch.

Like its companions at the end of the square, number eight was a semidetached example of lofty Victorian architecture possessing a basement. At the back a flight of ten steps, bands of white painted on the treads for guidance, led down from the garden to the kitchen, and four steps more, crossing the well of this flight at a right angle, formed an ascent from the garden to the back door at the top of the kitchen stairs. That door, locked like the rest, had its key, Archy knew, on the inside. He went down the basement flight and unlocked the door with the key he had taken from his pocket, locking it again behind him.

The kitchen struck one as chill and almost aggressively empty. With the flashlight on, the scrubbed boards and vacant, shining range sprang vaguely into view, with the glimmering window pressed closely by a bank of ferns outside, which even on the brightest day contrived to give a submarine effect to the light in the kitchen.

There was nothing here to linger for. Through an open door and across a strip of matting lay the breakfast room, and to your left before you entered it a curving flight of wooden stairs went up to the ground floor. Archy mounted them softly, listening with an attention that surprised one part of his mind to the sound of his own breathing, the pressure of his own feet and the tick of the grandfather clock in the hall, a voice crying in the wilderness with a sublime indifference to the fact that none heeded it.

It was curious and a little disquieting that the unpeopled quality of a house vacated for hardly more than a day should be felt so urgently. Not a board creaked, and now at once as Archy gained the short passage leading into the front hall all sound of the world outside was muted. At the angle of the passage the staircase to the bedrooms rose; beyond the foot of the stairs stretched the dense cavern of the hall ending at the front door.

Archy's business was not there. At his right hand, a few steps from the top of the basement stairs, the milky light of the torch picked out a closed door. He opened it with exaggerated care, putting out the light and pressing his body against the movement of the door as he went in. The blackness yawned in his face, silent and inhospitable as the rest of the house. Only the windows on his right that stared out upon the garden and the cul-de-sac by which he had come began to spill a gray, vapory light on the gloom.

He turned on his flashlight again and, going up to the windows, pulled across them the black curtains his aunt had provided in compliance with the rule. Then he went back to the door and pressed down the light switch.

In the glare of electricity the room looked at once harmless and civilized. It was a small sitting room pleasantly furnished and, to Archy, suddenly a box of brightness and security in a shaft of intolerable darkness. At thought of the obscurity outside this room he had a mastering desire to turn on every light in the house and by so doing to force upon it the habitation and comfort it lacked. But, remembering he would have to black out every window before indulging such a whim, he checked himself and stayed where he was, taking off his hat and overcoat and placing them on a chair.

In the light his movements had lost their tiptoe character. They were assured and quick, as though he knew exactly what he had to do but had little time to do it in. In the angle of the room between windows and fireplace stood a flat-topped desk, its surface clear of everything but inkwell and blotter. He unlocked the top drawer on the right and, from beneath other notebooks and papers, drew out a small, thick book bound in stiff red covers. He skimmed it lightly with a trace of pleasurable excitement in his eyes and parted lips. Then he sat down at the desk and began a close examination of those pages already covered with handwriting.

But over here the light, dimmed by shades recently painted blue, was weak and not conducive to comfortable study. Archy got up and, after turning on the electric fire, seated himself on a small couch beneath the pool of light thrown downward from the chandelier. He took a fountain pen from his pocket and after a moment's thought began steadily to write.

He looked up sharply. The initial stage of coming into an empty house and giving it a semblance of life by introducing light and occupation was wearing off. The surrounding silence now had swelled into something monstrously oppressive. The house was holding its breath. It might at any moment expel it, not in one mighty, reassuring shout, but in sibilant, fading whispers, as fearful of rousing his attention as he was himself of making his presence known.

Had it begun, the whispering? Something, not so much sound as a ruffling of the smooth silence, had jerked his head up and made his pen scratch wildly across the page. But as soon as he listened for it he could neither define nor recall what he thought he had heard. The great wave of silence had washed back over the house. He bent his head, but now it was tilted at a stiff angle, and his gaze remained lifted to the black curtains obscuring the windows, giving him a queer look of grim watchfulness that swamped fear.

The flow of composition was gone, and even when he lowered his eyes to the page once more he did not go on writing but began instead idly to make small marginal sketches.

He glanced at his watch. It was ten minutes to ten. Time he got back to the Pells. He added a few squiggles to the tiny drawing he had just scratched in and looked at it thoughtfully with a kind of vindictive satisfaction.

The knocker on the front door sounded three sharp raps.

Archy's hand flew wide, and the book slid from his lap. But he caught it before it fell. His legs were trembling as he stood up, but all at once he was angry at the cold which assailed him and the miserable fears he had been prey to since climbing into the garden. The house had broken silence and with it a tension he had not realized was unbearable until it was over. It was probably the warden. He glanced at the curtains. A chink might be gleaming. They had been here before.

He opened the door. In the dark passage outside he heard the bell shrill shortly.

It must be the warden, or else the police, impatient to douse his light. To turn it out now and do nothing would only arouse suspicion; besides, it had been detected from the back, and whoever had come round to the front to tell him about it would not know it had gone out. He stepped out into the smothering blackness of the hall.

As he groped for the latch of the front door he felt against the wall the hard pressure of the torch in his pocket. It gave him oddly an access of courage that made him open the door wide to his unknown caller.

The dark square was light by contrast to the blackness of the house. But the figure that confronted him was invisible except as a shape. A shape that wore no uniform. Regardless of rules he turned his flashlight boldly on its face.

In the brief silence that was like eternity there was no footfall in the road to give him courage.

"Oh, it's you, is it?" said Archy Mitfold, and laughed in a way that choked the breath in his throat as he admitted his visitor to the house.

CHAPTER III: DING, DONG, BELL

Dro. S. Do you not hear it ring?
Adr.   What, the chain?
Dro. S. No, no, the bell.
THE COMEDY OF ERRORS.

NETTA TRAILL, the Beatons' maid at number seven Mulberry Fountain, was a girl of intelligence and spirit. Victorian employers would have dubbed her a treasure and left it at that; her present ones were only too thankful to know that she regarded them as treasures it would be inexpedient to exchange.

She woke on Sunday morning, October 15, with an indefinite memory of something left over from last night. Whatever it was had been queer and unexplained. She chased it in vain for a few minutes, then when she was thinking of something else it suddenly returned to her.

A bell had rung last night in Miss Leaf's house next door. Not the front doorbell. That wasn't audible in number seven. It had been one of the service bells in the kitchen, and Netta, who had been in her own kitchen before going up to bed, had heard the unmusical tinkle clearly, three harsh little clangs. It had given her a turn. She had not liked it at all, still less carrying to bed the thought of it and the conjectures it raised. And now, with the sun shining and a fine day ahead, it was really no more agreeable.

Netta was neither abnormally superstitious nor in the least hysterical. It was true that she dutifully observed certain procedures following the spilling of salt, the sight of a single crow or the presence of a ladder straddling the pavement. She enjoyed studying the horoscopes of Herr Hitler, President Roosevelt and Miss Shirley Temple, and still more her own weekly forecast thoughtfully supplied by the *Daily Call*. But, even while she indulged herself, one part of her mind, and a part to be reckoned with, told her quite firmly that everything would be just the same, if a little less exciting, if she didn't bother with any of it. It was admittedly nice to imagine from time to time that one was compassed about with devils and crystals and fates, inexorable stars and malevolent spirits, but it was easy to see that they had no more to do with real living, as expressed in terms of washing up and walking out with a boy, than had Snow White or Ferdinand the Bull.

So when Netta heard a bell ring at night in the kitchen of a house left empty and locked up for the weekend, she was wholesomely skeptical of a super-natural explanation. Insistence on reality raised, of course, a number of difficulties. If you decided it was a ghost, well and good—you must leave it at that. You might be as jittery as you like, there was nothing you could do about it. Ghosts were permitted to ring bells, rap tables, toss pats of butter about and indulge in all sorts of unseemly tricks with impunity. You just had to feel your goose flesh and put up with their prankish foibles. But if a human being started the same practices, that was a different matter entirely. There were things that in spite of fear one could and ought to do. But it was not always easy to decide what.

Up to now she had taken neither Dr. nor Mrs. Beaton into her confidence. The doctor, in fact, had been out to all hours on an exacting case, and Mrs. Beaton, who hadn't been Mrs. Beaton overlong, was inclined to be anxious about his comings and goings in the blackout. Though she remained cheerful, practical and uncomplaining, her apparent unconcern never deceived Netta. And such occasions did not seem appropriate for drawing the attention of a worried wife to odd happenings next door.

However, the thought that her silence might have helped a burglar to decamp with his spoil weighed upon her as she went about her light Sunday duties. Eyeing the array of bells in her own kitchen, some of the clappers rusty from disuse, it occurred to her how easily a strange man in a dark house might accidentally stumble against a bellpull. Her imagination went further. Number eight, though she had never been inside it, was probably twin in most respects to number seven; and in the dining room and drawing room were ornamental bellpulls, brass handles that you jerked down, each side the fireplaces. How natural, then, for a burglar, groping toward the mantelpiece for clocks and brass candlesticks to stuff in his bag, to grip one of these in passing! Netta sighed. She liked Miss Leaf, and it was a shame, that it was, that she couldn't turn her back on the house a couple of days without something happening.

At ten o'clock when Mrs. Beaton came in from the garden with a few late dahlias for the dining-room table Netta could keep it in no longer.

Frances Beaton drew her thick, dark brows together, puckered merry eyes and gave generous attention to the dramatic rendering presented to her. When it was over Netta waited a moment for her verdict.

"Mice," said Mrs. Beaton firmly. She had a blunt, crisp form of expression that was reassuring because it carried conviction. "They run over the wires, you know, and make them jangle."

"In *some* houses they do," said Netta, jealous for the good name of Mulberry Fountain, "but they never did here, not till now. And this wasn't a jangle or a whirring. It was a proper ring. It would take a big fat mouse to do that."

"Well, why shouldn't it have been a big fat mouse?" Mrs. Beaton rejoined. "There's not much you *will* believe, is there? We get to your faith by a process of elimination, Netta." She went out laughing.

Netta had no idea what she meant, but it was Mrs. Beaton's way, bless her, and she returned to her own jobs sufficiently fortified to put the bells at number seven right out of her mind.

They came back in another guise at half past eleven.

Six weeks ago the Beatons' cat had presented her annoyed household with another quiverful. That her gesture was deemed superfluous and treated as such by the most direct method in no wise disturbed her complacency. Self-congratulation was just as apparent in the care she lavished on the twins left to her as it would have been for the original family of five. As far as the Beatons were concerned none of them would have rejoiced in names more specific than "Puss" and "Kitty"; but Netta had not been content with a haphazard christening. Influenced no doubt by the *Daily Call*, which had surpassed its own starry efforts in the last week of August, she had not failed to remark something portentous in the arrival of these infants on the thirty-first, and had promptly dubbed the black one "Crisis." After all, there was no gainsaying it was a domestic one of a sort. Mrs. Beaton had retorted with "Pax" for the tabby, to equalize the situation, as she explained.

After that the perversity of feline nature asserted itself. Crisis turned out a damp squib. There was nothing in the least sinister about him except his pale green eyes and ebony fluff. He was a dull, tame, unadventurous, smug little mama's darling. Neither Satan nor Berchtesgaden could have had a finger in his composition. It was left to the demure Pax, tabby and white like his mother and of uninteresting appearance, to demonstrate how unpeaceful was any so-called settlement in these days. His imp of curiosity and enterprise impelled him indoors and out into situation after situation which would have ensured speedy expulsion but for the happy English trait of turning a blind eye on culpability as soon as it was done with. So Pax left behind him a trail of spilt milk over which nobody cried for long. What was perhaps his mildest form of exacerbation was what he was indulging in again this morning.

Glancing up through the kitchen window because she thought she had heard a plaintive sound, Netta caught sight of him on top of the wall dividing their own garden from Miss Leaf's. His mouth was opening and shutting in the too-familiar way as he cried to heaven the impotence of things pacific.

"Drat that Pax," said Netta. "That's the umpteenth time he's got up there and can't get down. Won't, I believe it is. However the little beggar manages it beats me."

She wiped her hands briskly on a drying cloth and ran up the basement steps into the garden. With a nimbleness that came from practice she opened the door of a toolshed near the tradesmen's entrance and hauled out a short pair of wooden steps.

"You can get down yourself next time, my lord," she said. Pax had heard the same remark frequently.

The kitten stopped wailing and arched his back slightly as soon as he saw the steps being propped against the wall. This was following the customary formula. At the prospect of a more comfortable descent than by the espalier pear up which he had climbed he began a tentative kneading with his front paws—coming unstuck, Netta called it. Behind her on the grass Crisis was receiving concentrated attention from the maternal tongue. His head and neck groveled obediently to this determined instrument, his whole body spelled submission. Netta sighed.

She stretched out her hands and clasped the now purring Pax to her bosom. From this point of vantage she had an uninterrupted view at close quarters of the garden and back windows of number eight. And something over there was wrong.

Netta frowned. Toward noon on a fine autumn day the sun would shine on the backs of both houses. And an oval mirror in Miss Leaf's sitting room would catch it and throw it back and wink at you if you happened to be watching and liked to turn your head different ways to make the light shoot out. But this morning there were no bright rays.

For a moment Netta thought that Miss Leaf must have changed the position of the mirror. The next, with a gasp, she was sure the burglar had gone off with it. Even then there was something peculiar about the window. In spite of the play of light and shadow on the glass there was an impression of solid darkness behind.

The window was blacked out. That was it. Somebody had pulled the black curtains across. But Miss Leaf had gone away Friday afternoon, and yesterday—yesterday morning—

Netta scrambled down with a precipitancy that made Pax decide to take his life in his paws and jump. He uttered a final wail before making a beautiful landing within an inch or two of his family. His mother, without batting a whisker in his direction, acknowledged it by a moment's pause in her onslaught upon the unfortunate Crisis. Then she prosecuted the attack with renewed vigor.

Frances Beaton, warm from preparations for Sunday lunch, shut the oven door on the joint and listened gravely to the latest development. She admitted it was odd.

"And you're sure about Saturday morning, Netta? Because if you're not there's the chance, don't you see, that Miss Leaf never drew the blinds after Thursday night. Nobody may have used the room between then and the time she and her nephew went away."

"But what about their girl?" Netta asked quickly. She was not the less respectful because for the most part "sirs" and "madams" did not figure in her vocabulary. "Vera didn't go till evening, and she'd have tidied up, and you know what it is to try to do anything by day in a blacked-out room. Besides, I'm positive it wasn't like that this time yesterday."

Mrs. Beaton scrutinized her for a few seconds in silence.

"All right. I think, anyway, it's time we brought the doctor into this."

Dr. Beaton was not so much skeptical as resolute for the optimistic view. A tall, quiet, practical young man, he heard them out without interruption.

"Funny, perhaps—but only if you conclude directly that something's wrong. The black-curtained window doesn't necessarily mean the house was broken into. Yes, I know Netta says it wasn't like that Saturday morning, but suppose Miss Leaf came back later yesterday—with or without young Mitfold and the maid. She might still be in bed."

"But she told me on Thursday," Frances said, "that they'd be gone till Monday."

"She could have changed her mind," said Dr. Beaton.

"I know. But none of us saw her come back."

"That's an easy one. I was away most of the day as well as at night. You and Netta were both out at different times."

"Well, I'm like Netta now. I don't like it. Couldn't you take a look at their window? A close look, I mean, not from this side. You could get over the wall into the garden."

The doctor demurred. "I don't hold with making so free and easy with a neighbor's landmark, especially on a pretty flimsy pretext. If you don't mind, I'd rather go in the front way and ring the bell."

"A waste of time, Rod. If nobody's at home—and I don't for a minute think anybody is—you'll find the garden gate locked and won't be able to get round."

"Then I'll come back and climb the wall after all. But I'd really rather be the polite caller first. You hadn't guessed how conventional I was at heart, eh?"

From the dining-room window they watched him walk briskly past the railinged front, in at Miss Leaf's gate and up the steps to the front door. In the porch he was lost to view. A couple of minutes went by. Though they could not hear the bell ring, the sound of the knocker reached them once distinctly. Dr. Beaton reappeared. He glanced in their direction, shook his head slightly and went round to the garden entrance on the far side.

"He can't climb that," Netta said, unconsciously dropping her voice to a whisper.

They waited for him to return. When nothing happened Netta made an inarticulate remark and hurried out. Mrs. Beaton could hear her opening the back door. She herself went downstairs to her cooking. The matter was in Rod's hands now, and she had no manner of doubt that he would see it through.

When they both came in five minutes later she heard the bang of the garden door at the top of the stairs, then the doctor's steps making quickly for the surgery. The telephone was in there. There was something wrong, then. On the stairs she met Netta, a little pale and breathless.

"I don't know, ma'am," the girl forestalled her, with respectful emphasis for the gravity of the situation. "Doctor didn't say. But he's in a hurry. There's something queer, like. I said there was all along."

Frances motioned her to the kitchen and hurried upstairs. By the little table outside the surgery door Rod stood, tense and quiet, fingering its polished surface. She had an idea he was waiting for her. Their eyes met, and all at once he dug his hands sharply in his trouser pockets and gave his shoulders the backward hitch that was his habit when something had to be faced.

"Netta's right," he said slowly. "There's something damned odd next door— worse than odd. I've sent for the police. I—"

"All right, old thing. I can take it. What is it?"

"There's a man there. Dead, I'm afraid. I can see his leg and a part of the shoe where the swing of it's displaced the black curtain."

"But—"

"He must be hanging from the rod above."

CHAPTER IV: QUEST

Speed.   *Why, man, how black?*
Laun.   *Why, as black as ink.*
                    TWO GENTLEMEN OF VERONA.

"PRETTY HOW-DE-DO for a soo'cide, ain't it?" Dr. Tawney had remarked at sight of the official group in Miss Leaf's sitting room. "Proper gathering of the vultures, eh?"

He was a shabby little man with the police surgeon's usual lack of concili-ation in his manner, but while his appearance continued grubby his efficiency remained unimpaired, and in a short time he had found cause to revise his opinion.

They had cut down Archy Mitfold's body and laid it on the couch. With the absence of fuss a routine job imposes the camera had gone to work, the fingerprints man had completed his methodical round, the divisional surgeon was carrying out a swift examination preliminary to the autopsy that would follow. In the background Dr. Beaton, a little sick in spite of his training, failed for the first time to watch with an impersonal air a fellow worker do his stuff. This corpse had been a neighbor, and things like that did not happen to one's neighbors.

From his position between desk and window Dan Pardoe made a note of the measurements he had just taken and kept an eye on the scene before him. The youngest chief inspector at Scotland Yard, he was a tall, lithe man of easy carriage and unpretentious good looks whose prematurely white hair belied his forty years. Under his hand on the desk lay Exhibit A, the rope they had taken from the dead boy's neck. It was a thin, tough, soiled cord, darker in color in one half than the other, both ends neatly sliced with a knife showing the fresh, contrasting fiber.

All at once Pardoe felt the familiar sense of weariness. Routine enquiry into what looked like murder had clicked into motion. Slow motion, if he knew anything about it. This momentary pause was like the drop in the buffeting of a high wind. It had blown. It was going to blow. Now was the time to take a breath before the gale renewed its force and swept with it heaven alone knew what tragic or beastly burden. He had long ago stopped questioning his initial reluctance to handle a murder case. It was something one had to accept, like the nose on one's face, with the cynical consolation that in an hour or two one would probably be as keen as mustard. It wasn't, he believed, mere fastidiousness that made him hang back. The road to a chief inspectorship had had to lead away from all such niceties. He was no more of a sissy than the next man. But he had heard writers confess to a similar unwilling submission to their work. They were ready, so they said, to resort to every shifty trick in the calendar to avoid starting a new thing. But once let them get their teeth into it—well, then the hunt was fairly up. Some of them went so far as to say that the story itself took charge, willy-nilly driving 'em on. That was where policeman and novelist came to the parting of the ways. Scotland Yard could not afford crime to take charge—not like this Sampson Vick case was doing, if crime it were.

Pardoe glanced through the window from which the black curtains had been drawn back. At the bottom of the garden Detective Sergeant Salt, who had gone out there after a cursory examination of the other rooms, was bending down in close inspection of the foot of the wall bounding the cul-de-sac, with now and again an upward glance at Low, the divisional superintendent. They were chatting together with the amity of men who understand the job they handle and do not question its implications. The inspector's mouth quirked to an affectionate smile. It was Tommy's sort who should reach the winning post, not bad starters like himself.

"Here a minute," said Tawney when photographer and prints expert had withdrawn. His invitation included Dr. Beaton. They joined him at the couch and stood looking down at the dead boy. Tawney stooped and pulled back an eyelid. "Have a look at this."

"The pupil's contracted to a fine point," Beaton remarked, answering the police surgeon's interrogative glance. His gaze went involuntarily to the curtains now hanging in folds.

"He died in the light," said Pardoe, following the look.

Tawney nodded. "In a blaze of light. Not earlier than ten last night, not after midnight. An' you found him in a room with no electricity on—what's more, with all natural light excluded too. Seems like soo'cide's gone west. Unless it was a pact, an' the partner couldn't face up to it but thoughtfully turned out the lights before scramming—don't ask me why. But there's other things, too."

"The evidence was against suicide from the first," said Pardoe. "This only confirms what the superintendent saw at the start. It's a pretty well-established fact that suicide in the dark is rare enough to be practically unknown. Men choose to die in the light. And in these days one doesn't black out a window for any other purpose than lighting up inside."

"And dead men don't plunge themselves into darkness," Dr. Beaton finished.

"Exactly. What's this you were saying about other things, Tawney?"

The police surgeon grimaced. "You ghouls must have your murder. All right. He had a bump on the head—here." He touched a spot above Archy's right temple, partially hidden by hair. "Before death. Be able to say more after the P.M. But looks like he didn't die of the rope at all."

It was Dr. Beaton who looked up sharply and Pardoe who nodded acceptance. The inspector checked what he was going to say and, after a glance at his watch, turned to Dr. Beaton.

"There's no point in detaining you here, Doctor. The ambulance will be along in a few minutes. When I've finished here for the time being, I'll be glad to look in on you and have a talk. And I'll want to see that bright girl of yours."

"Right," said Beaton, who was recovering his spirits sufficiently to miss his lunch. "I'll cut along now and look out for you as soon as you care to drop in, Inspector."

Avoiding a further glance at the couch he went out into the hall, followed by Tawney, who hung back a minute to dig Pardoe in the ribs.

"Not giving anything away, are you? Oh no, I didn't miss the hands—he'd've had the devil's own job to hang himself without assistance."

When he was alone Pardoe closed the door and, taking a look through the window, saw that, though the superintendent had disappeared, Salt, like a stout but determined bloodhound, was still nosing up and down the strip of earth beneath the wall. He went back to the body and stood looking down at the strangely pale face. Except for the livid ring encircling the flesh above the collar line, there was little to suggest how Archy Mitfold had met his end. Over features which might have been petulant in life, Death had dropped his customary veil of dignity. The young, sensitive face was untroubled, the mouth even touched with faint humor. The shadow of risibility in the room struck sharply on Pardoe. It struck unpleasantly. Here was a secret, suggesting the possibility of a disclosure that now would never be made. For dead men tell no tales. Or do they?

He raised first one, then the other of the hands Dr. Tawney had mentioned, and looked again at the left from which the index and middle fingers were missing. The stumps showed the marks of amputation that was fairly recent, Pardoe thought. The rest of the hand was scarred but clean, the remaining nails polished. He put it down and took up the right. For the second time that afternoon the inspector looked thoughtfully at the heavy ink smudges it bore, a smear on the inside of the thumb at the top and a corresponding one on the index, and down the inside of the middle finger from the quick of the nail to first knuckle a thick, blackened mess. He frowned and laid the hand down. He examined the soles of the shoes. They were dry, but the toes were a little scraped, and there were marks of recent damp, with traces of something pulpy that looked like crushed fruit and, stuck to it, a dead leaf.

A medley of small articles from the dead boy's pockets had been assembled on the desk. Pardoe went across and, without touching, looked them over; a fountain pen properly capped, two latchkeys, a tear-off memorandum book with five blank sheets left, a small German-English dictionary with worn covers, a clean handkerchief from the breast pocket, a soiled one from the overcoat, a piece of modeling clay about the size of a walnut, a packet of cigarettes, a lighter, a bill from an Oxford bookseller and some loose silver and coppers amounting to eight shillings twopence. A flashlight of the sixpenny-battery size had been on the desk when the police first entered and had been tested for fingerprints.

The room was tidy, unnaturally tidy, it seemed, for the scene of violent death. Only a chair, its seat unmarked, lay overturned near where the body had been found hanging, and the pile of the carpet was a little rucked in a line running more or less from beneath that side of the window to a point beyond the desk and close to the electric fire. Superintendent Low had had the ready sense to spot it directly and see that it was not trampled. A wastepaper basket stood beneath the desk. It was empty except for a few screwed up pellets of inky blotting paper, one or two of which lay outside on the rug. In a shallow alcove behind the desk hung an oval, slightly concave mirror in a carved gilt frame, giving space and perspective to a small room. Pardoe recalled Conan Doyle's fine story in which a mirror had nightly revealed to an overworked clerk the cloudy image it had received of murder long ago. He could have wished Miss Leaf's glass so endowed.

A picture rail ran round the room, carrying watercolors by different hands and of unequal merit. A few caught Pardoe's eye. They were animal and bird studies in clean spare lines, depicting their subjects in characteristic but exaggerated poses. They had originality and wit. One of ducks in Indian file cocking mildly timorous eyes at a hawk overhead, and another of mice considering from the outside a handsome piece of cheese in a wire trap drew a chuckle from Pardoe. He looked for the artist's name, but beyond what might have been a single illegible letter they appeared to be unsigned.

The garden door shut noisily as Salt came in. At the same time the sergeant posted in the hall let the ambulance men in by the front. When they had left with their burden Pardoe turned to Salt.

"Get anything?"

"Wall's scraped a bit 'ere an' there. Looks fresh, but it mightn't be," the sergeant admitted. "An' there was this trod into the ground." He spread out his hand, disclosing a pat of garden soil and embedded in it a flattened out piece of modeling clay similar to that they had already found on Archy Mitfold.

"There's something odd about the ways in and out last night," Pardoe said when he had examined it. "This seems likely he got over the wall and came in the back way. But he had the latchkey of the front door in his pocket, and when Low got in by forcing the door into the garden the front one was found bolted as well as latched—which is queer in more ways than one. For if that door was bolted when the family left the house Mitfold couldn't have come in that way, latchkey or not. And in any case the murderer couldn't have gone out that way. Even if the bolt could have been shot from the outside, and I'm pretty sure it couldn't, he wouldn't have dared risk fiddling with it, and dead men don't bolt doors after one."

"If the other chap went away by the garden door," Salt said, "he must'a turned the key from the outside, because it was inside when it was forced."

"There's still the way out from the kitchen up the basement steps. There's no key there at all, but the door's locked. It's not on Mitfold, so if it turns out Miss Leaf hasn't got it either it's on the cards the murderer used that door and chucked the key away. And the tradesmen's entrance near the top of the basement steps wasn't bolted. Dr. Beaton was able to get in that way this morning."

"Bloomin' hide-an'-seek," Salt grumbled. "With the front door bolted since Friday, if it *was*, the tradesmen's gate 'ud have to be unfastened, else 'ow'd they get out an' in again? But if this fellow wanted to escape the back way why didn't he go through the garden door 'stead of roaming downstairs in the dark only to come up again?"

"Perhaps he did. We'll find out. What we've got to do now is have another look for what Mitfold was writing in here last night. Yes, I know we've been over the room once, but that was a quick look-see with every man jack of us fearful of disturbing something before the camera got it. This has got to be a thorough do. We'll take the place to pieces if necessary."

"Right," said Salt, but he looked puzzled. "Why you so sure he was writing in *'ere?*"

"Meaning he wrote it perhaps before he came here?"

"Sure. Why not?"

Pardoe shook his head. "Whatever and wherever he was writing, it was after his last meal—call it dinner or supper. Except for the ink smudges his hands are clean and manicured. He was well turned out, dressed with almost foppish attention to detail, and it's highly improbable, to put it mildly, that a young fellow as careful of his personal appearance as he must have been would have sat down to table with badly inked fingers." He broke off. "You going to say something?"

"Granted he was writing after he fed, it needn't 'a been here. Tawney says ten was the earliest he could 've died. There was time for him to have eaten his supper and inked his fingers before coming 'ere, wasn't there?"

"Of course, but for this." The inspector picked up the waste paper basket and tilted it toward Salt so that the little balls of inky blotting paper were in view. "This room was obviously left in order when they went away on Friday. Now no girl as conscientious as Miss Leaf's maid appears to be would leave the basket unemptied, still less these bits scattered about the carpet. They were dropped here by somebody who came in after Friday. Did you ever use a leaky fountain pen? Penwipers aren't much in vogue nowadays, and you'd find to tear a bit of blotter to wipe off the excess of ink round the nib was about the handiest thing you could do."

"That's right," the sergeant conceded. "But it wasn't this stuff he used, unless he pinched a whole sheet to mop up his ink."

He indicated the leather-bound blotter lying on the desk. The top was virgin white and untorn.

"No," said Pardoe, "it wasn't. There's another piece of blotting paper some- where, or what's left of it, along with the writing that's gone astray. What's more"—he made a dive after another pellet a foot or two away from the desk—"he didn't sit here to write, either. Hence your clean blotter. Hence his bad shots. He flicked these bits at the waste paper basket and some of 'em hit the bull's eye and some didn't. Now where—? Let's try the sofa."

But though they punched and peered and shoved hands into the back and corners, the sofa yielded nothing; and nothing was concealed by the snugly fitting cushions.

"If it's in this room," Pardoe said, "it was hidden so the other fellow shouldn't get it."

"Which the other fellow's done, I'll take my oath," Salt said with gloomy relish. But he applied himself to the search with a will his foreboding did not suggest. For the next ten minutes, while Pardoe gave meticulous attention to the desk, a tooth-comb could not have raked the room more exhaustively than Salt.

There were six drawers in the desk, three on each side the kneehole. The two top ones only were furnished with locks. Both were unlocked, but a key had been found sticking in the closed drawer on the right. It had been tested for prints. Pardoe went systematically through the drawers. Those on the left were tidy and completely impersonal: in the top one was a stack of clean notepaper and a depleted packet of envelopes to match, a rubber stamp, a small perpetual calendar and an almost empty box of drawing pins; in the middle were five manila envelopes, foolscap size, a little glass bowl containing a now dry piece of sponge for moistening stamps, and an unused picture post card of Harlech castle; a new ball of string was the sole contents of the bottom drawer. On the right the second and third drawers were crammed with several quires of clean foolscap paper, a bundle of quarto manila enve- lopes, the empty covers of a looseleaf notebook, a two-shilling book of stamps with a single halfpenny stamp remaining, and a small metal gadget for punching holes in paper.

The top drawer was more interesting. The inspector took out several notebooks, mostly of the school exercise book type, with a few of superior binding. One or two were blank, another contained what appeared to be a couple of undated essays in French, evidently first drafts, for they were penciled in a fine, irregular, but perfectly legible hand, with various scribbles and corrections made by the writer himself. Another had *Aufgaben* scrawled across its cover and inside a number of exercises in German script, mostly dated, written by the same nervous hand, now in ink, now in pencil. The book was almost filled, and Pardoe observed that the last date was "d.11.Oktober," four days ago, and that the exercise beneath had been done in pencil.

The margins of many of these pages in more books than one were characterized by the same drawings. Instead of the usual aimless circles or half-formed human features, Archy Mitfold had chosen to decorate his books with bird sketches. There were literally scores of them, both in ink and pencil, some rough and incomplete and as lacking in design as a child's first attempts, others delicate and finished. They were mere thumbnail sketches, and all, so far as Pardoe could tell, depicting the same bird, though what it was he did not know.

In drawing out the top books the inspector had got the impression of something else with them, a loose piece of paper, perhaps, that had fallen back inside. He found it now, standing flat against the front of the drawer. It was an ordinary, square white envelope addressed in a bold, foreign hand to Archy

Sketches on the envelope found in Archy Mitfold's desk

Mitfold at the Mulberry Fountain address. The postmark was clear and announced that it had been posted in Chelsea on the evening of October 9. There was nothing inside, but the back was covered with penciled sketches of the bird again, this time larger and with some speckled and barred feathers added. Pardoe studied them idly for a few moments. Then he locked the drawer and slipped both key and envelope in his pocket.

There was nothing else. There was nothing else in the room. Ten minutes' intensive search in which Salt had not omitted to examine the chimney and turn up the edges of the carpet had failed to produce the evidence for which they looked. Whatever Archy Mitfold had been writing on the night of his death it was no longer in the room where he had died.

"Maybe," said Salt, "he went out to post it an' came back to the house."

"And brought his murderer in with him? It's an idea," Pardoe agreed. "I hope you're right. If that's so there's the likelihood we shall get hold of it. About the safest place a piece of writing can be is in the post."

CHAPTER V: ROPE'S END

Rather, the prophecy like the parrot, "beware the rope's-end."
THE COMEDY OF ERRORS.

"WE DON'T KNOW THEM very well," said Dr. Beaton, when Salt had returned to the Yard to receive the fingerprints report and the inspector was sitting in the dining room of number seven, looking out on Mulberry Fountain. "We're not old stagers in this part, you see. It's only five months ago we moved in, and ever since there's been no time for the social amenities, only for coddling a practice that's a bit on the slow side."

"Don't exaggerate, Rod," Frances put in. "Mr. Pardoe will take us for hermits, else. And I know Miss Leaf quite well—it's the nephew we haven't seen much of."

"Well enough, anyway," remarked Pardoe, "for Miss Leaf to tell you she was going away for the weekend. Did she say where?"

"To Essex. But I don't know what part. She told me on Thursday when I was picking pears from the wall, and she was in her garden—a cousin was ill, I think she said, with no relatives near, so she was going next day till the following Monday."

"And her nephew with her?"

Dr. Beaton broke in. "That's what we don't know. My wife and I were discussing it just now. Miss Leaf didn't tell Frances that young Mitfold was going too."

"No, but she was quite definite about the house being shut up, and Vera—

that's the maid—going home for the weekend."

"I wonder," Pardoe said, "if you can more or less recall her own words about it?"

"Well, it was something like this—'we're going away tomorrow till Monday; the house will be locked up as I'm sending Vera home for the few days'— then the bit about her cousin's illness. That's as near as I remember it. She didn't mention Archy at all, but if I thought anything about it I concluded he was going with her."

"One would. And so far as we know now he may quite well have done so. It could have been from Essex he returned last night. Can you give me Vera's address?"

Frances Beaton shook her head. "She's a Londoner, I know. That's not very helpful."

"Half a jiff," said Dr. Beaton, stretching a hand out to the bell. "Netta knows, I believe. They're rather friendly—"

"All right," Pardoe said, "don't ring for a minute. I'll want to see your maid anyway. Tell me first the little you know about young Mitfold. Was he living here when you first came?"

"Oh no." It was Frances who answered. "We moved in in May. Miss Leaf had other people in the house then, and we didn't hear anything about Archy till he came. That would be early in August. At first it seemed as if he'd come on holiday, then he stayed on."

"Do you know why he was in London?"

"Yes. A week or two later his aunt said he was up receiving private tuition in languages—with a view to a Foreign Office job, I believe."

"He had a maimed hand, as you've seen," Dr. Beaton observed, "which cut out his chances of the army."

"Know how it happened?" Pardoe enquired.

"I don't. I'd only a nodding acquaintance with him. What I meant about not knowing them well, we don't drop in on each other or anything like that."

"Quite so. That reminds me. Have you noticed a difference in the number of callers since the nephew's been living here? Do you notice the people he brings home with him from time to time? Sorry to sound so inquisitive, but policemen always do."

The doctor, looking somewhat blank, left Frances to deal with this.

"I think there were more," she said. "Yes, of course. I've seen people coming and going who didn't turn up when Miss Leaf lived by herself. That was only to be expected. Not so many, you know. A few young men and a girl or two. Archy didn't run a car, but some of them did, and I've heard them drive up occasionally."

"That's helpful. Another thing: can you or the doctor recall anything in the least odd or outstanding that's happened next door in the two months since Mr. Mitfold came there?"

"Not a thing," said Roderick Beaton at once.

"You've forgotten, dear," Frances said firmly. "There *was* something." She turned to Pardoe. "Archy was taken ill one night lately, and was pretty bad for a day or two, I think. He looked ghastly when he got about again."

"Oh, that?" Her husband smiled. "So you call the collywobbles odd or outstanding? Been on a binge, most likely."

"When was this?" Pardoe asked.

Frances frowned thoughtfully. "Last week—no, this is Sunday. About the middle of the week before, it would be. I woke up soon after going to sleep and heard somebody moving about next door. Miss Leaf's bedroom joins mine, and the wall isn't thick. I didn't think much about it then, but in the morning the maid told Netta Mr. Mitfold had been taken ill in the night."

"Were you ever told the nature of the illness? I mean—"

"I'm not in professional attendance at number eight, Inspector, if that's what you mean," Dr. Beaton interrupted. "I've no idea if a doctor was called in."

"He wasn't," Frances said quickly. "Miss Leaf told me so herself. Archy didn't want one, I gathered. But he was really bad at the time, and his aunt was worried. He's never looked properly well since, do you think, Rod?"

"Tell you the truth I've seen so little of him I wouldn't know."

"It doesn't matter," Pardoe said. "Anything of that nature I shall learn from Miss Leaf once we get in touch with her. Now, is Netta downstairs?"

"I'll have her up," said Frances, and rose to ring the bell.

"No, don't. If I may I'd like to speak with her in her own province where she heard the bell."

Netta was in the breakfast room, where little diversion was possible. As this was the top of the square, the pavement was less frequented than the two rather longer sidewalks, so that even the trousered and stockinged legs one rarely saw were easily identifiable; nor was Sunday afternoon in Mulberry Fountain conducive to activity. The *News of the World*, however, made up for any deficiencies of entertainment, though unable to compete with the real, live member of Scotland Yard who now walked in upon her.

For the third time that day Netta, who was now convinced that poor young Mr. Mitfold had rung the bell himself, told her story. Here was a listener who proffered no explanation nor denied its oddity, but was silent a moment or two when she had finished speaking.

"When the bells are rung next door do you always hear them?" he asked.

"Oh no. Not much in the daytime; not if I was making a bit of a clatter, say. But this was night, and no sound anywhere."

Pardoe nodded. "Yes, that would be different. Tell me why you are sure the bell rang at a quarter to eleven exactly."

"Because I'd looked at the clock a minute or two before, and it was gone twenty to. I usually go to bed about half past ten, and I was just thinking it was time I went when I heard the tinkle through the wall."

"I see. Presently I'm going to ask you to let me sit in your kitchen just where you were sitting last night, while we carry out a little experiment in the other house."

"Pleased, I'm sure," Netta said, thrilled. She looked at him with a touch of hesitation. "I'm real sorry about Mr. Mitfold. I can't think—I mean, why would he want for to go and do a thing like that? He was a gentleman. But he was good to Vera."

Pardoe, accustomed to following with facility apparent *non sequiturs*, accepted the testimonial without bewilderment, and found it a little moving. He liked this girl, her intelligent response to the enquiry and fearless, unflustered attitude to himself; most of all for the questions she did not ask. He decided to let her in a little on what would after all not be a secret for long. In any case Dr. Beaton had got hold of it.

"We're not sure that Mr. Mitfold was alone when he died," he said ambiguously.

Her mind leapt to meet his more quickly then he had anticipated. "That would be murder if—"

"If there was someone else in the house last night too?" he finished briskly. "Yes. Has Vera ever mentioned to you any particular acquaintance of Mr. Mitfold's who was in the habit of coming there?"

"She wouldn't do that." Her tone admirably combined reproof for the suggestion with appreciation of the inspector's difficulty. "She's been with Miss Leaf too long to be gossipy, though she's friendly enough with me."

"Quite right, too." Pardoe tacked at once. "Can you tell me where Vera is just now?"

"At home. She lives in Clerkenwell. Wait a minute and I'll think of the address. No—I don't remember the number, but it's Brotherhood Street, and their house is the left-hand side near the top if you go to it off the Farringdon Road, if that's any use."

"It is, thanks. Now tell me how you knew the sitting room next door had been blacked out some time later than Saturday morning."

"Because I was picking the last of our pears yesterday before lunch, the ones on the wall Mrs. Beaton was after on Thursday. And I had a proper view of their window and there were no curtains across it."

"But isn't it hard to tell by day from the outside—I mean whether the black stuff is in place or not?"

"No. It might be for some windows, but not for theirs, because of the looking glass. It hung in a corner, sideways, like, to the window, and the sun made it flash. It was there all right Saturday but not today, same hour and with the sun shining just the same too."

"That was a nice piece of observation," Pardoe said, and meant it. "Now you and I are going to listen to some bells ringing."

P.C. Lawson, awaiting further instructions in the hall of number eight and finding his vigil less of a sinecure every minute, welcomed Scotland Yard's suggestion of a little action. Even the necessity of moving from room to room would mitigate the oppression of this dark passage. The last hour had confirmed his opinion that empty houses were unhealthy places. He groped for a clear definition of the idea in his mind that they were never really uninhabited. Something troublesome and vaguely antagonistic lingered on to make short work of one's good spirits; and when folk showed, as well, a queer preference for huge oil paintings, whose very tilt toward you held menace, darkening still further an already dismal hall, it was time for a plain constable to think with longing of his own cheery kitchen brightened by the innocent calendars a thoughtful baker and gas company had provided.

His orders were simple, but sufficiently important to be gratifying. He had to ring in turn every bell in the house except the one on the front door, and make a written note of the order in which they had been rung.

"Some of these old-fashioned bells don't clang properly, they only whirr. So this may help us to check up not so much on which of them was rung last night as which were *not*. Not that I expect much from it. At best it won't be conclusive, because a good deal depends on the strength of the tug. Ring the bells at intervals of two minutes—that 'll give you time to get from one room to another, including upstairs. If we don't do something of the kind I shan't be able to tell which bells I missed hearing. Give me five minutes' start to get into the next-door kitchen, and then do your stuff. Where there's two pulls in a room for one bell—you'll see 'em by the fireplace—pull only the one. Don't drag the doings now, but don't be too feeble either; it's a moderately strong pull I'd like."

P. C. Lawson went cheerfully to work. Tame as the job was, it smacked of the offensive, and that was acceptable after squatting on one's hams an hour and more musing on a man's death and what made him come to it.

He started on the breakfast room in the basement, working his way up with a hearty tread that reiterated, "Here, what's all this about?" to the sullen house.

After setting the clock by the constable's watch, Pardoe sat by the hearth in the Beatons' kitchen at the spot occupied by Netta the night before. Netta had found herself in the delightful position of issuing orders to an inspector of Scotland Yard, and the equally delightful one of participating in the fun, for the inspector had suggested that she, too, take paper and pencil and jot down results by the clock, O representing failure to hear a bell, with an X for each audible tinkle.

As Pardoe had half anticipated, the experiment from an auditory standpoint was a failure. Each of the seven bells rung came through with amazing punctuality, Netta discounting only one on the ground that it was too muffled to be what she had heard last night.

"A washout," Pardoe began when he joined Lawson in number eight a few minutes later, and was going on to explain why when the satisfaction the constable was displaying checked him.

"It's like this, sir," Lawson said, growing red as if at his own presumption in making the discovery. "I wouldn't say but what your idea for ringing the bells hasn't turned out fine. You don't need to test the sound of 'em, though. It's as plain as a pikestaff which he rang, an' why."

"Which? Out with it."

The constable jerked a thumb toward the rooms above.

"Bedroom at the top of the stairs. There's a bell rope—I should say there *was* a rope there—but it's bin cut, clean as a whistle. It's missing all but near a foot. I gave that piece a tug so as not to put you out of your reckoning, but I guessed soon as I clapped eyes on it where the hanky-panky lay. That 'll be the rope he hanged himself with, sir."

His concluding remark was made on the way up in Pardoe's wake. The inspector, who had with him a bag in which Exhibit A lay in a careful, sinister coil, wasted no time. It was exactly as Lawson had described. They came into a medium-sized bedroom which Pardoe judged lay directly above the sitting room. Its narrow windows overlooked the garden. Like the rest of the house it was tidy and, at first glance, featureless. The head of the bed was against the wall past which the stairs ran, its foot toward a small gas fire. Close to the head of anybody lying in bed and at his right hand, a rope should have hung. A piece of it did so still. About nine inches dangled from the pull by the ceiling, the end sharply cut as had been the ends of the rope which had hanged Archy Mitfold.

Pardoe mounted a chair and compared the remaining piece with the coil he took from his bag. They were apparently identical; expert examination would decide. The cleaner portion belonged to the upper part of the rope that was out of reach; where it had been handled it was darker in color and the fiber more slick. But the rope he held in his hands had been cut both ends, therefore—

Pardoe went down on his knees and groped beneath the bed. It was there, the knot and worn tassel, with an inch or two of cord attached to it. Whoever had appropriated the rope had discarded the knotted end as superfluous and liable to be in the way. He had not troubled to dispose of it, but had let it lie where it fell. Why not? After all, the murderer might have argued, if Archy Mitfold had filched the rope to hang himself he would hardly have taken pains to conceal the fact.

Before leaving, Pardoe had a look round. This had clearly been the dead boy's bedroom. A wardrobe revealed clothes hung with fastidiousness and shoes neatly disposed on trees. Books stood in a row on a small bureau, *The Fate of Homo Sapiens* shouldering two sixpenny thrillers, a library book, and a French novel in the usual flimsy paper covers, flanked by a German *Aufsatzbuch* and a little manual on British nesting birds. Everything appeared undisturbed, but Pardoe was taking no chances. He locked the room when he and Lawson came out and took away the key, regretting only that any telltale prints the knob may have carried must have disappeared by now.

Across the landing, at a right angle to the room they had just left, two doors faced them. Pardoe opened each. The larger of the rooms was a drawing room, furnished with an eye to comfort rather than taste, light and cheerful, with a large gas fire and plenty of watercolors about the walls. The other was a bedroom, presumably Miss Leaf's. A long bell rope hung beside the bed, proving on examination exactly similar to the one Pardoe carried. The windows of both rooms looked out on Mulberry Fountain, a pleasant vista of the fine old Regency houses of which it was chiefly composed; only this end block appeared to be of later date. A short flight of stairs went up from the landing to the floor above.

"What's up there?" Pardoe asked.

"A couple of bedrooms, sir—the one looks like the maid's, the other a spare. There's a bell rope in the spare, nowhere else. There's a bathroom, too, and w.c., and a linen cupboard. They're all in apple-pie order, no doors locked and nothing out of place."

When Pardoe left the house the square was as tranquil and deserted as Sunday afternoon in autumn could make it. He paused for a moment by the fountain which gives its name to the place, a pompous marble structure at the bottom where Trumpeter's Row runs into Smith Street. Eighteenth century infants of highly muscular physique and simpering demeanor, whose stupid attempts to clutch the thrashing hooves of Neptune's horses had kept them in jeopardy a century and a half, made a not unpleasing group in those quiet surroundings. No water played now; only blown leaves and a drift of dust, like the last whispers of its century, lay in the basin.

At Scotland Yard Salt greeted news of the rope with a grimace of self-reproach.

"An' to think I went over the place top to toe," he muttered. "Lawson's got 'is eyes skinned."

"You weren't looking for bells. Lawson was."

The identification of the rope raised a number of suggestive points both men were quick to remark, but for the moment Pardoe put off discussion of them. The fingerprints report was in, eloquent enough by reason of its very niggardliness. Prints were conspicuous by their absence. A few rather indistinct ones had been found on the top of the desk, with only useless smears on the drawers and key, and an excellent set belonging to a right hand and a left thumb on the wooden framework at the back of a small easy chair by the fireplace. Those were all. None had been taken from the chair found overturned near the body. The few prints recorded all belonged to the dead man.

"I'll have 'em go over his bedroom too," Pardoe said. "But my guess is they won't find much. This chap's a clever devil and took his precautions. Yet there's something that doesn't fit there—for the further we go into it the more unpremeditated the whole thing looks."

Salt remembered something else he had to report. A quarter of an hour after his return to it, Scotland Yard had been rung up and its help solicited to trace the whereabouts of Mr. Archibald Mitfold, whose absence since eight-thirty the previous evening was causing grave anxiety to his hostess.

The caller had given her name as Mrs. Byron, of eighteen Alma Square, Old Brompton.

CHAPTER VI: WITCHES' SABBATH

A witch, a quean, an old cozening quean!
THE MERRY WIVES OF WINDSOR.

WHEN PARDOE presented himself at the house in Alma Square that evening, a harsh-featured maid, looking older than her years, he thought, showed him into a dining room replete with the sort of tasteless opulence that is always oppressive. He had not till now thought an alliance of mahogany with a Turkish carpet and dull brown curtains necessarily disagreeable, but the atmosphere of this room was charged with a weight not entirely attributable to the heavy meals successive generations had eaten here. The very daylight appeared discolored, as if filtered through layers of glutinous matter before penetrating to the interior. Enormous steel engravings depicting the more ferocious events in Old Testament history hung from the walls, their background a dull crimson paper little calculated, Pardoe judged, to stimulate the appetites of those who sat at table.

He would not have been surprised at that early hour to find Mrs. Byron at church, but either she was not in the habit of attending at this time, or was perhaps staying at home in anticipation of just such a visit as his.

Presently she came to him, a tall, heavy woman with a thick neck and commanding bust, and yellowish-brown eyes that fixed their gaze on him immediately and kept it there.

"Inspector Pardoe? It's about Mr. Mitfold, isn't it? How quickly you've gone to work. Tell me what he's been doing."

Her manner was an odd mingling of courtesy, condescension and anxiety. For all that, there was something spurious about it. She wants me to think that *she* thinks he's been up to something and we've got him in jug, was Pardoe's instant reflection. And I don't believe she does. He shook himself mentally, however, with the reminder that prejudice at the outset would get him nowhere, and answered frankly.

"We, too, should much like to know what he was doing, Mrs. Byron. It has now become our business to find out."

"You mean—?" She motioned him to a chair, herself taking one a foot or two away in such a position that the light fell in a slant across her shoulder and not directly on her face.

Pardoe met her rather expressionless stare. "Mr. Mitfold is dead, madam."

He realized before uttering it that for most women the announcement was unnecessarily brutal. With this one he felt merely curious to know how she would take it.

In that somber room it was hard to say whether the horror on her face was simulated or not. For a moment she did not speak, then broke out hurriedly.

"*Dead?* But—but—it can't be! I don't understand. I—he was perfectly all right last night. I tell you it can't be!"

"I'm afraid it is," said Pardoe, and gave her a wary account of the bare facts. She listened with every appearance of genuine dismay.

"But how *dreadful*—this is terrible—his poor aunt, whatever shall we say to her? There was nothing wrong with him when he left us last night."

This was the second time she had given the assurance. "He was staying here while Miss Leaf was away?"

"Until Monday. She'd been rather insistent, I think, that he should go with her. But you know what boys are, they like to be left to their own devices. Silly to fuss them too much—though how I wish now he had gone with her. But he had some school or college function he wanted to attend, and in the evening he was off again, to a coaching. Why in the world he was at Mulberry Fountain, and died there, I can't conceive. It's all perfectly dreadful."

Pardoe, who had noticed before now that shock, whether real or assumed, frequently made people talkative afterward, fastened on one of these remarks before she could continue. "A coaching? Where was that?"

"I don't know. He was learning languages."

"What time did he leave your house last night?"

"Soon after eight. I gathered he was due at his tutor's at half past. But as he told us nothing at all of any personal interest I'm unable to give you details."

"He left on foot?"

"So far as I know."

She sounded resentful, Pardoe thought. Something about her haunted him persistently, like a long-buried memory there is little hope of resurrecting. The light, glassy eyes, too much on a level with her face, the bland features lacking animation, disturbed and nagged at his mind. He harked back to an earlier phrase she had used.

"Mrs. Byron, just now you referred to Mr. Mitfold as 'our' guest. Your husband—your family are living here?"

"No. I am a widow, Inspector." Was there a hint of amusement in her voice? "My mother, Mrs. Pell, lives here with me. She is an old lady in indifferent health, and I'd rather you didn't bother her, if that's possible."

"It may not be necessary. But she met Mr. Mitfold, I suppose? She's not bedridden, or anything like that?"

"Oh no. She met him, of course. Marian Leaf is her godchild. That's why we asked him here. But he talked no more with her than with me. In fact—I don't want to criticize the poor boy now this awful thing has happened—but my mother thought him very unmannerly, and so did I."

"You've known him a long while?"

"Well, hardly. He only came to London in the late summer, I believe, and we didn't meet him immediately."

"That accounts for it, perhaps," Pardoe said, anxious to keep this ball rolling. "He was reserved because he didn't know you very well."

"Not at all." There was a new note of sharpness in her voice. "It wasn't the kind of self-consciousness you suggest. Besides, young people nowadays have lost all sense of reserve. That wasn't the impression Archy made. It was more a deliberate withholding of normal, harmless information. We've seen little of him, really, and it was only natural while he was staying here to ask questions touching on his work and recreation, and one thing and another. My mother leads a very secluded life—she gets out and about rarely, and she's inclined perhaps to take a special interest in her fellow beings when she comes in contact with them. But no, this boy repulsed any advances made to win his confidence—literally *repulsed* us."

Portrait of a pair of Nosey Parkers meeting their match, the inspector reflected with some enjoyment, though if it were true this reticence might make his own task more difficult.

"It's characteristic of a good many of us, Mrs. Byron," he said, "to be unresponsive in face of any sort of inquisition, however well intentioned. Leave us alone, we'll often give gratis the very information that couldn't be got by questioning. Besides, perhaps Mr. Mitfold was modest enough to feel that he had nothing interesting to divulge."

"You don't understand, Inspector. We shouldn't have noticed Archy's rudeness to the same extent if it hadn't been that he obviously had something to conceal."

"Something on his mind, you mean?"

"Well, perhaps. But that usually means something worrying, doesn't it? I'm pretty sure this wasn't. When I said just now that he was quite all right when he was here yesterday, I didn't mean that exactly. I've no reason to suppose he wasn't well physically—but mentally he was in a high state of excitement that grew on him while he was here."

Interesting, Pardoe thought. Always providing, of course, that the woman was speaking the truth. On the other hand she might be trying to justify her own and her mother's curiosity by fabricating a reason for it. It was never safe to assume that these smooth, indolent folk, who looked so little prone to excitement and exaggeration themselves, were necessarily sticklers for veracity. They sometimes had hard-working imaginations, and were liable to erect on a substratum of fact a lively decor that would, they hoped, supply the vivacity they themselves lacked. But even in those cases it was his business to dig to the frail foundations.

"Which day did Mr. Mitfold arrive for his weekend visit?" he asked.

"Friday. After tea. He wasn't then so noticeably secretive, only impatient and rather sulky. To be quite frank, we thought him a little ungrateful. My mother is not accustomed to young people about the house and it was something of a concession on her part to offer the boy hospitality at all."

"I understand. Then there wasn't any of this suppressed excitement in evidence till yesterday?"

"No, not really. It was on Saturday he began to be so much on edge—by night he was simply bursting with something, I've no idea what."

"That would be by the time he left to go to his tutorial?"

"Yes. I didn't actually see him after dinner which was over about half an hour before he left. I was really thinking of his spirits when his friend brought him home at six o'clock. The behavior of both of them was childish in the extreme."

Pardoe pricked his ears. "Which friend was that?"

"Mr. Wynkerrell."

"And who is Mr. Wynkerrell?" he asked patiently.

She shrugged ample shoulders. "A gilded butterfly, one is tempted to say. But I don't know him well enough, perhaps, to dismiss him so harshly. He's a bookseller—I shouldn't be at all surprised to hear that the partner does the work while Mr. Wynkerrell dissipates the profits."

"Remarkably foolish of the partner," the inspector said pleasantly. She sounded rather vicious, he thought. "Where is the bookshop?"

"I can't tell you. I must have heard, too. Somewhere off Regent Street, I believe Marian said. It has one of those fancy names, I think, but I'm sorry I've forgotten that too."

In the last minute or two Pardoe had observed how once or twice her glance slid toward the door. As if sensing his attention, she looked back at him coolly.

"You met Mr. Wynkerrell before yesterday then, I take it, Mrs. Byron?"

"Oh yes. I should imagine he was frequently in and out of Marian's house. Mother and I met him there once at tea, and another time he called for Archy on an evening when Marian and he were here playing bridge. Archy was at school with him, I gather." She broke off impatiently. "But really I know very little about Mr. Wynkerrell. I must admit he's not the type of young man we admire. As Mrs. Pell has pointed out to him more than once, khaki would suit him very much better than the lounge suits he affects."

"You say he brought Mr. Mitfold home. Would that be from the school function he'd attended?"

"I hardly think so at that time of day. It was an Old Boys' lunch, or something of the sort, he went off to. But I can't say how he spent the time between. He wasn't in to tea."

"And they were both hilarious when they arrived?"

"Horribly. Archy had an unpleasant habit of making free with one's house, as if he were an undergraduate in lodgings. He thought nothing of bringing this noisy youth in and taking him up to his room. There they stayed till after the gong had gone for dinner. Then Mr. Wynkerrell went away."

Pardoe, who thought he had never seen a place that smacked so little of it, was about to utter a tactful cliche concerning Liberty Hall, when the door opened wide with such astonishing suddenness that he got the idea there had been none of the usual preliminary of approach from the other side. With the precipitancy of Aladdin's it swung back, to reveal, like a *dea ex machina*, an old and belligerent lady.

"*Who* is this man, Kathleen?" the apparition blustered, and swung up the thin black stick on which she leaned to thrust it at the inspector. The vigor of the gesture carried it too far, so that Pardoe, as he rose at her entry, had the uncomfortable feeling he ought to be splayed out on the ceiling like a gigantic fly.

He took a good look at her. Dressed like that in black, with two heavy Spanish combs stuck in her hair, she was not unlike an insect herself. Her flat, shining eyes, darker than her daughter's, and the wide, purplish lips were too large for the shrunken face. Pardoe dismissed the tortoise simile as outworn, yet her skin was reptilian, hanging in formless pouches from features that had once been plump. He had the disagreeable notion that its ocherous hue was not entirely the result of senility; her hands were plainly unwashed.

Mrs. Byron introduced them with a bored air that seemed designed to annoy the old woman.

"This is the inspector, Mother, of course. My mother, Mrs. Pell. It's about Archy Mitfold he's come."

Her complete indifference was bewildering. As far as Pardoe was concerned she was the only person in the house to know Archy was dead, but the knowledge was no longer affecting her in the slightest. If filial duty came uppermost in her relation with her mother she would, he judged, have been anxious to spare her shock; if, as he suspected, they were linked by a sort of reciprocal spite, she would still have been maliciously intent on being first to blurt out the news. She was neither. She preserved a provocative calm and left Pardoe to handle the matter as he pleased.

He tried to persuade Mrs. Pell to a seat, but she evidently believed she had command of the situation only as long as she could keep them both standing. She listened to his brief and suitably watered account of the discovery of Archy's body, her eyes unwinking, thumping her stick at intervals on the carpet, whether to applaud his own remarks, summon spirits, or in sheer enjoyment, it was hard to say.

"I told you so!" was her surprising comment when she had heard him out. But it was addressed to her daughter. "*This* is what you get for calling in the police! They were never any good to us. You wouldn't be advised by me, and now see what we've got on our hands!"

Pardoe smothered a grin. "We are hardly responsible for sudden death, madam. Unfortunately Mr. Mitfold would still have been dead if Mrs. Byron had not rung me up. And I'm sorry we're never of any use to you—may I ask why?"

"You may. I was a suffragette, my good man."

"That sufficiently explains it," Pardoe said with what urbanity he could summon. He was always nettled at having his piety and his manhood coupled in the vocative. "But in spite of your dislike of the police, you were anxious, I suppose, to have Mr. Mitfold traced?"

She paid no heed. She was the kind of woman who would always be thinking up some new, ridiculous assertion while the other person was speaking. Adders, Pardoe reminded himself unkindly, watching the apparently lidless eyes, were notoriously deaf. She was an exhibitionist, it was clear; a monopolist for whom the give and take of conversation meant nothing. If he turned to her daughter she exerted herself to recapture his attention for herself. If he failed to show interest she metaphorically capered before him in the strenuous hope of reviving it. She was vain and unveracious. In any case she fell into the category of bad witnesses who, from the kickoff, try the temper and weary the larynx; and in this particular one she was, he felt, as bad as they make 'em, trying deliberately to mislead him by silly evasions and extravagance of language. Her callousness toward the boy's death was even more repellent than Mrs. Byron's acceptance of it.

As a matter of form, though hoping little from it, Pardoe took her through the same questions he had put to her daughter. Her answers were at random, so charged with irrelevance as to show her mind occupied only with the image of Archy Mitfold in relation to herself. She would make everything a personal issue, Pardoe thought. She's triumphant now, the nasty old bitch, because she's convinced his death has paid him out properly for an indecent lack of loquacity as her guest.

He asked for Miss Leaf's address.

"No, no, *no*," she said with a horrible simulation of archness. "Oh *no!* Like nephew, like auntie—we mustn't give *anything* away—not even a few lines of writing for poor old godmother to find us!"

"Do I understand," Pardoe said to Kathleen Byron, "that Miss Leaf didn't say where she was going?"

"Not exactly." She showed no sign of perturbation at the disgraceful exhibition her mother was making. "She's got an elderly relative living the other side of Chelmsford, in the country. We didn't know her, and she didn't leave the address. It wasn't necessary."

"But it *was*," Mrs. Pell went on with the same unpleasant waggishness. "It was *very* necessary—very necessary *indeed*. Marian should have been more considerate than to give the inspector so much trouble. She——"

"Mother," said Mrs. Byron, severe but unruffled, "think well what you're saying. How could poor Marian possibly know that Archy was going to be killed while she was away?"

There was a short silence. Pardoe who had been careful to confine himself to the mere method of death, permitted a mild surprise to appear. Being killed was not the commonest way of describing suicide. "You have reason to suppose that Mr. Mitfold didn't take his own life?"

Her eyes narrowed a little. "None."

"Then——"

"Scotland Yard isn't as a rule interested in—suicides."

The old woman started laughing. The sound of it betrayed senility more than the strident voice. Its feeble huskiness was vilely suggestive. It would have been more tolerable if Kathleen Byron had appeared shocked at her mother's lapse from decency, but not a muscle of her face stirred while she kept her shallow gaze on the inspector.

He rose to go. The sickly brown light in the great overstuffed room where too much emphasis had been laid on material possession was only a degree less nauseating than the human contacts he had made here. Besides, he needed to be alone. In the last few minutes his mind had been making more lively efforts to pin down the memory that had eluded him earlier. Mrs. Byron's last words had reached him as a sort of echo through her mother's cackle; his inattention was due to a preoccupation with the idea that somewhere in not too remote a past he had encountered this woman before.

They both went with him into the hall.

"Yes, I'm afraid you'll be required to give evidence at the inquest, Mrs. Byron," he said in reply to a question.

For some obscure reason the old woman gave another derisive cackle. Then she nudged him violently, and croaked in his ear.

"If you're looking for somebody to fasten it on, you needn't go very far. Keep your eye on *Mister* Wynkerrell. *You* know the sort that Satan finds some mischief for."

Pardoe, meeting the stare of the basilisk eyes, was privately certain that he did.

CHAPTER VII: CURIOUS BEHAVIOR OF A YOUNG MAN

Why, here walk I in the black brow of night,
To find you out.
KING JOHN.

BROTHERHOOD STREET before the war was not the same place as it was now with its curtained windows and doused lamps. In the old days, as the adaptable Briton was already beginning to call them, or perhaps old nights would have been nearer the mark, a certain animation had been perceptible in after-tea hours. On Sunday evenings especially boys and girls had found mutual enjoyment in discovering together the excitements that lay underneath its drab familiarities, and their elders a vicarious one in merely looking on.

But Pardoe saw none of that when he went to look for Vera Moffat's house. Dusk was settling down, and besides himself nobody but a boy curvetting aimlessly on a bicycle from gutter to gutter was to be seen the whole length of the street.

Vera herself opened the door to him. Convinced of his bona fides, she led him to a front parlor where the sudden change from half-light to glare made him blink. Evening chapel, she explained, was at an earlier hour now that the dark nights were here, so her parents, taking the opportunity of their daughter's visit to attend together, had left her at home with her grandfather who was poorly and asleep upstairs.

At her invitation Pardoe removed his coat before sitting down beside a generous coal fire. He saw at once that this girl was older than Netta Traill, less self-reliant perhaps, but probably still more reliable. Her small, earnest face, framed in straight bobbed hair, was made to appear even smaller by the steel-rimmed spectacles she wore. Behind them her shortsighted eyes scrutinized the inspector politely as she waited for him to explain his errand.

Pardoe, avoiding circumlocution as far as was compatible with respect for her feelings, told her shortly what had happened. Her first reaction was an incredulity which found no vent in exclamations of horror. Instead, she frowned slowly and deeply and lifted her fingers in a wavering gesture to her mouth. She asked no questions, but all at once, to Pardoe's discomfort, her features crumpled uncertainly and she broke into quiet weeping.

He picked up the poker and knocked the fire into shape, letting her cry without interruption for a few minutes. When next he looked at her she had taken off her glasses and was dabbing her eyes with a large handkerchief. Without their shields they looked bright and luminous. It pleased him that she made no reference, apologetic or otherwise, to her tears, but sat trembling a little, applying the damp handkerchief first to her wet cheeks, then to the spectacles in her lap.

"It was bound to be a great shock to you," Pardoe said gently. "Better hear of it this way before returning to Mulberry Fountain. When are you due back?"

"Tomorrow morning. I was going in about eleven." She brushed away a wisp of hair and replaced the spectacles, fitting them carefully behind her ears.

"And Miss Leaf? When did she expect to come in?"

"In time for tea, sir. There's a train in at Liverpool Street just before four. Then she'd get another to Victoria, and be here in no time—but, oh—however are we going to tell her?"

"Don't worry now. Leave it to us. And there's no need to hurry Miss Leaf back in that case. It will be best for her to arrive the time she arranged, and I'll be glad if you'll come with me to meet her train at Victoria. That all right? Well now, there's one or two things you can tell me, if you think you're up to it?"

"Oh yes. I'll try." At some memory or other she blinked back fresh tears.

"To begin with," said Pardoe, resolutely matter-of-fact, "how were you going to let yourself in to number eight when you went back tomorrow?"

She seemed puzzled. "How—?"

"Which key had you been given?"

"Oh. The front door latchkey. That's the one I always have."

"So Miss Leaf wouldn't have bolted the front door when she went away?"

"No, never. None of us did. It was enough to drop the latch, you see."

"Of course. How many latchkeys are there to the front door?"

"Three. There were two to begin with, then about a year ago Miss Leaf felt lonely, like, and let part of the house as a sort of flat to friends of hers. She always kept one key and the Doyles—those were her friends—had the other. But—but Mr. Archy coming made it a bit awkward about keys. He went out to lessons in the evenings, and the time Miss Leaf wasn't well, she'd go to bed early and maybe I'd be down in the kitchen. So she got another for him to use."

"But the Doyles aren't living here now, are they?"

"No. You see, none of us knew there was going to be a war. Mr. Archy came the beginning of August when things hadn't got so hot, and it wasn't till the end of the month the Doyles packed up and went off to the country."

"That's quite clear," Pardoe said, remarking how composed she was while she was kept talking. "So when the house was shut on Friday each of you took away a latchkey to the front door?"

"That's right. If—if only I'd stayed."

"Stayed in the house, you mean? Was it suggested that you should?"

She shook her head. "It was like this. About the middle of the week when Miss Leaf made up her mind to go away she told me I could have the weekend for a holiday. She made sure then Mr. Archy was going with her. But then at the last he wouldn't. He was very firm about it. Miss Leaf—she was disappointed. So I said I'd stay and look after Mr. Archy, but they wouldn't hear of it. Said I was to have the weekend I'd been promised, and Mr. Archy could go to friends."

"Did you gather why it was he wanted to stay behind?"

"He *said* it was because he wanted to go to a lunch on Saturday—something to do with the boys from his old school. But that was funny too."

"Why funny?"

"Because about a month ago he had an invitation to this lunch, and he was making fun of it—said they were like proper hen parties, even if they were old boys, and some of them were so old he didn't know where they'd dug 'em out from. He said he wasn't going to talk ga-ga to a lot of old men who were kiddin' theirselves they were boys again."

"Very understandable," said Pardoe, who had experienced something of the sort himself. "And then he changed his mind."

"Well, seemingly. But I don't think he did really," Vera added quickly.

"You don't?"

"No. I think he said he was going to the school meeting to have an excuse to stay behind, but—there was something else at the back of his mind all the time."

She stopped, abruptly. A tinge of color in her face and the cautious glance she gave him told Pardoe that she had run on unintentionally. He did not want to alarm her into silence, but he must go deeper into this.

"You can perhaps guess what the real motive was?" he asked gently.

"Oh no, I can't. He wouldn't have told me nothing of that—though he trusted me." She was winding her handkerchief round her finger, then unwinding it again. Pardoe was afraid a growing agitation was bringing her to the verge of tears again.

"If Mr. Mitfold trusted you," he said, deliberately casual, "it was, of course, because you deserved his trust in some way."

She nodded unhappily. "But—Miss Leaf wouldn't like it."

"You're not telling Miss Leaf now," said Pardoe, grasping the sense of this apparently random observation. "You're telling me. And you're telling me so that I can discover why Mr. Archy died. You want me to do that, don't you?"

An inaudible remark that might have been, "Of course," escaped her. Pardoe was inspired to create a diversion that would allow her to relax. Chancing whether the sight of it would evoke fresh emotion, he drew from his pocket the envelope he had taken from Archy's desk and, turning it over, presented her with the bird sketches.

"Did you ever see Mr. Mitfold drawing pictures of this sort?" he asked lightly.

She peered closely, then exclaimed with a zest that banished tears, "Why, of course—dozens and dozens of them in the last week or so! He's made little clay models of them, too, an' stuck them about his room. I'm always finding them. Then he pinches them out of shape and makes instead little men with horns and a tail—devils, you know," she added primly as if in necessary, though improper, explanation. She looked again at the envelope and frowned. "But the hatchet isn't here."

"The hatchet?"

"Yes. He usually draws a row of little birds, and above them a row of little hatchets—or maybe sometimes it's one hatchet. I asked him why he wanted to butcher the poor little things. He'd laugh and most likely scribble them all out, and once he said, 'Some day that hatchet, as you call it, is going to get that little bird, V.'—he always called me V.—'an cut him right in two, the blighter.' He says a lot of things I don't understand."

She looked to Pardoe for enlightenment, he thought. It seemed a favorable moment to take the plunge.

"What were you going to tell me about the confidence Mr. Mitfold placed in you—just when I interrupted with that envelope?"

"Oh." She flushed again, but she did not look unhappy. The revelation when it came was innocent enough, so far as her own participation went, though Pardoe could well understand how an irrepressible conscience had been unable to reconcile it with her duty to Miss Leaf.

It appeared that a short time ago—oh, a bit more than a fortnight, perhaps—she had gone to bed at her usual time, but had woke up about one

Sketches on the envelope found in Archy Mitfold's desk

o'clock to hear a noise downstairs, "sort of stealthy it was, like somebody that didn't want to be heard." She had put on a coat, crept down the top stairs and, without disturbing Miss Leaf, knocked on Archy's door with the intention of rousing him to an encounter with a possible burglar. There was no answer and, because she had been afraid that persistent knocking would wake Miss Leaf, who had not been well for some time, she had opened the door a foot or so and momentarily switched on his light. It did not need more than the flash to tell her that the bed had not been slept in since she had made it that morning.

Her next move had been one of rare courage, Pardoe thought; for at the moment she made her discovery in Archy's room, a door closed somewhere downstairs. Instead of scurrying back to bed, as well she might have done, she nerved herself to go alone down to the basement from which the sounds had come.

"I didn't have time, you see, to think that if Mr. Archy wasn't abed, it was most likely him downstairs—and my heart was in me mouth. There was a bit of a light under the kitchen door, and water running. I opened it, and there was a candle end burning on the table and Mr. Archy drawing himself a glass of water from the tap in the sink."

It was a vivid enough little scene as she presented it. Archy was wearing a raincoat, and his hat was on the table. He made no attempt to take refuge in fibbing or excuse. Indeed, it would have been impossible to deny the obvious fact that he had just come in, and with Vera so clearly conscious of her responsibilities to the Leaf household the matter could not be left there. Archy Mitfold, as Pardoe saw it, made up his mind to admit his aunt's maid to partnership in a mystery he did not mean to elucidate.

This was the third night, he explained, that he had absented himself from the house at a time when the others thought him in bed and asleep. On the first occasion he had managed to let himself in without being heard. His chosen exit and entry had been by the basement door, because Miss Leaf's bedroom window was situated directly above the front door, and he did not want her to hear him.

"She wasn't there in August, of course," Vera added. "Her room and the drawing room next was the flat the Doyles had, and she was up on the top floor near me at that time. But when they left she moved back to her old room, being more comfortable with less stairs, an' that."

Archy had taken care to oil the basement key, but had not reckoned with the unpredictable tricks acoustics may play. A lavatory window open on the top landing at the back of the house, with the door left ajar, had carried to Vera's ears the sound of his return. Afterward, as she gravely informed Pardoe, she had seen that both were closed nightly, in case Miss Leaf should be roused in the same way.

For the nocturnal excursions had continued. Archy had explained to her with an earnestness her own simple version did not obscure the necessity for him to go out. Why, he would not say; nor where he went, nor what he did. Only that he had to find out what "they" were up to.

"No sir, he wouldn't say no more. I asked him. All he said was, 'I stumbled upon it by chance, V., and I've got to go on with it. Patience does it. Be a good kid and don't ask questions, and don't say anything to my aunt—an' when I've finished you shall know all about it."

Her lower lip was trembling. When she spoke again, however, her voice was calm and flat.

"So that's how it was. Sometimes I'd think I heard him coming in. I used to leave the kitchen window blacked out, and a candle and matches handy on the table when I went to bed, and some cocoa in a thermos. I'm always down first in the morning, so I knew it was all right. And sometimes I'd know he'd been out, and sometimes not."

"How many nights would you say he went altogether?"

She thought. "Five or six."

"And you never had any talk with him about it again?"

"Only once. One day he said to me, 'Thanks for the cocoa, V. By gum, it was cold out last night.' And I asked him if he was any nearer to finding out what he was after. And he didn't say anything for a minute or two—then he laughed—very jumpy he was—and said yes. But he didn't look like telling me more, so I didn't go on."

All this was far more than Pardoe had anticipated he would get. But for one phrase she had used it would have looked like the triangle business, with murder as its ugly apex. But, "I stumbled upon it by chance," had the ring of authenticity; and that did not sound the kind of thing to end in a killing at the hands of an injured lover or husband.

Feeling his luck might be in, he pressed his advantage. There was the matter of Mr. Mitfold's illness. But here she could help him little. Miss Leaf knew far more about that than she; she had attended him herself, had indeed made a point of doing so, excluding Vera from the sickroom. Yes, he had started to be ill in the night. He'd stayed in bed all next day and part of the next, and when he got up looked very white and pinched. Gastritis, Mr. Archy had called it. She didn't know, she was sure, but whatever it was it was a shame it should have happened on his birthday.

This was interesting. "Which day was that?"

"Last Thursday week. October 5. All right he was in the day, happy too—then to think of this coming on him at night."

"Perhaps he celebrated too well," the inspector suggested.

"Mr. Archy wasn't much of a feeder."

"Well, these bad turns will come along. After this one did he go out as usual at night?"

"Not at first he didn't. And he told me not to bother to put anything in the kitchen any more. But I think he went once just before Miss Leaf said she was going away."

"You're being a great help, you know," Pardoe said, and meant it. "You can understand it's important for us to know something of the state of Mr. Mitfold's mind in the days before this happened. Now, was there anything else—I mean anything peculiar besides his absences from the house at night?"

"There was nothing like that. Not to say mysterious. There was the old newspapers he started raking up"—she hesitated—"but he was quite open about it."

"I'd like to hear all the same."

"Well, it was this Mr. Sampson Vick affair, sir, that there's been so much in the papers about. You know how he's been missing from his home for a long time," she explained, as if Scotland Yard might not have heard about it, "and all the to-do there's been. Well, we never thought Mr. Archy took much notice one way or the other till all at once he began trying to get hold of back numbers of the papers and bothering his auntie and me which date it was Mr. Vick got lost."

"And could you tell him?"

"No. It was sometime in September, wasn't it?"

"Mr. Vick was last seen on September 25. Three weeks tomorrow."

"Well, we didn't remember. And we couldn't see that it mattered either—I mean for Mr. Archy to know just when. But he fussed and fadded about it, and then he found some of the old papers. We'd been asked not to waste paper, being wartime, but save it for the collectors to call, and Miss Leaf had tied some of them up and put them in the toolshed. So what must Mr. Archy do but pull 'em all about again."

"Did he find what he was looking for?"

"Yes. He cut out pieces from the papers about Mr. Vick. We asked him why, but he only said he always liked mysteries and fancied hisself as Sherlock Awmes. He did, too."

Pardoe smiled. "Well, a lot of us do. Was that the end of the matter so far as you know?"

"Oh yes. He seemed satisfied when he got all that litter round him. We didn't hear about it any more."

"Miss Moffat, this may be important." Pardoe leaned forward and spoke urgently. "Will you think carefully and tell me whether Mr. Mitfold's interest in the missing Mr. Vick was *before* or *after* he started going out at night?"

"I don't have to think hard, sir," she said simply. "It was after. About a week after. The day before his birthday, it was."

She could not tell whether her answer pleased him or not. He frowned.

"Then he was ill before he got hold of the papers?"

"No. He routed them out next day, his birthday, and started reading them.

But it was in bed, when he was feeling better, that he took the cuttings he wanted."

"Think back to the day before his birthday," Pardoe said. "Can you recall the first thing he said to you about the Vick case? Had he had a visitor just before, or been out, or reading, or what?"

Vera, without knowing why, had caught a little of the inspector's interest. Her small face was flushed. "He'd been to the pictures, sir. That I do know. In the afternoon. He came in as jumpy as a flea—the way he'd get sometimes—and caught his auntie round the waist and swung her round and said, 'Aunt Marie'—that was his name for her—'Aunt Marie, what day did this millionaire bloke disappear?' If she hadn't been used to his ways it would have sounded funny, coming sudden like that. But, being Mr. Archy, we didn't take on much."

"No. I see. What cinema did it happen to be, do you know?"

She did not. There was a slender chance Miss Leaf could tell him, though it was unsafe to conclude that Archy's interest in Sampson Vick was to be traced to that source. There may have been an encounter on the way home, a remark overheard, a poster that caught the eye—anything may have happened to quicken that curious excitement. It was not going to be easy to reconstruct the movements of a man who had taken pains to avoid publicity in the conduct of the least of them. But Vera Moffat's evidence was almost an *embarras de richesses*, whose proper sifting and bringing to order promised adequate reward for labor.

Pardoe's swift mental picture of the dead boy on his way back from the cinema was succeeded by another of less definitive outline. As he turned over a fresh page of the notebook in which he had pencilled occasional memoranda of the conversation, it prompted him to say: "There's one other thing you can tell me—I'll have to get in touch with Mr. Archy's friends. Can you give me the names of those he knew best, especially any who visited him at Mulberry Fountain?"

In a few minutes he had what he wanted, a list of half a dozen visitors to number eight since Archy's arrival two months ago.

Pardoe cast a speculative eye over them.

Mr. Tony Winkerell. (Spelling contributed by Vera.)
Mr. Lake. (Christian name unknown.)
Miss Hatty Bemrose.
Miss Anna David.
A young man (name unknown, certainly a foreigner) who appeared from time to time in the company of Mr. Lake and/or Miss David.
Mr. Beltane. (Christian name forgotten.)

These, Vera had pointed out, might be termed frequent, if erratic, callers at the house. All, that is, except Mr. Beltane. She could not remember that he had been more than once, but his name came easily to mind because Mr. Archy often spoke of him. She proffered it doubtfully, but Pardoe added him to the list nevertheless.

He noticed she was hesitating as if on the verge of further disclosure.

"Something else come to mind, Miss Moffat?"

"Well, no, not exactly. Only when you asked me about his friends I was wondering if I ought to count the professor."

"I should," said Pardoe cheerfully, prepared to count everybody. "That the tutor?"

"Yes. Professor Speyer. He—he's a German, sir," she added dubiously, "but he goes on just the same since the war came, so p'raps he's one of these friendly a-leens."

"Perhaps he is. He comes often to the house?"

"N-no. Not often. Not like Mr. Tony and Miss David and them. And it's Mr. Archy goes to the professor for his lessons, he doesn't have them here. But he's been to tea a few times, and I thought—if you wanted to see Mr. Archy's friends, well, he'd know something perhaps what was in his mind—at the last, sir."

Her voice fell to a whisper.

"Quite right. That's sensible of you. Where does he live?"

"Close by. At least, I mean not far. In Rossetti Terrace—he's got rooms there, by the river before you get to Oakley Street. It's number sixteen. I know, because I've had to ring him up before now. But he hasn't long moved in."

"Oh. Where did he live before?"

"Earl's Court way. Mr. Archy was pleased when he came here, he didn't have so far to go."

That concluded Vera's evidence. Pardoe thanked her heartily, made arrangements for the next afternoon, and went away cherishing the not unpleasurable if confused sentiments of a legatee who is unable to make up his mind as to the best use to which to put his unexpected access of wealth.

The shadow of Sampson Vick, which in the past week had retreated into a background it yet haunted with disconsolate persistence, loomed up again, freshly disturbing. This time it fell across a path which death, sudden and unnatural, had closed.

Mitfold . . . Vick . . . Mitfold . . . Vick . . . The car, clocks, footsteps, a little pulse in his own brain beat it out that night in monotonous rhythm.

In the morning Mrs. Sampson Vick, who for ten days had not communicated with Scotland Yard, put through a telephone call and asked to speak to Inspector Pardoe.

CHAPTER VIII: A WORD OF MR. VICK

By this light of heaven, I know not how I lost him.
OTHELLO.

PARDOE TOOK THE PIECE of paper to the window of the pleasant drawing room overlooking the Green Park, to examine its penciled characters more closely.

The woman who sat at the table rested her chin in her hand and watched him. She watched without hope or fear. Three weeks of mental agony had at last blunted the finer edges of imagination. Letters . . . there were always letters . . . cruel letters, foolish letters, heartless, crazy letters, letters of vague sympathy that managed to convey still more vaguely their authors' yearnings to hobnob with the household of a missing millionaire, letters execrably written and nearly all anonymous. What difference did it make that she had received another this morning? Not one had offered a concrete basis on which to work. They had poured in for the first week or so and been dealt with quickly by the police, who were only too familiar with this curious social phenomenon. Anonymous letter writers were to them the jackals that moved, a miserable, jostling pack, on the fringes of crime. Where murder was concerned they kept a respectful distance from the kill, scavengers for the scraps of notoriety the beast of prey chucked aside. Some pickings they always got, if it were only mental gratification of a private lust.

Beatrice Vick was finding that they no longer had the power to hurt. She was not vulnerable any more. Sampson himself had at last receded to that distant region where memory seeks only penultimate records by which to conjure up the beloved. His activities in the spring and early summer, and in the years of their life together, were vivid and endearing; what were now of little consequence or reality were the last weeks he had lived in this house, with the shadow of his abrupt dismissal from it already darkening the scene. She remembered that that was how she had felt when her mother went. All the meaning that her mother had given to childhood and adolescence she had been able to take hold of and cherish like a warm, living thing. What had perished had been the last months of suffering; they remained blank, meaningless, without light. But her mother had died. And Sampson . . . ?

She pulled herself together as the tall, quiet man came back from the window and flattened the letter out upon the table in front of her, with the envelope beside it. In spite of the indifference despair had bred, confidence in him kept stubbornly alive.

His first remark was startling in its apparent irrelevance.

"Can you tell me, Mrs. Vick, if your husband was acquainted with a young man named Archy Mitfold?"

She frowned, but characteristically did not enquire his reason for asking.

"I don't think so." She glanced involuntarily at the letter, but there was no clue she could interpret. "As far as I know, he certainly wasn't. But there were—friends I hadn't met."

"I know. The American ones. But this is different—at least I think it is. Besides it might not be that Mr. Vick knew him personally—do you remember if he ever received a letter from anybody of that name?"

"I don't. But I can find out. That's Miss Channing's province."

She rang a bell and sent the maid for the secretary.

Pardoe had met Miss Channing before and admired her brisk attention to detail in the face of an event which had rocked her world. This no-nonsense, get-on-with-it attitude might or might not connote callousness; he only knew that it was in every way preferable to the vaporish sort of sentiment so often met with in cases of this kind, that got you precisely nowhere. She was a little spare woman, sixty if a day, with abundant gray hair amazingly well dressed. She put her head on one side to consider Pardoe's question.

"I'll look through the files again if you like," she said, "but I can say at once that no such letter ever passed through my hands. You can put against that what I told you before—that since the middle of February Mr. Vick has taken over a number of secretarial duties himself. I still answered his letters and still handled the bulk of them—but only *after* he'd sorted them himself, a thing he never did before. He didn't tell me why he was making the change, and I didn't ask."

The eyes of the two women met.

"It was after the threatening letters came from America," Mrs. Vick said.

Miss Channing nodded. "The time he made his largest donations to the hospitals," she added.

"All you can say for certain, then," Pardoe went on, "is that no letter was received from a correspondent called Mitfold at a time when you were handling the entire correspondence yourself. But there may have been one after February?"

"There may," she admitted. "In which case it wasn't brought to my notice at all. And no record of it exists. You've seen all there is to see of the correspondence."

"Thank you. We'll leave it at that." He placed his finger on the letter that lay open before them and looked at Mrs. Vick. "Has Miss Channing seen it?"

"Yes. I showed it to her when it came this morning."

"Miss Channing, you're familiar with letters written in every variety of hand. What do you make of this? Never mind about trying to preserve prints—it's been freely handled already, the envelope too, and this type of paper's a poor vehicle for them in any case."

She took it nevertheless with the scrupulous care the unknown, however valueless, commands.

Paper and envelope were, as the inspector suggested, of the cheapest brand, and could have been bought at any big store or railway station. The paper was faintly lined and so thin as to be transparent, the envelope inadequately gummed and of that absorbent quality that sometimes plows up under the nib or else causes the ink to run. In this case, however, ink had not been used. Both message and address were written in pencil, in block capitals.

Miss Channing's sharp eyes scrutinized them minutely, with particular attention for the letter itself.

This, undated and bearing no address, ran as follows:

MADAM—*if you want news of S.V. find out who was at the Hotel Roland in Mentone Sept. 30.*

A Friend

"Well," said the secretary drily, "a pity his amity couldn't go a bit further and tell us who *was* staying at the Hotel Roland on the date in question! Whoever it was it wasn't Mr. Vick, for you've raked the permit and shipping offices thoroughly, and his passport's been safe in his desk all the time."

"You were going to give an opinion on the handwriting, Brenda," Mrs. Vick said impatiently.

"Of course. Well, this isn't exactly handwriting, is it? I'm used to all sorts, it's true—you should see some of them, Mr. Pardoe—but block capitals, even in begging letters, haven't come my way before." She raised the paper a little higher in her hand and tilted it back so that its surface lay horizontally under her eyes. "Yes, there's something strikes me. The tops and bottoms of the letters don't lie evenly. They're out of alignment, as we say in typing. Perhaps the writer had something wrong with his eyesight."

Pardoe took the letter from her. "I don't think so. You're quite right about the inequality of the printing—for example, the R L of 'Roland' are considerably larger than the O, which seems to jump up between them; then the A drops below, and so on. But I fancy there's another explanation. This writer's method shows a slight variation of that usually employed by anonymous correspondents who favor block type. The ordinary thing to do is either sit down and write the message straightway yourself without more ado, or else cut out your letters from some newspaper or other and paste them on the paper. 'A Friend,' I think, did neither."

He paused, and Beatrice Vick who had been looking toward the window suddenly turned her head and said, "You mean he traced them?"

"Yes. Handwriting experts know that resort to block capitals doesn't always disguise the individual character of the writing. Certain peculiarities of the cursive hand continue to crop up. Also, as one writes, confidence gives speed, and speed always helps to betray the writer who wants to remain anonymous. Tracing, on the other hand, is a slowing-down process."

"That's interesting," Miss Channing said emphatically. "There's method in his madness. And tracing would explain why he used such very thin paper."

"I think so. And the reason the letters don't keep in line is because he moved his paper about over the surface of the newspaper, or whatever it was, in search of the ones he wanted. They weren't all the same size either. And I shan't be surprised if an expert doesn't spot how slowly he went to work—which again suggests tracing. Look closely, and you'll see for yourself the wavering of his pencil here and there."

"And a nasty pencil it was," the secretary said, delighted to contribute a personal observation. "An HH, it looks like."

"You're probably right," Pardoe said absently. He picked up the envelope. "Now it wasn't possible to trace with this. Here he *had* to do without the help of printed letters. And notice how hideously malformed most of his are—he's purposely done his worst so as to conceal the characteristics I spoke about just now, as well, I think, as to suggest he is an uneducated person, the kind of camouflage that's frequently overdone."

"Where was it posted?" Mrs. Vick asked in a voice gone suddenly harsh. "I didn't look."

"W.C.2's our only guide there—in time for the 8:30 collection last night."

A telephone's muffled trill came from close at hand.

"Excuse me," said Miss Channing, and left the room.

Mrs. Vick looked at Pardoe. From a haggard face that kept still the beauty she no longer regarded, her eyes shone strangely large in their dark orbits. With her elbows on the table she spread her hands a little in a gesture precluding speech.

"You'll—you'll—?"

"We shall make enquiries in Mentone," he said quickly.

She dropped her forehead on her hands.

"Before God," she said softly, more to herself than to him, "I don't know why he went without a word. And you think—you all think——" She was silent.

"Mrs. Vick," said Pardoe gently, "if what we think is true, you have the courage to bear it. Actually you've borne it in the weeks gone by, over and over again. Reality, if and when we've got to face it, won't be worse than that."

"You're right," she said, lifting her head. She added, "I wish I could have helped you more."

Pardoe put out his hand, but she went on.

"But I do. I mean, it must have seemed strange to you that there were no photographs—literally none—since he was a young man in the States years before I knew him. And not a scrap of handwriting—for, though he grew better of the arthritis I told you about, habit still held, and he would never write unless to sign his name. That's why I don't think, even after February, he answered any of his letters himself."

"That may be," Pardoe admitted. "It's possible that after receiving the threatening letters from America he merely wanted to sort his correspondence to eliminate anything like that before his secretary saw it—a natural defensive measure against confiding unpleasant news."

"Yes. But he hadn't minded Miss Channing seeing the first ones, and he discussed them freely with me." She passed a hand across her forehead.

Pardoe sensed her weariness. "I'm not going to ask you to hope where we see little room for hope, Mrs. Vick," he said quietly as he took his leave. "But I do ask you to remember that if the solution proves the worst we have thought, he is out of reach of further suffering."

At the time of the disappearance of Sampson Vick, Detective Sergeant Salt had been hard at work on the Walworth robberies, a series of minor smash-and-grab activities carried out under cover of the blackout and punctuated by rather more serious bodily assaults. The Fascists attributed them to the Jews, the Jews to the Fascists. Salt went stolidly to work and by solution exonerated both parties from blame, to their mutual dissatisfaction. The job had kept his nose to the grindstone for the best part of three weeks while Pardoe was handling the Vick case with what delicacy he could, and now that he was released to work with the inspector in the Mulberry Fountain business he found he knew little of the earlier affair beyond what he had had time to gleam from the less reticent organs of the press. For the newspapers, tenderly concerned for a public they deemed undernourished on war news, had served up with savage gusto the necessary vitamins extracted from what they called the "Lost Millionaire Mystery." But Salt, who shared the common knowledge that Sampson Vick was one of the three richest men and most lavish dispensers of wealth in England, had not spared time to digest their fare.

"You'd better get the facts clear, Tommy," Pardoe said, "before the fairy tales have corrupted even your tough mind. It's like this.

"Sampson and Humphrey Vick were brothers, coming from a Wiltshire family of small country squires—the sort who live decent, unrecorded lives from one generation to another, never expecting, and not often getting, a breakaway from tradition. What's that? Oh yes, he's English right enough, didn't see the States till he was sixteen. When he was that age, and Humphrey about three years younger, they were left orphans by the father's death—the mother had died a year or two before—and penniless ones at that. Bad speculation, agricultural setbacks, and the Vick boys with not two red cents apiece, and certainly nothing to complete their schooling.

"Then an uncle who'd settled in America in his young days and not regretted it offered to take them. He wasn't a Vick—he was the mother's side of the family. Remember hearing tell of the Vick Seaman hardware stores? Seaman was the uncle, and he took Sampson into the business, and started to push his stores, already thriving, all the way from New York through Pennsylvania out to the furthest parts of the Middle West. He had a fine business head, and he soon found that his young nephew had a still finer. Between 'em they flooded the markets with cheap, reliable stuff, from nails to plowshares, and did for the manufacture of farming implements what Ford did for the car industry."

"Ah! That's where the brass came from," said Salt.

"Yes. Seaman was a bachelor, there weren't any other relatives he'd kept in touch with, and Sampson Vick took over. Let's see"—Pardoe made a mental calculation—"he was fifty-five last birthday. Seaman died in 1911, so he was twenty-seven at that time. He carried on the work, scrapping, expanding, modernizing, till at last pile was added to pile in the way money, after a certain point is reached, seems to make money independently of human effort."

"What about the brother?" the sergeant said, frowning. "There was something—"

Pardoe looked grim. "There was. And if you've done no more than skim the papers you've seen it. They've kept quiet about it while Sampson Vick's been living here as a munificent donor to every conceivable cause, but they've unleashed the hounds now. It's been splashed across every rag in the country for the past three weeks."

"I know," Salt said quickly. "Humphrey was the gangster."

The inspector nodded. Salt thought he looked worried all at once, but the Vick case was like that, rising like a wraith to trouble every new job in hand.

"Yes," he said, "Humphrey was the gangster. In the real Al Capone tradition—though he was never a leader in that sense. But he was the next best—or next worst thing—the right-hand man of Vincent Balthasar, called Vinny the Backer, who was Capone's only serious rival in those palmy Chicago days. They ran neck-and-neck in the liquor and blackmail lines, till Vinny slipped up on murder and cut his career even shorter than Capone's."

"They killed one of their own pals, didn't they?"

"Well, an unofficial pal, p'raps. A rich fellow called Bulmann who'd 'contributed' to the racket for a year or so, most likely at pistol point. He turned nasty and held on to the dibs at last, and was plugged one night for his pains when his car got held up in a jam as he was leaving the opera. There was a fog at the time, and his killer slipped away, but the police traced the murder—so they said—to one of Viny's men a fortnight later."

"Vick?"

"No. Not the murder. That was another chap, I forget his name. But they netted the whole gang. And it was easy to take Humphrey, anyway."

"Why?"

"He'd quarreled with the Backer in the fortnight the police were hunting 'em, over the murder, it was said. He accused Vinny of it in front of some of the others in a night club the racketeer owned, and all hell broke loose. Vinny got the idea he was going to rat, you see, and knifed him before you could say Jack Robinson—or whatever it is they say over there."

"He didn't die of it though, did he? I remember—last Sunday's *Meteor* said they put him in Alcatraz for—I forget how long."

"That's it. They left him for dead and cleared out, but the police turned up and hustled him off to hospital where they got him round. It was touch and go though—he'd a tearing wound in his chest, and Vinny nearly had two murders to his account."

"And then Vick squealed—wasn't that it?"

"They said he did. The police said not. Whichever way it was the gang was cleaned up three days later."

"Ah," said Salt with gloomy satisfaction. "An' Vinny went to the chair."

"With the fellow he'd told off to do the murder. The rest got varying sentences. Vick got five years—in Alcatraz."

Salt lifted his brows to a comical height above his small gray eyes.

"Not too bad, was it, if he *didn't* squeal?"

Pardoe was silent for a minute as though he had not heard.

"You see," he said slowly, "Sampson was his brother. It was the end of 1929. At the beginning of the year Sampson had resigned the chairmanship of the Vick Seaman board of directors and made a clean break with the whole vast concern. Rumor, which is more often right than's imagined, said Humphrey's goings-on had made big business too hot for him any longer. Sampson was a decent chap always, not priggish, but he liked to be quiet— the more publicity his brother got the keener he was himself to get away from the limelight."

"How was it the fellow only got a five-year packet?" Salt repeated doggedly.

"Because he was Sampson's brother." The inspector sounded patient. "I just said so. It's what we enjoy calling graft. I don't know—there are circumstances, maybe, when it's nearer real justice than justice itself."

The sergeant snorted with subdued skepticism. There were times when he privately questioned his chief's ethical standards, and was thankful that in practice he did not as a rule conform to his theory.

"Good conduct earned Humphrey remission," Pardoe went on, "so he didn't serve his five-year packet, as you call it. They released him in the autumn of '32—a sick man. He never really got over the knife attack, and Alcatraz isn't much of a pick-me-up."

"And then Sampson had him to live with 'im," Salt said.

"In the shack he'd had built in the Salmon River mountains in Idaho—yes. By this time Sampson, in rotten health himself, was living the life of a hermit, no company, no servants, none of the devices we're slaves to and are positive we can't do without, nothing, in short, that we understand as civilization. He was happy, though. Of course it made his doctors and old business associates mad—they said if he'd only gone to live somewhere on the Mexican gulf instead he'd've rid himself of the arthritis that was crippling him."

Salt chuckled. "It took England to do that. Gosh, our darned old climate that buckles us all up with the screws—an' it goes an' cures a rich Yank that's dyin' of 'em!"

"He wasn't a Yank. So p'raps it was a case of the hair of the dog that bit him. Anyway, he took Humphrey to live with him, and the G-men ticked off to see their old enemy didn't run amok again found they had nothing to do. The two lived the simple life with a vengeance, never stirred out, or wrote or talked to anybody except when business demanded some sort of personal contact, and then Sampson would manage to get as far as Challis perhaps and put through a trunk call to his banker or solicitor."

" 'Umphrey didn't carry on long, did he? I mean, he soon pegged out."

"Humphrey died the middle of 1934. And in the winter of the same year Sampson, with the natural desire, I think, to cut himself adrift from the old life, sailed for England. On the voyage home he met his future wife, and they were married the next spring."

Pardoe paused, and made some idle marks with his pencil inside the cover of his notebook.

"That was another jolt for the folk he'd once known. Everybody supposed him a hardened bachelor—Humphrey had been the one with the charm. Oh, you can stare, Tommy—he had. Charm, built on sands. It was just that deadly combination, an engaging personality and no grit behind it, that had led him to Alcatraz."

"I'll take your word for it."

"You don't have to. I didn't know him. Take common report."

"His wife left 'im, though. I'm talking about Humphrey."

"Yes—there was a woman—an Italian cabaret singer. I don't know if they were married. Well, I suppose she had her future to think about. It's true she cleared out."

"But the fellow had a tidy bit, they said. From the beer racket."

"If they weren't legally spliced she had no claim to it. Yes, rumor had it he'd got a fortune, which he left in his will to Sampson. And Sampson's will left everything to Humphrey, with the stern disapproval of his lawyers. But he'd done in his lifetime all he meant to do in the charitable line, and he wasn't to be moved. The early will I'm talking about, of course. There'll be another since Humphrey's death and his own marriage."

"If there's anything left over," Salt grunted. "Soon as the brother died he started again on the charities. Must 'a' given thousands upon thousands in the four or five years he's been here."

Pardoe, scribbling with apparent concentration, nodded. "A systematic round of every charity deserving of the name—his last gift before he was reported missing was £30,000 to provide comforts for merchant seamen in the war."

"Blood money," said Salt.

"Maybe—not on his own account, though."

"I mean he was trying to pay for Bulmann an' all the rest of 'em."

"P'raps. Sampson had a highly developed sense of family responsibility."

"Social too, by gum."

"You're right. He seems to have found a sort of restless pleasure in constant giving away—especially in the simple, unorganized giving that most people enjoy best. The putting one's hand in one's pocket business. He couldn't do it with the immense sums, but with lesser amounts he liked to see for himself the happiness they brought. It's by that habit of his that Mrs. Vick had the secretary explain the frequent checks drawn to self." Pardoe paused and looked up quickly, as if he expected a comment from Salt. When the sergeant said nothing, he went on: "He didn't spend much on himself. You know he bought up the little family holding near Devizes? They lived there part of the year, the Piccadilly flat the other part. But he and his wife do no entertaining to speak of and keep a minimum staff. All the same—"

"What?" Salt asked in the pause.

"I was going to say there *was* a sort of activity on his part in the last year or so. He went places and met people Mrs. Vick knew nothing about. She knew he was doing it, that is—but he didn't let her in on it, and she says she never bothered him. There's no doubt he was leading a sort of double life, in a quiet way. He'd go out nights."

Salt grinned. "These things will 'appen in the best reg'lated families—an' nobody can say the Vick family was that."

"Sampson's part of it was," Pardoe objected quickly. "He'd say sometimes he was going to play bridge, or whist or what not. Mrs. Vick hasn't a fancy for those things, and she says she sensed early on that he was relieved when she didn't offer to come. Now the night he never returned home—the night of September 25—he'd said he was going to drop in on Sir George Ling in Carlyle Square to make up a four—he did sometimes. And that's where the taxi put him down. *But* the driver swears Vick didn't enter the house before he drove off, and Sir George has said he didn't turn up that evening. Indeed, he goes further and says bridge hadn't been arranged for that evening, though had Vick called they would most likely have played—his wife and her brother occupy the house with him."

"Is 'e O.K.?"

"Who—Ling? Absolutely. Traveled a good deal—not in Vick's hemisphere, though. Australia and the South Seas. Feels irked at settling down in the old country and finds the average Britisher sticky. So he welcomed the friendship of a man like Vick."

"What about 'is other friends? You overhauled 'em?"

"That's just it. He hasn't got any. None we can lay fingers on, that is. He wasn't the sort that encourages friendship. The whole thing's been one hell of a nightmare—and, keep this under your hat, he's due for a baronetcy in the New Year."

Salt whistled sympathetically. "I hate these clams," he said with feeling after a minute. "Look at Mitfold. There's no give an' take about it with a corpse an' a missing bloke who won't cooperate with yours truly."

Pardoe laughed. "We haven't got to look for cooperation in our line. We can think ourselves lucky to have picked up the Vick trail again in this new job. There's the chance running the two cases together will simplify both."

"If Mitfold's interest in 'em wasn't jes' the Sherlock 'Olmes stuff he told the girl," was Salt's dubious rejoinder.

"Dammit all, Tommy," Pardoe said irritably, because a suspicion which had crossed his own mind assumed larger proportions now that it was voiced, "have you *got* to be the unfailing pessimist? Is it likely it was mere amateur sleuth fever when it began nine or ten days *after* Sampson Vick was missing? Why, he'd troubled so little about the case previously that he didn't know which day Vick was reported missing. And he'd been carrying on some private mystery of his own beforehand, so you can't say he was only looking round for something to exercise his detective talents on."

"All right." But the sergeant felt called upon to defend his position. "We're not dead certain, though, that Mitfold was murdered. Why shouldn't a suicide—a freakish guy, say—once in a while turn out the light?"

Pardoe stared at this fresh heterodoxy. "I don't know why he shouldn't— I only know he never does. Hanging, above all, which may prove a deuced awkward business in the light when you've only one completely good hand to do it with, is practically out of the question in the dark. Besides, bumping yourself off in the dark would be different again from doing it in a room you'd had to *make* dark—for the blackout curtains prove there'd been lights on. The house had several gas fires—an easier and altogether more painless way of passing out. There's the evidence of the prints. There's the evidence of the chair lying near the body—in the first place its weight suggests that the distance it was found from Mitfold's feet is too great for it to have been kicked over by him. Secondly, no prints have been found on it; and what's more, though his shoes carry traces of damp earth and squashed fruit, the seat of the chair on which it's suggested he stood to hang himself is perfectly clean."

"I'll hand it to you on the chair count," Salt admitted, "but 'e could 've faked the rest to look like murder."

"You pull yourself together, old man," the inspector said kindly, "and sit up and take notice again. That Walworth business got you down, and no mistake."

" 'Your courage, your cheerfulness, your resolution.' " Salt grimaced. "O.K.

But you can't get away from it—the fellow *liked* making a bloomin' mystery of things."

"And Tawney's said he had a blow on the head before death. Wait for the autopsy report, you old grouser—that'll settle your hash." Pardoe stood up and looked at his watch. "We'll get a move on before Miss Leaf's train's in. Better take Tony Wynkerrell first—he can put us wise to a bit, and—"

He stopped short, then brought his fist down on the desk with a violent movement that ended softly. "Got it," he said with a satisfaction that mystified the sergeant. "I knew I'd seen the woman before somewhere—Mrs. Byron, I mean. Wasn't there a Mrs. Welkin who was mixed up with a notorious inquest and a coroner who thought he was the Almighty?"

"Garage affair," Salt said laconically. His obstinate and random memory was at times a treasure house. " 'Er husband died in it—carbon monoxide an' shut doors, same old mixture. They tried for 'er to give herself away, but she wasn't having any. The coroner was right, though," he added darkly.

"P'raps he was. All the more reason he should have behaved himself, the jackass. That's the woman. She must have married again. See if you can get a line on her. Find out what happened after the inquest."

The telephone rang. Pardoe stretched for the receiver and listened impassively for a few seconds after the first hellos.

"Yes—what? Well, we might, if there's anything to go on—depends what you can tell us. I see—Saturday afternoon, was it?—Yes—yes. No, I see—somebody shall come down tonight or in the morning. Let me have the address—what, *Whitby?* No—will you repeat that?" Receiver to his ear, he scribbled something on the pad beside him, then read it slowly into the telephone. "Right? Thank you, we'll be along."

He hung up and looked at the attentive Salt.

"We move, Tommy. That was a Mr. Philip Beltane, a master at Rowan House Preparatory School, Witley-in-the-Holt, Kent. He's seen the report of Mitfold's death in the papers, and he's got some information he says will be of use to us."

"How far's Witley?"

"Surrey border, he says—north of Westerham." Pardoe narrowed his eyes a little in thought. "Tommy, why give us a call?"

"Why not?"

"Because all the press had was a little paragraph that didn't so much as hint it wasn't suicide—and our interest wasn't mentioned."

Salt shaped his lips to a soundless whistle. "Must be 'is own information then. He knows what's 'e's got is meat for the Yard."

"It might be that." Pardoe picked up his notebook, opened it and glanced at one of the pages. "We've got him on the list, Tommy, we've got him on the list. He was a caller at Mulberry Fountain."

He was turning the leaves as he spoke. When he got to the cover he stared hard. Then he laughed shortly.

"I've got the fever too. I've been drawing Mitfold's birds."

The sergeant gave the sketches a solemn glance. "Now all you've got to do is put *salt* on their tails," he said, with gloomy relish for his pun.

CHAPTER IX: AT THE SIGN OF THE JUNIPER

I'll have them very fairly bound:
All books of love.
THE TAMING OF THE SHREW.

"THAT'S HOW I LOOK AT IT," said Tony Wynkerrell an hour later, flicking off the ash of his rapidly consumed cigarette. "He wasn't worried in the way you suggest, not a bit of it. Only in an excited, I'm-not-telling-you-all fashion that Beltane and I found wearing after a bit. Somebody was feeling spiteful toward him, without a doubt—and thinking it over afterwards I haven't a doubt either that the poor beggar knew who it was. But he wasn't telling." He sighed. "Good lor', to think it's only a couple of days since he slung us the tale—and now this!"

A chain smoker, Salt decided, as he listened to the throaty voice and watched him light another fag before crushing the stub underfoot. He didn't envy the blighter who had this room to clean. If it ever was cleaned. It was a small, dark cubbyhole of a place behind the Juniper Bookshop where some sort of untidy business was obviously carried on. The wooden floor, gritty and ink blotched, was innocent of matting, the little window set too high and laced by the dismal skeleton of a fire escape that ran down the outside wall and shut off still more of the inadequate light. The table was smothered in packing paper and dirty cord, among the debris some copies of a quarterly review; a few files stood about in corners; the chairs on which the Yard men had been invited to sit were of the less durable office variety. Stacks of business envelopes steadily collected the week's dust on a packing case against the wall, whose only adornment was a damp-ravished paper that even in its pristine days could not have been other than hideous. The only comfortable feature in this disordered abode was the electric fire, which burned with an extravagant resolve to combat the prevailing gloom. Indeed, its cheerfulness was a little overpowering in surroundings where the supply of oxygen fell short of the demand.

All of it, Pardoe thought, was in ludicrous contrast to the ornamental young man before them. Whatever else might be said of Tony Wynkerrell, he was unquestionably a credit to his tailor. He reminded Pardoe of a gorgeous pea-cock butterfly he had once disentangled from a dust-laden cobweb; but the simile, of course, was falsely colored by Mrs. Byron's prejudices, for here was not the mind of an aimless dilettante but one that leapt to meet his questioner's and anticipated the drift of interrogation in a way peculiarly disconcerting.

He had listened intelligently to the guarded account Scotland Yard had thought fit to impart, and had responded with a frank and apparently unguarded account of Archy Mitfold's last day alive so far as it concerned himself. The only jarring note in his statement was a want of feeling that expressed itself now and again in an irritating flippancy. But Pardoe was used to this brittle quality in the modern young; it seemed to be the kind of emotional disturbance of a piece with their odd appreciations and surface enthusiasms that were so bewildering to follow, and as often as not signified nothing at all—unless it were regimented and employed by a government alive to its potencies, and then it could be dangerous, as all the world knew. Wynkerrell himself sensed the official attitude to his witty departures, and made no attempt to ignore it.

"I'm sorry if I seem to have no heart," he said with graceful apology. "It's not that I disliked Mitfold. But, well—I didn't come upon him dead as you did, and perhaps I'm wanting in a sufficiently lively imagination. It's the same thing as sympathy, after all. Besides, I was never really friends with Archy. We went to the same school and all that, and were co-sufferers in the last year we swotted in the Sixth. Then it was Cambridge for me, Oxford for Archy. We've only picked up the threads again since he came up here—so you can't expect me to feel any deep regrets. I see it in the more detached way, you know, a highly interesting, even exciting problem—and that, of course, is his own fault."

Pardoe, who thought him unnecessarily defensive, agreed.

"I understand. Now when you took him home, or rather to the house where he was staying, did he add anything fresh to the story he'd told you and Mr. Beltane?"

"Not a word. In fact, he didn't say much at all on the way—I can't remember a thing. Driving in London these evenings doesn't encourage talking."

"No—but I think you talked when you got to Alma Square, didn't you? Mrs. Byron has a rather lively recollection of the noise."

Wynkerrell stared, then laughed. "She would. Old Mother Pell too. I won't say we didn't kick up a bit of a shindy—but the old girls would complain of the row a fly made walking on the ceiling if it suited their little book. And this did. Look here." He leaned forward, his lips twisted wryly and a gleam in his eye. "Bet you anything they've fixed the murder on me already. I've only run across them about twice, but they hate me like henbane and arsenic and prussic acid rolled into one! And do I care?"

Salt had grunted a response to this uncanny insight into the bent of mind of the Pell household, but Pardoe merely smiled indulgently and let it pass.

"So you admit the clatter," he said. "What was it all about?"

"Why, nothing at all." Wynkerrell frowned. "I don't know what Mrs. Byron may have said, of course. Archy took me upstairs to show me the perfectly awful pictures hanging in the room they'd given him—ghastly things, Day of Judgment, and Last Trump, and churchyards yawning, and I don't know what. No wonder the poor kid thought he was for it. Of course we got a giggling fit and whooped a bit—wouldn't you?"

The inspector looked noncommittal, though privately of the opinion that whooping was not the emotion roused in him at sight of the dining-room pictures.

"As a matter of fact," Wynkerrell went on, "I believe our silly ragging was simply reaction from the morbidity of the afternoon. We were inside a lighted house, you understand, after the dark streets, and I do believe Mitfold had the feeling it was rather a miracle to have reached it safe and sound."

Pardoe accepted this as probably true. None had known so well as the boy himself the degree of danger in which he had stood.

"Mr. Wynkerrell," he asked abruptly, "did Archy Mitfold mention to you that he was going out again Saturday night?"

"Yes."

Salt looked up in quick surprise.

"He said he was going to a tutorial," Wynkerrell continued. "He took German lessons, you know, from a Herr Speyer."

"Oh yes? He didn't mention the hour, I suppose?"

"No. But the Pells should have been able to say, surely."

Pardoe admired the dexterity with which he had pounced upon the obvious flaw in the question. He ignored the remark, however, and met Wynkerrell's suspicious eyes calmly.

"What did you yourself do that night after you left Mrs. Pell's house?" he asked, pursuing the policy of in for a penny, in for a pound.

Wynkerrell, his suspicions crystallized, relaxed with a certain satisfaction.

"I thought it was coming. The old woman's at the bottom of it, of course. She's like that thingummy in *Hamlet*—you know, play within play, that drops poison in the king's ear. Still, I don't bear malice."

"Well, I wasn't asleep in an orchard," Pardoe said. "Aren't you a bit inclined to overdo Mrs. Pell's hostility? This is only ordinary, common garden routine, you know. Enquiry into movements isn't synonymous with being suspicious of them, though the layman in his ignorance always thinks it is. But I'd have thought you'd sense enough to know that half the time we're only clearing the decks."

Wynkerrell flushed slightly at the implied reflection on his intelligence.

"All right. It's nothing to tell. After dropping Mitfold I went home—I don't hang out here. I've got a cottage at six Grail Street, in Mayfair. I let the top part as a flat. A woman comes in by the day, and gets my supper—when I don't dine out. She puts something handy for breakfast before she goes, but I'm not much of a breakfast bloke, and for the most part I live alone. Actually the place is nothing much more than a bed-and-brekker. Well, I didn't stay long because I had an appointment to view a library the owner was disposing of—that was in Eaton Terrace—but it didn't take me long to see there was very little stuff of use to us, so I was back at my place by a quarter to ten."

"You seem sure of the time."

"Why not? There was a murder one-act on the radio at ten, *Slippers on the Stairs*, by Hanley Kirbston—grand stuff that fellow puts across—and I didn't want to miss it. It finished at ten forty-five and after a drink I went to bed. I had a spot of headache, and anyway the Old Boys' gambols had killed any other yearnings for jollification I might have had."

Pardoe was thoughtful. "You have a partner, Mr. Wynkerrell?" he asked irrelevantly.

"Yes." Wynkerrell's surprise made him sound curt. He added, "Leofric Williams. He's got digs Baker Street way." He gave an address in York Terrace. "He's out just now—but he wouldn't be any use to you. I believe he met Archy once, way back in August, but that's about the sum total of their mutual acquaintance."

"And Mr. Beltane? He was another contemporary at St. Crispin's?"

"In a way. What I mean is, he left a year before Archy and me—to go to Oxford. A year's a fairly big gap while you're still at school, you know." He laughed mirthlessly. " 'Fraid as far as he and I were concerned there was nothing of the Damon and Pythias about us—but Archy, who was a fresher at Latimer's when Bel was in his second year, knew him far better, of course."

"I see. And what other old friends did you three pick up on Saturday at the reunion? I'm wondering if you can give me their names—I gather it wasn't very well attended?"

"No, it wasn't. A round score, I'd say. But as for giving you their names—well, I didn't know half of 'em myself. You mean you want to get in touch with anybody else Mitfold may have told the tale to?"

Again the swift anticipation of purpose, Pardoe thought.

"I had it in mind," he admitted. "It's clear he was particularly strung up and talkative on Saturday, and there's at least the chance that one or two details you didn't hear from him may have been given to somebody else, and vice versa, of course."

Wynkerrell considered. "There's that about it. On the other hand—well, I think you're barking up the wrong tree. Mind, I've no proof whatever—Archy may have blabbed it to all the old dodderers at lunch. I didn't see much of him till later. And it's none of my business. But I got the impression that what he told Beltane and me at teatime was confidential—or, shall we say, had been reserved for our ears; that he was making a point of telling us and no-body else."

"P'raps. But you admit yourself that's only supposition. And in our line we can't afford to leave it at guessing."

"Quite. But I don't know where those fellows came from. A museum, by the look of 'em. Wait a bit, the best thing you can do is to apply to the secretary of the O.C.A.—Old Crispians' Association, you know, though our feebler wits are always trying to make Christians of us. In vain."

He got up and, after some jerking, pulled out a drawer in the overladen table and rummaged in it impatiently. Presently he found what he wanted, a small address book which he opened and took across to Pardoe.

"Here it is. He'll be able to put you on their track. He must have a list of the acceptances—and anyway those are always in excess of the fellows that eventually turn up."

Pardoe made a note of it and thanked him.

"There's nothing else you can recall, I suppose—he didn't, for instance, give you the dates of these alleged attacks?"

"Not that I remember. I gathered they'd all been pretty recent, but if he mentioned precise days then I didn't register them. You may get better luck with Beltane."

He was taking it for granted, Pardoe thought, that Beltane had not been questioned, an assumption possibly based on communication held with one another since Archy's death had been noised abroad.

"Do you know when Mr. Beltane returned to Witley?"

"Last night," Wynkerrell said briefly. "Well, I won't say I could vouch for it this time, not as far as personal knowledge goes—but whenever he has a weekend in town, which is pretty often, he says he comes up on a Saturday and goes back on Sunday, so I conclude he followed his usual practice last night. He's a towny old bird, you know—no, I said towny, not downy." He glanced at Salt with a mocking air. "I suppose he thought it was more or less a duty to look for a better 'ole than Witley when he could get out of the cage—and who'd blame him?"

Pardoe, who had never seen Witley, politely refrained from doing so.

"How's business these days?" he asked, as Salt and he prepared to leave. "One hears conflicting opinions of the effect of war on the book trade."

"Does one?" Tony Wynkerrell gave an exaggerated shrug. "Well, it's bad with us—and no doubt of it. Half London's in the country, anyway. It mayn't be bad with the chain libraries and the big stores—they've had a fillip of a sort, p'raps, from the fresh habits the blackout's forced on their subscribers. People who've had to curtail their night life may've intensified their reading—of a sort. Escape stuff, and all that." He waved a contemptuous hand. But we're rather different. We don't run a lending library, and here in Hobby Court we're right off the beaten track and even darker than the big streets by evening.

Besides, we depend on specified rather than on catholic taste, as you see, and when evacuation or the army loses us a customer he's not so easily replaced. Our appeal is—well, limited."

Pardoe, who had taken careful stock of the place on coming in, believed it. Certainly the unhealthy combination of precocity and dust made no appeal to which he could respond.

They returned to the shop, Wynkerrell shepherding them with a touch of patronage. It was a long, low-ceilinged place, in autumn artificially lit at the back even in daylight hours. Properly handled, it would have exercised the peculiar fascination that is the prerogative of obscure bookshops. But here was no compulsion to linger. Erotic verse bound with lack of chastity and at its author's expense was not Pardoe's line at all; and this seemed to be the chief supply of the sparsely stocked Juniper. Its forlorn nakedness was further emphasized by a plentiful array of empty shelves. A few at the back of the shop were crowded with a litter of magazines and periodicals and what appeared to be an uninteresting and probably outdated collection of school textbooks, jumbled together without attention to shape, size or subject.

The ivory towers of the poets occupied the vanguard. Across the back of the window a black velvet curtain was pulled. When they came in Pardoe had observed that it formed a not ineffective background to the kind of dressing usually associated with a Parisian modiste's establishment. For a single volume in ivory and gold was triply represented on indelicately carved stands in the window. It was *Flight from the Philistines*, by Priam Pastell, which one critic had incautiously described as "a burning revelation of the poetic soul in subjection to the mundane and purblind." Judging by the specimen pages revealed by the two opened copies flanking a closed one that formed the centerpiece, "burning" was right enough, Pardoe thought. Come to think of it, it was rather surprising, the muck that sidled round the censor, as well as the sometimes less mephitic muck he contrived to stop.

Behind and to the left of these subject souls rose a shapely bronze vase, its stem the writhing limbs of a sexless being whose upraised arms embraced the rim. It was occupied by one or two imitation branches of the juniper tree, the rigid spiny leaves and blue-black berries, a few of which had dropped near the bookstands, handsomely and truthfully copied.

Intelligence had clearly been at work behind a misguided taste. But the nineties, thought Pardoe, who supposed he must himself be the mundane and purblind factor present, would have blushed to be guilty of such vapidity.

Wynkerrell was speaking as they opened the street door.

"Archy's aunt's been away—of course, you know that. I mean it's going to be a bit of a shock to her. Especially as Archy said he never let her know what was going on."

CHAPTER X: —OF ACCIDENTS

The story of my life,
And the particular accidents gone by.
THE TEMPEST.

IN SALT'S OPINION there was something vaguely improper in Miss Marian Leaf's resolute return to Mulberry Fountain within an hour of receiving news of her nephew's death there. Small, physically frail ladies should know better. Their qualities ought to harmonize more comfortably with their appearance; and an indomitable strain was altogether out of place where one was led to expect appealing dependence.

"Tough," the sergeant epitomized, and would not have minded if it had been a big, strapping wench he was describing. He shook his head. When Dresden shepherdesses of Miss Leaf's generation let you down, the Victorian age was not only dead but buried. Well, it was none of his business. He had his own job, to seek out the O.C.A. secretary whose contribution to the case would, he was sure, after unremitting investigation prove utterly useless. After that there were the visitors to the house in Mulberry Fountain, whose Saturday-night activities and possible motives for hanging Archy Mitfold would have to be probed. All, that is, except Professor Speyer. The special relationship in which he had stood to the dead youth called for a particular enquiry at which the inspector must be present. Salt set off on his round of visits in dreary anticipation of the worst, unless his chief's interrogation of Miss Leaf produced results so fruitful as to negate some of his own efforts.

Pardoe, seated in the upstairs drawing room at number eight, confronting Miss Leaf's composed little figure, felt that of the two he must himself present the less calm appearance. Prepared to cope with a distraught, possibly inarticulate, woman it was at first disconcerting to find that anything in the nature of first aid was entirely superfluous. Miss Leaf was clearly mistress of the situation.

She was a small, delicately shaped lady of about sixty who must in her youth have been ravishingly pretty in the style of an older century. Her face and figure and trifling elegancies of gesture were perfectly at home in the regency atmosphere of the square in which she lived. Her bright silver hair was dressed rather high, her eyes were large and melting and an unfaded blue, her face heart shaped, with the over-curved lips and undershot chin of an eighteenth-century belle. She had reached home, accompanied by Vera, an hour before the inspector had ventured to disturb her for the second time, and when he arrived it was to find that she had changed her traveling costume for a black dress that made her look more than ever fragile and in need of protection. It was a shock to have her greet him in mourning for the youth whom, up to the moment her train drew into the station, she must have imagined alive and well. Of course, her composure might, as he knew from experience, be only a mask for bewildered grief which, control snapping, would find vent at last. Meantime, Vera Moffat was by far the more upset. She crept about her duties, red-eyed and subdued in manner, and had now retreated to the kitchen to prepare an early supper for her mistress.

Pardoe, recalling Wynkerrell's parting words about Miss Leaf's ignorance of the earlier attempts on her nephew's life, did not plunge immediately into the subject. There was another matter about which he was so far in the dark.

"Miss Leaf, are your nephew's parents living?"

She looked surprised with a pretty arching of eyebrows.

"Why, yes, of course. His father is, I mean. He's married again, though. The present Mrs. Mitfold is Archy's stepmother."

"Oh. Where do they live?"

"In the lake country. Archy's father is a doctor. The address is the Old Stone House, Rowdale—it's by Ullswater." She paused. "There's a second family, two small children. Archy was the only child of the first marriage. His mother was my sister. She died when he was ten."

Pardoe made a note or two while she continued.

"It was his stepmother he'd gone to meet at Sloane Square station the day he nearly got pushed under the train."

Pardoe jumped, visibly, and broke the point of his pencil.

"You know then?" It was half involuntary.

"Know? Of course I know. Somebody has been trying to kill Archy for a considerable time."

The inspector expelled a quiet breath of relief. No great finesse would be required here.

"But, Miss Leaf," he said sternly, "why, if you knew this, didn't you or your nephew tell the police?"

"Archy was against it—very much against it. He said except for the chocolates, anyway, there was nothing to show for it all but his word, and he assured me over and over again that the police wouldn't be interested."

"You say he was against it from the start. I want you to tell me when the first of these attacks took place and as much about them as you are able to remember. A great deal now may depend on your memory."

"It's a good one. And after the second queer accident we took more particular note of the first. The first time anything unusual happened was on September 28, in the evening. You'll find it was a Thursday. Archy went to his coach Mondays and Thursdays. The hour was occasionally changed to suit Professor Speyer, and this time it was 7:30. Quite often it was a little later than that. Archy set off on foot. Since the professor moved into his new house he usually walked there, as it's fairly close. Well—this is what he told me afterwards—just as he was turning out of Mulberry Fountain into Trumpeter's Row a car was coming along slowly in the opposite direction. It passed him and turned into our square. We don't get many cars here, and as Archy didn't recognize this one he says he turned his head and was surprised at the way it was behaving."

She sounded a little breathless, and Pardoe waited.

"He got the impression," she went on, "that all it did was simply to turn round the fountain at the bottom of the square and come out again the way it had come. But after that he hadn't time to think of anything else. He'd started to cross the road at the very moment he was turning his head, when all at once the car accelerated and drove straight at him—with deliberation. He says it was all over in a minute or two, but there can't be any mistake about it—it made for him with a screeching sound and seemed to be right on top of him when somehow he managed to jump clear. But he fell sprawling, half across the opposite pavement, half in the road. The car swept past in the direction of the Avenue and King's Road, and was out of sight directly."

"Did anybody witness this?"

"There was nobody in the road at the time. It's very quiet here, as you see—and especially since most of the houses are evacuated. But the horrible noise of it and Archy's shout as he leapt brought one or two to their windows, and then a man from the nearest house came out when Archy had picked himself up."

"Who was the man?"

"The name's Runyon. I don't know the number of their house, but it's the other side of Trumpeter's Row. You'll be able to tell it by the religious banners and texts stuck in the windows. They belong to some fiery sect or other."

Pardoe agreed he would be able to identify it and enquired if Archy Mitfold had been injured by his fall.

"Not really. He was badly shaken, of course, and the shock went rather deep because he was so sure that somebody had done his best to run him down. But beyond bruises and a grazed cheek and a little damage to his clothes, he was all right. He went on to Professor Speyer's without first turning back home, and I didn't hear anything about it till he came back that night."

"And he had, of course, no idea of the driver's identity?"

"Oh no. He said the car was a black saloon, and described it as snaky."

Pardoe nodded. "By the way, can you tell me how your nephew lost two fingers on his left hand?"

She was surprised. "Oh, *that* was no attack, it was pure accident. It happened a year or more ago, when he was at home in the early summer. He was roaming about not far from the house when he got in the way of a man with a rook rifle. At least, so it appeared—though the man, who was pretty well known in those parts for a poacher and vagabond, swore he wasn't aiming in that direction at all. But there was nobody else about. Archy had to lose his fingers to save the hand."

Pardoe made an additional note to the Rowdale address. A man with a rook rifle might well have been instrumental in the deadly scheme that had worked itself out on Saturday night. But if so, the Vick case, surely, was going to remain a separate problem after all. That was only three weeks old, but Archy had lost his fingers eighteen months ago.

"Before we go on to the second of the accidents, Miss Leaf, will you tell me if his only purpose in coming to London was to receive language instruction from Professor Speyer?" he asked abruptly, and looked at her keenly.

She was silent a moment, returning the look with a kind of critical inspection that reminded Pardoe of the intent, unemotional gaze of a bird.

"I don't mind telling you, Mr. Pardoe," she said at last, "in fact, I think I *ought* to tell you—there were difficulties at home. Archy was a sensitive, stubborn, temperamental boy—he took after our side of the family, and—well, when one parent marries again after a child has passed the infancy stage, relations with the new parent aren't always happy. You understand."

"You mean your nephew and his stepmother were not on good terms?" Pardoe translated bluntly.

"That would describe it," Miss Leaf said without hesitation. Pardoe was quick to notice that she made no effort to mitigate in family interests the domestic situation.

"So the opportunity to polish up his language in view of a future diplomatic appointment was, after all, of secondary importance?"

"Oh no. That certainly came first. Dr. Mitfold is an old school friend of Sir Ritchie Adam at the Foreign Office, and it was understood that Archy would be taken on as soon as he was proficient in certain branches. But I won't say that difficulties at home didn't hasten his coming to live with me."

The inspector nodded, and passed straight on to the circumstances of the second alleged attack on Archy.

Miss Leaf's observant eyes grew a shade brighter. "It's strange you should speak of it just after what we've been saying. Because indirectly—oh, very indirectly—it was connected with his stepmother."

She paused. Pardoe made no comment, and after a minute she went on.

"One day at the end of last month Archy's father wrote that Mrs. Mitfold was coming to London on October 2. I am sure of that date, because Archy kept the letter and, if necessary, I expect I could still find it. Mrs. Mitfold has a widowed sister living in Old Queen Street. She pays her an occasional visit and does a little shopping at the same time. October 2 was a Monday, and my brother-in-law said Gertrude proposed staying two nights at her sister's and returning Wednesday. She wanted to fit in one more visit before the war made traveling still worse in the autumn and winter. And she didn't like weekends— Sunday is a waste of time if you come up here just to shop; Saturday afternoon, too. His father was always anxious that Archy should show courtesy to his stepmother, even though he couldn't feel affection. And as Archy didn't mind anything so much when he wasn't living at home, he was quite agreeable to meeting Gertrude and lunching with her, or whatever they might decide to do."

"Wasn't Mrs. Mitfold in the habit of calling upon you when she was in town?"

"No. She usually made such a very short stay." The words dropped with a tinkly coldness.

A suspicion Pardoe had entertained a minute ago was fast hardening into certainty. Archy was not the only member of the Mitfold family who had failed to agree with the doctor's second wife. Her sister's successor was no favorite with Marian Leaf, it was plain.

But when she spoke again the subtly frigid tone had gone.

"Archy sent a postcard home to say he would meet his stepmother at Sloane Square station between half-past two and three on Tuesday afternoon. That would be October 2. He suggested they have tea somewhere and go to the cinema."

"And the meeting took place as arranged?" Pardoe asked, picking up his cue.

"No, it didn't." She sounded bright. "Archy did just as *he* said—went to the station, and had—an accident. Well, a curious one, as we all thought. But never a sign of his stepmother. She didn't turn up at all."

Pardoe was interested. Here was the covering for the bare bones of Wynkerrell's story.

"Tell me about the accident first," he said. "Then, if there are any explanations of Mrs. Mitfold's failure to come, I'll hear them afterwards."

"Oh, there were explanations, of course," she said quickly. "But the nasty experience Archy had at the station pushed everything else to the back of our minds—till later."

For the second time that day Pardoe listened to the story of the misadventure at Sloane Square station. This time there were trimmings that had been absent from Wynkerrell's carelessly pithy narrative. Archy's friends had clearly not been given to understand that he had gone there to meet his stepmother, nor that he had been waiting some time when the push occurred which had nearly sent him sprawling beneath the wheels of an incoming train. On Saturday afternoon, it was evident, he had confined himself to the minimum of facts bearing on the incident.

"You are certain," Pardoe said with a frown, "that your nephew said the platform was not crowded at the time?"

"Positive," Miss Leaf said crisply. "*I'm* not certain it wasn't, of course. I wasn't there. But Archy was quite sure. He said the previous train to go out had taken the bulk of the waiting passengers, and he thought there weren't more than six or seven there at the time. He admits he was near the edge of the platform with the other people behind him. But there was no reason, so far as he knew, why he should keep watch on them. When it happened they were moving in the usual drift toward the train, with Archy, of course, in front. It was gone three by then, and he was getting impatient at not seeing Gertrude."

"So, as he was looking toward the line and not around him, other people, or say one other person he'd not previously noticed, might have joined those behind him?"

"They might, I suppose."

"Your nephew didn't overhear any remark from those who helped him up suggesting how it might have happened?"

"Oh no. Well, if he did he didn't say anything to me about it. They were frightened, and when he wasn't killed before their eyes they were too relieved to worry. You know how it is. Besides, they were all intent on catching their train, you see."

"Of course," said Pardoe, and sighed. That was the devil of it. There can be no moment, he reflected, psychologically more perfect for the commission of a crime in the presence of a number of witnesses than that at which a train is due in to a station. Place, time and circumstance conspire to play into the hands of its author; for train catchers, whose peculiar reaction to the sight of advancing wheels nails their visual and mental attention to one object only, are the least observant of mankind. Mitfold's attacker, with his intention clear before him, had been free to keep a wary eye on the group in whose company he had moved and to gauge with precision which second of that psychological moment he must act. All the same, an attempt at daylight murder in the presence of perhaps a dozen people calls for cool nerves anywhere, and even that degree of knowledge about X's character was so much gain.

He wondered why Mrs. Mitfold had failed to put in an appearance.

"Oh," said Miss Leaf helpfully, "that was very simple. She didn't come to London at all. It came out later when I wrote—Archy wouldn't have bothered to say anything—that just at the last she had a wire from Derby to say an aunt of hers who had practically brought her up from babyhood was dying. So she canceled the London visit and went there instead. She says a postcard was sent to Archy about the change of plans. But he never had it."

As Pardoe raised his brows she repeated, "No, never. Cards don't always get delivered, of course." Her tone faintly suggested that such failure, however, was unheard of in her experience.

Pardoe made a note at the bottom of the page and turned over a leaf.

"And the third accident?"

"Nothing like the other two. It happened in the house. It was illness. The date is particularly easy to remember because it was his birthday—October 5. He was twenty-two. And it was only two days after his fall at the station."

Only one clear day between the attacks. That looked like desperation. Why? What had happened in between? The inspector knew of only one thing—a visit to the cinema. And something else—a sudden interest in Sampson Vick. Pardoe felt a curious elation as he put a question about the nature of the illness.

Pressed to describe this as minutely as possible, Miss Leaf produced a tolerably vivid account of the symptoms. She produced it with apparently little strain on memory or feelings.

She had been aroused at nearly two o'clock in the morning by sounds of distress from Archy's room, and had found him suffering with what they at first took to be colic pains. But it was not long before she suspected something more serious. There had been severe stomach cramp and vomiting, a low pulse and a constant feeling of cold. "Even with two more hot-water bottles he went on shivering." She had been puzzled and frightened, but too busy trying to relieve his pain to allow alarm to master her. No, she had not called Vera. And Archy had asked her to give out next day that it was gastric trouble keeping him in bed.

There had been nothing wrong with the boy all day before. He had been, it was true, a little quieter—more thoughtful, perhaps—since the Sloane Square episode, but the good spirits he had enjoyed for the past week or so were not really subdued. The birthday had been spent almost as any other day, for Archy had declined to have any of his friends in on the grounds that he was no longer a kid who felt birthdays incomplete without parties, and that in any case they would most likely get too rowdy for his aunt's peace of mind.

"I haven't been well for the past month or two," she explained, "and perhaps was saved on that account from the pain and discomfort the poor boy suffered that night. For I was on a diet and couldn't indulge in chocolates."

"Chocolates?" Pardoe queried encouragingly, as if hearing of them for the first time. "You consider his illness due to the chocolates he ate?"

"What else could it have been? It's true that at one or two meals he ate things which I didn't touch. But in each case of that kind I made it my business to find out if Vera had had some too, and in each case she had—with no ill effects. Only the chocolates were left."

"So neither you nor your maid ate one of those?"

"It was like this, Mr. Pardoe. Among the presents which came for Archy that day were two boxes of chocolates. They were both pound boxes, of different make. One of them contained a short letter from an aunt of his in Worthing, a sister of Dr. Mitfold. After taking out the letter Archy left the box unopened and gave it as it was to Vera. He said that as I couldn't share them with him two boxes were too much. Besides, Vera is a very good girl, and Archy was always pleased to make her a present."

A tear glittered at the corner of her eye. She lifted her handkerchief and wiped it away with a small, dignified gesture. Pardoe wondered if, after all, a grief one had not guessed waited to break through the assumption of calm.

"And the other box?" he reminded her gently.

"Ah, that was different. It was certainly queer that the sender should have forgotten to sign his name to the greeting message. There was nothing inside but a little plain white card, and written on it, 'Best wishes.' "

"Written—not printed or typed?"

"Ordinary handwriting in ink. Archy didn't recognize it. Yet, though it was odd, you must remember that at first finding that greeting card suggested to our minds that the gift wasn't entirely anonymous."

That was reasonable. Even a word or two of friendly writing would destroy the feeling of anonymity to the extent, at least, of lulling suspicion. It might even suggest that one's own memory was at fault in failing to recognize a friend's hand. And arguing the identity of the giver would certainly not prevent one from sampling the gift.

"Did you examine the postmark?"

"Archy did. But you know what brown paper is—there was nothing clear about the impression made. Even the address was poorly written and only just legible. It looked as if it had been posted in London, though. And of course Archy's friends often did silly things."

So they might, Pardoe thought, but an anonymous line of greeting was hardly to be included in that category. Puerile pranks on a birthday aimed at something a little more freakish than a nameless gift.

"How many chocolates did your nephew eat?"

"Five. One when he opened the box and four after supper."

"What became of the rest?"

"We saved them. At least, I did. It didn't occur to Archy till he was feeling much better that the chocolates could have had anything to do with the sickness. I thought of it in the night when I was attending him, though I didn't bother him with it then."

"Were you able to save everything—including the outer wrapping?"

"No, I'm afraid that went directly. I questioned Vera, but it couldn't be traced. I'll fetch you the chocolates."

She started up, but sat down again as Pardoe put out his hand.

"One moment, Miss Leaf. There's something you can tell me first. Why wasn't a doctor called in to Mr. Mitfold, especially as you have one living next door?"

She spread her hands in a pretty, melancholy gesture. "You may well ask. I was most anxious to do so, but Archy was *insistent*, really frantically insistent that I shouldn't. The fear that I was going to threw him into such excitement and renewed the pain so much that I had to promise I would do my best without a doctor. Luckily my efforts made bad better instead of worse."

Pardoe looked at her intently. "Do you know why your nephew had such an antipathy to calling in a doctor?"

"Yes. He was quite sure, you see, that this was another 'accident' staged by the same hand that had twice before tried to kill him. He thought—as I think—that he had been poisoned. He knew a doctor would know that, and would set enquiries on foot, and because he was anxious to cope with this attacker himself he wanted to keep the matter entirely secret from outsiders."

"You were both doing a very incautious thing."

"I know," she said frankly. "But as it happened Archy made a recovery."

"To be struck at again," Pardoe said, not sparing her, "and this time successfully."

Her lip trembled. "And you think—?"

"I don't know, Miss Leaf, whether we could have saved him. But you can see for yourself the chance we should have had of doing so if you had come to us earlier. Enquiry into these attacks on him while Mr. Mitfold was *alive* would have given us a distinct advantage over his murderer."

She shuddered at the word, and Pardoe added: "But that time's gone by. May I have the chocolates, please?"

She crossed to a little table and took a key from a handbag lying there. With this she opened the doors of a graceful china cabinet in inlaid lacquer, and stooping, drew out something from the back of the lower shelf. She brought it to Pardoe and sat down in silence, watching him while he examined it.

It was as she had described, a pound box, square, light blue, with wisps of paper sticking out under the hastily jammed-on lid. Inside were two layers of chocolates, by the look of them the usual mixture of creams and hard centers. Five were missing from the top layer where their crumpled containers lay. Though he did little more then than glance at them, Pardoe saw at once that the coating of several of the remaining chocolates was split as if they had been pressed between finger and thumb and then replaced. He put the lid on and looked back at Miss Leaf.

"I'll take charge of these. They'll be analyzed, and you'll get the report. Now, what do you make of this?"

He took from an inner pocket the envelope on which Archy had sketched his birds. She glanced down at it, then met his eye with a slightly puzzled look.

"I don't think I make anything of them," she said slowly. "Archy was always drawing birds, especially lately." She pointed to a couple of watercolors hanging near the door. "Those landscapes are his. He's an artist, you know." She caught her breath quickly as she remembered that the present tense was no longer applicable.

Pardoe nodded. "And the pictures downstairs?"

"Oh yes—the animal studies. Everyone thinks them amusing. He was very interested in birds. That's probably why he scribbled so many of them at odd moments."

"But only lately?" the inspector insisted.

"Well, yes—perhaps. But there's nothing much in that, is there? I think myself he was missing Westmorland—not his home so much as the country. He loved it all—all the birds and plants and wild scenery. And if you're missing a thing it may be natural to draw little pictures of it."

"Do you know what bird it is?" Pardoe asked, tapping the envelope.

"I'm afraid I don't. I'm town bred—all birds are alike to me. Is it *anything* special? But if you want to give it a name I should say Professor Speyer could help you."

"Mr. Mitfold's German tutor?" Pardoe metaphorically sat up straight.

Miss Leaf showed a touch of ingenuous pleasure at being able to impart a piece of news to the police who were always so tiresomely forearmed.

"Yes. He's a—an— Oh, what does one call a man who studies birds?"

"An ornithologist." Pardoe could have shouted it. He felt like a small boy who, dipping into a bran tub, pulls out the largest package there.

"Yes. What a clumsy word. It was a kind of hobby of his, you see, bird watching or whatever it is they do, from the time he was a boy, he told me."

"How did you come to talk with him about birds?" Pardoe hoped he did not sound too eager.

She stared. "Oh, I'm telling you the wrong way round. Professor Speyer has been in England a long time. Before he came to London he was German master at a grammar school up north, and he used to spend part of his holidays in Westmorland to study the birds. That's how my brother-in-law got to know him, and why he decided to let Archy study under him."

"I understand. So Herr Speyer and your nephew were not strangers?"

"Not really. That's not to say they knew each other well. Archy had met him, but he was the merest acquaintance until he started taking lessons from him."

"You say Mondays and Thursdays were the evenings for his coachings. Do you know if Mr. Mitfold had arranged to go last Saturday too?"

She seemed puzzled. "Saturday? There was never a tutorial that day. No—at least, he said nothing about it."

"It's all right. I didn't think he would have. Is the professor a frequent caller at your house?"

"Oh no. Infrequent would be more correct. Archy has asked him in occasionally."

She watched him, perplexed. Pardoe sensed how industriously her mind was at work to follow the course of his, and changed the subject. He did not want her thoughts to run exclusively in one channel.

He leaned forward and spoke in a lower voice that gave emphasis to his words.

"Miss Leaf, can you suggest a reason why somebody should want to kill your nephew?"

"No." She softened the brevity of her reply by adding, "I've thought about it, and thought about it—as Archy himself did, I know. But nothing ever occurred to me that would really explain such a diabolical plot."

"Yet you have an excellent memory, and I am going to ask you to use it again to help to unravel this. Can you remember anything odd—*anything* at all out of the way—which happened to your nephew or in which he took part *after* he came to London and *before* these attacks started?"

Almost at once a change came over her. Before he had finished speaking she gave a little anticipatory nod. The bewildered air with which she had just now met his interrogation vanished, and she sat taut with bright, assured eyes.

"But of course," she said calmly. "There have been several—odd things. I have been waiting to tell you about them."

CHAPTER XI: —OF INCIDENTS

There is occasions and causes why and wherefore in all things.
I KING HENRY VI.

WHEN Pardoe came to thrash out Miss Leaf's evidence with Salt the sergeant's first reaction was precisely what his own had been.

"How the devil'd she keep 'em all in 'er head so clearly unless she knew a time was coming when they'd have to be fetched out?"

In his own fashion Pardoe had wondered the same thing. For this was evidence so neatly tabulated, and presented well on in the interview with such a nice sense of the dramatic, that the inspector's insufficient acquaintance with her had at first persuaded him that Miss Leaf could not be entirely innocent in the matter. Her disarming narrative style, however, would have lulled suspicion in the mind of any but a listener who had had before now to evade the pitfalls spread by apparent frankness.

"There were three things," she said with a certainty precluding possibility of error, "that were—well, not exactly the kind of thing one expects to happen every day. Should I give them to you in order of time?"

Pardoe, deciding with some amusement that if Archy Mitfold's aunt had ever been a schoolmistress her timetables must have been things of joy, agreed that chronological treatment might be the best. Their relative importance to what followed might then more easily be judged. It struck him all at once how extremely well timed, apart from the dramatic angle, was this contribution to the evidence; for had it been offered early in the interview he would have been inclined to discount it as perhaps the somewhat nebulous impressions made on an old maid's mind, in retrospect superstitious. Now that he had some idea of the unsentimental personality with which he had to deal and the neat pigeonholes from which memory drew its data, he listened with respect.

"The first thing," said Miss Leaf, clearly aware of his attention and pleased at it, "was something which might happen to anybody and yet be considered odd—you might say unique, if you can see what I mean. It was the middle of August. Just about a fortnight before war came. A police message was broadcast appealing for witnesses to a motor accident that had happened at the corner of Pandulf Road and Concord Street in Hammersmith."

"I know," said Pardoe, "between the police station and the electricity works. What happened?"

"An elderly man was knocked off his bicycle. There was no question of the car not stopping, nothing like that. On the contrary, it helped him up—I mean the driver did. It seems he said he was all right and refused offers of help, even of a lift in the car, and went on his way pushing his bicycle. The afternoon of the next day he died. The doctor said something about delayed concussion and cerebral hemorrhage, and they started looking for the car and any possible witnesses."

"And Mr. Mitfold?"

"He was the only witness. It had been early in the afternoon and very quiet just when the accident happened—indeed, Archy said it was always quiet there. He used to visit a friend in Pandulf Road. All the same he was quite sure another man was passing at the same time as himself, though if he was he didn't come forward in answer to the broadcast."

"That's very clear," said Pardoe. He did not press for details of hour and date, as these would be under his hand when he returned to the Yard. "Can you give me the name and address of the friend in Pandulf Road?"

Miss Leaf hesitated. "You don't think what I've told you is unimportant then?"

"Nothing in connection with sudden and unaccountable death is unimportant from our point of view," he said easily. "At present, with everything but the manner of his death unexplained, we can't afford to ignore any item of evidence bearing on your nephew's actions since he came to live here. On the other hand there's no need to attach particular importance to any questions I may put in this instance, as I'm seeking from you only the information our own records won't have dealt with. You can put it this way: you're helping me to fill in the gaps."

"I see," she said simply. "Then the friend is Mr. Benjamin Lake, and the address twenty Pandulf Road, where he lives with his father."

"Can you remember if your nephew told you about this accident *before* the police broadcast occurred?"

"He didn't. I remember quite well, because as soon as he exclaimed, 'Oh, I was about when that happened!' I said, 'Why didn't you tell me, Archy?' "

"And why hadn't he told you?"

"Because, he said, it had seemed so trivial. The mudguard of the car, which wasn't traveling fast, had grazed the cycle, and the man had fallen off sideways, quite slowly, not in any violent or alarming way. But his head struck the curb."

"Mr. Mitfold came on the scene then, did he?"

"Oh, he saw it all. He was walking along Concord Street pavement and just going to turn into his friend's road when cyclist and car passed him. Archy, together with the motorist, went to the man's help—but, as I say, he left them in rather an offhand manner that convinced them there was nothing wrong with him. It was when Archy was picking up the cycle that another pedestrian came by, he said."

"From which direction?"

"He didn't say—or I don't remember. But it will be in his evidence, won't it?"

"It may," said Pardoe dubiously. "Well, that's clear. And what was the next thing you thought odd?"

"The next thing that happened to Archy?" Her tone sharpened a little as she shot him a quick look. "You've heard tell of the 'Nordic Bond'?"

Pardoe had. Most people knew nothing about it until the war had put an end to its apparently mild activities, but the Yard had had an eye for it from the days of its inception in 1935 when its first badly attended meetings were held in a back room of the now defunct Hardbake Night Club.

"It's dissolved now," he said. "You mean your nephew was a member?"

"No. But he went to one or two meetings—only two, I think. Politically he had an inquisitive mind—he'd go with the same readiness to a communist gathering. People said the 'Bond' was definitely pro-Nazi, but the club itself, so Archy told me, said all it was trying to do was to promote Anglo-German understanding, and that with complete impartiality. I don't know anything about it myself."

"Well, it didn't conduct itself toward the Jews with complete impartiality," Pardoe remarked, with a lively memory for some unpleasant anti-Semitic business that had kept the police watchful in the summer. "I understood, Miss Leaf, that only members were admitted to the club premises—how then did Mr. Mitfold get in?"

"On Professor Speyer's ticket. The professor joined in the beginning, four or five years ago, but he said he was disappointed at the way it developed. He thought a fine chance for useful work was thrown away, and that they simply frittered away their time in pointless spites or else back pattings. He said he seldom attended, so the only times Archy ever went it was on a borrowed ticket."

"I see. And the incident you have to tell me about happened at one of these meetings?"

"At the very last. The club was closed just afterward. It must have been the end of August. Archy left the house about eight-thirty and didn't get back till after midnight. It worried me a lot, as he hadn't been nearly so late on the previous occasion he'd gone there. Besides, I hadn't liked his going. I mistrust all political gatherings that aren't of an official nature, whatever color they are, and I wanted Archy to have nothing to do with them. But he was so keen to follow up anything new, and he got talking to Professor Speyer, and there you are."

As far as Pardoe saw, where they were was still a long way from what Miss Leaf was proposing to tell him.

"Mr. Mitfold returned safely, however?"

"Oh yes, but very annoyed at the stupid mistake he'd made. I expect you know that the Nordic Bond held all their later meetings in a private house belonging to one of the members, off the Pimlico Road, for membership dwindled a lot after the seizure of Czecho-Slovakia, and they had to practice economy, they said. It was fairly near, and Archy walked there. He left before they closed down because he was bored—we were fast drifting into war by then, and he said everybody seemed afraid to commit himself, and—to use Archy's own words—the fireworks had gone damp, and it looked as if they were getting ready to shut shop."

"They did almost immediately."

"Yes. And a good thing too. I expect they were all a parcel of spies. Well, it was dark in the lobby when Archy went to put on his coat. There weren't many coats about, and he went instinctively to where he'd hung it, put it on and came away. And it wasn't till he was actually turning into Mulberry Fountain that he discovered he was wearing somebody else's. I think he felt in a pocket for something, and knew immediately it wasn't his own—and then there were plenty of details to confirm it. He wasted a few moments hesitating, then turned to go back to the club, which he thought would still be in session as he'd left early. But his luck was out. It was closed and in darkness, not even the household in residence about, or if they were they didn't reply to his knocks. So he came back home again."

"And returned the coat next day?"

"Yes. He didn't visit the club, though, to find out the owner, because he came across a notebook in the coat with the name and address. A very funny notebook it was, too, written in a queer sort of shorthand, not the name, I mean, but all the other pages. And what's so annoying now is that I've completely forgotten who he is and where he lives, though I remember Archy's description of him quite well."

Pardoe smiled. "You're human after all, Miss Leaf. Your memory's such an excellent one I was beginning to doubt it. Well, if it's necessary to trace him we shan't have much difficulty in doing so. Tell me as much as you can remember."

"I've a vague fancy," she said reflectively, "that he lived somewhere in the Albert Bridge Road direction—but let that pass, I'm not sure. Archy wasn't kept waiting a minute at the house before the owner came bustling to him, just as if, he told me, he'd been looking out for him with the utmost anxiety. He was an old, thin, white-haired man, rather the retired colonel type, but nervous in manner, quite humorless and rather hostile."

"Hostile?"

"Yes—that was Archy's word, hostile. It seems he implied Archy had done it on purpose to get hold of his property for the night. He wasn't at all reasonable about what was after all a genuinely easy mistake to make, and it appears he asked Archy a lot of sly questions—that was how Archy put it—and didn't properly wait for his answers nor believe them when he did listen."

"What sort of questions?"

"Archy didn't tell me."

"Can you remember if he said whether the old man laid particular emphasis on the notebook when he showed himself so disagreeable?"

"That's exactly what he did say. It made Archy curious, because the old fellow literally snatched it from him and then went hastily through the pages with a *most* suspicious glare in his eye."

"Well, well," said Pardoe mildly, and then, "Hadn't he made any effort himself to recover his property before Mr. Mitfold turned up with it? In any case he must have missed it when he left the club."

"Oh, he'd carried on that night, I suppose—made a fine to-do by his own account. They'd promised to ring up members and must have got rid of him as quickly as possible. Archy was sure afterward that that was why nobody opened the door to him when he knocked that night. They probably thought it was old Mr. Caffey again—there, the name's come back to me!"

"Splendid," Pardoe said approvingly. "You'll have the address, too, in a minute."

She shook her head. "That's really gone. Well, I can't be sure it was ever there. I've a misty impression it was the Bridge way, that's all."

"It doesn't matter." Pardoe looked at her closely in silence for a moment. "You tell me these things, Miss Leaf, because you believe they may have some bearing on the series of attacks made on Mr. Mitfold later on?"

"You asked me to tell you any out-of-the-way incidents."

"I know. But you intended telling me these in any case."

"Yes—well, perhaps so. It's true I did think there was a possible connection. I said as much to Archy after the chocolates affair, but he wasn't much impressed."

"He made no alternative suggestion, though?"

"No—simply accepted what I said and dismissed it immediately. I thought he seemed not to want to discuss that side of it."

There was a short silence which the inspector broke.

"Didn't you mention three things just now as having happened before the attacks? You've told me two of them."

"Yes. There was something—but it's less unusual, I think, than either of the other two, and it happened much later."

Pardoe looked up quickly, and she nodded.

"More than a month after the police message. In the blackout it was—indeed, the blackout was the real cause of it. Again I can't tell you the exact date, but it was late last month. Archy walked into an empty house one evening by mistake."

She saw at once that she had secured his attention and smiled wanly.

"Poor boy, it's not an unusual thing to do—I don't mean to go into an empty house, but to go in the wrong one. People do it in fogs, of course. And one doesn't see why it should give such deep offense as to provoke murderous attacks upon him."

"Not in an empty one, on the face of it," Pardoe agreed. "Where did he think he was going at the time?"

"To a coaching at Professor Speyer's. That's how you can get hold of the date—I'm sure the professor will remember, because Archy was late for his tutorial that night. I'll tell you why it happened. The professor used to live in Earl's Court, but he was wanting a change, and when war broke out and people evacuated in large numbers more houses were available. So he took one in Rossetti Terrace, near Cheyne Walk, and had only moved in a week or so before this happened. It was because Archy had never seen the house by daylight that he blundered in finding it."

"Do you mean this was his first coaching after the professor moved house?"

"No—he'd been once, perhaps twice, before, but always in darkness, and it's still possible to make a mistake like that after being right several times before."

"There's an unoccupied house near the professor's, then?"

"I suppose there must be. I've never been there. Professor Speyer doesn't like his pupils knocking—the housekeeper's deaf, and anyway I believe it's quite usual for tutors expecting pupils at stated hours to ask them to walk straight in. So Archy never announced his arrival."

The inspector was frowning slightly. "Miss Leaf, do you notice something odd about what you've just told me?"

"No—what?"

"Isn't it unusual for an empty house to have an unlocked outer door?"

She had been looking puzzled but now her face cleared. "So it is. I hadn't thought of that, nor Archy, I'm sure. As a matter of fact, he never mentioned the thing to me till a couple of days later. It must have been—yes, it was—the morning of the day he was nearly run down by that car. I remember him saying, 'I hope I get to the prof's all right tonight. Last time I went I walked into an empty house.' "

"How could he be sure it was empty?"

"I asked him that. He said, 'Oh, I had a good look at it next day. Besides, it struck so chilly.' "

"It's strange neither of you were impressed by the unfastened door. Did he tell you the number of the house?"

"No. But it won't be hard to find. Professor Speyer's is sixteen, and this should be close by."

Pardoe, glancing at the notes he had made, nodded. "Since you tell me you've thought over these incidents in connection with your nephew's accidents, Miss Leaf, to which one of the three are you inclined to attach most significance?"

Her reply came readily. "Oh, the Nordic Bond business, of course. I was always convinced its doings must be sinister, though the professor tried to laugh me out of it, and I couldn't bear Archy going near the place. Besides, what can old men like Mr. Caffey want with such things?"

Pardoe, who had not as yet met the old gentleman, found this unanswerable.

But, "Dabbling in amateur politics," he observed, "and getting mixed up, perhaps, with odd people, doesn't necessarily imply something worse. Still, we shall look into these things, as they reflect Mr. Mitfold's activities in the last weeks. One thing strikes me at once, though—two of these incidents took place in August, yet the attacks on Mr. Mitfold didn't begin till the end of September. If we are to accept the view that either his response to the police broadcast or his visit to the club was in some way bound up with those, we shall have to explain why there was a lapse of a month and more when presumably nothing happened."

Miss Leaf's melting gaze grew brighter. "Which makes you think—?"

"Nothing much at the moment. I hope for more, if it's only negative knowledge, when I've looked into all three cases. Now there's something I'd like you to tell me: did your nephew, as far as you know, ever have dealings with Mr. Sampson Vick?"

It was deliberately he made the question abrupt. Her mind was so clearly running on what she had narrated that subterfuge was improbable.

She looked startled. "The missing millionaire? No, never, I'm sure." She hesitated. "Of course, the silly way the papers have run the affair roused his curiosity, I think—a week or so ago he was reading up all about it."

She gave him an account of the research among back numbers of the newspapers, much on the lines of Vera's, and Pardoe was able to lead the subject round to Archy's excitement about Sampson Vick on his return from the cinema the day before his birthday. But here she could be of no help. She could not say what cinema he had visited and, it was plain, attached little importance to his sudden interest in the millionaire.

"Archy was like that, you see—prone to sudden enthusiasms for the very things which had bored him before. And of course he loved to be mixed up with a mystery and feel he was contributing personally to an investigation. I quite think it was some such amateur-detective work that has led the poor boy to his end."

Pardoe, who guessed she was thinking of Mr. Caffey's notebook, refrained from pointing out that such a surmise was highly consistent with the interest shown in the Vick case. In his job it was not always wise to rivet the attention where it was not itself inclined to halt.

"There's a chance," he said quietly, "that further evidence of Mr. Mitfold's activities these last few weeks may be lying about in the form of writing, or something of that sort. I've taken charge of the contents of his desk, and we've been through what clothes we found. Can you suggest anywhere else we might look—did he correspond much with relatives or friends?"

She shook her head. "Very seldom. He hated writing letters, and Dr. Mitfold has often complained that he only heard from him when Archy wanted something." She frowned in an effort to remember and, looking at him intently, added, "But what about his diary—wasn't it in the desk?"

Pardoe wanted to whoop all at once, an impulse which brought sudden recollection of Wynkerrell and the grim pictorial taste displayed at Alma Square.

All he said was, "There was no diary. He kept it regularly?"

"I don't fancy so. He wouldn't have had the patience. But I know he was keeping it lately, because he told me so when I saw him writing in it one day. He said now he was in London he wanted to put down a few first impressions. It was a red book, not very large. You couldn't overlook it."

"We must look again, though. Did he ever allow you to read in it?"

"Dear me, no. He used to lock it up. He was always most secretive."

Pardoe, to his cost, was aware of it. Anything that might now be of value in laying his murderer by the heels the dead boy seemed to have gone out of his way to conceal. From the evidential standpoint the story he had told to Wynkerrell and Beltane on the afternoon before his death was entirely inconclusive. It threw no light at all on his own actions or possible relations to his murderer, and Pardoe was irritably puzzled to know why he had bothered to regale them with it. According to Wynkerrell, Archy was as ignorant as they were why somebody should be trying to kill him. But was he? For, according to Archy, his aunt had known nothing of the peril in which he stood. The inspector was finding that apparently pointless lie as intriguing a poser as any.

Before leaving he introduced the subject of Mrs. Pell and her daughter by, as he flattered himself, a subtle gambit. "When your nephew declined to go away with you in the weekend did he want to stay here—did he raise any objection to going elsewhere?"

Miss Leaf interpreted the query more frankly than he could have hoped.

"I wondered, too, at the time," was her oblique reply, "because he didn't like Godmother at all. But I'd not supposed he was going to stay behind at the last, and it seemed the best thing to do in a hurry. But, really," she spread her hands again with a wavering movement, her eyes suspiciously bright, "he was so different the last week, so drawn into himself—I can't explain it properly—that he'd have accepted anything without protest, except, of course, the suggestion that he should leave London for a night or two. He seemed *absorbed* by something, so that everything else outside it was trivial and unimportant."

That was vivid, Pardoe thought. He knew what she meant. He had met it before, a curious acquiescence in everything, in the very things, perhaps, which before had roused opposition. When you marked it in somebody, you were conscious of a secret force in control, creating indifference to all outside its range. Love, especially when degenerating to infatuation, was its commonest cause. But there were others—some of them the sphere of the psychiatrist rather than of the police—and it was his business to discover what overmastering obsession had persuaded the impatient, temperamental Archy Mitfold to stay without demur in the house of a hateful old woman like Agatha Pell.

Miss Leaf was crying quietly now, and Pardoe, who wanted a few minutes upstairs before going away, fetched Vera to her while he slipped up to the dead boy's room.

He unlocked the door, and with practiced economy of time and effort went again through the few clothes and books the room contained. It was labor unrewarded; everything was depressingly tidy. Inky fingers . . . blotting-paper pellets . . . "a red book, not very large." Small enough, perhaps, to leave Mulberry Fountain in a murderer's pocket.

On coming downstairs he did not expect to see Miss Leaf again. But she was in the hall where the pictures tilted their dark shadows, no longer weeping, but looking, he thought, old and tired.

"It wasn't there?"

"No. Never mind, we shall try elsewhere. I've left the room unlocked now—the fingerprints man did his job this morning."

In the open doorway he turned to her gently.

"Miss Leaf, on Friday afternoon when you left the house who actually was the last to come out, and by which door?"

"Well, Vera stayed on an hour or two. She had only the front door to fasten behind her. I'd locked the others. But of Archy and I, Archy was the last to come out—through this door. We each had a key to it. He and I took a taxi to Victoria where he saw me off."

"And what did you do with the key of the basement door?"

She looked a little bewildered. "Why, left it inside the door after I'd locked up. But it's disappeared."

He nodded, satisfied.

On the way back only a trained mind prevented him from stopping dead in his tracks as memory put things neatly into place. On September 28, a Thursday, Archy Mitfold, said his aunt, had been run down by a car. That morning he had told her that the last time he went to Professor Speyer he had entered an empty house by mistake. His tutorials were on Mondays and Thursdays. It must, therefore, have been on September 25 he had walked into the wrong house. And September 25 was the last evening on which Sampson Vick had been seen alive.

CHAPTER XII: SALT IS DOUBTFUL

I fear I am attended by some spies.
TWO GENTLEMEN OF VERONA.

SALT TURNED IN the first part of his report that night and felt sour about it. It had the dismally negative character that connotes in the investigator fatigue without attendant compensations. Nor did thirty years experience of the pound's- worth-of-drudgery-to-ha'porth-of-thrill that makes up a detective's life preclude a sense of personal responsibility. He felt a little self-conscious about the lack of excitement in it all.

To begin with, the O.C.A. secretary, who seemed to have roused the sergeant's resentment by wearing a squint together with an air of aloof reproach for the Yard's interference, had furnished a list of eighteen names and addresses exclusive of those of the dead man, Tony Wynkerrell and Philip Beltane. Fifteen of these proved to be out of London and were, therefore, undealt with up to date. Visits to the other three justified Salt's worst hopes. None had been a contemporary of Mitfold in the peculiar scholastic sense of the term. If, in a general sense, a miss was as good as a mile, Salt learned that as regards school and college a year is as good as a decade. His name was received with blank stares, news of his death obviously for the first time. One of the three was a boy of nineteen who had only left St. Crispin's in the summer and was too preoccupied with the war's blighting of his own immediate university career to feel much interest in the Mitfold catastrophe; another was a middle-aged A.R.P. warden who had been on duty about three miles away at the time at which the murder had taken place; while the third was an elderly bank cashier, fussy, impatient and entirely unsubtle, whose quite glaring impeccability and lack of motive put him out of court at once, unless, as the sergeant, clutching at straws, suggested, " 'E's one of these Jekylls an' 'Ides."

Pardoe, who never found Salt's reports unrefreshing, received this lugubrious account with equanimity and asked after the frequenters of eight Mulberry Fountain. Here again the sergeant, by his own reading, had drawn distressing blanks.

The Misses Hatty Bemrose and Anna David shared, or rather, had shared, a flat in Bayswater, where Miss David painted some startling nudes and even more startling dressed-ups, and, most startling of all, contrived to sell them. From Salt's sketchy but not ungraphic description Pardoe built up the portrait of a forthright, talented young Jewish woman, with a one-track mind and a little money of her own that secured the independent tone of her work. She had had, it was plain, no use for Archy Mitfold, whom she thought the type of dilettante incapable of achievement in any line, and who had finally forfeited her last shred of respect by "messing around with the Nordic Bond scum." Asked if she could throw any light on his death, she admitted that he had never confided in her; that she knew nothing of any accidents that had befallen him, and, if you asked *her*, would attribute everything to one of the Nordic spies whom he had by chance unmasked. That he could have done such a thing wittingly was clearly from her standpoint impossible, and as this view agreed with the victim's own remark, "I stumbled upon it by chance," Salt had accepted it readily. Her attitude to the whole affair was one of resolute indifference that was rather naive, and her implication that Archy may have cornered only one of many spies was meant, the sergeant knew, to suggest that she could contemplate a whole nest of them without turning a hair.

As to the other names on Vera Moffat's list she had shown no diffidence in dissecting them for the sergeant's benefit. Tony Wynkerrell she knew slightly and was as positive as the rest of their "crowd" that the bookshop was not the source of the money he threw about with, at times, such ostentation. Mention of the foreign young man who had occasionally visited at Mulberry Fountain in her own and Ben Lake's company roused the only emotion she had shown throughout the interview. He was, it seemed, a Central European Jew—Miss David herself appeared vague as to the precise country of his origin, and Salt who had faithfully noted it down refused to pronounce his name—who, exiled by the Nazi drive eastward, had ever since expressed with passionate frequency his abhorrence of everything pertaining to his persecutors. Notwithstanding, three weeks after the outbreak of war he had, she indignantly explained, been interned, and neither individual nor concerted effort since, though unremitting, had secured his release. As for Benny Lake, she dismissed him as "not a bad kid" who wrote execrable verse in the belief that he would one day be a great poet. Sometimes he thought he was now. His pen name was Priam Pastell. She had not seen him for about a week. Philip Beltane she had never met.

"A young woman of taste," said Pardoe firmly at this structure on *Flight from the Philistines*. "And the Bemrose girl?"

Salt, failing to understand official approval of Miss David's discrimination, said he hadn't seen her. She had, by her friend's account, joined the Women's Land Army more than a week ago and had given up her share of the flat, a patriotic move that had not entirely commended itself to Miss David who had now the sole expense to bear and was afraid she could not sustain it. Hatty Bemrose had held a job in a travel bureau whose staff had been considerably cut down by the turn of international affairs. In Anna David's phrase she was now "grubbing turnips" somewhere in Lincolnshire, and though Salt found this account of her duties and domicile rather inexact it was a verifiable alibi;

and, as Pardoe pointed out, no woman anyway could have carried out a murder conceived on these lines without masculine help.

"What you grumbling about?" he added as Salt brought his gloomy narrative to a close. "You're never alive to the value of elimination. We'll look into these alibis, of course, but an internment camp and the Women's Land Army aren't bad to go on with."

"I've got one as good as those," the sergeant retorted, slightly cheered. "That Lake fellow. I went round there. He lives in Hammersmith—his pa's senior partner in a real estate business, and he don't think too much of the young un'opeful. But one thing's sure. The boy's been in bed since Thursday with a mighty good attack of the 'flu—father says the doctor can prove it, but I didn't press it, not wantin' 'em to think then that we'd be checking up to that extent. I went up an' had a look at 'im, an' it didn't look like a fake to me. He said 'e didn't know Mitfold was dead—'e seemed shook up by it. Couldn't throw any light on it; no confidences or hints, and so on. He described Mitfold as 'dam' close about his own business,' and suggested that a Nosey Parker attitude to the Bondites 'ad got him into trouble. Seems to be the general inf'rence."

Pardoe nodded. "And what about Anna David's own alibi?"

"Bottle party—till after midnight. A handful of 'em at mutual friend's flatlet. They were roused by a warden about 11:30 who told 'em they'd be reported for showing a light. Seems a pretty good checkup."

"It does. We'll rake it over a bit, but I'm thinking this lets out the Misses Bemrose and David and Mr. Priam Pastell, not to say our unknown friend they've interned. Never tell me again you grub about for nothing—crossing 'em off makes a tidier job of it every minute."

In face of this stubborn optimism the sergeant's spirits rose.

"Who're we left with?" he asked hopefully.

"A good fat collection," said the inspector, unconsciously damping revived ardor, "including Wynkerrell and Beltane, Mesdames Pell and Byron, the tutor Speyer—*he* crops up at every turn—the Mitfold family in Westmorland—all right, I'll tell you about 'em in a minute—a fair sprinkling presented to me by Miss Leaf, including a wrathful old fellow with probably pro-Nazi sympathies, and, if you want to be scrupulously thorough—Miss Leaf herself."

Salt stared.

"Yes, I know, a small, frail lady with a sound alibi. But I'm not suggesting her as a single-handed murderer. If a woman had a share in it there was a male partner to the crime who did the dirty work. We've got to consider everybody, for as long as *motive* is absent nothing but personal prejudice on our part can make one of 'em a more suspicious character than the rest." Pardoe beat his clenched hand gently on the desk. "It's motive I want, blast it. We know *how*—and the autopsy report will furnish details—but there's nothing concrete that tells us *why*. Only surmise and whisper and hint and little mental snapshots as sketchy as those birds he drew—and until we know why we can't know *who*."

Salt considered it. "I'll say the Nordic Bond business gives us a pretty good lead. It touches more sides of the affair than anything else. After all, 'e *was* aimin' at a job in the foreign office, and war *was* on the way, and 'e *did* 'ave a German prof—"

"An' Mrs. Pell *is* a true-blue totalitarian," Pardoe grinned. "No, I'm not ragging—that's pretty good, old man, and it's two to one at the rather blank moment that the N.B. wins. You'll think so still more when you've heard me out."

The next forty minutes were spent in concentrated discussion of the points raised by Miss Leaf. Pardoe's report of the interview confirmed Salt in his conviction that the club was at the bottom of it and gave him a new angle on young Mitfold's aunt who had pigeonholed her nephew's London life with such chronological precision.

"Suppose she was in it with the professor?"

"We can suppose fast enough," Pardoe agreed cheerfully, "but unless we give 'em a motive we're only chasing our tails."

"They're a coupla spies," was the sergeant's firm suggestion. He could always be relied on to support his own theories, however wild—a quality that was never permitted to interfere with the impartial handling of his job and which endeared him to his colleagues.

"Whom Mitfold unearthed?"

"That's it."

"All right—but then aren't you overlooking the clumsy way they went about getting rid of him? If Miss Leaf was in it why a string of apparently unconnected accidents *outside* his home when polishing him off *inside* should have presented small difficulty?"

"Prof might have been in it on his own at that time, an' only brought Auntie in later. After all," the sergeant added shrewdly, " 'e wouldn't want attention drawn to her if she was in the spy business with 'im."

"You're right there—make the trial lead away from home? But the murder itself did just the opposite. And what about the discrepancies in time? The earliest attempt on his life—assuming it was a murderous attack—didn't take place till a month after the Nordic Bond had been dissolved. Old Caffey—or Speyer, Caffey's boss, if you want it that way—was cherishing his revenge a long time, and spies can't afford to."

"Suppose there'd bin more of these accidents before the car run 'em down?"

"But why suppose it? Then we'd have to suppose that Mitfold preserved a hush-hush policy toward the first ones while telling his aunt freely about the last, and that's being wilfully irrational. We've nothing to go on. And that's another thing I'd like to clear up—why did Archy Mitfold tell Wynkerrell and Beltane that his aunt knew nothing about his mishaps?"

"Because," said Salt triumphantly, "he wanted to catch her out unbeknownst, an' 'e thought if he let on she was ignorant of it all his suspicions weren't so likely to reach her ears."

"You're a plausible old devil, Tommy," Pardoe said, but he sighed. "Look here, all this has made you lose sight of Sampson Vick—and there *is* a date there that dovetails nicely."

"Well, you can't say we ever 'ad 'im *in* sight," the sergeant retorted with heavy jocularity. "As for dates, don't tell me you're suggestin' 'e's shut 'isself up in an empty house to play 'ide-an'-seek with the underworked police?"

"He's in the picture," said Pardoe unshakably, "and I mean to put my finger on him."

"Mebbe 'e is." Salt looked sly. "He 'ad some queer friends, you said? As Mrs. Vick knew nothing about? Well, say 'e was a member of the Nordics an' kept it quiet? Then you don't have to leave 'im out of the picture. He can be in it with Speyer an' the rest of 'em."

"All right. There'll be no proof nor disproof till we've turned up more. But I'm going to find out which cinema Mitfold visited and what he saw there."

"An' those dates *don't* dovetail," was the relentless reminder. " 'E'd bin having 'is 'airbreadth escapes, an' going places nights, an' sayin' some mighty queer things to the girl some time before 'e started messin' about with the Vick case."

"That's the devil of it."

"Well, I know what you think," said Salt, "but I'd say it was a whole lot simpler if we was sure there was no connection with Vick, an' that September 25 was jes' coincidence. After all, a fair number of phony things must be 'appenin' in London on the same night, any date you like to choose."

There was no gainsaying this. Pardoe laughed, and laid on the desk the envelope Mitfold had covered with bird drawings.

"There's still this, Tommy. I'd give something to know why he drew them with such repetitive zeal and, for an artist, so monotonously. For rough as these are it's plain to see they're always the same bird, and so are those in his notebooks. It isn't just *a* bird either—at least, I don't think it is—it's a particular bird. I've got to know what, and why."

Salt, who could not distinguish one bird from another, was insensitive to the question of identity; but he thought he knew why.

"It don't seem to me much of a puzzle," he said with a sort of patient exasperation. "Why any of these pencil scribblings you see in books and blotters? Some folk are jes' bitten with the bug—that's why."

"But margin illustrators of that kind don't make little clay models of their pet subjects, nor remark on the probability one day of said subjects being chopped in two."

"What with?"

"A hatchet." Pardoe described the additional sketch of a suspended instrument which Vera had said appeared in most of the bird drawings.

The sergeant stared at the envelope for a few moments with the first real attention he had given it. Unlike Pardoe, he had not the imagination to which evidence of this type readily appealed, but, once secured, his interest remained. When he looked up the inspector was surprised to catch a gleam of exultant pleasure on his stolid features.

"Got it, b'gum," he said, with such delight that Pardoe, ignorant of its source, experienced quick enjoyment too. "It all boils down to the Nordic Bond business. I knew it would. You said Speyer was a bird man, didn't you? An' was a member of the N.B.? An' Miss Leaf said 'ow Mitfold went to a communist do with the same keenness 'e showed for the others? Well, suppose 'e was a communist, an' suppose 'e kept it quiet an' went to the N.B. because 'e 'ad suspicions of Speyer, an'——"

"On Speyer's ticket," Pardoe reminded him.

Salt brushed this trifle aside. "An' found out enough to put the professor on the spot, only Speyer got wise to it in the end an' got 'is in first. Then this bird is Speyer, an' the 'atchet, which we only got the girl's word for, represents the 'ammer an' sickle dealin' 'im one. Of course," he hastened to add, "that would be before old Stalin came in with the Germans."

"Of course," Pardoe agreed gravely. "But if you're right I'd expect the victim not to be a bird but a swastika."

"Ah, but not if it was personal, like. You said Speyer was the bloke for birds. An' I'm thinkin' Mitfold knew 'e was a spy. Who'd have a better chance of pickin' something up than a pupil going there twice a week an' with 'is eyes skinned for the sort of Edgar Wallace mysteries 'e liked to poke about in?"

"Meaning the wish was father to the thought in the first place?"

"Something like that."

"Well, if we keep it to the personal rather than the political angle he needn't have been a communist. Wynkerrell hasn't hinted at it, and he's sharp enough to have got hold of it however quiet Mitfold kept the fact. Besides, it isn't, I believe, the customary prelude to a job in the F.O. And if the hammer, why not the sickle too? But it's a hunch that's got its points, Tommy. Only we can't lose sight of dates—sorry to nag, but the fact is the whole thing buzzes with 'em. Now, the N.B. Club was closed at the end of August and the very first feelers in this affair don't appear to have been put out till a month later: not the só-called accidents, nor the nocturnal outings, nor the bird sketches—nothing."

"Mebbe it took 'im that time to size things up—sort 'is evidence an' make it shipshape before he took action," Salt said, but he sounded dubious.

Pardoe was thinking along another line. If Salt were right in fundamentals, the boy might never have discovered anything suspicious until *after* the dissolution of the club. Or else he was occupied the early part of September in watching the professor in the hope he'd betray himself by a further move; and in the cat-and-mouse game being played out in the first weeks of war the roles had been finally reversed. The diary . . . it was perhaps the key to the whole business. If he could get his hands on that he had not a doubt he would have what Archy Mitfold had been writing the night of his death. But it was equally certain to be in the murderer's possession—or rather, if the murderer were as shrewd as he appeared, completely destroyed by now.

"Where d'we go from 'ere?" came the sergeant's philosophical interruption.

Pardoe returned to the reality of routine.

"We're going to call on a German ornithologist in the morning. We're going to look for an empty house. And then we're going to visit the obliging Mr. Beltane."

CHAPTER XIII: PARDOE IS UNSUCCESSFUL

There wants no diligence in seeking him.
CYMBELINE.

BUT IT WAS NOT to official pattern that things worked themselves out on Tuesday morning.

For Herr Speyer was absent from the house in Rossetti Terrace when the Yard paid its call. A muscular housekeeper with dry, sallow features and an uncompromising stare met enquiry with the apparent hostility not uncommonly experienced in a first encounter with the deaf. A fund of patience was expended before the unprofitable facts were dug out. Indeed, it occurred to Pardoe that a pose of stupidity was as responsible as poor hearing for her inexpansive manner; a feeling that was confirmed when she gave with lucidity the information they sought as soon as their intention not to enter the house in her master's absence became plain. The professor's tuition, it seemed, was not entirely of a private nature. He still attended a few schools where he took German classes some mornings in the week, though evacuation had reduced his work in this respect. He had such an engagement this morning. She could not say whether he would be in much before lunch, because he took no pupils at his house in the morning hours and when his class was over at school did not often return straight home. But she suggested times when one might expect to find him at home.

Rossetti Terrace itself held a greater surprise for them. For there was no empty house in it.

It was a little road of quiet charm linking Flood Street and Manor Street. North of it lay Pentagon Square, and south, Hammer Street. Along each side rose about a score of mid-Victorian houses, semidetached, dim and solid,

pardonably dignified with their basements and railinged fronts and touches of
Gothic fussiness that a bungaloid age could no longer dub pretentious. Though
it was plain they were all occupied, Archy Mitfold's story might still be explained on the ground that one of them had been vacant on the date in question. Salt was for a systematic door to door enquiry that cleared up as it went
along and left nothing to later, but Pardoe felt that a little deductive work might
make this fatigue unnecessary.

The ground front of each house was occupied by a large window with, in
most cases, the front door, approached by a short flight of steps, beside it.
Since the houses were semidetached the doors were at the outer sides of each
pair, on the left of one window, on the right of its companion. The door of
number sixteen was on the left. Therefore, the inspector argued, unless Mitfold's
sense of locality had been hopelessly at sea, he had entered by mistake in the
darkness a house with a similarly situated door. Salt agreed and pointed out
that this eliminated both fourteen and eighteen, the houses immediately flanking Herr Speyer's. The numbers began at the Flood Street end, all the even
ones occupying the professor's side of the road, so that assuming Archy
Mitfold had approached the house from Flood Street, the natural route for a
foot passenger from Mulberry Fountain, number twenty was probably the
house if he had overshot his objective, number twelve if he had undershot it.

Enquiry at each made it almost ludicrously conclusive that neither was the
house. Number twelve had been occupied for fourteen years by two middle-
aged sisters, the younger of whom received music pupils and was definite in
her assurance that from six o'clock to nine on Monday nights the front room
on the right of the hall was occupied and the piano in action, and that even if
she or her sister had been unaware of someone entering from the street the
intruder for his part could never have supposed he was in an empty house.
The last week of September had been like every other week, and neither of
them had been absent from home for so much as a day at that time. Pardoe
tried number twenty.

This was eliminated even more effectively. On the night in question the
front room opening off the hall had been occupied by an old gentleman with
severe heart trouble, the nature of whose illness and its sudden onset had
necessitated a bed downstairs. At the hour at which Archy Mitfold had entered
the wrong house the day nurse had been still in attendance, as she was not
relieved until nine o'clock, and with four other adults in the house and a light
burning in the hall nobody could have taken it for an unoccupied place. The
invalid had since died. Pardoe thanked his informant for what, in the absence
of the formidable conspiracy his rational mind refused to envisage, was watertight evidence, and came away crestfallen but still undaunted. Archy Mitfold's
miss must have been a yet wider one, that was all, and while Salt tackled
number twenty-four he himself rang the bell of eight.

But it was no good. A timid widow who combined fear of the blackout with a stubborn contempt for the probability of air raids, was horrified at Pardoe's suggestion of an unlocked door. It was with pained reiteration she assured him that the latch was dropped and the bolt shot at six every evening; that there were two maids in residence and a good light in the hall, and that nothing, no, not a mouse, could enter her house without her knowledge and permission. Pardoe left with the feeling that the portcullis was falling hastily behind him, to encounter an equally chagrined Salt. As additional protection number twenty-four, which had twice been burgled in the present family's nine years residence, boasted an Airedale terrier whose vociferous temper had won him a reputation and was exercised nightly not earlier than ten o'clock. He had undoubtedly been on guard as usual at the close of September.

There was nothing for it but to adopt the sergeant's first suggestion of a house to house call, not now with any real hope of dropping on the house that had struck "so chill" on its intruder, but simply to clear the job up tidily and ascertain if any one of them had been vacant late last month. So Salt carried on with the even numbers while Pardoe, a faster worker, began on the odds on the other side of the Terrace. When, half an hour later, the two joined one another in Manor Street, it was to find that only one house in the road had been entirely evacuated by its inhabitants on the outbreak of war, to be reoccupied by newcomers as early as September 12.

"If it wasn't for his remark, 'I had a good look at it next day,' " Pardoe grumbled, "I'd be ready to think Mitfold dreamed the whole thing, or else was pitching the tale with some ulterior motive. Our luck's out." The neighborhood stirred a memory of yesterday. "What about a look at old Caffey? If Albert Bridge Road is right we're next door to him now."

He slipped into a telephone box and rang up the Pimlico Road number where the Nordic Bond had formerly met. The man who had been its secretary was living there and, if he knew Caffey's address, was at present in the frame of mind to recognize the expediency of obliging the Yard. This time fate tipped the scales the other way. Mr. Caffey lived just off the Albert Bridge Road.

A taxi took them in a few minutes to a large, neglected house south of Battersea Park. An untidy girl admitted them to a room without a fire and went off, with apparently little hope of success, to find Mr. Caffey. In a short time he came in, a haggard, irritable old man much as Miss Leaf had described, with restless, protruding eyeballs and an untrimmed moustache, stained by tobacco, which he clawed furiously throughout the interview. Pardoe summed him up correctly as a nervous, stupid old fellow with the natural antagonism bred by that combination of qualities and fortified by the knowledge that members of the defunct Bond were still being watched by the police. The best thing was to disclose one's hand at once.

But no sooner did he learn the identity of his visitors than the old man's testy manner gave way to frank bewilderment. Pardoe, with a vigilant eye on him, did not doubt its sincerity. He was palpably no actor.

"But—but, gentlemen," he stammered hoarsely, "if I owe this visit to my former membership of the Nordic Bond, why—I—I can only assure you that any connection I may have had with the club ceased—"

"Our present concern isn't directly with your membership," Pardoe broke in, and went on to explain in terms as concise as possible the necessity for enquiry into Archy Mitfold's movements, an investigation which had led them to look into the appropriation of Mr. Caffey's overcoat about six weeks ago.

"Was there perhaps," the inspector asked blandly, "anything missing when the coat was returned to you?"

The old man gave his mustache an extra tug and eyed Pardoe with a less choleric expression. It was possible that for once the police were adopting a helpful attitude.

"N-no, not really," he admitted, reluctant to commit himself wholly until he knew what treasure trove the inspector might have up his sleeve.

"Perhaps there was very little in the pockets at the time?" Pardoe continued, without probing this inconclusive reply.

"Fortunately, yes," Mr. Caffey said hastily, adding with unintentional veracity, "one doesn't know whom one's rubbing shoulders with at places like that, and I was particular never to leave my wallet or money or anything of that kind in the cloakroom. It didn't do. But it's queer you should ask me that, decidedly queer. Because the night I missed my coat I *had* done a stupid thing, an inexcusable thing, a thing which added considerably to my anxiety while I was waiting for my property to be returned."

"What was that?" But while he put the question Pardoe guessed that their search had run into another blind alley.

"I had inadvertently left my diary in the pocket."

Pardoe sensed the deflation of hope at work in Salt, and grinned slightly.

"Ah, your diary. Will you let us see it, please? It must be the book Mr. Mitfold came across when he was going through your coat to find the owner's identity."

For no apparent reason this mild remark fired the old gentleman to a surprising display of temper.

"That's it, that's it," he spluttered, plucking venomously at his upper lip and jigging a disagreeable staccato dance while the veins of his frail temples swelled and reddened. "I guessed it—I knew it—I was sure of it—— My good man, I practically *accused* him of it! He had been retaining my diary for the set purpose of prying into its contents, of decoding the entries for the satisfaction of his very vulgar curiosity—and I've no doubt, no, not a shadow of doubt, that he filched my coat deliberately, sir! Dis-*grace*ful. The young-er generation, if you please. And you, I am sure, are making these enquiries because he has now been caught red-handed in a similar theft?"

"Mr. Mitfold is dead," Pardoe said shortly, and remarked with some satisfaction the sickly fading of color from the malicious old face. "And now may I have a look at the diary?"

It was noticeable that Caffey raised no protest. With a muttered invitation to follow him he led them into a small room across the hall, as moldy and chill as the one they had left, where damp paper bulged on the walls, and a bust of Bismarck dared them enter. Here he unlocked the dusty glass doors of a bookcase and revealed, with a touch of recovered vanity, two shelves packed closely with notebooks of varying shapes, sizes and colors, though the last half-dozen or so in shiny black covers were of uniform pattern. Some bore in faint, others in conspicuous figures their years. The first was 1879.

"My diaries," the old man said. The self-conscious introduction was not without its dignity, and Pardoe knew that he must have made it many times and always in anticipation of the inevitable astonishment. The inspector's at least was not simulated.

"But there must be—"

"Sixty-four, my dear sir." In the presence of his achievement, he bore himself with arrogant confidence. "That number is in excess of the years I have kept it, which are only fifty-one. I began as a lad of fourteen, and I am now in my seventy-fifth year. But a single volume did not always suffice for one year, hence the thirteen extra books."

"And the volume in use?"

"You would like to—read a little of it?"

The words were informed by a sly, childish glee as he drew out the last notebook and put it almost eagerly into Pardoe's hand.

But the inspector was prepared for the script in which the entries were made, a hybrid form of shorthand, as it appeared, interspersed with numerals, and the glance he gave it was without surprise. The old man was anxious to explain.

"Until 1932 my record was made in longhand. Then, conceiving a plan which ensured greater secrecy, I invented a code which I have since used. The great Pepys himself is my preceptor."

Little remained for Scotland Yard to interest itself in after that. One or two other volumes were cursorily inspected, but they were so obviously what they claimed to be that Pardoe felt his lingering a thought ridiculous. A few neatly disposed questions drew replies that convinced him that in the matter of Archy Mitfold's fate Mr. Caffey was as innocent as the proverbial unborn.

Before they were clear of the house, however, he knew, too, that Salt was not satisfied.

"It don't make clear why he mixed 'imself up with the Bond," was his obstinate objection.

"But it does, Tommy. It's all a matter of character. Your diarist—and particularly your faithful, plodding, break- the-record kind—is about as near as you'll get to the supreme egotist. It's probably, in old Caffey's case certainly, vanity that eggs 'em on, based on the half-conscious belief that a record of their own trivial round is indispensable to the larger one. The diarist's world revolves on his own axis. And that means the necessity for private satisfaction of a lust for assertion, power, call it what you like. The very same qualities that turned Caffey into the complete diarist made him a member of the Nordic Bond, where he got vicarious enjoyment kiddin' himself he was pulling international strings. See?"

Salt, who saw nothing of the sort, said, "But what did he get out of it bein' in code? Nobody can read straight off what a fine fellow 'e is if 'e dresses it up in them fancy curls."

"That doesn't signify. The more secretive the greater the private satisfaction—like secret drinking. Besides, he doesn't himself suppose it's indecipherable, no more than we do, else why his rage at the thought of Mitfold reading it? No, Caffey's mental age is about that when he began his diary—fourteen, say. And to him and others like him diaries and Nordic Bonds are just safety valves."

"Well," Salt clinched it, finding the world more and more unpredictable, "seems like old 'Itler could've got it off 'is chest same way, an' saved all this mess."

Pardoe, whose anticipation of a useful morning in the company of Herr Speyer had not been realized, was keeping the Rowan House School visit until the afternoon, when a fast train would get him there about the time that small boys exchange classrooms for playing fields, and some masters are at leisure. This meant there was still plenty of time before lunch to pursue the enquiry at its London end, and in Mayfair there was Wynkerrell's alibi to check.

"Do you know, Tommy," Pardoe remarked as the taxi swung them from Hyde Park Corner into Hamilton Place and thence into Park Lane as far as its junction with Mount Street, from which point they had elected to walk, "Do you know there's a bird in this case after all—independent of the professor's interests, too? Only I can't make it fit those realistic sketches Mitfold made. I mean it isn't the same bird."

"What is it?"

"Tony Wynkerrell's shop is in Hobby Court—know what a hobby is?"

"Ah. A pastime," said Salt, who thought it a balmy sort of question. "An' the prof's is birds."

Pardoe laughed. "I hadn't thought of it that way. All right, there's three hobbies then—Speyer's ornithology, Wynkerrell's business address, and the one I'm thinking of. It's a bird—a falcon, sort of hawk, you know."

Salt grunted and turned it over thoughtfully. "An' why couldn't these scribblings be 'awks?"

"They're not." Pardoe was definite. "I don't know a great deal about them, but enough to recognize the distinctive characteristics of birds of prey; and

Mitfold, who drew well, hasn't reproduced any of them. But I shall ask Speyer, and I'll get hold of some good illustrations of the hobby falcon to make sure."

"It'll be a bloomin' nature-study ramble in the end, if you ask me. What *ho*, is this the 'ole we're after?"

The sergeant hardly did justice to the expensive obscurity of Grail Street. It might be a mere lane over which modernity and mechanization had muttered their spell, converting stables to garages and grooms' quarters to flats, but to Pardoe it suggested just the sophistication and tedious way of life with which it was best acquainted. Even its unobtrusive smartness was faintly repellent, for it had the smugness not of gentility but of its opposite; as if it made a point of being raffish. As Wynkerrell himself made a point of unsentimentality. And its dumb, sunless aspect this morning hinted at nocturnal business less drowsy.

Number six was a narrow cottage in white and green. There were two bells. Pardoe rang the one marked "Mrs. James." When the house remained unresponsive he pressed it again.

"Out," said Salt laconically, with resigned memory for the call on Speyer.

Pardoe glanced at his watch. "It's 12:20. These are the night birds, Tommy. They roost by day."

As he spoke the door opened and a woman in a gaudy, soiled kimono looked at them in hard silence. Art, that had once made her a platinum blonde, was ruthlessly turning her over to nature. She was putting up no fight about it. Her puffy face was so swollen that Salt surmised a scrap in which she'd got the worst of it.

"Mrs. James?" Pardoe enquired.

She looked him up and down. "What do you want?"

The inspector proffered a card. "I won't keep you many minutes."

She looked at it with narrowed eyes and a faint compression of the lips that tucked in the corners of her mouth.

She's had the police before, thought Salt, as she held the door wide and in silence stood back for them to enter. They went past two doors painted white— Wynkerrell's, Pardoe assumed—and up stairs laid with drugget and with a white handrail. At the top a small dark landing led to a door which faced them. On their left a bedroom door stood wide open. They came into a sitting room whose two windows on the street had their light hopelessly blocked by a tall, lifeless building opposite. Pardoe's sense of locality told him it must be the back of business premises at the Grosvenor Square end of South Audley Street. The gloom of the room was emphasized by closed windows, an atmosphere of fug, and a sprawl of cinders and cold ash in the grate. For the rest it was stuffed with floppily cushioned chairs and divans disposed with an air of salacious ease.

Mrs. James was a woman of few words, or else her swollen jaw was unconducive to conversation. She waved them indifferently to chairs, took a packet of cigarettes and a lighter from the mantelpiece, flumped on a settee, proceeded to add to the general frowst puffs of smoke from a long scarlet holder and subjected Pardoe to the fishy stare of one normal eye and one partially closed one that watered at intervals.

"What's wrong?" she said.

"Nothing here, I hope," Pardoe answered. "But if you were at home Saturday night it's likely you can help us on a question of time which has cropped up in the course of an enquiry we're making." As she made no response he added: "Were you here at ten and after on Saturday evening?"

"What if I was?" The tone was more inquisitive than offensive, and as people who are curious, Pardoe reflected, are not usually fearful, there was hope of breaking through her reticence.

Without reference to the Mitfold affair he explained briefly what he wanted. "It's simply that we have to check up on all such statements, and I'm wondering if you can corroborate what Mr. Wynkerrell has told us."

A gleam of satisfaction replaced the earlier expression of wariness on her face.

"Blast my landlord," she said with a burst of vindictiveness. "I hope he's in trouble, good, thick and running over. You can jug him just about as fast as you like. I'm clearing out, and so's my sister—we'd sooner dig in a pigsty than in this house any longer."

"Your sister shares this flat?" Pardoe made mild enquiry. Her spiteful attack on the bookseller reminded him of Mrs. Pell. Tony Wynkerrell might be an ornamental young man, but all women, it was plain, were not attracted by him.

The ice having been broken, largely by Mrs. James's own illusive sense of being ranged with the police against Wynkerrell, she explained readily enough.

Her sister, it appeared, was "Melilot," the dressmaker. She obviously considered the name sufficient enlightenment. They had occupied the flat at 6 Grail Street for ten months now, and wished they had never seen it. Why? Because it was horribly expensive, badly equipped, cold and depressing. And it was impossible to squeeze the smallest concession out of Wynkerrell without a disproportionate degree of unpleasantness and fatigue. He was oozing with money and as tightfisted as they made 'em. But this weekend had been the limit. After this they wouldn't hang on another minute once they'd got a place to go to. After this—

"What happened?" Pardoe stemmed it with, he hoped, the right touch of sympathy.

She launched out on a furious diatribe that set her voice trembling. On Friday evening she had fallen prey to an attack of neuralgia which had increased in ferocity all day Saturday and had only begun to grow better when the swelling appeared. Until that had subsided the dentist would be unable to do anything for her. Fortunately her sister left business early on Saturdays and had stayed with her and done what she could to allay the pain. She herself went to bed immediately after lunch, which she hadn't taken. She had not been able to touch food all day and was anticipating a night as sleepless as Friday when, soon after ten o'clock, she fell into a doze. She couldn't have slept a minute or two, or so it seemed to her, before she was awakened in a most outrageous manner by a hideous din in the flat below.

"What, a fight?" said Pardoe. Salt looked hopeful.

She stared at him. "We thought it was. It wasn't though—not in reality. The blasted fool downstairs had got his radio on full pitch—some fool play, and everybody scrapping in it. Maida got the paper and said it was one of these murder plays. I said I wished it was Wynkerrell being murdered. He'd got the volume on as far as it'd go, and what it must've been like in his own place the devil knows, for anybody else would've had their eardrums bust. Wynkerrell must've been tight, of course—that, or it was a fancy bit of spite because he knew I was ill. Oh yes, he's capable of it, the tripehound. I was in agony. My head was raging, and all the jumpiness I'd have cured by a spot of sleep had come back ten times worse. Maida went down and hammered at his door. She says she yelled at him, but I don't know—she's quieter than me. She tried the door and it was locked. And he came up to it and gibed at her."

"What did he say?"

"He didn't. He whistled at her through the crack."

"Very unamiable," said Pardoe. "What happened then?"

"She came back up, and it went on just the same. I thought I should go mad. I was pretty near screaming. It was gone ten, and all I had in front of me was the prospect of another night like the last. I got out of bed and huddled myself in a coat and went down. I was ready to beat the door in. But I could see the more row we made the worse he'd carry on, so I put my eye to the keyhole first to see if he was too drunk to take anything in. And then I told him all over again about my toothache, and that I'd fetch a copper if he didn't tune down—"

"You saw Mr. Wynkerrell plainly?"

"As plain as I'm seeing you. Hanging over the thing, seeing if he couldn't squeeze a bit more din out of it. And in the middle of what I was saying he made a run backwards and took a flying kick at the door with his heel—slap in my face, you might say. But when I'd gone away he tuned in lower, so I bet he took me at my word about the copper."

"And things were quiet for the rest of the night?"

"Not to say quiet—but it was more like it was any other time he'd got the radio on."

"You mean it was making an altogether exceptional din on Saturday?"

"I'll say it was. Never heard anything like it since we took the flat on—nor Maida. And we've had something to put up with one way and another."

Pardoe nodded sympathetically. "I wonder if you can tell me what Mr. Wynkerrell was wearing—could you see what it was through the keyhole?"

"What he pretty well lives in when he's here, a peacock blue dressing gown. And slippers." She added with spiteful reflection, "I'll bet the kick he gave bruised him good and hard."

"About what time was it when he reduced the volume?"

She thought. "Ten-thirty. Near enough."

Pardoe put a few questions about Wynkerrell's callers at the cottage, but he put them cautiously. The woman was suspicious enough as it was, and he had no wish to loose abroad her exacerbated tongue on the subject of Wynkerrell's alibi. In any case she could tell him nothing useful about the bookseller's associates, nor were there any carousals to report. Her meagre information was all the more genuine when coupled with her reluctance to make admissions favorable to Wynkerrell; she would have been only too delighted to damn him if she could have done so with any hope of getting her lies accepted as truth. As it was, except for Saturday night, her grudge against him was less, it seemed, on account of personal interference with her rest than for the unsatisfactory relationship existing between them as landlord and tenant.

Pardoe came away with the conviction that Wynkerrell had told the truth when he described 6 Grail Street in terms that made it little more than a *pied-à-terre*.

CHAPTER XIV: THE MOST UNLIKELY PERSON

I promis'd to inquire carefully
About a schoolmaster.
THE TAMING OF THE SHREW.

THE AUTOPSY REPORT awaited them at the Yard. It established Tawney's first diagnosis, that a blow on the head had been received prior to death, and supplied the details which made murder unquestionable. The inspector ran over them with Salt: fracture of the skull a little above and behind the right temple, laceration and slight hemorrhage of the brain, damage to the meninges.

"That's the lining of the brain," Pardoe translated. "If death had been brought about by hanging alone, Tommy, the brain would be in a bloodless state because of interference with its blood supply by constriction of the large vessels in the neck. The report says there certainly is partial anemia of the brain, but evidence of hemorrhage is present all the same, which merely suggests that suspension of the body accelerated, without causing, death. There's rupture of the inner coat of the carotid artery too, and though that's a post-mortem finding in cases of hanging, as in judicial hanging, it can equally well occur where the rope's auxiliary to and not the cause of death." He broke off and glanced at the report. "The usual blunt instrument's suggested—I mean for the blow. There was no blood externally."

Salt took him up promptly. "The right temple? That'd be a left-'anded bloke hit 'im, eh? Or else he came up behind an'——"

"It's a small room. Coming up behind wouldn't be too easy, and by then, remember, Mitfold was on his guard against queer—accidents."

"But what if 'is killer was a different fellow altogether, not the one, I mean, that'd been having shots at 'im before?"

Pardoe was thinking of something else. "I wonder—look here, I want another go at the room where he died. Not now; when we've seen Beltane. But I've got an idea—suppose he fell, was knocked down, say, and got his blow that way? There were some funny prints of his on the back of that chair—they'd have come that way if he'd thrust out at it when he was falling. It'll bear looking into anyway."

He was still turning the notion inside out in the carriage they had to themselves on the way to Witley. It strengthened, he argued, the case for unpremeditated murder. A knockout blow with all its element of luck wasn't the best preparation for planned murder.

"That's what I'm gettin' at," Salt said. "Looks like somebody else killed 'im after t' other'd tried three times. An' that's a dizzy complication."

Pardoe shook his head. "We don't have to see it that way. There's no reason why it shouldn't have been the other fellow all along. So far as we can tell now the murderer wasn't to know he'd return to Mulberry Fountain for some private reason that night. Well then, say the murderer came upon him there and was let into the house *unprepared* for immediate action? Then we'll say there was a flare-up, blows, and from his point of view the luck of a k.o. for Mitfold. Then he finished the job."

"A bit risky goin' in the place unarmed."

"You mean for the murderer? Why? Perhaps he knew, or thought he knew, that Mitfold hadn't discovered the identity of his attacker. Besides, he was probably sure the boy had nothing to defend himself with in the house."

The sergeant was worried. "But, say, apart from the k.o.—*if* he knocked him down—why's it got to be unpremeditated? If he sloshed 'im with piping, f'r instance, it'd look *pre*meditated, now wouldn't it? Unless 'e's one of these gents that always carries a bit round with 'im for company."

"The rope, Tommy—keep your eye on the rope," said Pardoe, with a sudden grim vision of a second one at the end of the story. "That was a piece of smart improvisation—quick thinking, speedy action, but improvisation all the same. Else he'd have brought rope with him, and if rope, why not a simpler weapon? As I read it it means the murderer had to think up that method at the last to ensure Mitfold died, and it tells us, too, that he's a man familiar with the run of the house in Mulberry Fountain."

The station at Witley-in-the-Holt was half a mile from the school. It was not impossible, the booking clerk who seemed to be the solitary genie of the place explained, to get something or other on wheels to convey one to the

Rowan House; but the suggestion was that at three o'clock in the afternoon the expectation was presumptuous and the probability slender. Pardoe and Salt elected to walk.

On the slumbering road they covered there was neither house nor traveler. After a bright morning the sky had turned steely, and a few drops of rain spattered them as they reached the extremity of the wall that ran on their right between the school grounds and the road. It marched with them for a distance of more than three hundred yards, an uncompromising guardian ten feet high permitting no glimpse of what lay the other side. A pine plantation hugged it closely its entire length, the dark motionless boughs encroaching over the roadway. At its other end the road suddenly dipped into a bay that lay at a lower level than the road itself. At the bottom were iron gates between disproportionately large pillars smothered in ivy.

The very devil for bringing a car out, thought Pardoe, considering the gradient as he pushed open a gate. He wondered if there was, perhaps, a second exit. A short semicircular drive heavily arched with limes led to the school, a chaste white house with a classical face that looked from the outside tidy and comfortless. There was everywhere such unnatural silence that Pardoe concluded the playing fields must be at some distance from the house; but when he had pulled the handle of the bell in the porch, and they had been admitted by a businesslike maid, the sudden uprush of small boys' voices as suddenly quelled reached their ears from behind a closed door. Then they were maneuvered into a sparely disposed room like the prelude to an experience with the dentist and summarily left to themselves.

"Things are done with dispatch here, and in their proper order," Pardoe murmured to Salt, who was looking as if he didn't know how he got there. "We shall be vetted by the headmaster first."

In less than a minute the H.M. came in, a small, dry man with an academic manner his humorous eye suggested was largely assumption. The warm undertones of his speech were Welsh.

"Yes, Mr. Beltane told me he knew the young fellow who'd hanged himself," he said, and Pardoe sensed a relationship between head and assistant staff that was first of all human. "I believe the boy came down here once."

He was admirably incurious, and not, Pardoe thought, much interested. When it was suggested that if Mr. Beltane were at liberty they would not detain him long, he offered them a private sitting room for the interview.

"Mr. Beltane's bed-sitter's remote as the antipodes," he said, waving an arm to indicate miles of corridor, "and the staff common room's out of the question—you'd be barged in upon every other minute. Come with me, and I'll send him along."

They were taken to a little room stacked with amiable photographs of self-conscious children grouped about soccer balls, and a fine assortment of what appeared to be Mr. Edwards' own family. A coal fire burned on the hearth, and french windows opened on a broad graveled path and an expanse of turf that appeared to drop away in terraces. It was an altogether more genial view than the pine copse and the approach to the house.

When Beltane joined them, Pardoe, he could not have said why, was at once surprised. He had seen Mitfold in death and gauged with what accuracy one could the slight, fastidious, secretive being he had been in life. He had met Wynkerrell and found his elegancy not out of place in an associate of the dead youth. But the third member of the triumvirate who had met and talked on the last afternoon of Archy Mitfold's life struck for him a false note in the picture he had formed.

Philip Beltane was tall, muscular, heavily built. His clothes were good, but he moved uneasily in them as if they were tight. This tentative quality implied, Pardoe thought, a reserve of strength, and emphasized a certain defensive note in his manner. His hands were large and workmanlike, with long, spatulate fingers. He had a sun-reddened skin the autumn had not paled and light gray eyes so widely open beneath thick, fair brows that they gave him a troubled look younger than his years. A bucolic air about him impressed Pardoe immediately; anyone less like Wynkerrell's "towny" individual could not, he thought, be well imagined.

Beltane sat down and looked uncomfortably from one to the other. He seemed surprised to see two.

"Bringing you down here," he said stiffly, "looks as if I'd something definite for you to handle. I haven't. I thought it over last night and decided I'd been a bit impulsive. I'm afraid you'll think I'm merely wasting your time."

"Suppose you tell us all about it? We'll decide whether or not we're wasting time."

Beltane looked anxiously at Pardoe for a few moments before blurting out: "Look here—I've been bothered—I'm bothered now, ever since I saw Archy had been found dead at his aunt's house. There's something wrong—something desperately wrong about it. I'm not being melodramatic or anything like that, but—well—"

"Yes?"

"I don't believe it was suicide. Even if it *was* hanging. I—I think somebody killed him."

He shot a worried look at Salt, but the sergeant, thumbing his shabby notebook, was impassive. Pardoe waited for more.

"Why do you think so?"

"Because Archy thought somebody was trying to. To kill him, I mean. He tried to convince us of it, and I *was* convinced. And then I pretended I wasn't because I thought the whole thing was giving him the jitters—and by the time he left me I really didn't believe him."

"You mean you pretended so hard that in the end you convinced yourself it wasn't true?"

"Oh no. It was Archy's manner at last that put the idea into my head he was pulling our legs, not perhaps so far as the foundations of his story went but in all its lurid implications. I'm not fanciful, and if I can I must have the rational explanation. But then, dying like this directly afterwards—I'm bound to believe he was speaking the sober truth."

"I see. Now will you let us have the full story?"

In fact it differed in no respect from Tony Wynkerrell's, for which it was admirable corroboration up to the point when they had left in Wynkerrell's car. From the psychological standpoint, however, it was a more valuable account. Beltane seemed at once to have been specially interested in and more observant of the play of personality and Mitfold's mental condition when he had given them his grudging confidence.

"At first I felt increasingly that Archy wasn't telling us all he could have told. It was as if he had something in reserve up his sleeve which he *might* produce at any moment he judged best, but never did."

"And you thought later on he'd been lying to you?"

Beltane hesitated. "That's blunt, isn't it? If you'd known Archy you'd have recognized how closely reality and fancy were associated in his head. He wasn't a liar in the ordinary sense of the term. But his imagination—"

"Was uncontrolled?" Pardoe put in as he fumbled for a word.

"Perhaps." He added shrewdly, "It might be that he controlled it too well— in his own interests. Wishful thinking, and all that."

"But he wouldn't want to wish somebody was trying to murder him?"

"Archy would. Take my word for it. He had a childish passion for mysteries and the sort of vanity that makes you positive you can solve what's baffling other people. When we were at Oxford he was forever dabbling in, or hoping to dabble in, what didn't concern him. And if nothing trotted along of its own accord he'd invent it. Anything on the lines of the 'Fly, all is known' message to the revered cardinal or whoever he was, filled him with glee. He wasn't practical—nor, poor kid, particularly sensible. He'd got detective fever all right."

"I never had it," Pardoe said.

"Real ones don't."

The inspector smiled. There was more perspicuity in the young man than appeared on the surface. "Well, his fever didn't send him to the professionals for a consultation. Why didn't he come to us?"

"That's just it." Beltane was eager. "We suggested it, Winkle and I did, I mean. Hang it all, if he thought he'd got a determined murderer on his heels it was the only thing to do—the only common-sense thing. It's exactly why I rang you up yesterday. But Archy was instantly against it, wouldn't hear of bringing the police in. And it was that as much as anything else that gave me the idea he was romancing. If he really was leading us up the garden path it was natural he wouldn't want you people exploding his myth."

DEED WITHOUT A NAME

"Well reasoned. On the other hand if, as you suggest, he fancied himself as a detective he would have been on that account, too, reluctant to call in help."

"Yes. That's my view now. Because now I believe what he told us."

"When you started to doubt his story was there anything besides his refusal of the police that made it seem incredible?"

"Oh, two or three things. Well, for one, his aunt didn't know anything about these attacks on him, he said. Now that didn't seem feasible. I mean, he was living with her, and if anybody knew about them it would surely be she. But—and this was how I looked at it when I thought his story wouldn't wash—if the whole thing was an invention it was more than likely, of course, that he wouldn't tell Miss Leaf because she'd have more opportunity than anybody else of finding out it wasn't true."

Pardoe nodded. "Yes. But now you're convinced he was telling you the truth, can you think of any reason why he should say Miss Leaf didn't know?"

Beltane frowned. "Well, because she really didn't, I suppose. Mitfold could have kept it from her if he'd been careful, and that's what he must have done."

Pardoe was silent. Salt watched Beltane. Then the inspector said, "Anything else to support your theory that he was romancing?"

"Yes, there was. I can see now, though, that his ignorance could have been perfectly genuine. But at the time I thought it odd that he couldn't guess at a motive for these attacks on him. Wynkerrell and I pressed him to say why anybody should be so keen to get rid of him, but he couldn't—or wouldn't—tell us."

"Which of you first suggested that Archy Mitfold should go to the police with his story?"

Beltane's rather full stare widened. "Dash it all, does it matter?" he said with the first impatience he had shown. "I don't properly remember. I believe it was me, but if it was, Winkle backed me for all he was worth—for a wonder."

"He usually disagrees with you?"

Beltane smiled. "We don't like one another a lot. He thinks I'm pedantic—I probably am—and I think him wasteful of his talents, which he in his turn thinks smug of me. So there you are. Of course I'm getting on for two years older than he and Archy."

"Of course." It was time, Pardoe thought, to lay down his cards. "Mr. Beltane, you may as well know that the police share your opinion of your friend's death. He didn't hang himself. He was murdered. We were handling the case when you rang us up."

Beltane turned rather red and momentarily looked as if he thought he had been tricked.

"Then I *am* merely wasting your time," he said, offended. "You don't want me to tell you what you know yourselves. I wondered why it was worthwhile two coming. Wynkerrell was a jolly sight handier to get at and could have given you precisely the same story as myself."

"He's done so," Pardoe said. "That doesn't detract from the value of yours. Corroborative evidence is essential, and if you'd not given us a call we should in any case have approached you. You've been, and can be, extremely helpful, Mr. Beltane, and now we're here there are some more questions I'd like to put to you."

"Anything I can do." The mutter sounded mollified, but he still looked rather hot.

For some seconds Pardoe watched Salt's pencil tracing an idle design in his notebook. Even while his mind was busy in another quarter he saw with amusement that the sergeant was trying his hand at a bird.

"There's a possibility that somebody killed Mr. Mitfold for political—or semipolitical—reasons. Do you know if he was a communist?"

Beltane's astonishment was unconcealed. "Lord, no. Whatever put that idea into your heads? He wasn't anything in particular. Tory outside, I suppose, but nothing deep."

"He attended communist meetings, didn't he?"

"Possibly. I don't know. But that wouldn't mean a thing. Archy attended anything that gave him the chance to poke his nose into something new. I believe he'd have gone to a Mothers' Meeting and glamourized it the same as he did everything else. Most of his time he was simply one large query mark. He was the Elephant's Child."

"Any Nazi sympathies? Or, for that matter, would you say he was actively anti-Nazi?"

"Honestly, I can't say. And because I can't, it looks, don't you think, as if his feelings weren't violent either way? His whole temperament, I think, would have made him range himself against them—he was rather a brainy boy, artistic too, and what you might call undisciplined in the dreamy way. He had no political ideal, I'm pretty sure—not strong enough to make him die, or make somebody kill him."

He spoke with unmistakable earnestness.

"Do you know Herr Speyer?" Pardoe asked.

"August Speyer, the language tutor? I saw him once, when I was with Archy. That's all. A remarkable-looking man."

"Did Archy ever talk about him?"

"Not that I remember. Nothing that sticks, anyway. But look here, d'you mean Archy was mixed up with spies?"

"I don't know. I'm going to find out. Does Herr Speyer bring spies to mind?"

"Not at all," Beltane said indignantly. "I don't know him. I wasn't hinting at any such thing. I meant—"

"Yes, I know," Pardoe said patiently. "I didn't think you were. Association of ideas is impersonal enough. Tell me, did Archy Mitfold ever talk to you about Mr. Sampson Vick?"

"Not once," said Beltane, after a momentary flounder in these new waters. "I really am sure of that. It's a wonder he didn't too, because this 'Lost Millionaire' business is exactly the kind of thing I've been trying to tell you was meat and drink to him."

"So I gathered," said Pardoe who, remembering the six hundred odd letters that had reached Scotland Yard propounding theories their writers believed squared with the disappearance, privately agreed it was a wonder Archy Mitfold's had not been one of them. "Let's try something else. We want to find out which cinema Archy visited on October 4. Is there a chance you can help us trace it?"

The bewilderment on Beltane's face made him smile.

"There's a serious purpose behind all this, though to you it may sound a mass of unrelated nonsense. Have you any idea where he may have gone that day?"

"The fourth? Today's the seventeenth. That would be a week last Wednesday—what a hope." He spoke thoughtfully, however, and seemed annoyed with himself for his unfeigned surprise a moment ago. "Except for one occasion when he came down here I only saw him weekends. Wait a minute—I can tell you the picture houses he most often went to. I've been to both with him—that's the Fantasia in Ebury Street, which he said he liked best, and the Aladdin in Fulham Road. But he wasn't as keen on the flicks as you'd think."

"All the better. His patronage of the cinemas wouldn't be so wide, perhaps."

"Oh, and there's another thing," Beltane broke in. "A couple of weeks ago there was a talkie he very much wanted to see—enough to talk about it anyhow. That rather ghastly thing called *Repeat the Dose*—Grand Guignol stuff, but subtly acted, no bludgeon effects or overtones, I believe. Archy liked that kind of thing—he had rather good taste in the macabre. I don't like it in any guise."

"But wasn't the premiere of that in the West End in August?"

"That's right. Archy didn't see it then, though. He said so. He got a belated enthusiasm for it after hearing it talked about, as one does."

Pardoe nodded. "Thanks. You've helped a lot."

"But I don't know that he ever did see it," Beltane observed hastily. "Though if you can find it was showing at the Fantasia or the Aladdin on October 4—"

"Exactly. Though it's possible he saw it before the fourth?"

"I don't think so. I was in town a fortnight ago, the weekend September 30 to October 1, and that was when he talked about wanting to see it. I wasn't in London again till the Old Boys' dinner on Saturday."

"I see. That narrows it." Pardoe cocked a mild eye at him.

"You come up nearly every week?"

"Almost." Beltane's manner was at once a little distant. "That is, when I'm free. There are six resident masters here—we've each roughly two weekends a term on duty. One of mine fell on October 7, so I remember quite well it was the week before when Archy talked about the movie."

"Excellent," Pardoe said cheerfully. "Now what about your own doings Saturday night and Sunday? We've got to check everybody, as you know."

"Yes, I know." Beltane accepted the fact quietly. He gave them the address in Victoria Street they had already learned from Wynkerrell and a complete account of his own movements from the hour he had parted from Archy until his return to Witley on Sunday evening. The only period furnishing an alibi was one of no particular value to the case, from two to four Sunday afternoon when he had paid a visit to a relative in a North London nursing home. He did not offer the address. Pardoe asked for it, to recognize with reluctance for pressing the point a home for mental diseases. At the crucial period from nine-thirty till 11 P.M. on Saturday Beltane admitted that it would be hard to produce anyone who could positively support the statement that he had stayed in his room at the hotel and read solidly before going to bed.

He added as Pardoe made no comment: "I haven't an alibi, I'm afraid, but I believe nowadays the innocent seldom have."

"Well, the innocent needn't worry," the inspector said mendaciously, and took from his pocket Archy Mitfold's bird envelope which was acquiring a shopsoiled appearance.

"Ever seen these things, or similar ones, before?"

Beltane, who had by now schooled his countenance to indifference, took the envelope and examined the drawings. When he looked up he was frowning.

"What am I supposed to say now? Is it a new sort of riddle, or something?" He turned it over and read the address. "What, you don't mean it reached Archy like this? Sort of hieroglyphic threats, eh? Sorry, but this is the first time I've met 'em. And I've no idea what the birds are meant to be."

When Pardoe had described the discovery of the drawings, Beltane said: "It's like the *Adventure of the Dancing Men*—only in this case it's the dead man and not his murderer who's made the pictures."

Pardoe nodded. "And by the number he's drawn in the last few weeks in his books and on scraps of paper it's possible there's some significance in them beyond mere scribbling. We've evidence, too, that occasionally he adds a hatchet or some such instrument to the bird drawings."

"The hammer and sickle?" Beltane said, and wondered why the detective sergeant bestowed an approving glance upon him.

"Except that the bird isn't a sickle," said the inspector. "No, I hardly expected you'd know much about it. But what I'm wondering is whether you know anybody connected with Archy Mitfold whose nickname, surname, or any name he's known by is that of a bird? You were at school and college with him, and those are the places where nicknames flourish."

"By Jove, that's interesting," Beltane said. "And it's in character—with Archy, I mean. Just the sort of superfluous camouflage he delighted in. Let me see—there must have been, there *were*—one or two Birdies, but they're in some limbo far from here long ago and I can't think they've resurrected themselves so as to murder Archy. And there was a master at Crispin's named Cock—the boys called him Rooster. That's all I can think of—except schoolmasters are sometimes known as beaks, I believe, but we never called 'em it that I remember, nor the kids here."

Pardoe smiled. "That would be putting too fine a point to it. There's more to this bird than a beak. What about yourself—did you have a nickname?"

Beltane shook his head. "Not really. Only my own cut down. Schoolboys are rarely inventive, you know. They take the short cuts. So I was just Bel."

"And the Dragon?" Pardoe finished.

"I don't know where he came in. That's right—Bel was a brass idol in Babylon. But I don't think he took the shape of a bird."

"No." But Pardoe was curious. "Isn't Beltane itself—doesn't it mean a forge or something of the sort?"

"It was a Celtic festival held on the first day of May. And Mayday itself got to be called Beltane. You must be thinking of the fires they kindled that day, and the rites the Druids performed at them. There were the Beltane games too."

"What's in a name? A fair amount by the sound of it. And what was Mr. Wynkerrell called?"

"Oh, he was Winkle. You can't turn a shellfish into a bird."

"I won't try. And Mitfold himself—any name attached to him?"

"Only Archy. And the unimaginative Mits sometimes."

"Do you by any chance know the date of his birthday?" Pardoe slipped in casually.

Beltane was silent overlong. He said absently, "I don't," then looked apologetically at the inspector. "Sorry, I'm thinking of other things. Archy himself had a sort of sporadic trick of calling people odd names just for a time, you know. Then he'd let 'em die down again and invent something else. Half the time nobody knew what the names meant, and he enjoyed being secretive about them. I know at school he called Wynkerrell 'Lacky Mo,' or some such thing, for a whole term, and Winkle was disgusted because the other kids said Archy meant 'Ikey Mo.' Nobody found out what he really meant, though. And at Oxford he used to call me Beltenebros, an awful mouthful—in the story of Amadis of Gaul, you know—only it was a disappointment to him when I recognized the source of it, because he was a conceited kid besides being a well-read one and it tickled his vanity to keep us guessing."

"Yes. And now he's dead he's got us guessing again."

"Well, none of that's any use to you, I know. But honestly, I don't remember a thing relating to birds. Have you tried your luck with Wynkerrell?"

"Not yet," said Pardoe, noting that he made no reference to Speyer's ornithology. "On the contrary, Mr. Beltane, anything you tell us is welcome when we can get hold of so little that's tangible. Where it hasn't direct bearing on the case—and that has to be proved—it's evidence as to character, idiosyncrasies, habits, and part of our job is to construct from a dead man a living one."

The library at Rowan House School was a handsome, well- equipped room whose invitation was honored, alas, as much in the breach as in the observance. This afternoon Rowlands major, whose fifth-form status entitled him to do his prep in inspirational surroundings, sat huddled up at the end of the central mahogany table trying to pad out to at least two pages an essay on Cromwell. It had to go in tomorrow to Mr. Blunt, and Mr. Blunt unfortunately lived up to his name in the matter of criticism and had a deadly eye for padding. All Rowlands major could comfortably recall about Cromwell at the moment was the wart on his nose, which had always seemed to him a most powerful wart, very suitable for a dictator. But he knew that Mr. Blunt would regard as superfluous even half a page about a wart, so there was no salvation there.

Rowlands major sighed, fidgeted, wondered what new dodge there was for getting a rise out of Tubby Moxham and decided he hated the first half-hour after tea with two or three preps in hand and supper such a long way off. What was more, the lack of consideration shown by people who kept barging in and out the place and snapping on and off the light at the other end of the room was certainly foul. They seemed to think the place existed for them to rummage in moldy old books, and not for Rowlands major to remain in undisturbed while he wrote about Cromwell.

It was true there was only one person in the far bay now. It was Mr. Beltane. He was being pretty quiet about it, except he hadn't got hold of what he wanted because he kept returning books to the shelves and pulling others out.

Rowlands major hooked his left ankle round his right calf and wished Cromwell had never been born. He cut off Charles's head, of course, but the first page seemed a bit premature for—

Whatever was up with old Beltane? The light down that end was brighter than the one illuminating his own virgin paper, and it was plain to see that Bellows was jolly well het up about something. His face wasn't as red as usual; it looked quite skinny like people did on the pictures when Something Awful was just going to happen. And first he'd shut the book he had his nose in, and then he'd open it again for another peep, and then—

Rowlands major assumed the attitude of a paralyzed rabbit confronted by a stoat. For Bellows was fixing him with a singular and, to the rabbit, highly disagreeable expression on his usually tolerant mug. It could only mean T-R-O-U-B-L-E. That he was invisible to the eyes which seemed to bore into his head would never have occurred to Rowlands major, for small boys have their vanity too. In the flash of a second this one was raking an infrequently goaded conscience and finding nothing in the medley turned up that was pertinent to old Bellows. The next moment Beltane had hastily shoved the book into place and gone out without a word.

Emotional disturbance in a master was worth investigating. When it was related to the contents of a book investigation became imperative. Rowlands major, considered to have a healthy mind by all the adults who had never seen inside it, slipped off his chair and made his way to the bay of books while he could still memorize the shelf Mr. Beltane had been consulting.

Gosh, it was the nature-study section! Rowlands major, who thought of it as bugs and slugs and had never looked inside one of its books, tentatively drew out a volume from about the spot he had noticed old Bellows' hand hovering.

Birds . . . what a bore. He tried again . . . more birds. *Golly*, what was there in a *bird* to put the wind up a great, hulking bloke like Bellows? For his own part the only mental association their image evoked was that of his own catapult, a view, he was aware, on the whole unpopular with adults whose odd, unnecessary prejudices were such a trial to a boy.

A maid crossing the lower hall at five-thirty on her way to the front door passed Mr. Beltane seated at the telephone in earnest conversation. At her approach he stopped speaking and leveled a look at her she did not like at all and which Rowlands major would at once have recognized. Funny thing, she had seen him in the very same spot doing the very same thing an hour ago, the time she went to beat the gong for tea. Only then he'd looked a sight more cheerful than he did now.

Well, even a schoolmaster might have a girl, she supposed, and even a schoolmaster might have a tiff with her.

At 5:10 Pardoe and Salt got into the London train, their departure watched by the solitary pundit of Witley-in-the-Holt, who thought their business had been concluded with unseemly haste. As they rumbled past fields where the last light drained from a brooding sky, the sergeant turned to Pardoe.

"Not so good, eh? He *could've*—"

Pardoe interrupted quickly. "You don't like character as evidence, do you, Tommy? But on the strength of it, know who we've been talking to?"

Salt did not commit himself.

"To the most unlikely person in the case."

CHAPTER XV: AT MULBERRY FOUNTAIN

> Tim.   *What have you there, my friend?*
> Pain.   *A piece of painting.*
>
> TIMON OF ATHENS.

ON THEIR RETURN from Witley Pardoe sent Salt to Trumpeter's Row to get a story from the man Runyon, so far as they knew the sole witness of the car assault upon Mitfold, while he himself examined the reports which had come in during their absence.

The first he picked up was negative but not on that account disappointing, since to eliminate it from consideration helped to clear the ground. It referred to the Pandulf Road accident resulting in the death of the cyclist. Further enquiry had established it as a genuine accident incapable of producing the reactions suggested. The driver of the car, a Suffolk engineer, had readily given evidence at the time, been exonerated from all blame, and engaged since early in September on a job of work in Ayrshire. Apart from his alibi, which in any case made it impossible for him to be the attacker they were seeking, it was out of the question that he could have nursed any grievance against Archy, whose testimony had corroborated his in every respect; while, since he had himself suffered no such molestation as Mitfold had complained of before his death, the theory of revenge on behalf of the victim was ruled out. The cyclist had been a retired school inspector living in lodgings at Turnham Green. His few relatives were out of touch with him and apparently indifferent to his fate. No previous connection had existed between the victim of the accident, the driver of the car and Archy Mitfold, or between any two of them; the other man alleged to have passed by at the time had not been traced.

Pardoe pushed the report aside with relief. He had never imagined there was anything in it, and now that old Caffey, too, was disposed of the empty house was the sole survivor of Miss Leaf's "incidents." And that at the moment looked like the most fanciful figment of all.

The second report he took up dealt with Salt's enquiry into Mrs. Byron's matrimonial adventures. Within a year of Mr. Welkin's untimely decease in his garage, she had married Percy Byron, a well-known bookmaker of excellent repute. Two years later he collapsed when getting out of bed one morning and died in a few minutes. The doctor, though puzzled, had shown no demur about granting a certificate, since Mr. Byron's heart had been in an uneasy condition for the six months preceding his death. The most that could be said was that death, when it came, was unexpected. And Mrs. Byron, who had found herself a rich woman by her first widowhood, was now a richer.

In fairness Pardoe had to admit that the Byron case was not in itself sinister. It might be so only when regarded in the light of what had gone before and after it. But where in the world would be found the woman's motive for plotting Archy Mitfold's death? After a minute or two one possible motive insinuated itself into the inspector's mind. If Archy had stumbled on something pointing to Kathleen Byron as a murderess on at least one occasion, and she had got to know of it, his elimination might well have seemed imperative to her. Pardoe did not think much of the idea, but it was worth keeping in mind.

The third statement under review was brief, positive and deadly. The chocolates received by Archy Mitfold on his birthday contained potassium cyanide. Of those submitted for analysis a minority had not been treated with the poison, of which the total amount, confined to the top layer of the box, exceeded four grains. It was therefore not only possible, but probable, that of the five chocolates eaten which had contained a quantity of poison insufficient to kill, cyanide had been introduced to only some, or even one. A mercy, thought Pardoe, that chance in the shape of an exacting diet and a second box of chocolates had intervened to prevent Miss Leaf and Vera from sharing them. Cyanide in chocolates . . . a hideous sidelight on the determination of a killer careless of the indiscriminate results of his crime. He might have killed at least three people with a single instrument.

Or might he? Pardoe was suddenly pulled up short. Suppose Miss Leaf's indisposition had been instrumental in the choice of chocolates as a weapon to kill her nephew? If so it hardened more than a little the suspicion of her own complicity in the plot.

But this was catching at straws, and Pardoe, who knew it, clapped a hat on his head and went out to have another look at the room where the body had been found.

It was nearly eight o'clock, and at Mulberry Fountain only Vera was in. Miss Leaf had gone to see Mrs. Beaton next door and was "making an evening of it, to take her mind off." Vera, who declared that nothing would induce her to stay in the house alone, had for company in the kitchen a cousin of hers who was a cook nearby and whose half day it was. Neither of them, it seemed, had had the courage to come upstairs before Pardoe rang; for when he was at last admitted the hall was in complete darkness, an omission which Vera, who appeared to have lost her nerve, made no effort to rectify. After bumping his head against one of the overhanging oils and barking his shin on an umbrella stand, the inspector mildly suggested a light. Vera complied in the subdued, oblivious manner he attributed to shock, then bolted down the kitchen stairs like a rabbit into its warren, and he was left with a free hand in the sitting room.

There was not much he wanted to do, but little as it was it reconstructed a scene for him. First he drew the blackout curtains and turned on the light. Then he spread out on the desk the photographs of the room as the police had recorded it on Sunday afternoon. He studied these in comparison with the original, particularly the one revealing the long ruck in the pile of the carpet from the corner of the brass fender to a spot immediately below where the body had been hanging. A foot or two in front of the hearth the mark described a curve or angle projecting toward the middle of the room. Pardoe paced out the distances and felt confident of the deductions made. If a dead or dying body had lain on the carpet with its head resting on the end of the brass fender rail, and hands beneath its armpits had subsequently dragged it to a point under the window, marks exactly like these would have been made by the heels of the corpse. Nor was it too difficult to infer the murderer's next move. While it would have been pretty well impossible to put a dead or insensible man into a standing position on the chair they had found overturned, he could have been lugged into a sitting pose on it and the rope then fixed. The next thing for the murderer was to stand on another chair, get the rope round the curtain rod and proceed to drag on it until he had maneuvered the body into position. That would not have been so difficult as it sounded. It had been at once noticeable how close to the ground the feet of the corpse had been, his toes barely brushing the carpet and a good play of rope from the rod, so it was clear the murderer had not exerted himself a jot more than necessary. He would, too, have enjoyed the distinct advantage of standing above his victim, and this, allied to the dexterity and resolution he must anyhow have employed, should have made up for any want of physical strength; though there was no evidence to suggest he was lacking in that.

Pardoe next sat on the couch and eyed the now empty waste paper basket which had been the Aunt Sally for Archy's blotting-paper pellets. Its nagging image brought another in its train . . . the missing diary. The diary that might be the key to the whole thing. As he sat there the kitchen door below closed. The next minute there were quick steps on the basement stairs and Vera's voice calling him.

"Your light's showing in the garden, sir," she said, out of breath, as he opened the door to her. "I just popped out to make sure."

"Dear me," said Pardoe contritely, going over to the window, "and I pulled your black curtains across, too."

"Ah, but they won't do by theirselves. We got to draw the ordinary ones first, and then the black ones, else you can see a faint sort of ray in the garden—the warden came about it once or twice in the beginning, and he was real cross about it the last time."

Vera could not imagine why a Scotland Yard officer should look pleased at being caught out in a serious misdemeanor like that. After all, if the police were going to show a light, why haul ordinary folk over the coals for it? But pleased he was.

"I'll put it right directly," he said hastily, brushing past her on his way to the garden door, "and I'll stand the racket if they knock you up about it in the next couple of minutes. But I've got to have a look at it from the garden."

The light certainly showed, not as a beam, or blatantly, but as a sort of diffused cloudy glow that was a hiatus in the surrounding blackness. The further off you moved the easier it was to see, so that by the wall at the bottom of the garden and therefore from the cul-de-sac on the other side it appeared as a luminous patch. That was good, thought Pardoe, as he walked back to the house. For when Dr. Beaton had fetched the police on Sunday they, too, had found only the black curtains pulled across. Could not the murderer, snooping around the back of the house for reasons best known to himself, have seen the same dull light and taken his chance then and there? If he had known Miss Leaf was away he could reasonably count on the occupant being Archy. If not, and the door was answered by someone else, he had his excuse ready in the form of a warning that their light was visible at the back.

Pardoe not only approved the idea as probable; it fitted the facts, for it explained better than anything else the extempore nature of the killing.

When he came in Vera was again waiting for him outside the sitting-room door. She held something in her hand.

"I just picked it up in the hall, sir. I can't think at all how it come to be there."

It was a piece of cartridge paper such as artists use, removed from a drawing block measuring about five by seven inches. On it, meticulously executed in watercolors, was a portrait of the bird Pardoe had previously seen sketched only in pen and ink. Here every feather, you felt, had been given its true value, every color and nuance of color delicately applied. In the right-hand top corner the artist had added, evidently as a hasty afterthought, some pencil drawings of the hatchet Vera had described. Seeing it for the first time, Pardoe would have called the thing an axe. In the right-hand bottom corner Archy had signed his name with the same pencil in a cursive hand identical with that found in the copybooks. The paper was a little thumbed, and the edges top, bottom, and right side bent back at an equal width all round.

"Where," said Pardoe when he had looked at it closely, "did you say you had found this?"

"Here." Vera took him into the hall and indicated a spot on the floor a few inches away from the umbrella stand. "Soon as you'd gone into the garden I came to see if I'd dropped the latch of the front door behind you. I've grown that nervous now, and the last day or two I don't seem to remember things like I used to. And as soon as I come into the light I saw it looking so funny and white there on the floor where it didn't ought to be."

"But," said Pardoe, who saw no other reason for doubting the veracity of this, "it wasn't there when you let me in."

Vera looked dubious. "No—maybe not. But where could it have come from?

And we wouldn't know in the dark, would we?"

This was true but, as Pardoe remembered it, the light had been switched on before he had got past the umbrellas.

"Look here, I must pull those other curtains. Come in the sitting room a minute, will you?"

She followed him reluctantly, darting sidelong glances at the familiar walls as if she expected them to close in upon her. The blackout attended to, Pardoe turned to her.

"Have you ever seen this sketch before?"

"No, I haven't. I know Mr. Archy colored a few of them on bits of paper, but he used to throw them away."

"And *was* the latch dropped when you went to look?"

"Yes, it was." She looked puzzled.

"And you've not let anyone in even for a minute since I came?"

"Oh no, sir." She was frightened now. "You—you don't think somebody left it there?"

"I think it's extremely unlikely anyone from outside did, if that's what you mean," Pardoe said. "But you realize, don't you, that it's a serious thing to plant evidence—that is, in this case, leave things about for the police to find?"

Vera gave him an admonitory look. "I'm sure it is," she said with dignity. "I never did no such thing."

"All right, Vera. Thank you."

He did not really think she had. It would be a clumsy device for anybody in the house to adopt when there were so many other simpler and more credible ways of bringing a thing to his notice. Besides, it did not need a Scotland Yard detective to see that duplicity was foreign to the girl's nature. Yet, if she were to be believed, the paper had been lying on the hall floor at 8:30 in a spot where Pardoe could have sworn it was not lying half an hour earlier. And on testing the matter when he left the house he found that the distance the sketch had been found from the front door made it impossible for it to have been put through the letter slit.

So irritating was the new mystery that in its initial stages Pardoe gave secondary importance to the value of the detailed sketch as a certain means of identifying the bird that had haunted Archy Mitfold.

Back at the Yard his own good temper was restored by Salt's shaken one. The sergeant had had a bad time with Mr. Theodore Runyon of Trumpeter's Row, in the course of which he had given away about ten times as much as he had received. As official confidence in this case had been confined to the state of the sergeant's soul and the probability of saving it, a very exiguous one in the eyes of Mr. Runyon, no harm had been done.

At first Mr. Runyon professed to have forgotten anything so trivially mundane as a young man's escape from death outside his house almost three weeks ago, but had finally agreed that such an event had taken place. Once warmed up, he even described with fervor Archy Mitfold's shaken appearance, the swooping passage of the car, and his own alarm at the sight and sound of it, but he had been unable to take the number and his tale amplified Miss Leaf's in no particular. It was plain that he was to be classed with those unobservant witnesses whose preoccupation with their own private interests blurs every detail of what is going on under their noses. Archy Mitfold's spiritual condition had concerned him more closely than his proximity to physical extinction, conclusive proof of which lay in his indifference to the belated interest the police were taking in the affair.

The inquest, arranged for ten o'clock Wednesday morning, occupied in its opening stage less than half an hour. It was of a purely formal character with a police request for adjournment, made to a week later.

Rossetti Terrace was next on the bill, but before setting out there Pardoe had sent in to him the reply cabled from Mentone. A list of the guests at the Hotel Roland on the date stated was supplied, and the suggestion made that in view of the circumstances the name of Signora Tommaseo might receive particular attention. For Bianca Tommaseo, widow of a rich Neapolitan merchant, had been Bianca Vick, the wife of Humphrey Vick, the Chicago gunman. She had left Mentone for England on October 2, asking that any letters which arrived after her departure should be forwarded to an address in Holland Park. This address was now sent on to Scotland Yard.

The message stimulated Pardoe to immediate action. He detailed a man to shadow the signora, and himself took from a drawer and studied again certain photographs and information sent to him a fortnight ago by the New York City Police Department and the Federal Bureau of Investigation of the U.S.A. in connection with the Vick enquiry.

CHAPTER XVI: THE MOST LIKELY PERSON

If there be here German . . . let him speak to me.
ALL'S WELL THAT ENDS WELL.

"THE CRIME EXPERT seeks the bird expert. A strange union of interests, *nicht wahr?*"

Professor August Speyer spoke correct English with a foreign inflection. He had disposed his visitors rather pedagogically at the table in the study where his pupils worked, and himself seated at the end gave polite attention to their requests.

Beltane had described him faithfully, as a remarkable looking man. He was such a man as made staring not merely pardonable but turned it into a kind of homage. Over six feet in height, his gaunt physique matched the long, leonine head and immense, partially bald skull. The vigorous quality of his dark-gray, curling hair, worn longer than fashion dictated, gave Pardoe the idea that he perhaps deliberately shaved the crown to accentuate the height of his brow. The lines of his face were craggy, the temples hollow, the dark eyes slow and sombre, sunk deeply in orbits stained with fatigue or worry. He had a sardonic mouth that never lost its rigidity and look of faint contempt however agreeable its words, and this curious blend of the innocuous and the derisive again and again suggested speech issuing through a mask. He had been inevitably pre-pared for their visit and showed not the least sign of embarrassment at either scrutiny or questioning.

"But you don't come only to the bird man. A foreigner is naturally under suspicion. So?"

"Of what?" Pardoe was wilfully obtuse.

"Of murder." The inflexible mouth smiled a little.

"Of whose murder?" would, Pardoe thought, be a somewhat vapid ques-tion in the circumstances. But the fact was the word had not been mentioned. Something of what was in his mind must have appeared on his face, for the professor spoke again.

"It would be childish indeed to pretend that I don't know. Childish of you, childish of me. My pupil dies on Saturday. Here is Wednesday, and clever, able, resourceful Scotland Yard"—Salt, who never heard the Yard called clever without scenting sarcasm began to grow red in the face—"still at work on his death. Also, he dies in a darkened room, which is not only contrary to every human instinct but is deliberately making suicide by the rope a very difficult labor. Also, he has a maimed hand of which he has not yet learned to make adequate use. Hang oneself with one hand? In the dark? When there are easier modes of death not so far to seek? I think not. So it is not so clever, eh, to deduce that some other has killed him?"

"No," Pardoe agreed, "not if one is in possession of all the necessary facts."

There was a short silence while this double-edged remark sank in.

The professor said smoothly, "I expressed my profound regrets to Miss Leaf, of course, poor lady."

The inspector was suddenly appreciative of the delicate innuendos of the conversation. They were like the beautifully oblique exchanges between two Chinese gentlemen in which elaborate courtesy is never routed by the deadli-est intention. While he himself had implied that Archy's murderer would have possessed the facts enabling him to scout the idea of suicide, Professor Speyer's riposte was to the effect that he had learned from Miss Leaf the condition of the room at the time. Amusement got the better of Pardoe, who grinned openly, but the professor, whose long residence in their country had not persuaded him to acquire the peculiar sense of humor of the English, remained unmoved.

The inspector took out the bird envelope and pushed it toward Speyer. For the moment he kept the colored drawing in reserve.

"There it is," he said. "You saw the marginal drawings in his notebooks I spoke of. Will you let us have your opinion of the bird as it appears here?"

The professor drew the envelope close and smoothed imaginary wrinkles away. His hands, Pardoe observed, were long and spare, the fingers combining sensitiveness with great strength. They were the hands of a creator who is conscious of their power to destroy.

He gave the sketches his calm attention for more than a minute without speaking. Then he looked up.

"They are well drawn."

"Yes. That helps you to identify the bird?"

"Per-haps. It is of the order *Ralliformes*."

"Oh. Does that include many birds?"

"Not so many. The best known are the moor hen, the coot, the water rail and the crakes."

Pardoe ran over the names mentally. Not a very hopeful collection.

"And has this one distinctive enough features to be picked out as one of those?"

"Who shall say? There is not enough to tell. It might, perhaps, be a coot, but here are some spots, and the coot has none. Also, in these quick, light sketches, there is nothing which suggests the uniform coloring of the coot. So again I say—it may be a corn crake."

"On the evidence of this alone then you can't commit yourself to naming any one bird?"

"No. It is accurate, you understand, in outline—as one would say, as far as it goes. But it is not sufficiently filled in for me to know what precisely was in his mind when he drew it. And in a police case it is better that one should be convinced, is it not so?"

"Certainly," said Pardoe, conscious of the sardonic mouth. "What about a hobby falcon—can you be certain it's not that?"

He had to repeat his question before the professor would believe his ears.

"My dear sir," he said gently, "give me a duck and say that it may be an owl—there will be equal reason in it. A hobby falcon? *Falco subbuteo?*" He broke off. "You know what a hobby is?"

"Roughly," said Pardoe, unabashed. "Since it was obvious Mitfold drew well I never really supposed it was. But I am assuming, sir, that these birds were drawn with a purpose, that they're not random or even absentminded scribbles. He drew them because the bird, or, as I believe, the *name* of the bird—there's an important distinction between them—was constantly in his mind the last week or two, because it was also the name of something else, some person or some place, closely connected with him at that period, the important period of his life from our point of view."

The professor looked at him curiously. "I see you are in earnest, Inspector. And you would like this to be a hobby? It would give substance to a theory you have formed?"

"Not at all. Hobby occurred to me because it is the only bird name to have cropped up in the course of the case so far. But as for wanting—well, I would like it to be only exactly whatever it is."

"And one of the birds it cannot be is a hawk of any description."

"No—even my slender knowledge of the birds of prey tells me so."

Speyer got up with a long uncoiling movement that made so little disturbance it struck Pardoe as peculiar until he remembered he was an experienced bird watcher and therefore practiced in changing position with economy and silence.

"I want you to see for yourself some colored plates of the coot and the moor hen," he said, crossing to a bookcase in the corner.

"One moment, sir." Pardoe signed to Salt, who opened the folder he had brought with him and took from it the watercolor picked up last night. "I haven't shown you this. Does it help in giving the bird a name?"

The professor came back carrying a heavy tome which he laid down unopened. Now he stood erect, only his head bent, the tips of his bony fingers splayed out on the table with the painted bird between them. Pardoe noticed that everything he did had the slowness of deliberation. As a characteristic of those resolute not to be taken off their guard he had met it before. Speyer was nodding, slow heavy nods that reminded Pardoe of a mandarin.

"That is better," the professor said, and lowered himself into his chair, still nodding. "That is good—very good. Why haven't you shown it to me first?"

"I wanted to see if the others were good enough for identification, and then if you thought they were the same as this."

"But yes, they are the same. He has here elaborated his rough sketches. It is the finished article. So finished that now it is certain what the bird is."

Pardoe curbed his impatience as the professor stroked with one finger the painted plumage.

"You see—the warm brown tinted with olive, black barred and white spotted, the richer brown of crown and nape with grayish neck spotted white, white belly and under-tail coverts, the yellowish-green legs and feet. Then the beak, yellow with its scarlet patch at the base. And see the inconspicuous tail; how well he had drawn the forward, rather fearful thrust of the head—timorous, alert. It is good, very good."

"And what is it?" Pardoe asked. "Because it's nothing I've ever seen before."

"You would not have seen it. I have seen only one on the nest, and others that were each but a brown ripple across the meres, though I have heard its voice many times. Sometimes it is a throbbing cry like the beat of a small engine. Its name? *Porzana porzana*—in English, the spotted crake."

Salt, who had been holding his breath in expectation of he did not know what revelation, expelled it now with the too-familiar sense of having been had. Another hope gone west. Not that he had ever shared the chief's enthusiasm for it. It was all too sure there were no crakes in this show, spotted or plain.

"I don't think that helps you," Speyer was saying. "But see, there is no mistake."

He thrust the book he had fetched toward them, deftly turning the leaves till he came to a plate of the bird in question.

No, there was no mistake. There it was, "Spotted Crake (*Porzana porzana*), order *Ralliformes*"—in every detail Archy Mitfold's bird. Pardoe read the brief text on the opposite page.

"It's rare, then?"

"One of the rarest birds in Britain, and extremely localized. It is a migrant due in March, perhaps the earliest to arrive. It nests—so far as we know, and there is much yet to learn—only in desolate marshy places, as in Westmorland and remote parts of Wales, and in still fewer numbers in Scotland and the Irish bogs. It is a shy, secret, lonely bird that knows well how to keep its secrets, for no bird has a finer protective coloring—those white spots, the black bars, the olive-russet hues in the sedgy tussocks and on the water where it makes its home—think how hard it will be to detect. And none depending on his eye alone will find it."

Quite true, thought Salt grimly.

How warmly the fires burn, thought Pardoe, when a man's discourse is of his true love. Birds were this man's passion. For the first time something unguarded shone through the inscrutability.

"Herr Speyer," he said abruptly, "on the one occasion when you saw this bird where were you?"

The professor gave a faintly contemptuous smile. "In Westmorland, Inspector, close to Ullswater. Indeed, I was staying at the home of Dr. Mitfold, my late pupil's father."

As this was the answer Pardoe expected he felt no surprise. Salt uncrossed his legs and grunted a little.

"It would be seven years ago," Speyer continued. "I was resident master then in a North Riding school and used to spend the English part of my vacation in Westmorland with its rare and lovely water birds. And there Dr. Mitfold was kind enough for several years to offer me a hospitality I do not forget."

"You got to know his son too?"

"A little."

"Have you been back there in the last seven years?"

"Not once. London has me now, and from here I go chiefly into the Broads for my birds."

"And when you said just now that the English part of your holidays was spent in the Lakes, you meant—?"

"That until now I have been each year home to Germany. My sister, who is married, lives there, in Wertheim on the Main. What then shall I do now, Inspector?"

"Now?" Pardoe echoed, he felt stupidly.

"Yes, now—when I must report myself without fail, when five miles is my radius of travel. Westmorland is a little farther than that, eh—and the Broads too, and Germany? What birds shall I study here? The sparrow, maybe, and the starling—who chatter, no doubt, and give away vital secrets to the enemy."

Not a bad bluff, thought Salt, if he is a bloomin' spy.

Is he rattled? Pardoe asked himself. And if so, why? Because the police are in the house, or because we found that drawing?

Speyer was watching him austerely. Then he glanced down at the watercolor and flicked his finger at it.

"What are those things?" He tapped the crudely drawn hatchets in the corner.

"We ask the same question," Pardoe said. "What would you call them?"

"Hammers," said the professor promptly.

Pardoe looked again. "They could be. They've been called axes, hatchets and hammers. Mr. Mitfold sometimes added them to his sketches of the spotted crake."

The professor frowned. "Ver-y mysterious. That is outside my domain. A psychologist may perhaps discern his meaning. Though one might hazard a guess."

"And yours?"

"You suggested an axe, Inspector. The poor boy was perhaps thinking of execution being done on—the spotted crake."

"The execution of a bird?"

"But you have yourself said the bird is probably symbolic."

"But we hang people in England, Herr Speyer."

"And in my land we behead them. Especially traitors. Where is the difference?"

Pardoe shrugged. "None, ultimately. But in the pictorial use of one or the other there seems to me some significance in the artist's choice."

Speyer was silent, eyes veiled in apparent contemplation of the drawings. Even Salt, on whom the oblique statement was lost more often than not, recognized the delicate thrust in the words. The thing was something of a duel, for though Speyer's own definition of the instrument had been at once a hammer, as if he shied away from the axe simile, he had then boldly carried the war into the enemy's gates by quoting Pardoe and suggesting execution as the artist's intention. That, of course, would be part of the bluff Salt was ready to swear he was employing.

"You can help me in matters other than ornithological, Herr Speyer," Pardoe went on. "Except for Miss Leaf, probably nobody in London saw Mr. Mitfold so frequently and with such regularity as yourself. Did he make you any confidences which seem likely to throw light upon his death?"

The professor looked at him, unmoved. "I would like you to particularize."

"Yes. Has he, for instance, ever spoken to you about the disappearance of Mr. Sampson Vick, the millionaire philanthropist?"

"You need not enlarge on the name, Inspector. Everyone knows, *nicht wahr*? No, Archy did not speak of him once." He knotted his hands together loosely and sprawled his arms on the table as he leaned toward Pardoe. "And tell me, don't you think that odd? Was it not stra-nge"—he dragged at the word—"that he should be silent about that affair when the world talks of it, from the charwoman and the dustman to cabinet ministers and the great people this shy rich man did not want to know? Was it not queer that Archy alone should hold his tongue on this *cause célèbre*?"

"Wasn't it for that matter queer you shouldn't have introduced the subject yourself?" Pardoe retorted.

"I am not a gossip exchange," said the professor loftily, and leaned back again.

Thinks himself a cut above 'em all, char to cabinet minister, considered Salt. These Jerries always do.

"Then there's the question," Pardoe went on, "of alleged attacks made on Mr. Mitfold before the fatal one. I wonder if he talked to you about them."

He was going to elaborate this a little, but there was no need. It seemed that Archy had kept Speyer informed of each chapter of jeopardy through which he passed.

"It is only last Thursday he told me about the chocolates he had received the week before. You understand, he was absent from a tutorial on the Monday—that is, a week ago last Monday—and a message came for me that he was ill with gastritis." He picked up the bird envelope and turned it over. The bold foreign script stared up at them again. "Here is the outside of the letter I sent him that day, commiserating on his misfortunes. Then he returned on Thursday, looking still not well and saying he had been upset by some chocolates. That is the last time I saw him. Next comes news that he is dead."

"When he mentioned the chocolates did you gather that he suspected somebody of trying to kill him?"

The professor was silent as if trying to arrange his thoughts for expression. "That is rather hard to answer. Because yes, and no. Yes—I gathered just that by my own inference. No—I gathered from his own words that he supposed there was by accident an ingredient in the chocolates which had made him ill. It was, you see, as if he were anxious I should not think a malicious attempt had been made on him."

"Yes, I understand." That was in line with every other implication of Mitfold's reticence and purposeful obliteration from the trail. "And did you play up to what he wanted you to think?"

"Oh yes. I said the chocolates should be analyzed and if anything were found the manufacturers must be held responsible."

"What did he say?"

"He smiled—as I have seen children smile who plot a trap for others—and said he supposed that would be done."

It rang true. And the rest of the story was scrupulously consistent with the gradual withdrawal of confidence which had marked his attitude toward the people he knew best. To Speyer Archy had described the car assault as a deliberate attempt to run him down, but his subsequent misadventures at the station and with the chocolates as mere untimely accidents. A reserve had come over him after the first attack, which could be explained on the grounds that he had got hold of something he had every intention of keeping to himself.

The thread of Pardoe's thoughts was spun longer by the professor's next words.

"He was vain, you see, a little proud that these unpleasant things should happen to him. So he could not be wholly silent. His vivid and, what we say these days, wishful imagination must provide falsities to conceal a truth he did not want to show me."

"Do you know why he should have wanted to conceal the truth?"

"No."

"Would you say that on the whole he talked to you freely?"

"Within the limits I have suggested, yes. So long as one accepted his own interpretations I think one might say he was a ready, even an eager talker. But always of himself. What he really wanted was a listener, not a conversationalist. And he was lonely. He was fond of his aunt, but"—the professor shrugged—"there was little in common between him and Miss Leaf, naturally. On the other hand, he had known me from time to time when he was quite a small child, and he would talk—without giving himself away."

A sound bit of psychological insight, Pardoe reflected. It rounded off with a polish all he had learned about Archy Mitfold from other sources. The boy's character stood out for him as substantially familiar as if he had been intimate with its vagaries in life. That was the black-and-white nature of the whole affair: while he could not recall a case in itself so baffling, so muffled in obscure deed and even obscurer intention, the figure of its victim, whom he had seen only in death, had been made for him as vital as that of any living actor in it.

"While we're on the subject of confidences, or half confidences, Herr Speyer," he said, trying a shot in the dark, "did Mitfold talk to you about the cinema any time during the last week you saw him?"

The random shot found its mark. The professor sat up straight and gave him a peculiarly searching look.

"*So?*" he said softly, with the slurring emphasis he gave to a word here and there. "You are then better informed than we know? Have walls ears indeed? In that case one must not make denial. Yes, Inspector, Archy spoke to me about the cinema in the last week that I saw him."

"Please tell me exactly what he said."

"With pleasure. It was his birthday—"

Pardoe interrupted. "You knew when his birthday was?"

"Indeed yes. I have known it years ago."

"Yes?"

"It was his birthday. When tomorrow comes that will be a fortnight past. I had thought he might want to cut his tutorial that evening, but no, he came. And when we were talking he asked me if I would not care to go to a cinema in Ebury Street that week."

"He referred to it as 'a cinema'?"

"No, he did not. He had a name for it, but it eludes me—a Palace or—ach!" He snapped his fingers loudly. "It was, I think, the Fantastic."

"Does Fantasia sound more like it?"

Speyer brought the palm of his hand down quietly on the table. "That was it. These names, they mean nothing to me. I thought it one of the queerest things he had said to me."

"Why so?"

"Because I never visit a cinema, never. Seldom a theatre, never the cinema. And it is something Archy knew."

"Then it was queer, I agree. I suppose he explained why he had made the suggestion?"

"There could be no explanation when I am not moved by reports, however good, of these silly films. He knew I would not go. But he said he had been yesterday—that would be a Wednesday. I said, 'Which picture is it you recommend to me?'—you understand while I do not share my pupils' enthusiasms I encourage them to speak of them—and he answered me in a rather funny way.

" 'I recommend the whole program,' he said. 'I cannot say what I liked best.' "

"Not so funny, perhaps," said Pardoe, "if he found the program consistently good."

"Ah, but not so—it was not what he said about it. It was the sly, thoughtful look of him, you see. He did not look at me, but down at his book, again smiling. I thought him excited."

One more who had been conscious of the excitement . . . Wynkerrell, Beltane, Miss Leaf, Mrs. Byron, Vera Moffat and now, his tutor.

"Well, it's good news," Pardoe said, "for we believe that visit to the picture house on October 4 has some bearing on his actions later. Now we come to something very important. First, can you tell me when you moved house?"

"On September 19."

"Do you remember Mitfold arriving late for a tutorial soon afterwards?"

"Quite well I remember. He was more than a half-hour late the following Monday. He walked here, as he did each time after I came to live in Chelsea, and that night he came without his torch because he had forgotten to renew the battery. He told me that in the dark he entered the wrong house by mistake."

The following Monday. That was right, September 25 . . . the night Sampson Vick had left home and failed to return.

"What else did he tell you about that mistake?"

"Nothing. But then, what else was there to say?"

"He didn't, for instance, describe the house in any way?"

"But no. I did not question him. It is not so rare to walk into the wrong house in London in a fog, and this blackout has been equally troublesome." He frowned. "He was unusually silent. I remember that. Preoccupied, you understand, his mind not on his work, yet disinclined to chatter which was his more customary fault."

"And could you gather which house it was he had entered?"

"But I have already said he did not tell—"

"I don't mean that. I mean, can you suggest the most likely house for it to have been?"

The professor lifted his shoulders almost to his ears in a slow exaggerated shrug. "But no better than yourself. Up and down this side of the road"—he waved a hand to and fro in front of his face—"why, any house would do, *nicht wahr*? Provided, of course, he found the back door unfastened."

Pardoe sat up mentally. "The back door? That was the way he came in to his tutorials?"

Speyer caught the surprise. "Why not? Until lately when the darkness is frightening them off I have had pupils until late in the evenings, as late as ten o'clock. My housekeeper is deaf and does not like the front door unlatched after dark. Also, one cannot fetch her to the door every hour, and, as you see, this room is at the back of the house, close to the garden entrance. So what more simple than that my pupils come in by the garden door?"

Of course. They had reckoned only on the front way in. Was it possible after all that entering at the back Archy had taken an occupied house for an unoccupied? Pardoe quailed at the thought of a second examination of Rossetti Terrace. Speyer, it was clear, had not heard the place described as empty, an omission on Archy's part which fitted in with Miss Leaf's statement. According to her he had found it to be empty when he went to look at it next morning; that probably meant he had not been sure about it the night before. But again, that morning visit negated the possibility that he had really stumbled into an inhabited house. The unambiguous daylight would have discovered its vacancy to him. Pardoe sighed—with pleasure at the thought of not having to rake the Terrace once more, with fatigue at the still unraveled tangle.

For where in the world was the house? You couldn't lose a house which somebody had accidentally located only three weeks ago. Besides, there was a peculiar boundary set to one's possibilities of error in this direction. Archy Mitfold could not have blundered into any house in London, nor for that matter into any house in Chelsea. His mistake must be confined to those houses within reasonable proximity to 16 Rossetti Terrace.

When he came to the Nordic Bond business Pardoe was inclined to handle it with gloves on. It brought things a little too close home to be comfortable, and he did not want Speyer suddenly to become uninformative. His fear was unfounded. The professor described with sarcasm his own impatience at the club's tedious futilities and his nonattendance over a period of many months. He admitted that Archy had gone there several times on his ticket and said that he didn't see, in view of the work the boy proposed taking up, how a nodding acquaintance with such an institution could possibly do him any harm. His own impression was that Archy had been bored. He had gone there looking for mystery and intrigue and had found a collection of people moved by the usual small personal issues to scramble for the limelight and forget the ideals they had originally set before them. No, he had never heard of Mr. Caffey.

Pardoe had one more question. "Herr Speyer, Mitfold told several people on Saturday evening that he was going to a tutorial that night. Did he, in fact, come here?"

The professor looked at him steadily. "I have told you that the last time I saw Archy was on Thursday."

As they rose to go, the bird drawings safely bestowed in Salt's folder, Pardoe asked if they might leave by the back door.

"It will give me the hang of the place as Mitfold knew it when he came for his lessons. He left, of course, by the same way?"

"Of course."

The professor was courteous and helpful, accompanying them through the garden door and round the side of the house to the front gate. Pardoe noticed that all these houses contemporary with one another varied hardly at all inside and out. In all of them the basement stairs ran down close inside the back door, with the area steps correspondingly near outside; but unlike Miss Leaf's house the professor's lacked the additional tradesman's gate shutting off the back of the house from the front. Here one could pass freely along the path round to the back door.

They had not gone many yards before Salt gave a dry chuckle.

"Know who we've been talkin' to?" he innocently enquired.

Pardoe surmised that a reply would be neither welcome nor necessary.

The sergeant, gratified, answered himself.

"To the most likely person in the case."

CHAPTER XVII: AT THE CINEMA

Look here, upon this picture, and on this.

HAMLET.

MR. ALLBRIGHT, manager of the Fantasia picture house in Ebury Street, was at once helpful.

"We want," Pardoe said, "the full program you were showing on the afternoon of October 4."

That was easy. He took them into his office and provided it almost immediately. *Repeat the Dose* had been one of the pictures showing, the other being *Hunter's Moon*, billed as "A Spectacular Western Drama." The remaining item had been a newsreel sandwiched between them.

"The next thing," the inspector said, "may be a little more difficult. I want to see these pictures as your audiences saw them the week before last. That won't be possible here, I know, but perhaps the identical program is now running in some picture house?"

The manager, who was beginning to show a little human curiosity, was doubtful of the likelihood of seeing all three items on the same screen. He explained the technical improbability in simple terms, but was confident that visits to several cinemas would quickly give them what they wanted. Pardoe, pointing out the inevitable waste of time, agreed that if necessary they must adopt that course; whereupon Mr. Allbright seized the telephone and engaged in a masterly, if somewhat involved, conversation which produced speedy results.

The Fantasia, it seemed, was one of a group of privately owned cinemas. Another member of the group situated in King's Road was at present showing *Repeat the Dose*, while the Western figured on the program of a smaller picture house in the same ownership in the Vauxhall Bridge Road.

"Of course," said Mr. Allbright, "you'd have a fairly wide choice of cinema at present showing *Repeat the Dose*, for the box office returns are still steady, but I thought you might prefer one in the neighborhood."

And that will secure a little extra patronage for Mr. Allbright's employers, supplemented Pardoe, and thanked him. The newsreel was not so easy to follow up. The very nature of the feature, Mr. Allbright implied, gave it a venerable air after the lapse of a fortnight, so that its more topical successors had by then crowded it out of the principal houses. Pardoe's disposition for thoroughness made him reluctant to give the thing a miss. Whatever revelation that particular program held for him he believed to lie in *Repeat the Dose*. Yet he could not rid his mind of Archy's peculiarly unspecific recommendation of the show to the professor. On that account, if on no other, he felt it obligatory to see each item the Fantasia had shown on October 4.

Finally, after an exhibition of efficiency resulting in remarkably little wear and tear of patience, Mr. Allbright ran the hoary thing to earth in a turning off Kingly Street. What was more, he secured for them the hour at which each of the three pictures they wanted to see was showing. On the principle of the laborer being worthy his hire, Pardoe thereupon outlined for Mr. Allbright something of their reason for all this. So delighted was Mr. Allbright at having this new, exciting light thrown on his unglamorous occupation that he parted from them in the firm conviction that he had received far more information than he had imparted.

On a question of observation Pardoe believed in the greater efficacy of two pairs of eyes. As luck would have it, however, the times at which *Repeat the Dose* and *Hunter's Moon* were showing, though not precisely simultaneous, made it impossible for him and Salt to watch together. On the other hand, they would both be free to see the 4.50 showing of the newsreel.

Since separation was inevitable, the inspector dispatched Salt to Vauxhall Bridge Road. By the sergeant's own confession the films had a soporific effect on him, so Pardoe judged that the type of picture least calculated to make him nod was that known as "a good Western." Its guileless qualities were much in keeping with Tommy's own character. Besides, it was necessary for himself to see the crime picture to which he had largely pinned his hopes.

Nothing doing, was Pardoe's subsequent verdict. From every point of view the thing was a flop, and he was disposed to envy Salt who had unreeled before him those wide-open spaces and unflinching he-men. If this wishy-washy, affected nonsense were the result of subtle acting and direction he decided he would henceforth plump for the blood-and-thunder every time. Even custard pies would be a relief.

As far as he could make out the plot turned on the conspiracy of a small group of people of indeterminate sex and relationship to one another to poison an unpleasant old man who stood between them and the enjoyment of an immense fortune, and who never once opened his mouth throughout the film. The scheme misfired: a manservant who had looked cut out for it from the start took the fatal dose instead, the disagreeable old man continued to sit about in disagreeable silence and then the conspirators, with the first consideration they had shown, began to drop off one by one from the effects of poison in one form or another. It was all very naive and ridiculous, and when the speechless elder was at length convicted of all five murders, confirming Pardoe's guess made in the first quarter of an hour, the inspector decided that if this was the adroit production it claimed to be he was indeed a back number, one of Mr. Priam Pastell's Philistines. Most important of all, there was not by the furthest stretch of imagination anything in the film to have sent Archy Mitfold home in a state of excitement to hunt up all he could find on the Vick case.

In the bus on their way to Kingly Street an hour later Pardoe listened to Salt's equally unfertile experiences. "Pullin' quick ones" and performing incredible equestrian tricks had little to do with a millionaire whose fate was nameless, except perhaps for their common American background.

Salt, whose spirits seemed permanently to have touched zero since the identification of the spotted crake, communicated something of his despondency to Pardoe. The inspector knew quite well what Tommy was visualizing: a vast conspiracy inspired by the Nazis against the forces of law and order in Britain, in its midst the figure of August Speyer whose satellites were engaged in the profitable task of pulling hank upon hank of wool over the eyes of the police. But it was no good dwelling on a theory until it swelled to monstrous proportions and became a dangerous certitude. He glanced at his watch and saw that they would be too early for the newsreel if they went in now; and, not hankering after further surfeit in that direction, proposed a walk down Hobby Court to see Tony Wynkerrell.

"It's only a few minutes away, and he won't have put the shutters up yet, and"—with a sly glance at Salt—"there's always the chance he knows a fellow named Crake."

They turned down Conduit Street and in another minute were in the narrow, unfrequented court where the bookshop lay. Hardly anybody was about, but a man stood outside the window of the Juniper looking in. As they crossed the road he took a few quick steps backward to the curb and considered its contents from that vantage point.

" 'Distance lends enchantment,' " Pardoe murmured. Aloud he said: "Good afternoon, Mr. Wynkerrell."

But the man who turned round was not Tony Wynkerrell.

Pardoe was a little nettled at the mistake, for there was actually, he decided, no resemblance. This man was about forty, a stringy fellow with an unhealthy skin and eyeballs like those of a restless horse. He stared at them nervously and a sudden inspiration came to Pardoe.

"Mr. Leofric Williams?"

The other nodded, retreating to the door. Pardoe followed.

"Is your partner here?"

"He's gone to his tea," Williams said in a grudging voice. He darted a look up and down the empty court. "He'll be back any time now."

"It's all right," Pardoe began, "I won't wait—"

He broke off abruptly as he caught sight of the queerly appraising glance the bookseller was giving them. It was clear that he had no idea who they were, but, it flashed into Pardoe's mind, equally clear that he thought he should know.

"You've a message for Wynkerrell?" he said tentatively. "You can leave it with me, you know."

"Well," Pardoe said noncommittally, playing for time, "p'raps—"

Williams, whose eyes had never ceased to scan the length and breadth of Hobby Court, took alarm at sight of a leisurely pedestrian on the opposite pavement and plucked Pardoe by the sleeve.

"Inside," he whispered, and shuffled ahead of them into the shop.

Time was getting on, but the picture house wasn't three minutes away, and, exchanging a look with Salt, Pardoe, too intrigued to stop outside, followed him into the gloomy interior. The sergeant compromised by filling up the doorway, an impregnable figure at sight of which the bookseller's intention seemed to weaken a little. He slipped round the counter and faced them doubtfully.

It was darker than ever inside. A feeble bulb burned behind Williams' head, but the black velvet curtains drawn across the back of the window excluded any light from that source.

Pardoe looked from the practically empty shelves and dusty accessories to the man in front of him. His silence crystallized Williams' suspicions.

The bookseller licked his lips and said huskily: "You're not from the Pied Monkey, are you?"

Pardoe held his eyes steadily. "Not this time. I'm sorry if we misled—"

"I beg *your* pardon," the man said stiffly, but even in that murky light Pardoe could have sworn that he was frightened. "Anything I can supply you with today? No?—then—"

He came from behind the counter and almost shooed them out. Pardoe could not help wondering how far, if he had asked for book or journal, demand would have exceeded supply in that singularly understocked library. As they passed the window he saw that the Priam Pastell verse was gone. In its place, against the background of the juniper branch and the epicene statuette, were three little books looking jejune in blue and silver, whose gold- lettered titles he did not stop to read.

"That's a good one, that is," Salt said. "A pied monkey. Say, what is it—a pub?"

"It's a night club," Pardoe said absently. "We visited it once. Whom do we look like, Tommy?"

"Patchy baboons," the sergeant chuckled. "Well, not busies, for sure," he added complacently. "Our own mugs are our best disguises, after all."

"I'd like to meet the Pied Monkey again," Pardoe said.

"Not me. You've 'ad a spotted crake, an' where did that get you?"

The Palace Cinema was squeezed between a bicycle shop and a block of offices in a side street dipped in shadow. The bills that added a crudely formal touch to the blistered paint outside proclaimed their legend boldly; but it was a place that showed mostly reissues of the cheaper pictures and expelled its patrons with a sense of hunger they could not explain.

As they entered and a torch picked out their seats, darkness and music rose smotheringly to meet them. They were in good time. The last of a slapstick was spilling its indelicate backchat across the gloom. The comedy closed on a raucous note, the screen dimmed, grew bright again as the advertisers flickered by with a sort of apologetic haste, familiar shops borrowing for a second of time a foreign, slightly daring air. Then the shadows swallowed them all, cakes and fish and Corinne's perms; trailers of next week's films, headless bodies, bodiless heads, mutilated scraps of horror and excitement that swung their lures giddily and snatched them back again. Then darkness again—darkness melting to light and the newsreel.

In eight minutes, probably fewer, Pardoe guessed that he would have another blank to add to the mounting pile of blanks in the Mitfold case. That, or the thousand-to-one chance that they would strike a clue here. In three minutes he knew that they had struck it.

The running commentary had dealt with the usual royal visit, there was a swift succession of pictures of invaded Poland, a rugger match with some slow-motion shots that provoked a few giggles and made Salt restless. Then the white blaze of words: "WENBOROUGH ORTHOPEDIC HOSPITAL"—and "MR. SAMPSON VICK, FOUNDER, PERFORMS OPENING CEREMONY."

Pardoe felt Salt stiffen beside him. But neither made any sign. Together they watched the four or five inadequate shots trail past, the unctuous voice explaining coyly that they were fortunate to have these pictures of the least photographed man in Britain, that it was significant that Wenborough Orthopedic Hospital, Mr. Vick's magnificent contribution to the cause of healing and reconstruction, should be opened in September, when Europe was once more threatened by annihilation and crucified by the powers of destruction, etc., etc. Pardoe paid no heed. His whole attention was for the hardly discernible middle-sized figure that contrived to tilt a screening shoulder toward the camera. The blurb about the public's luck in at last beholding the camera-shy millionaire was sheer effrontery. The least photographed man in Britain was still determined to keep himself to himself. The face was invisible. Only an indeterminate profile was glimpsed for a second, so close to the camera as to be blurred. But it was at that moment that the one voice fell blissfully silent, and another spoke—the voice of Sampson Vick.

"It is—with great pleasure that—I declare—this hospital open."

The words were halting, deliberate, the voice rough and a little subdued, but curiously resonant. An extraordinary stillness, more electric than their customary silence, settled on the audience. A whisper pricked the darkness behind Pardoe. This was Sampson Vick, the modern Croesus, the man whose name had been for a few years a sort of open sesame for charity till mystery, more real than the mysteries of the screen, had invested it with a new meaning. Millions of tongues that had once made it the synonym of a bottomless purse, had uttered it in the past three weeks because it belonged to a man who had unaccountably escaped from the society of men.

A woman's voice in the row behind whispered, "They say he done it for publicity."

"You'd think he 'ad a packet o' that already," a man answered gruffly.

As the rest of the news flickered to its choppy end, Pardoe and Salt made their way out with the inevitable bumping of knees and impeding of vision.

"Got it at last," Pardoe said with quiet satisfaction when they had once more emerged into daylight. "Chasing from picture palace to picture palace isn't the sort of game I care about, but the thing's worth the loss of time."

Salt looked at him doubtfully. "But that thing—what good was it to Mitfold? With no proper face to 'im, an' a back an' shoulder as might've been anybody's, an' gone like a flash in the pan? What clue could there 've been in that?"

"That was the clue," Pardoe said. "That one couldn't see his face—that he looked like a thousand and one other men—that Archy Mitfold didn't recognize him by his features." He smiled. "Wait till we get in."

In his room at the Yard they got down to brass tacks. Pardoe had thrown off the incubus that had fastened on him since the close of last month, and spoke with a warmth and confidence not perceptible since before the Vick case opened.

"Tommy, you've put your finger right on it. Those miserably poor shots we've just seen wouldn't have afforded the ghost of a clue from the pictorial standpoint—featureless, indistinct, partially blocked out by other figures. But when you've eliminated everything that's normally of use from the photographic angle, what's still left?"

"Sound," said Salt with a certitude he was far from feeling.

"Yes—the doubtful blessing of the talkies. But not doubtful at all in this instance. Sampson Vick's voice—Archy Mitfold going home in the happily excited state of Jack Horner when he got the feel of the plum between his fingers, not because he'd seen a face he recognized but because he'd heard *a voice* that was unmistakable. Tommy, one of the best things that could have been handed us was the poor quality of that photography—if it had been good and distinct we still shouldn't know whether it was face or voice that gave him what he wanted, and the natural inference, I think, would be that it was the face. But there's no alternative here. We know it was the sound, the only thing that came over well—" He broke off. "Would you say it was a voice to remember?"

"Sure. Queer, like."

"So that somebody listening might have said, 'That's the voice I heard when—' " He drummed his fingers on the desk. "It fits. It explains a whole lot. You remember you were bothered about the way dates didn't seem to hang together, how things were working out wrong way round? Like this— we know that Archy Mitfold didn't concern himself with the Vick case till

October 4. We've evidence for the precise hour when that interest was first shown. Yet for more than a week before that he'd been engaged on a mysterious investigation of his own, involving going out at night and the dropping of all sorts of dark hints that led nowhere and told nobody a thing—because he didn't choose that they should. And in that first period, when he plainly wasn't interested in Sampson Vick, two attempts were made on his life, one in Trumpeter's Row, another at Sloane Square. These attacks, like his own nocturnal excursions, took place *after* September 25, the last day on which Vick was seen by any living person who's cared to report it. Throw into the pot his remark to Vera, 'I stumbled upon it by chance, and I've got to go on with it—patience does it'—mix well, and what d'you get out of the stir?"

"A week or so when he'd got 'old of somethin' to do with Vick's disappearance an' didn't know the bloke concerned was Vick," Salt said without hesitation.

"Exactly. A week of uncertainty followed by a visit to the cinema that clinched the matter for him. So far as identity went. He still had a lot of spadework to do, since he wouldn't do the proper thing and hand over his information to the police, the dithering young ass. It's obvious he knew he was up against a crime—and a criminal—and he wasn't unintelligent, so that he must have known his persistent silence was making him an accessory after the fact. But he wouldn't divulge a thing, at first because he was by nature keen on making a corner in mysteries and could fairly consider he'd made this one his own by finding it—afterwards, because when he knew it was the Vick business he'd put his finger on he'd be more than ever reluctant to share its solution with us. Archy Mitfold, private detective, should have the honor and glory of solving a case that had rocked the country. Poor little mutt, he paid for his folly . . . and the payment tells us what the Vick case is."

"You mean—?"

"Murder."

Salt felt the cold drop of silence on the word which had broken it again and again in this room.

"There's kidnappin'—" he began gruffly.

"No. It's murder that has to be wiped out with murder. You can't be hanged twice, Tommy. The irreparable step's been taken—so take it again—and again—and again, if to you it seems necessary; you'll only pay one penalty. Look at the determination to kill Mitfold. There's no decline of purpose when three cold-blooded attempts fail. He had to go. Why? Because he knew enough to put a particular neck in jeopardy. Kidnapping? It's not a capital crime over here, and there's been no ransom notes, and three weeks gone. Murder—twice over—is our answer."

"But look here," said Salt excitedly, "you're jes' saying 'e heard Vick's voice. How—if Vick was murdered?"

"I didn't say Mitfold knew it was murder. He was somewhere where he heard Vick speaking, not knowing it was Vick. That's sure. As it doesn't make sense to suppose Vick was conducting a monologue we'll assume Mitfold heard a second voice. Whatever it was he overheard it put those two unseen talkers in a sinister light. Something was afoot, but I don't think Mitfold guessed murder. That happened afterward when he was out of earshot—perhaps immediately afterwards. But he'd heard enough to put him on the track of something, and he was rash enough or careless enough to give away just as much of what he'd learned as was necessary to put the murderer on *his* track. Mitfold didn't know at the time who Vick was, but—know what I think?"

"That 'e had an inkling of the other fellow."

"More than an inkling. I believe he was sure of what we'll call Voice Number Two. It seems to me pretty plain he knew one of them, because he had enough to go on to follow it up directly and, more telling still, to draw those birds *before* October 4. And after three days his snooping drew on him the first attack."

"On the twenty-eighth? You're reckoning, then, this business he chanced on *was* September 25?"

"If it was to do with Sampson Vick—and today's evidence proves it—it had to be. It wasn't earlier, because Archy wasn't behaving oddly till then, and it couldn't have been more than a day or so later because of the date of the first attempt on his life. And since the twenty-fifth is the date on which Vick disappeared it's more likely to have been then than in the first day or two he was missing, when—if he was still alive—precautions would have been taken against sight or sound of him reaching the outside world. Besides, we've something else to remember September 25 for."

"The empty 'ouse," said Salt, adding skeptically, "providin' there ever was such a place."

"There was. There's got to be. It fits so patly. The dark—and without a torch it would be smothering—the feeling of void and cold. Ideal conditions for hearing without seeing. And then the return to it next morning for a second look—not the usual thing, Tommy, when you've blundered into the wrong house, unless the attendant circumstances made you think about it afterwards. The house is somewhere, and we've got to find it."

"We better take Chelsea to pieces."

Pardoe was frowning, a remote look on his face, but Salt was busy on another line of thought.

"Something I can't make out 'ere," he said suddenly. "He was working at the thing on his own, keepin' it quiet from us, an' at the same time he was gassin' about 'is accidents an' the house 'e went in that night an' the cinema, an' drawin' all these birds an' leavin' 'em lyin' around—and tellin' people like Miss Leaf an' the girl an' the professor , an' finally Wynkerrell and Beltane, bits an' pieces of the story, for all it was so secret. Why?"

"More than one reason. Speyer put his finger on one—Mitfold was vain, and he was lonely. He wouldn't share what he'd got, but he had to talk to somebody because the thing was eating him. But there was more to it than that. I believe he thought there was the chance he wouldn't come out of it alive. Or perhaps, if we want to be very subtle, he got a kick out of pretending that he wouldn't come out of it alive. So he made sure there was a good sprinkling of clues left behind him, like a paper chase—for us to pick up the trail." Pardoe added slowly, "Here's something else to chew on, Tommy—among the people to receive what you've called the bits and pieces of the story is, I believe, the murderer. I thing Mitfold told him—or her—just as much as it pleased him to tell."

"Why?"

"P'raps in the hope of putting him off the scent. The killer, according to Archy, might argue that since Archy could drop hints of the affair openly to him he didn't suspect him. Or maybe it was vanity again—or a warning to clear out. But from what I know of Archy Mitfold I'd be more inclined to think it vanity—letting the other fellow know that he, and no other, was on his track."

Salt saw some shape in the story at last. It was the barest outline still, with at least one deed and one actor in it nameless, and all the details to fill in, but the fog they had groped in was thinning out. His small, shrewd eyes took on a sharper look.

"We're taking for granted," he said, "that it was 'is diary he was writing up Saturday night, an' that the murderer's pinched it. But it don't make sense, because why did 'e ever 'ave to go back to Mulberry Fountain at all? Why didn't 'e take the bloomin' diary with 'em when he moved 'ouse on Friday?"

"Not such a hard one, Tommy. It puzzled me too, and it's something we've got to keep in mind, but the answer's simple, I think. Turn it over yourself. Keep before you Mitfold's abnormally secretive nature, his obsession with the business he'd discovered which made him acquiesce in any suggestion made except that of leaving London for a night or two, and the—what shall we say?—nature of the house in Alma Square that was waiting to receive him."

"I see," said the sergeant, feeling a little cold at the glimmering of truth revealed to him, "an' I don't like it."

Pardoe gave him a quick look. "I wonder if you really see," was his cryptic observation. Before Salt could reply he went on: "There's two or three other things we've got to ask ourselves. I've been at 'em—now you take a turn, and we'll see what comes out of the bag. First, why did Archy Mitfold change his mind about attending the Old Crispians' lunch? A month ago he scoffed at it—but on the day he died he went to it. It's not enough to say that he stayed in London last weekend with an ulterior motive. Of course he did. All the more reason why he shouldn't waste an afternoon at a function he'd already dismissed as footling. The way he was snooping round then, he hadn't got time to kill. Since he was present at the lunch we've got to infer that being there was part of his plan for staying in town."

He paused. Salt said nothing.

"Next thing, why did he lie about Miss Leaf's knowledge of the attacks made on him?"

"I told you the answer to that once," the sergeant put in stubbornly.

"She plainly knew everything. She's been our best source of information. And Archy knew that she knew. Yet he made out she was in the dark about it. It's an extremely important point that clamors for an answer. I'll go further and say that the right answers to these two questions will probably give us all we need to build our case."

"*And* the birds," put in Salt, thinking these foundations rather slender.

"And the birds."

"Not to say the 'ammers?"

But that went unanswered, for Pardoe's telephone rang. He lifted the receiver quickly.

"Yes . . . put him through. . . . Yes, this is Inspector Pardoe. . . . *What?* Is he dead? Not dead? A pretty fair chance, eh? Fine. How long ago? . . . Oh . . . in Banklow Cottage Hospital? Right. Keep your man at the bedside without fail, and report directly there's any change. Admit nobody but police and doctor. . . . Oh . . . Yes . . . yes, I know him. Right. . . . If you report he's conscious before morning I'll be down tonight—if not, tomorrow early. . . . 'Bye."

He turned shining eyes on the impatient Salt.

"The Witley sergeant. Philip Beltane was discovered insensible in the school garage this afternoon with the engine of his car running, and the doors closed. Not locked, please note. They've rushed him to the nearest hospital, at Banklow, with a good stiff dose of carbon monoxide poisoning. The police surgeon can only say his chances of pulling through and going under are at present fifty-fifty. It's the headmaster put 'em on to us. He connected up our visit of yesterday with this calamity on the school premises and acted with his usual dispatch, good man. Twenty-four hours after we were there—think of it. Somebody's moving fast."

Satisfaction and disappointment wrestled for mastery on Salt's face.

"He's done it 'imself?"

"Looks like attempted suicide, Bailey reports. But we can't accept that without all the facts. Dammit"—he took a few quick steps up and down and beat his fist gently in the palm of his other hand—"remember what I said? 'The most unlikely person.' It doesn't fit—"

"Only in the storybooks," said Salt sagaciously.

"Not in mine. Mine's different. Why weren't the garage doors fastened on the inside?"

"P'raps there isn't no fastening. Anyway, if it's soo'cide, why fasten 'em?"

"That's an idea," Pardoe said. He sounded tired. "I'll send a man to relieve Bailey's at the hospital. If they pull him round we must get a statement or the next best thing. We can't afford to lose anything he may say, however fragmentary."

Salt emitted a low, clear whistle. At Pardoe's glance he said: "Old Welkin died in a garridge."

"The Byronic touch, eh?" The inspector frowned suddenly and said in a slow, doubtful voice, "Tommy, what were you saying to me when the buzzer went?"

Salt could not remember.

"Something about the spotted crake, wasn't it? . . . No, it wasn't—it was about the hammers. Old man, turn your mind back to Rossetti Terrace and our door-to-door jaunt. When I joined you in Manor Street and we walked on toward the Embankment, just before I put through that call about Caffey's address, what was the name of the street on our left?"

Salt shook his head. "Never looked."

"Well, I did." Pardoe hurried over to a table alongside the wall and in a few seconds had spread out on it a street map of Chelsea. He ran his finger down from the Town Hall, his breathing suddenly a little short. "Look—come on down. Yes, past Alpha Place, past that—*and* that. Here's Pentagon Square, see, immediately north of Rossetti Terrace—and here, directly south of the Terrace and parallel to it, *Hammer* Street." He repeated the word softly, "Hammer. Hammer—"

"On the 'ard 'ighroad," said Salt flippantly. "An' where do we go from there?"

"It's where Archy Mitfold went, not us," said Pardoe ungrammatically. "Call ourselves detectives—we didn't look an inch beyond our noses. We thought Mitfold got into the wrong house because in the dark he overshot (or undershot) his mark in the Terrace itself. He didn't. I believe he overshot it in Flood Street on his way down. Instead of turning into the professor's road he went past it and into the next one—into Hammer Street. If I'm right, the end of the chase is in view."

CHAPTER XVIII: GAS

Suddenly a grievous sickness took him,
That makes him gasp, and stare, and catch the air.
KING HENRY VI. PART 2.

THE AGENTS' BOARD leaned over the scabby railing with the intimate air of a drunken man. On application to Messrs. Froggatt and Kay at an address in

Fulham one gathered that number eight, Hammer Street, might be inspected with a view to purchase or rental.

Morning, perhaps the least sanguine period of the day, reserves a particularly uncompromising treatment for inference, theory and guesswork based on hope. So it was with a feeling of mingled astonishment and relief that Pardoe had come face to face with the empty house in Hammer Street.

It stood in precisely the same relation to its own street as Professor Speyer's did to Rossetti Terrace. Architecturally there was no difference in essentials. Here, it was true, the numbers ran consecutively down each side of the street, but that was no matter to anyone not relying on its number for finding the house. To a pedestrian coming into Hammer Street in the dark in the belief that he was entering the Terrace the house could have presented nothing to arouse suspicion.

Like Speyer's it was semidetached. Pardoe noticed that its companion, too, was vacant. But number eight had by far the more neglected appearance. The gate sagged uneasily on its hinges; the railing had lost most of its successive layers of paint; coarse grass ran riot, encroaching on the path and area; the large window downstairs turned to the street the curiously blind face that masks a void; the steps to the front door had an unscrubbed, moldy bloom.

At the moment Pardoe did not want to make himself or his intention conspicuous by lingering at the spot. He was convinced that he had located the scene of Archy Mitfold's mistake on the night of September 25. It was a good eight hours still before darkness set in, and though he intended to examine the place by daylight there was plenty of time yet to see what a less obtrusive watch upon it might result in. He must go down to Witley on the Beltane case and visit the hospital; meantime, this house should be watched back and front for anyone else disposed still to take an interest in it. On his return from Banklow he would call on Messrs. Froggatt and Kay, after which he and Salt would enter number eight.

On the other side of the street he noticed what appeared to be a block of offices recently vacated. Its frontage ran parallel to numbers three to ten of the houses opposite, and furnished admirable cover for the man he proposed to set there. The back of the house would have to be overlooked from Rossetti Terrace. Between numbers eight and nine Pardoe saw that a narrow alley ran, flanked by the walls of these two houses and blocked at each end by iron posts for the frustration of all but pedestrian traffic. There was, then, a short cut into the Terrace from Hammer Street? He took it and found himself almost startlingly, though he should have been prepared for it, confronting the professor's house. As he made his way out into Flood Street his mind worked busily about this simple juxtaposition of residence. Had August Speyer been prompted by a motive less innocent than it appeared to leave Earl's Court for a house in Chelsea so conveniently close to an empty one in the next street?

Pardoe traveled alone to Witley-in-the-Holt. Salt would be more usefully employed supervising the guardians of number eight and dealing with any reports that came in. The Signora Tommaseo's shadow, at least, was enjoying an exasperatingly easy job, for the lady seemed to be spending most of her time in bed.

At Witley Pardoe's first objective was the police station, a comfortable-looking cottage standing by itself at a short distance from the school. Sergeant Bailey was dark and pessimistic; his saturnine air lent an unintentional touch of mystery to the most innocuous piece of business, but Pardoe saw that the infrequent demands made on him in the village had not interfered with his skill in handling a case when occasion arose.

"Sheer luck they ever came across him in time," he said, and sounded regretful. "You'll see when we're there how cut off the garage is from the main block of school buildings. If it hadn't a' been for these two masters taking a stroll round . . ." He tailed off into eloquent silence.

"Then which way do they bring their cars out?" Pardoe asked. It was a point on which he had felt inquisitive on Tuesday.

"The back. Oh, I see, you came down the road day before yesterday? But coming from the station there's a lane on your right, not a stone's throw from the booking office it isn't. Not the way for Shanks' pony, unless you like a bit of country and got time to kill, but the school traffic uses it because it brings 'em straight round to the back and to the garage. Here's how it is."

His finger sketched a quick plan on the tablecloth.

"Yes, I see," Pardoe said. "I didn't get round there Tuesday. This lane—is it much in use?"

Bailey shook his head mournfully. "Nobody but the school—well, maybe a laborer or two who's making for the field path on the other side."

"Did you examine the place for wheel tracks?"

Bailey had. What was more, the rain of the previous night, which had started as a drizzle at the time of Pardoe's visit, had come to his aid. Where the drive from the garage turned into the lane the ground sank a little in a saucerlike depression that became a puddle in really wet weather and a soft patch of mud after a moderate storm. Neatly bisecting this oozy piece of ground Bailey had discovered the well-defined track of a pedal cycle, and the cycle itself a quarter of a mile along the lane in a ditch close to a field stile. Before the discovery of the machine Mr. Haldane, one of the masters, had reported his own bicycle missing. Interrogation of the boys had produced nothing, and indeed, now that the cycle had been found, a quarter-mile joy ride and a walk back seemed a singularly tame prank for any boy to play. Bailey, it was clear, was not inclined to connect the bicycle with the condition of Mr. Beltane in the closed garage and explained that he only looked for tire marks in any case because it had been rumored that Beltane had gone out earlier in the afternoon. He had found none, however, belonging to a car. He did not enquire what had prompted the inspector's question.

"Was he seen to leave in the car?" Pardoe asked.

"No. But one of the masters got the idea from Mr. Beltane himself that he was going out. When I put it to him, though, he admitted it was p'raps only an impression."

"I'll see him myself. Where was this cycle standing when it was taken away?"

"In a shed next door to the garage, with some other bikes. Doors unfastened, and Mr. Edwards thinks probably open."

"Pretty trusting lot at the school, aren't they?"

"Nobody's ever along the lane, that's why."

"And this stile where you found the bike—where do you get if you cross the meadow?"

"Onto the Banklow road. Banklow's about two miles further on; then Westerham."

"Anywhere near the station?"

"What, this station? No. If you go by the meadow you're gradually sheering off from the station, till when you come out on the road you're a good half-mile away. If you was to follow the lane all the way instead, now, you'd come on top of the station."

"So that if anybody leaving the school took the field path you'd say they hadn't got the station in mind?"

"I would." But Bailey was looking puzzled. "You don't think there's somebody else mixed up in this, do you? Because I've been looking at it like it was plain suicide—or maybe just the chance it could be accident."

"I'll tell you what I think when I've seen more. You tell me—why d'you think he did it himself?"

Bailey looked hard at the inspector. "Various things, sir. Well, it just jumps to the eye, you might say. Those garage doors—they're the sliding kind—they're real hard to budge. That's not hearsay—I tested 'em myself. Shutting 'em's an act of deliberation. Nobody could do it in a fit of absentmindedness. He'd be doing it of set purpose. What's more, none of the masters ever bothered about closing the doors. It was the gardener's job at night, and it seems more often than not he'd let 'em be—that's why they're so stiff. Then, another thing, they all say as how this Mr. Beltane's a specially clearheaded sort of young chap, practical and sensible, and the last to go pulling those doors together in a fit of abstraction and then starting his engine."

As it was plain that Bailey's only alternative theory was accident, on the face of it his deductions were reasonable enough. The fingerprint test applied to the garage doors, the car and the bicycle alike had yielded nothing useful. Nor, when they had arrived at the Rowan House and he had examined the scene with a microscopic thoroughness that commanded Bailey's respectful attention, could Pardoe light upon anything to suggest a third reading of the facts.

The garage was spacious and well built and accommodated three cars. Beltane's Morris Oxford still occupied the position in which it had been found, three yards from the doors, its bonnet pointing at the back of the garage. Beltane himself had been lying on the floor in the space between the back of the car and the garage doors.

Pardoe frowned. "A bit odd, isn't it? If he was bent on suicide, sitting at the steering wheel would have made him susceptible to the fumes sooner." The shade of Mr. Welkin assumed a more substantial form. "They're usually slumped across the wheel, I believe."

"Not always, sir," Bailey said respectfully. "There was a case right here in Banklow—year before last it would be—chap had done a spot of forgery and was generally at the end of his tether. He tried this on, and died of it. But they found him even further off from the car than what Mr. Beltane was, with his hand stretched out to the bolt of the door. That'd got an inside bolt, but there's none here. Sometimes they change their minds, you see, while they're still able to think, and try to open the door before it's too late."

Pardoe looked again at the doors. A rusty padlock hung outside. "As you say, there's no inside fastening. But with doors as weighty and stiff as these, closing would be enough—nobody giddy from the effects of the gas could get 'em open again without help."

He walked down the short shrub-bordered drive to the gate in the lane which, the sergeant explained, stood open all day. Only a few yards away the lane curved sharply enough to block one's view of its further course. On his return he observed how well hidden were the garage and bicycle shed from the house itself. Between the school and this back drive a small melancholy-looking quadrangle lay, beyond it the new stone of an additional wing pierced by narrow lancet windows. But those windows, said Bailey, ran the length of a corridor unfrequented during school hours, so that even if a watcher had been able to penetrate the screen of shrubs on the far side of the quad, there had been none there to do it.

In the headmaster's study Pardoe interviewed Mr. Jackson and Mr. Dunkerly, the two masters who had rescued Philip Beltane. They were both youngish men with a genuine concern for Beltane's misfortune, whether self-sought or accidental; that did not, however, preclude a measure of enjoyment of the position in which they found themselves.

"The sound of that car purring away chirpy as a cricket behind closed doors," said Dunkerly brightly, "struck me directly we got round the corner. If it hadn't been Jackson tumbled to it the very same time as me, though, I'd have said I was hearing things."

"As it was," Jackson went on, "I don't think either of us had the idea immediately that somebody was inside. I mean, our lunge for the doors was simply a sort of instinctive move. Without bothering to think about it we knew it was wrong for an engine to be warming up like that in a shut garage."

"What time was it?" Pardoe asked. "And how did you happen to be round there just then?"

"It was nearly four," said Jackson. "I know because the church clock struck the hour as we hauled Beltane out onto the drive. Then we phoned the doctor—the Witley one, I mean."

Dunkerly added, "We'd been strolling round discussing a matter arising out of three A's syllabus. Jackson's senior maths, I'm junior, and three A are the nasty little transition beggars that upset the applecart. So our peripatetic chinwag about their arithmetic brought us round to the back. Neither of us was on games duty, you see. It was the free period before tea."

"That's quite clear," Pardoe said. "Now was it to one of you gentlemen that Mr. Beltane mentioned he was taking his car out?"

They looked puzzled. Jackson made as if to speak when Dunkerly, who seemed a little quicker on the uptake, broke in: "I know what you mean—but it was only an idea he had really." He turned slightly to Jackson. "Old Franco, you know." Then to Pardoe, "It's Mr. Franklin you mean. Beltane got him to take prep for him this evening, and Franco got the notion it was because he was going out. We swap like that occasionally, you see, then Bel would have paid his debt by taking Franklin's prep for him another time."

"Yes, I see."

Pardoe's mind worked fast. Had Beltane planned some move for the after-tea hour then, and had a second player got his move in first? Or, intending suicide, had he some grisly foreknowledge of his absence from the prep room that evening, and provided for it in advance so as to delay the discovery of his body?

He put a few more perfunctory questions, chiefly relating to Beltane's behavior since Tuesday afternoon. But they had remarked nothing unusual, though Jackson contributed an interesting postscript.

"It wouldn't have been surprising," he said, "if his manner had been a bit odd. Nobody would have thought twice about it. He was quite moody at times and often short with everybody."

"Especially round weekends," Dunkerly added, and stopped short as if caught in an indiscretion.

Jackson flushed and looked a little annoyed. "So's anybody, for that matter."

"That's what I meant," Dunkerly said with a too-bright mendacity. "Tempers have worn a bit thin by Friday, and the time between's too short to make 'em mellow again by Monday."

"This is Thursday," said Pardoe. He added: "Mr. Beltane was away most weekends, wasn't he?"

There was a short silence.

"Yes," Jackson said coldly.

There was no more to be had from them. Their first loquacity had run dry.

Pardoe, who had an idea that Jackson was itching to tell Mr. Dunkerly what he thought of him, thanked them for their information and asked if they would find out if Mr. Franklin could spare him a few minutes.

The classics master was a gray-headed man with precise, legal features and a formal manner. At the moment he was somewhat testy at the factual value rumor had given to a mere impression he had received.

"I did *not* commit myself," he said with emphasis, "to the statement that Mr. Beltane was going out. Nothing of the sort. Really, one will be afraid to open one's mouth next. What happened was this. The boys do preparation from five-thirty to seven every evening. Yesterday—Wednesday—Mr. Beltane was on prep duty. He came to me directly after lunch and asked if I would exchange my Friday evening prep duty for his. I agreed."

"And he gave you some idea of why he wanted to do this?"

"Yes. He proffered it quite voluntarily, of course—I should not have asked. This is exactly what he said, and if you can read into it an intention of taking his car out, well, I can't. He said, 'I have an appointment, and I may not be here in time for prep.' "

"Haha," Pardoe murmured. "Then there was the possibility that he *would* be back in time?"

"I suppose so. But obviously he didn't think so."

"But your impression was that is this case the appointment was before and not after tea?"

"Dear me," said Mr. Franklin impatiently, "I can't say that I thought about it at all, but seeing that we don't finish tea till five and after there wouldn't, I should say, be much probability of his being back in time to take prep if the appointment had been after tea."

"That's what I mean," Pardoe said. "And that brings us to another point. Was Mr. Beltane free from teaching on Wednesday afternoon before tea?"

Mr. Franklin referred to the timetable for that. "There is a games period from three-thirty to four-thirty every day. Afternoon classes are from two-five till two-fifty and two-fifty till three-thirty. I understand that Mr. Beltane's second period yesterday was free—that is, he finished teaching at two-fifty. I presume he was not taking games, or else had already come to an arrangement in that respect."

Pardoe nodded. "And now, Mr. Franklin, have you the slightest idea of the nature of Mr. Beltane's appointment?"

The classics master lifted thin eyebrows. "None whatever," he said severely.

"Did you perhaps find his manner a little strange?"

"No, I did not." Mr. Franklin was sharp. "And if I were now to try to recollect anything of the sort, the result would be mostly surmise and conjecture colored by after events, Inspector, and I'm afraid that wouldn't be of any use to you and certainly isn't going to be indulged in by me."

Pardoe thanked him, and closed his notebook in the knowledge that he had extracted from Mr. Franklin all he ever would extract. Before leaving the school he spent a short time with the headmaster, who had clearly come to regard him as a bird of ill omen. It transpired that Beltane had not been in charge of games yesterday, so that from two-fifty on he had been at liberty to keep an appointment either at school or away, though he must have anticipated that the business in hand would take up a fair amount of time, else why had he arranged for his possible absence at five-thirty?

"Of course," said Mr. Edwards gently, as if reading the inspector's thoughts, "we mustn't exclude the possibility that this appointment was purely mythical. If the poor lad intended taking his own life he may simply have been playing for time, or concocting a tale to lull suspicions."

"Which nobody apparently entertained," Pardoe reminded him.

"That's true. I can't say I noticed anything peculiar about him myself. But if he was feeling odd he'd imagine the rest of us noticed it, wouldn't he?"

"He might. Mr. Edwards, why did Mr. Beltane go up to town so frequently?"

The headmaster shrugged. "His time was his own. It's natural for a young fellow to do so, isn't it? I really don't know any particular reason."

"What time did he usually go up?"

"Time of day? Always on a Saturday, usually afternoon. Last Saturday he went in the morning, though, because he was attending an Old Boys' lunch."

"But the weekends he wasn't on duty—if he'd wanted to he was free to leave on Friday evening?"

"Yes, indeed. Most of the staff taking a weekend off naturally get away Friday to make the most of it, seeing they have to be back Sunday night."

"Thank you," said Pardoe. "That's what I wanted to know."

The police surgeon in Banklow had news to impart.

"It only turned up this morning," he said, "on a second examination. Dr. Cowburn of Witley wouldn't have made a detailed one yesterday, of course— the job then was an ambulance and hospital as fast as you could make it. And when Doc Hiley here went over him with me in the evening we missed it, because it was plain as the nose on my face he'd got CO poisoning, and we didn't look for anything else. But there *is* something else—he's had a recent crack on the head, almost on the crown, as if he'd been struck sitting down. No fracture, mind you, and no blood, but definite contusion of a nature that suggests he was knocked out by it, and that the gas got to work on him before he came round."

"Self-infliction out of the question?" Pardoe asked.

The doctor eyed him quizzically. "Any idea it's not suicide? All right—not my province. Well, I won't swear he couldn't have done it himself. Say he started the engine, then ran his head like a bull at the closed doors of the garage so as to hasten insensibility, he could've got something of the sort. Sounds dotty to me as well as a bit superfluous under the circumstances., but there's no accounting for taste when they've made up their minds to bump 'emselves off."

The look accompanying the last remark made it something of a feeler, but Pardoe did not respond.

"Otherwise," pursued the doctor hopefully, "I can only offer you our old friend, the blunt instrument."

"And what's your own opinion of his chances?"

"The general one today. He'll pull through. We'll have him talking tomorrow or the next day. Now—don't be optimistic. Maybe you'll get nothing out of him anyway. It's no uncommon thing, remember, for CO gas to destroy the memory of anything immediately preceding its inhalation—or, at least, to render recollection pretty imperfect. And there's sometimes a tendency to mania and irresponsible language on coming back to consciousness. We'll do our best, but don't bank too heavily on what you're going to get when we've done it."

Pardoe thought about it on his way to the hospital. An imperfect recollection of things immediately preceding insensibility . . . yes, but a whole day had elapsed between his own visit to the school and Beltane's visit to the garage. If the latter had had a suicidal motive there was in itself evidence of guilt which negatived the importance in any case of what Beltane might have to say on recovery, unless he decided on confession. If, on the other hand, he were innocent and the victim of assault at the hands of Mitfold's murderer, then the appointment he had mentioned was genuine, and surely planned a sufficiently long time before he had been overcome by the gas to be remembered when the toxic effects had worn off. Either way Pardoe could not see the possible amnesia as a serious stumbling block.

In a private ward of the small country hospital the man in attendance at the bedside got up as he came in. Beltane lay quietly, after a period, the matron explained, of great restlessness, even violence. Pardoe observed at once the cyanosis of face and neck, the unfailing symptom of CO poisoning; his skin was still a bright cherry color with a faint bluish tinge, though it had faded, he was told, since yesterday. His hands now and again plucked aimlessly at the sheet.

Pardoe cocked an enquiring eyebrow at his man, whose notebook lay on a little table close at hand.

The detective shook his head. "Nothing, sir. Leastways, not of any account. He's been delirious on and off, but we can't get anything coherent. About a dozen times I caught the same word—seems as if he'd got a *crate*, or some such thing, on his mind."

Pardoe looked grimly at the bed. "Peg away—make a note of anything, however vague. I'll instruct your relief to keep his ears pricked too. It's not a crate he's talking about—it's a crake."

CHAPTER XIX: VACANT POSSESSION

A little little grave, an obscure grave.
KING RICHARD II.

"AN' THAT'S 'OW IT WAS," said Salt with a note of excitement in his voice. "Nobody with so much as a look for the place till Speyer rolls along just before one o'clock an' gives it the glad eye."

"Sorry to sound discouraging, old man," Pardoe said, "but the thing looks so pat and undisguised that it suggests he was putting on an act for our benefit."

"But 'e didn't know we was watching the place," Salt urged.

"Perhaps not. Well, looking at it another way, what's so odd in Speyer walking past the house any day of the week? He's next door, so to speak, in Rossetti Terrace, and right opposite his house is a cut into Hammer Street. He must use it pretty often. If he'd entered the place, now, or even put a hand on the gate, I grant you, we'd have something to think about. But he didn't—you say he went straight past?"

"And for why?" Salt flashed. "Walk past the 'ouse an' out into Flood Street, an' he can get to the same place in less time by turning out of his own gate an' goin' up the Terrace a dozen yards?"

Looked at that way it was certainly queer. Watch on 8 Hammer Street had gone entirely unrewarded but for the professor's appearance in the alley at 12:45. He had been hatless—a fairly usual condition, Pardoe gathered—and walking with decision, a conspicuous figure that in any circumstances would have attracted a certain attention. This morning he had instantly riveted the gaze of the man at the window across the road and of Salt who happened to have joined him a short time before.

As soon as Speyer stepped out onto Hammer Street pavement, he paused for a fraction of time to glance down the road in the direction of Manor Street, but did not aim to go that way. Those watching interpreted the glance as a precautionary measure, for, the next moment, walking at a visibly slackened pace, he was moving up the street past the frontage of the empty house, his face turned so completely toward it that his features were hidden from those who spied on him. So slow, said Salt, was his gait that they had expected, even when he passed it, to see him turn back and open the gate. But he touched nothing, nor did he actually halt; he simply subjected the whole front

of the house to a minute and leisurely scrutiny before making for the Flood
Street end at a moderately quick rate and with his gaze now ahead of him.

"You might 'a' said," Salt rounded it off, "that there was somebody up at
the windows waitin' to see 'im go by."

Pardoe was silent. He had a sudden uncanny prevision of a scene not far
ahead, vague in detail but disagreeable as a whole, when that remark would
return as an uncomfortable memory.

The representative of Messrs. Froggatt and Kay was mildly astonished at a
revival of interest in wartime in number 8 Hammer Street. As Pardoe, in spite
of his optimism, prepared for a mare's nest, did not see fit at present to
disclose that interest as Scotland Yard's, the key was handed over with the
hopeful gesture of an angler throwing one more cast. Nor was this the time to
pump for information which in the event of a fruitless visit would not be
needed. So the inspector came away richer only by the fact that the house,
whose owner lived in Fiesole, was unfurnished and had been vacant for two
years. Its companion, number seven, had been empty since the end of August
only, when the family had evacuated as soon as war became inevitable.

At five o'clock Pardoe and Salt together made quiet entry.

The path, patchy with lichen, was of a spongy nature that might have
retained a fair impression of footprints but for the recent rain. Now, as they
picked their way under the stare of uncurtained windows, it was merely a
succession of puddles.

"We'll try the back," Pardoe said, "in spite of our key."

But the back door was locked. They did not return to the front immediately.
The mildewed, overgrown path that ran here across the top of the garden
before turning down at a right angle by the wall of number seven, was subjected to a careful preliminary examination. Twitch grass scrambled unhealth-
ily across it, and showed here and there unmistakable signs of having been
trampled into the earth. The garden below them was a little jungle of decay
and neglect. A rambler rose trained over a wire arch not far from the door had
collapsed in an undisciplined mass of suckers and weak, trailing shoots. Pardoe noticed that one or two of these had been split underfoot and that the
bruises were comparatively fresh.

Near the dividing wall between the houses was a lilac bush large enough for
an effective screen. The grass approach to it was trodden down in such a way
as to suggest more constant passage than one or two casual journeys there
and back. Bending over it, Pardoe saw that in the small space between the
bush and wall the grass was partially worn away, as if somebody had kept
vigil there not once but a number of times. Snapped twigs and bruised, torn
and dropped remnants of leaves on that side of the bush testified to the watcher's
long wait and the aimless occupation of bored fingers.

"And this scrubby, caved-in part of the foliage," said Pardoe, "is so low it looks as if he'd squatted or crouched most of his time to hide himself the better."

In silence they returned to the front door, passing a flight of stone steps, green with disuse, that led to a basement door. In another moment they had mounted the front steps and crossed the threshold of the silent hall.

Its stripped walls and naked floor gave it a false appearance of loftiness. When the door closed behind them the light from the transom and from a small window on the first landing was its only illumination. At the far end the stairs rose to a twist and vanished in obscurity. On either hand were closed doors. Dust lay everywhere; not in the unequal distribution that marks a house neglected by its inhabitants, but in an even, orderly spread like the inexorable flow of the tide covering a void dwelling. The silence, suddenly localized and made intimate by the closing of the door, was so deathly as to give an airless quality to the place.

Pardoe had prepared beforehand a simple plan of campaign, and they went to work with the economy that only trained men employ. While Salt took the left-hand door the inspector opened the one on the right. For a few moments neither moved beyond the threshold; if the prints or any traces of recent occupants remained behind the fact must be ascertained before their own feet made fresh disturbance. But the virgin dust bore no mark. Only in Pardoe's room the crumbling cornice had dropped plaster. His was the large bow window on the street, Salt's two small ones looking on the alley. Taking up their stance at these and examining the rooms from those angles gave them nothing more. Whoever had made recent use of the place had not intruded into the hall or either of the front rooms. That meant an entry by the back. And that supported what Speyer had said must have been Archy's approach on the night of the 25th.

When they came out again into the hall Pardoe moved off in the direction of a little passage on the left of the stairs while Salt took the stairs themselves. For an ungainly man the sergeant could move when he liked with an incredible delicacy. He mounted the treads now with a precision aimed at fluttering not one feather of the ubiquitous dust, keeping his eye rather than his hand on the filmy baluster.

Pardoe found himself in a short passage about ten feet long with the garden door at the bottom and close at his left hand a door which in Rossetti Terrace would have belonged to the professor's study. The daylight here was feebler in effect than in the front of the house, for the back transom was of frosted glass, but he could see that the passage was laid with small red tiles, gritty and blurred from the cleaner's long inattention. Entering the little room on the left he got a view of the tangled rambler and the dank, unwholesome garden. Here, too, dust lay unruffled on the floor boards. Nothing more expressive of occupation than a few cobwebs met his eyes.

Closing the door behind him, he made for his real objective, the back entrance. He could hear Salt's faint, muffled movements upstairs as he explored the silent house. His own now were more wary, for here, if anywhere, should be signs of footsteps. About a yard from the door he stopped and switched on a pocket torch the better to examine the condition of the tiles. But the gray daylight was still enough to neutralize its gleam. On his right the passage, after meeting the back door, took a sharp turn and culminated in a flight of steps that made spiral descent to the basement.

Pardoe sat back on his heels and scrutinized the floor as minutely as he could in a line from the door to the top of the basement stairs. Once they had got the door open light, in more ways than one, perhaps, would be shed on his difficulty; but that action would depend on what they found elsewhere in the house. The tiles continued in a straight line as far as the door, but at the turn to the steps the passage was not paved. A scrap of linoleum with irregular, frayed edges and its original pattern worn away covered the boards at the top of the stairs. Pardoe found indistinct, earthy stains and the absence of the even film of dust he had found everywhere else. With the tips of his fingers he explored the surface of the linoleum. At the edge, where its tattered fringe revealed the boards below, he felt a small, hard protuberance. He inserted a finger and poked out what for a second he thought was a bullet. It was too large for that. It was a bead, bluish-black in color and slightly elongated. Not a very exciting find, for it might have rolled into its present hiding place years ago; but as it lay in the palm of his hand it looked all at once vaguely familiar, as if, he reflected, he had seen its companion only a short time before.

He got up, slipped it in his pocket, and began to go down the basement stairs. His pulses quickened a little as he saw that here and there on the treads dirty tracks were visible. At the bottom were three doors. The one straight ahead opened into a kitchen in the front of the house, as dusty and featureless as the other rooms he had seen. At a right angle to it a latched one gave on a shallow cupboard with shelves at the back. The third door stood beside the stairs facing the kitchen. Pardoe expected a scullery, but when he had raised the latch and opened it a sudden draught of cold, musty air met him, and he found himself looking down three stone steps into a lightless interior.

It was a cellar. Flags paved it, and the only light was through a rusty wire mesh half a foot deep that formed the top of a door in the far wall. That was the way, he knew, to the steps outside and the garden path. He went back to the kitchen door, opening that too. The result was a pale stream of light passing from front to back and in part relieving the gloom of the cellar. It had another result too. For there sprang into sight at his feet, on the bare boards between kitchen and cellar, a long, dull brown streak. He stooped to get a good look at it, not because he doubted what it was, but because the floor in its immediate neighborhood was interesting. It was clean, with a new, yellowish look in contrast to the surrounding grime. Somebody had made a valiant attempt to wash out the blood. But the blood had stayed. With the dreadful loyalty of its kind it stuck to the post it had been forced to take up. It looked like a sword, the blade directed at the cellar—no, not a sword, a pointing finger . . .

He went down the cellar steps and across the flags to that other door and shone his torch on it. Top and bottom the heavy bolts were shot home. They were red and flaky with rust and little cobwebs clung to the sockets. He could swear they had never been moved since the house fell vacant two years ago. He turned and surveyed the cellar, up, down and across.

Even in that twilight something odd about it struck him. It wasn't size or shape or the ghostly whitewashed walls that, devoid of everything that might have broken their monotony, stood out bleakly in the gray spill of light. It wasn't the cool, earthy smell either, that subterranean odor peculiar to all cellars. It was something that had unconsciously struck him as wrong as soon as he had looked at it from the top of the steps. All at once he knew what it was.

The cellar was unbelievably clean and tidy. While the rest of the house was as dejected as resignation to dust could make it, the cellar bore the air of a recent wash and brush-up. In a manner of speaking. On examination Pardoe was sure there had been no washing in here. On the other hand somebody's broom had gone thoroughly to work—so thoroughly that here and there in various parts of the floor its vigorous sweep had dislodged crumbs of earth from between the paving stones.

Pardoe felt a surge of cold excitement in his nerves. Salt was downstairs now, nosing about in the passage. Pardoe left the cellar and called to him. When he came down they exchanged a dozen words. Then they went to work. For nearly ten minutes they crawled on hands and knees about the cellar floor, each using his fingers as a second pair of eyes. They were especially interested in the cracks between the flags.

Salt found it first. He found it more by touch than sight, for it was near the far corner of the cellar in the darkest place. Here the earth packing in the crevices of a group of stones was of a different nature from that they had already explored. Instead of being dark and dry and crumbly and sunk a little below the level of the paving, it was pressed into smooth, rigid lines that rose to the level of the stones or above. Where the cellar mold was black and dusty, this was lighter and not so dry.

At the sergeant's grunt Pardoe rose from his knees and came up to him. Salt got up too, and together they shone their torches on the spot and moved the searchlights up and down.

There were five stones in the group. The last one was smaller, tapering off a little. It was, thought Pardoe, the shape of a coffin.

"Careful—take it steady. Put that lamp down there—no, not at the feet . . . here, where his head——"

Oh, poor devil. . . .

"Steady—steady—*now*. . . . Stand back a minute. Will you come over here, sir?"

The assistant commissioner's thin figure with its stooping shoulders moved forward from a dark recess into the pool of light that shone round Pardoe and Salt and the thing at their feet and left in deeper blackness the yawning hole from which they had taken it.

It was such a picture as Goya might have made. Except for the lamp in the corner the cellar was lit now by candles that fluttered to every sly draught and tossed ragged shadows ceiling high. Their dark gyrations made more macabre a scene where men waited to go about their jobs in a silence none would be the first to break. They were ready—fingerprints and camera man, Tawney with his mocking little mouth subdued to a hard line, the fellow with the rope who had helped Pardoe and Salt to raise their ghastly burden and stood now against the wall with hands that trembled in spite of himself. In the garden a couple more were systematically combing the tangles. They had already found the crowbar the murderer must have used to prise up the stone flags. There had been a bucket too, earth still clinging to it, and a patch of recently disturbed mold in the border by the wall. There might be other things.

"My God," said the A.C. softly, looking down at the tarnished clothes and the broken skull and thanking his stars that for the most part he was out of touch now with realities like this. "My God . . . the end of the quest—the last of Sampson Vick."

Pardoe looked at him quickly. The A.C. had a histrionic streak that found satisfaction in quiet utterances of a dramatic nature. Well, he should have his fill of the dramatic this time.

"No sir," he said in a flat voice, for he felt abominably tired, "not Sampson Vick. Sampson's been dead these five years and more. This is Humphrey—Humphrey Vick, the mobster."

CHAPTER XX: LAST WORD OF MR. VICK

Some violent hands were laid on Humphrey's life.
KING HENRY VI. PART 2.

PARDOE WOULD HAVE GIVEN MUCH to avoid what in the circumstances was unavoidable. His visit to the Green Park flat he found even less tolerable than the cellar ordeal of the night before; but the law demanded identification by a competent witness, and as identity in this case must be established by the great scar from Vinny the Backer's knife slash that had delved almost to the sternum, the condition of head and face precluding recognition, the onus of it lay on the wife. Pardoe had already ascertained that any medical attention Vick had received since coming to England had been of the most superficial character. He had more than once expressed an antipathy for doctors half-jocularly laid to the door of his persistent arthritis. For Sampson it was a reason that might have passed muster, but for Humphrey reluctance to call in a doctor would have been based on his fear of the betraying mark his body had carried to its grave.

Then there was Bianca Tommaseo. While Beatrice Vick would identify the man to whom she had been married for five years, the signora would be required to identify Humphrey. The Yard was already in touch with her, for Pardoe had some questions for the lady relating to her opportune presence in London; for the moment what was worrying him was a conjunction of events which had made the paths of these two women cross. It was Beatrice Vick herself who supplied an answer to his problem.

He could not have believed that any woman would have borne with such simple fortitude this last disastrous revelation. But he had not understood that for her the agony was finished. Now, Sampson or Humphrey, it did not matter. Memory of the man remained. In a big airy room with the park spread beneath it, where he had read the anonymous letter only four days ago, Pardoe came to the end of his story. He felt an abject coward, at a loss for words, refusing to meet the eyes of the woman, unable to break the clean, sharp silence that lay between them.

She broke it for him.

"I had thought . . . at times . . . there was something wrong. He never spoke of his brother. I, knowing a little, thought I understood why . . . and never asked. The scar—he said he had been attacked in revenge by a man who had a grievance against the family. . . . I understood he was referring to . . . Humphrey. We never spoke of it again."

After a minute Pardoe brought up again one of the things that was worrying him acutely.

"It has to be faced. It will be painful, I know. But it will be short . . . it shall be—and—it will be very little we'll want you to do. I wonder . . . could you bring Miss Channing with you—for company, I mean?"

She gave him a gravely compassionate look. It was an absurd thought, but to Pardoe it seemed for a moment as if their roles were reversed.

"Don't worry," she said. "I can do it. Other women have to. I shan't need Brenda." She paused, clasping her hands tightly in front of her. "And you say . . . Signora Tommaseo . . . she must too?"

He nodded, his gaze remote on the long vista of grass.

"Where is she living?"

He looked at her then. "Does it matter?"

"I should like to know. It is going to be hard for her, too, perhaps."

"You shall see her later, if you wish. There are things we must ask her first."

She was silent a moment. "And the . . . the people who have done all this?"

"They will be punished, Mrs. Vick."

"Ah, punishment . . ." Her voice broke. "I didn't mean . . ."

She suddenly caught his hand hard. "You have been kindness itself."

Two hours later Pardoe and Salt waited in the lobby of the long, squat mortuary while Tawney and a surgeon made the last preparations.

When Mrs. Vick's taxi came on the stroke of the appointed hour it was followed a minute later by that of the signora. A third that had halted at the end of the street turned round and drove off the way it had come. The signora's shadow had finished his work.

Pardoe had arranged that the two women should not be together in the anteroom. He accompanied Beatrice Vick down a stone passage to a second door of the mortuary while Salt took charge of the Italian and led her to a chair. She sat down, gazing round her at the nudity of the room with large, shining, oxlike eyes. Her fleshy figure, dressed with subdued flashiness, was showing now the rapid disintegration of beauty that not infrequently overtakes the Latin, but traces of a seductive loveliness still lingered in the camellialike skin and heavily fringed eyes.

Beatrice Vick said, "I'm ready. I'll get it over," and Pardoe took her inside. *How icy it is, and gray, and bare, the last negation. Steel yourself now. You've got to be brave. Try to pretend it's over. All the real things are over. This, too, will be done with in a minute. . . . That rigid, strangely swathed, shapeless mound on the slab . . . it's not Sampson. Sampson still lives and moves in a region beyond the control of murder and its avengers. . . . But it was never Sampson. . . . They've said so. This is Humphrey. . . . And the man at your elbow is still there, quiet and safe and rocklike, as he's been all through. But nobody can really help you but yourself. And the little doctor is murmuring something. . . .*

"Yes—yes, that's it. And—there was a burn—I can't see it. . . ."

"It doesn't matter. You need not see it. On the arm, was it?"

"Yes—the right forearm, outside. Close to his hand. Some acid . . ."

Not what you thought. Not an accident to Sampson. But Humphrey flinging up an arm in self-defense, and the corrosive acid burning through his sleeve.

More questions, formal and quiet, their very monotone kind.

"Yes, it is Sampson. . . . I mean . . ."

Then the anteroom again, its occupants mercifully silent, and the sudden sense of purity like that of well water in the air outside, and the inspector putting you into the taxi . . .

Pardoe returned and motioned the signora into the inner room. She got up with a voluptuous movement that was unstudied, and only shrank a little at the threshold. But they did not lead her immediately to the slab. One of the doctors came forward and began to question her. She thought how unexcited these English always were.

"Can you describe to us the scars left on Humphrey Vick's body by Vincent Balthasar's knife attack?"

That must be a catch, of course. Or else they believed she'd joined up with Humphrey again after he'd come out. Because the last time she had seen him alive he'd been in a jail hospital ward and the scar wasn't a scar at all but a gaping wound muffled by dressings.

"No, I can't. I never saw it. I haven't seen him for ten years, and then nobody thought he'd live after what Vinny had done to him."

They seemed satisfied.

"Did he have any distinguishing marks at the time you knew him?"

"Yes, a nasty burn—here." She touched her right arm just above the outer bend of the wrist. "Con Walter's gang it was did that. They muscled in on one of Viny's rackets, and there was some acid throwing."

"Yes. Did you ever know Humphrey suffered with arthritis?"

"There was never anything the matter with him."

"Thank you. Will you come here, please—it's only for a moment—and tell us whether you identify this burn on the right arm?"

She came with extreme reluctance, her creamy skin blanched to a sickly tint, and halted too far away.

Tawney said firmly, "A little closer, please. It's only for a moment."

Her full dark eyes fixed themselves in a kind of hypnotized fascination on the spot indicated.

"Oh—oh, yes—that's it." She clenched her plump hands slowly. "And— I've just remembered. There was a mole—a very dark mole—on the back of his neck, just below the hair line."

She shot them a sudden pathetic glance, as of a child that has said its lesson and now seeks approval. The doctors nodded at her gravely, but they did not tell her that it would have been impossible to look for that.

The question of formal identification was put to her.

She gulped, and moved away uncertainly.

"Sure, it's Humphrey."

She covered her face with her hands and broke into passionate tears.

Pardoe got a taxi and returned with her to Scotland Yard. Tears still glistened on her lashes, but she had recovered with the facility of her race, and seemed almost eager for enquiry. This readiness to oblige was explained as soon as he began to question her.

"Why did you leave Mentone for England on October 2?"

"Because of this," she said, and took from her handbag a letter which she handed to Pardoe. "I was coming to you people anyways, only you happened to spot me first."

Pardoe looked at the cheap envelope and badly indited block capitals that formed the signora's address at the Hotel Roland. It was postmarked London, September 27, and was twin to the one received by Beatrice Vick four days ago. He drew out the single sheet of flimsy paper, faintly lined, and here again were the painfully traced letters in pencil, unequal in size and uneven in alignment. He read:

Why not get news of Vick from the other woman at 12b, Grenacre Mansions, Piccadilly? Things are not always what they seem nor husbands neither.

There was a short silence. Pardoe tapped the letter with his finger.

"But why take the trouble of a journey to England—for this?"

"I thought there might be something in it for me," she said frankly. "I've had anonymous letters before now, and there's not one of them that hasn't meant something. I'd believed he was dead these five years, but this looked like it wasn't so, and if Humphrey was alive it was worth seeing him again. He'd likely do something for me. He—he was one of the best. And I'm not so well off as all that since Tommaseo died. I wasn't married to him much more than a year before he handed in his checks, poor old geyser, and you can run through a whole heap of dough in eight or nine years."

"You mean," Pardoe said bluntly, "you thought here was a heaven-sent chance for a little blackmail on the side?"

She looked sullen. "Nothing like it, mister. Get that clear. What hold would I have on him anyways?"

"You were married to him," Pardoe insinuated.

She rose to the bait. "I wasn't. We weren't ever spliced. I'd got a husband living when I took up with Vick."

"Alive now?"

This meant that Beatrice Vick's marriage was legal, after all.

"Not him. He died twelve years ago, eighteen months before Viny's gang was broken up. I could have married Humphrey then, but by that time we weren't so stuck on it. It was wearing a bit thin between us, and anyways nobody thought he'd live to come out after the Backer had got at him. I cleared out—you got to stand on your own feet, nobody 'll do it for you—and whichever way it went with Vick it looked like he wouldn't be able to do anything for me for a mighty long time to come. I married Tommaseo, properly this time, too, before Humphrey was sentenced." She added defiantly: "I got the papers to show."

Pardoe was looking at her not unkindly. "I appreciate your frankness. Tell me this—how is it you've not tried to get in touch with 12b, Grenacre Mansions, though you've been in England more than a fortnight?"

She stared. "Because I pretty soon found out who it was lived there. Mrs. Beatrice Vick was Sampson Vick's wife. I never had any dealings with them and I wasn't going to begin. That sort of thing don't get you anywhere. It wasn't for me to know—no more than for you," she put in slyly, "that Sampson was really Humphrey."

"So you thought the anonymous letter writer was putting you on Sampson's track by mistake instead of on Humphrey's, as he intended?"

"That—or it was a bit of spite to lead me a dance. Or," she added thoughtfully, "maybe whoever wrote the letter had got his facts muddled and took it I'd been married to *Sampson*, not Humphrey, and could make plenty trouble for Mrs. Vick."

"Ingenious," said Pardoe. "But that would have been a big howler, and these anonymous scribes usually get their data correct before they start circularizing it. Have you any idea who sent the letter?"

"Nope. There was always plenty of that sort of stuff flying about in our line in the old days. Tommaseo got 'em, too, after I married him, all about what a wicked woman his wife had been—you know the dope they hand out—but he knew about it all along, so it didn't make the difference."

"I'm wondering how the fellow who wrote this traced you to Mentone so soon after Vick's disappearance. This letter was posted two days after he was reported missing. Have you had a correspondent in this country lately?"

She shook her head. "I don't know anybody hereabouts. But I can tell you this—I was in the news in September."

"What way?"

"Middle of the month I had some stuff stolen, cash and jewels, while I was staying at the Roland. It was one of these hotel thieves—he had a regular big haul from one and another of us. They recovered a bit of mine, not all. The papers had it, of course."

"Where you'd be mentioned as the widow of Signor Tommaseo?"

"Oh yes—but one or two had the cheek to add, 'former wife of Humphrey Vick, the celebrated American gunman.'"

Pardoe nodded. "That's probably the explanation. Did any more letters like this one come after you arrived in London?"

"No."

"Any visitors or telephone calls?"

There had been none. It looked as if the writer of the letter had been curiously content with the one shot that had brought the signora to England.

"You said just now that in any case you intended showing this letter to the police. Then why haven't you done so in the two weeks you've been here?"

"I don't like the cops," she said frankly, "and while I thought there was maybe something worth while in it for me I wasn't going to bother 'em with a little thing like that. They turn you inside out anyways, and I'd rather my time in the States was let lie doggo now. Besides, I was waiting for something else to happen. It was only when all this fuss about Sampson didn't get any better that I thought it wouldn't look so good for me to have a letter of this kind that might be evidence, seeing it mentioned Grenacre Mansions and all. But I was putting it off, and I'm glad you folk picked me up first before I could go to you."

An interesting sidelight, thought Pardoe, on the crook mentality which continues to maintain a respectful distance between itself and the arm of the law long after the necessity is past. It was clear that Bianca Tommaseo, however innocent in the matter, had preferred the initiative to be taken by the police.

Before leaving she gave him again the half-fearful look he had glimpsed in the mortuary.

"They've bumped Humphrey," she said. "How do I know they won't get me?"

Pardoe reassured her. "As a material witness for the prosecution when that stage is reached, you'll be under our protection from now on."

He did not point out that "they" had had every chance of getting her in the past fortnight and had held their hand, nor that the watch kept on her would be as much in the Yard's interests as her own.

CHAPTER XXI: A BUMP ON THE HEAD

This cuff was but to knock at your ear, and beseech listening.
THE TAMING OF THE SHREW.

"JUDGED BY HER OWN STANDARDS," Pardoe said, "the woman's honest enough—and a bit of a moron, perhaps. It takes a brilliant and subtle mind to put up a story that's at once naive and convincing, and I'd say she isn't brainy at all. Enough of a sucker, at any rate, to make a snap at the bait in that letter and come on a little gold-digging expedition to England."

"Which she didn't pursue once she'd got here," the assistant commissioner reminded him.

"I know. She hadn't the courage. It's one thing to land here in the belief you're going to renew contact with an American racketeer with plenty to hide up of his past career, and quite another to find that the Vick in question—to all intents and purposes—is the highly respectable brother who, with his wife, has every right to show you the door as free as look at you. No, this inaction on the Tommaseo's part helps to establish her innocence. Guilty, she'd have known that Sampson, missing or not, was actually Humphrey."

"What I can't understand," the A.C. remarked in an uncommonly testy voice, for this horrible equation of Sampson and Humphrey which he felt had plumbed the extremity of bad taste had shaken his self-control, "what I *can't* understand is what Vick's murderer or accessory thought he was going to gain by writing those two letters."

"I agree it doesn't jump to the eye, sir. But if you think it over, motive does appear. Here you've got a man reported missing on September 26 and, to the murderer at least, known to be dead. But the police who are at work on the problem are looking for one man, namely Sampson, while the murderer has dealt with another, namely Humphrey. Now it would be to the advantage of the murderer—"

"Damn the fellow. Call him X."

"To the advantage of X for the police to find out early that Sampson is Humphrey—"

"Why the devil?" the A.C. interrupted sharply.

"Because it might safely be assumed that Humphrey had plenty of enemies in the American underworld from which he came, and once the police had tumbled to the identity of the missing Vick X banked on their attention being diverted *from himself.*"

"Which means," said the A.C., recovering his spirits a little, "that X isn't associated with Humphrey Vick's past. Isn't that rather a daring theory?"

"I don't think so, sir. Apart from the assurances we've had from New York City and the Federal Bureau that the large and small fry alike who might be considered enemies or hangers-on of Vinny the Backer's old crowd are safely accounted for in the States, this inducement to get Bianca Tommaseo to England supports the idea. X might reasonably hope that if he could get her to London on the strength of an anonymous letter which, mind, he'd like her to show to the police, she'd fall under suspicion. But if he were really connected with her, belonging, that is, to the American end of the business, it's the last thing he'd try for. Criminals working in collaboration are individually safer the greater the distance between them."

"I see your point. But suppose X is a gangster who is the woman's enemy as well as Vick's—wouldn't he like then to get her convicted of his own crime?"

"I still think her presence unduly stresses the mobster side of it, if he really belonged to some such fraternity. And there's the letter to Mrs. Vick to consider, too."

"Yes. And why two and a half weeks between the posting of them?"

"The delay is important if we accept the theory that he wrote the letters to create diversion. Note the dates—all along dates are of the utmost importance whether they relate to Vick, Mitfold, or both. Bianca Tommaseo's letter was written on September 27, directly after the murder of Vick. Mrs. Vick's letter, posted last Sunday, was written a matter of a few hours after the murder of Mitfold. The implication is he's laying a false scent at each crisis of his own affairs."

"It can be, I agree. It's a bit puzzling, you know, why he put Mrs. Vick on the Mentone trail when the other woman had been in London a fortnight."

Pardoe shrugged. "Look at what it meant to us, sir. Enquiry abroad instead of at home, and consequent delay. X no doubt argued that every minute he could keep us busy elsewhere was a minute gained for himself. So it was, in a way."

"Then he knew the Tommaseo hadn't been to the Yard with the letter?"

"He must have known. He probably kept some sort of watch on her from the time she landed to see how far she was going to be an asset to him. It didn't suit his book to know that we were ignorant of her presence here."

In the silence that followed, the A.C. directed at Pardoe a long, acutely worried look from eyes that were usually lazy and cynical. Even in comparatively innocuous matters his was the nature to which a hush-hush policy makes the readiest appeal; and it was dawning on him that there could be no question of hush- hush in this appalling affair. There would be instead no end of a yapping, and something of a stink, and soaring newspaper sales—every manifestation, indeed, that his training and outlook most deprecated.

"Don't think I'm completely batty, Pardoe," he said abruptly, "if I put a question to you for the last time: is there no possible chance that the body is Sampson's after all?"

The inspector was sufficiently immune to surprise to answer calmly.

"None at all, sir, I'm afraid." His tone held the right note of regret, for, though he did not share his preference for camouflaging the ugly, with the New Year honors looming unpleasantly near he sympathized with his superior's anxiety. "The medical evidence alone would be enough, and we've much more than that. Sir Lewis Blayne is definite that the body found in Hammer Street wearing the clothes Sampson Vick wore when he left home on the evening of September 25 has never suffered arthritis in any degree. Sampson was racked with it. The miraculous cure, too, supposed to have been effected, would still remain a mystery—for his American doctors know he was a victim to it at the time of his retirement to his mountain shack, and since he's been in England he's had scarcely any medical attention at all, certainly none for arthritis."

"Exhumation of the body buried over there would settle the question, wouldn't it?"

"Of course, sir," Pardoe said, marveling at the stubbornness of hope, "but that's a last and unnecessary resort. The identifiable scars are Humphrey's. The American photographs are irrefutable evidence of that. And so many things that clamored for attention when we started out to look for Sampson are explained now that we've found Humphrey."

"For instance—?"

"His reluctance to write anything beyond the absolutely essential signatures. Why? If he were Sampson and had recovered from the disease which had prevented him writing before, force of habit isn't a good enough answer.

But since he was Humphrey, whose hand differed so noticeably from his brother's crabbed and painful one—you've seen specimens of both we've been sent—well, the unwillingness simply becomes an imperative precaution."

The A.C. nodded. "The photographs too," he contributed with a sigh. "I mean, the absence of any pictures of Sampson in middle life—though we know some to have been taken."

"Yes. Humphrey would have had to destroy them. The resemblance between the brothers, though strong, couldn't be gambled against the camera's possible betrayal. Look at his shrinking from publicity—oh yes, I know Sampson was a quiet enough chap, but his dislike of the limelight when he was in the States had nothing abnormal about it. Again, worth thinking about if the missing man were really Sampson, but perfectly explicable once you grant he's Humphrey."

Picking up a pencil the A.C. ground its point thoughtfully into a piece of blotting paper under his hand.

"You're not even connecting up with the murder those letters Vick got in February, are you?"

"We've proved they were the usual hot air. There's nothing remarkable about them—any prominent public figure's likely to be squirted at in the same way. He got them after he made a New Year gift of £100,000 to Magnus City Hospital. Three of them came one after the other in two consecutive weeks—badly written, dirty notes, asking for money and uttering vague threats. They carried the New York postmark, and there are two rather important things to note in connection with them—first, the writer obviously didn't know that Sampson wasn't Sampson, for if he'd known he'd have used his knowledge as a weapon; and secondly, Vick treated them lightly and had no objection to discussing them with both his wife and his secretary."

"So that you believe his sudden decision to sort his letters himself had nothing to do with the American letters?"

"I'm sure it didn't. I'm equally sure, though, that Vick wouldn't have minded that interpretation being put upon his action—it would have served to hide the real motive. Because I fancy something else had begun to happen soon after the New Year."

The A.C. cocked an eyebrow at him and stuck the pencil through the blotting paper.

Pardoe answered the unspoken query.

"Blackmail."

The A.C. depressed his chin and lifted his thin melancholy eyebrows into his hair.

"Those checks to self," he murmured dreamily, waggling the pencil. "But he liked the sort of charity that sees what it's doing, didn't he?"

"I know. Funny, isn't it, we've been unable to trace any of these casual beneficiaries? And the amounts on the stubs range from £100 to £1000, and—

a very significant feature—rise steadily from the first cheque drawn to self in January to the last at the end of July. Sums paid out for charitable purposes aren't likely to show this smooth crescendo. But blackmail is—and does."

"And that accounts for Vick taking over the secretarial duties?"

"That's what we think. It must have occurred to him—" Pardoe broke off, and then went on eagerly, "I say, why shouldn't those letters from the U.S. themselves have suggested it to him? I mean, that it was possible X would add written to verbal blackmail, in which case whatever it was he wanted to hide—which we now know to have been his identity—would in all probability come to light, at any rate as far as Miss Channing was concerned. So he took steps to preclude any such disaster."

Blacker and blacker, thought the A.C. This fellow, with a baronetcy in the offing—and, by gad, that made it a degree worse than if it had been a knighthood—doing all he could to maintain his perfectly monstrous imposture in the eyes of the world. And yet—

"Pardoe," he said quietly, "blackmailers are murdered more often than they murder. Why do you think X killed the goose that laid the golden eggs?"

"Because, sir, I think the goose in desperation refused to lay another. Not only that, I think he may injudiciously have turned the tables and become a menace to X."

"How?"

"By threatening to disclose X's blackmailing proclivities. Vick was probably not the only victim. And if he was pushed so far that he was prepared to let X give him away rather than dance to his tune any longer, that same courage of desperation was certainly equal to betraying X. In short, he may have become both a negative and a positive loss to the blackmailer—and better eliminated."

"It's only too convincing, dammit," said the A.C. reluctantly. "And they used the Hammer Street house for winding up the business? Sorry, that's grim in the circumstances, but you know what I mean."

"Yes. The agents can't help there, as they say no prospective purchaser's been over the place since last May. Besides, X didn't use the front door and so never needed to apply for the key to take an impression, or anything like that. The back door was far less conspicuous. He had only to chance on a key that fitted—and look how alike all those doors are—or, more probably, use a skeleton. Anyhow, I doubt they made use of the place more than two or three times at most. It would have been running too great a risk even in the blackout to make it a regular rendezvous."

"Why not only the once?"

"I was thinking of X, sir, not Vick, when I said two or three times. He had to be there, you see, at least once, and I fancy oftener, before September 25, to—dig a grave."

The A.C. suppressed a fastidious shiver and looked up.

"Considering Vick turns out to be the racketeer, don't you think it odd that anybody was able to lure him like that into an empty house?"

"You mean he should have been wise to such tricks? Ah, but don't underrate X. He's no fool. As soon as he made up his mind to get rid of Vick—say, any time after the end of July when that last check was drawn, and Humphrey got obdurate—he drew in his horns, we can be sure, and somehow lulled the other into a false sense of security. Humphrey *was* a bit of a sucker, you know. That's how Balthasar got hold of him. And beside the enormity of his own secret which X had been holding over his head all the year, his own threat to inform against X as a blackmailer must have seemed small beer indeed. I mean, he wouldn't have suspected X was plotting his murder. But X had a ten years' stretch to think about. Once Vick had counter- threatened, with the resolution the turning worm can show, and convinced X he meant it, he'd signed his own death warrant. But it's just from that time that X would have played him ve-ry gently."

After a pause Pardoe added: "The house was excellently placed as regards Carlyle Square."

"Sir George Ling's place?"

"Yes. Vick was in the habit of going there now and again—and you remember the taxi man on September 25 has sworn he didn't ring the bell while he was watching. He had only to come out of the gate as soon as the taxi was gone, leave the square, cut a little way along King's Road and down Manor Street and he was there. Another thing, sir—he need never have known the tryst was at an *empty* house, especially if his last was his only visit."

The A.C. agreed. Then he frowned. "Funny thing, y'know, for a wary devil like X to leave the back door unfastened that very night."

Pardoe was silent a moment. Then, "That very night's our answer, sir. He was waiting for his partner in the crime—enter Second Murderer, in fact. They were going to kill Vick. And it would take two of them at any rate to tidy up the job. And looking at it from X's point of view, what grave risk was he running after all in merely closing without locking the back door of an empty house on a night of late September? It was clear to him that nobody ever came there. Why should they? And there were no possible means by which he could have foreseen Archy Mitfold's blunder in the dark."

"In fact," said the A.C., "he probably thought it was his partner arriving when Mitfold opened the door."

"Which is why the voices didn't stop immediately the boy came in."

"It's the very hell of a business," the A.C. said gloomily after a minute. "And you think you've got—?"

Pardoe sketched for him the indications of the evidence to date. In the course of doing so he produced two small, dark, round objects which rolled a little way as he put them down in front of the A.C. and explained what they were.

The A.C.'s saturnine expression cleared. "Good enough, my lad, good enough. One, I know, you got from under the linoleum. Where was the other?"

"In the grave."

The A.C. picked up one of the balls, rolled it between finger and thumb, and said nothing.

"I'm glad of that," Pardoe added in a low voice. I'm not a vindictive bloke, but I'm glad that bit of evidence comes from the grave."

The A.C., pursuing a logical line of thought, filled the pause with a question about Philip Beltane.

"We shan't have him talking till tomorrow at earliest, sir," Pardoe said. "He was nearly a goner, you see. But his very delirium is revealing."

"The spotted crake?"

"Not precisely its identity. But a very interesting thing has come to light. It's this. His ravings tell us he knows the bird is a crake. How? Beltane saw only the sketches on an envelope which were not good enough for even Speyer to put a name to. If he was lying when he told me he didn't recognize the bird, then he had something to hide. If he wasn't lying, how and when did he identify it? At some time between my visit to Witley on Tuesday and his mishap in the garage Wednesday afternoon. Of course—but that doesn't tell us how, because whether he consulted a person or a book his reference couldn't possibly have been 'crake' or 'spotted crake'—you can't look up a name you haven't thought of. Therefore, it was *another name* he hunted up, and the answer was 'spotted crake.' "

"Q.E.D.," said the A.C. "Somebody he guessed at?"

"Or he was trying out names, as you might with a crossword—or——"

"Or?"

"It was his own."

The A.C. looked at him sharply. Apparently satisfied with what he saw, he said in a quiet voice, "You didn't by any chance leave the sketches with him?"

"You're implying, sir, he might have studied them at leisure or with help after I'd gone, and found out that way? Oh no, I held on to them. And I saw Beltane some hours before I picked up the colored one in Miss Leaf's hall."

Recollection of the tantalizing thing started Pardoe on the chase again. This time they hunted it together.

"It's like our paper war," the A.C. said. "Leaflet dropping, don't y'know? Of course a thing like that would skim a certain distance, wouldn't it?"

"I know, sir," Pardoe said with a touch of impatience, "but if you're thinking of the front door it's definitely out of it."

"I wasn't," the A.C. said in a tone of mild apology. "And you trust that girl?"

"Who—Vera Moffat? She had nothing to do with it."

"And Miss Leaf?"

"Was next door."

The A.C. sighed. "And those bent edges mean it was kept inside a book smaller than itself."

Pardoe agreed. Memory suddenly began to stir. Aural memory cooperated with visual—Marian Leaf describing her nephew's diary, "a red book, not very large"—himself returning to Mulberry Fountain last Tuesday night and coming into an unlighted hall.

The A.C. stared with amazement at the changed expression on his chief inspector's face. Pardoe was returning his look with bright, unseeing eyes, smiling mouth and clenched fist which he suddenly brought down on the desk to the imminent peril of the little round objects that still reposed there. The A.C. caught them in the nick of time.

"*Got* it, sir!" Pardoe was almost shouting. "I know where Archy Mitfold's diary went—and, gosh, the devilish simplicity of it!" He dropped his voice and ran on excitedly, "I bumped my head in the hall at Mulberry Fountain in the dark—on one of those ponderously framed oils. Then after the girl had lit up we found the sketch of the bird. Don't you see—I dislodged it when I shook the picture! It means the diary's there—Mitfold's diary. Here's top marks for the presence of mind that poor little devil showed. He hid his diary in the best and handiest place possible on his way to open the door to his murderer. I'll eat my hat if it's not there now—no, I won't—I'll put it on my addled pate and go see for meself!"

CHAPTER XXII: LEAVES FROM A DIARY

My tables—meet it is I set it down.
HAMLET.

IT WAS THERE. From the apex of the triangle formed by the wall and the tilt of the massive frame Pardoe drew out a notebook in thick red covers faintly clouded with dust. It was Salt who picked up the jagged, extremely dirty scrap of blotting paper that fluttered down at the same time.

"The remains of the penwiper," Pardoe said. "The watercolor sketch of the bird must have slid forward in the same way when I jostled the picture, but only partially. It didn't complete its fall until after Vera and I left the hall. I know that, because when she snapped on the light it wasn't on the floor."

"And the book was too 'eavy to get the jolt." The sergeant nodded.

They turned back to the room where Archy had died, Pardoe weighing the diary lovingly in his hand.

"It's plain what happened, Tommy. We can reconstruct it as clearly as if we'd seen it. Mitfold's writing here"—he indicated the couch—"flipping his blotter pellets at the waste paper basket. There's a ring at the door, or a knock—

we know his light's been seen. We can't say what degree of fear he felt at that moment, but the discovery of the diary tells us he foresaw the possibility of his visitor being X. He's not going to ignore him—there's always a chance it's somebody harmless—and if it isn't, well, the showdown's got to come sooner or later and he'll let X have it. Let him know that he knows he's responsible for the attacks on him, as well as for some shady goings on in Hammer Street. I don't believe Mitfold thought X would kill him then and there. I think his conceit was big enough to let him see himself coming out top that night. He probably imagined himself recovering the diary from its hiding place later. What he was determined to do, though, was to put it out of X's reach. Could he have chosen a better place? Or an easier? On his way to the front door—he wouldn't have to pause to do it—he simply slipped it behind the picture. X could turn the place upside down if he liked—you could still bet your boots he'd never think of looking for it there."

"Think it was 'im shoved that bolt home too?" Salt asked in a puzzled voice, with a parental eye on the diary.

"No, that was the murderer. It isn't hard to see why, either. Archy was somehow in his aunt's house when the place was supposed to be shut up and empty. Suppose, argues X, it's a put-up story, and there's more of 'em hanging around? Miss Leaf or the girl may come in unexpectedly with her latchkey. So X isn't content at having the latch dropped behind him. He slips the bolt while Archy leads the way in."

"And I'll say 'e didn't think of looking for the diary. Mightn't 'ave known Mitfold wrote one."

"That's probable. They came to blows, and X had the luck to knock Mitfold out, because, I fancy, the fender got in the way. In the excitement of improvising a murder after getting home an unpremeditated blow like that, it's not likely he'd pay any attention to the inky fingers and the evidence we found in and around the basket. He'd go through the desk as a precaution, but it's obvious he didn't grasp the significance of the bird drawings, else he'd never have left that envelope for us to find."

"Then he didn't know his own name was—?"

"Not then—he does now, though," Pardoe said cheerfully. "Come on, old man. Home's the proper place for a spot of serious reading."

Home being Scotland Yard, they were there in a few minutes.

The book at first glance appeared disappointingly blank. That impression, though, was chiefly due to its size. With the traditional optimism of the diarist at his first entry Archy had scorned a slender volume for the record of his experiences in London. A page inscribed "A.M. *Journal Intime.* Vol. 1.," was succeeded by comparatively few closely written leaves in the fine, economical hand of the exercise books. The margins of the later entries were profusely decorated with sketches of the spotted crake. Pardoe refused to allow

himself or Salt an examination of these until they had made the proper chronological approach to them. They began where Archy had begun.

He had struck out in flowing style early in August with the impressions
made on him during his first week at Mulberry Fountain. They were the usual
dull mixture of self-analysis, insincere appreciation and insufferable criticism,
with the meretricious twang of intimate thoughts itching for public reception.
This pomp and patronage continued for three or four pages; then the writer,
tiring, abruptly descended to laconicisms that had evidently struck Archy as
aphoristic gems worth preserving. When these, too, petered out there was a
considerable hiatus embracing, as Pardoe saw, the Pandulf Road cyclist's
death and the subsequent broadcast; Archy had plainly grown weary of his
diary or else had paid no attention to the incident. The next entry dealt with
Mr. Caffey's overcoat and book in a few pungent lines omitting comment on
the Nordic Bond meeting. The outbreak of war a day or two later got some
cliches markedly inferior to the diarist's usual standard. At the time, indeed,
they were in the nature of a final effort, for after September 4 the journal had
been laid aside for three weeks.

When it was taken up again the style had undergone a change. The change
was so complete that it was as if the diary were being resumed by another
hand. In a sense, thought Pardoe, this was true: what they had been reading
was the work of a *poseur* truckling to imagined approbation; what they were
going to read was an unforced record made primarily for the use of the recorder.

Sept. 25–26. Something worth sticking down here? I don't know. But I
shall find out. To do that I must make a few notes of the evidence to date, if
only to clarify things for myself.

A letter from Dad yesterday to say Mother's coming to town next week,
and will I be nice to her. What a bloody bore. He asked, too, if I'd keep my
eyes skinned for a copy of Barrough's *Method of Physick*, a seventeenth-
century medical tome he's keen to have. Thought I may as well give Winkle
the chance of a sale. Can't be often he makes one. Went around to the Juniper
where he had the window out and was dressing it in style, he said, for Benny's
latest outpourings. Hadn't got book. Never has. Asked him how he got his
bread and butter. He quoted Macduff's beastly child at me and then was
contemptuously astonished at my immoderate laughter. I retorted with *Titus
Andronicus*, Act 4, Scene 2, my hand thrust out in the right direction. He was
rattled because he couldn't place the quotation so served up Bel's old gibe
about me and the classics.

Home to lunch where Aunt Marie was off her feed again. I seem to do all
the eating. Spent afternoon wrestling with French essay. S. says . . . (*Rest of
this sentence scribbled out.*)

Then night, and time for my coaching, and something very odd before I
got it.

It happened simply because the blinking battery in my torch conked out, and I didn't know in time to get a new one. So I missed my way to Rossetti Terrace. It was infernally dark, and, as I've been late several times, and old S. is ungracious about unpunctuality, I put my best foot foremost with such a vengeance that enthusiasm carried me too far. I hurried by the Terrace and came into H. St. instead, though I didn't know it then. Turned into what I took for S.'s gate and round to the back as usual and never guessed anything was wrong till a whole lot of scratchy leaves brushed my face near the back steps. Even then I supposed I'd only sidestepped a bit in the dark, as I don't know his new house well. But with the doorknob in my hand it flashed on me this wasn't the right place. Some quite little thing gave it away—the way the door opened, perhaps. Next minute I was looking into a black, cold passage. Nothing was visible, but everything was *unfamiliar*. (If that sounds mad, A.M., you know you don't have to *see* to feel strange things.)

My first idea was the place was empty. It was only a passing notion then, though, because next thing I heard was talking going on. Very quiet talking, whispers really, and it seemed to be close to my left ear. It was coming from below. So there was somebody downstairs. I had the knob in my hand and was keeping still as death, because, though it takes a long time to write, I'd barely jumped to it by then that I was in the wrong house. If the voices had kept to that buzzy pitch I wouldn't have heard a word. But all at once one of them said aloud: "Try it and see. Two can squeal." It was a queer voice, rough but attractive. It reminded me of the voice of a Canadian *locum* Dad once had. Then another voice said, very slowly: "Not—in—this—case." And I nearly jumped out of my skin, because I knew who that was.

It's impossible that I can have made a mistake. You can't hear a voice as many times, on and off, as I've heard that one and not recognize it. Now this is where I've got to be very careful if I mean to keep this thing close. No real names. Not where I talk about H. St. I shall call him C. Nobody but I, not even C. himself, knows that that letter is the letter of his own name.

The other voice I didn't know said: "Why not?" It sounded defiant and confident.

C. laughed. It was the beastliest little laugh under his breath.

I've heard it before. I loathed it when I was a kid. Now it sounded right in my ear.

The Canadian voice said something I couldn't catch, but C.'s answer came distinctly: "Well, we can make it midnight next time." He sounded more conciliatory. But I always said that's when you've got to watch him.

Then the first speaker said: "Now your friend's here can't we go upstairs and settle this in the light?"

C. said on a high note, "Who's here? Nobody's here."

And the other said: "Somebody opened the door."

There was dead silence. I could hear one of them breathing. I think it was

C. I didn't like it. Thought it was time to scram. Slipped away and pulled the door to without shutting it. When I got round the corner of the house somebody was in the garden. Lucky I've rubber soles. Then the door closed properly. Perhaps they decided the wind had opened it. Hurried away and found out the name of the street from a passerby. Easy enough then to get to the Terrace, but I walked about a few minutes puzzling why C. was in the basement of a house in H. St. carrying on a phony conversation. Squealing always means ratting, doesn't it?

Went back to H. St. this morning to find the house. Amazed to see it *is* an empty one. Can be no mistake, as in the darkness I had to count gates to find S. What the devil can it mean?

Put into execution a really corking idea I got last night. It ought to mystify C. and will give me the chance to keep tabs on him without rousing his suspicions. After leaving H. St. I rang him up from a call box in King's Road. Didn't give my name, of course, but when I'd got his "Hello," assuming a voice as unlike mine as possible, said, "A Friend speaking. Sorry I barged in on you in Hammer Street last night."

There was no answer. I'd have liked to hear the gasp at the other end of the line they tell you about in the bloods. But there wasn't anything. Hung up and went home. Shall enjoy myself watching C.'s reactions.

Feel awfully excited. Childish, I know, but I do. This chase will ginger life up a bit, and anyway it's not bad being for once in a position of superiority to C.

Sept. 27. Am writing this in the afternoon because I didn't get to bed till 3 A.M. Pretended to go usual time but meant to be in H. St. at 12 in case C. and friend turned up for the midnight tryst C. hinted at. Renewed battery in torch and oiled the basement key. Find I can easily slip in and out that way with no chance of waking Auntie. Good for me this is an early-to-bed house.

Vigil useless. Quite likely, though, they wouldn't be there the very next night, unless business is pressing. Said good night to a bobby in H. St., which I reached just on midnight, and passed by number eight because I thought he might be looking. When coast was clear slipped back and approached the house very cautiously. Tried back door again. It was locked. Might mean they hadn't come yet or else were inside and had taken care to lock up after them. Found a bush commanding view of door and prepared to wait in spirit of Micawber. Would have liked to examine back windows then and there, but being round about 12 there was the chance they'd come and nab me if I did. So preferred to be Tar Baby and Br'er Fox for a while.

Nothing happened. Only the still night and tiny sounds one can't account for, and the black column of the house in front of me, looking grimmer in the mass than when I'd seen its empty face by daylight. I let an hour go by, feet getting colder and imagination livelier. Then I poked about the windows very delicately with my torch. As far as I could see none are curtained in any way, and there's one small one in basement looking onto what I think are stairs, which would have been on my left when I stood in the doorway Monday night. Query: when they come here how do they manage their lights? Improvised blackout screens that are moved afterwards in case they're noticed in the daytime? But there was no light Monday. And anyway you can't turn up lights in empty houses—they're not there. But even a candle would have shown me a glimmer, for their voices were so near there could have been no closed door between them and me. And what game is there you can carry on in the dark?

Any jolly old how, my game's assured—snoop, snoop, snoop, and then some. And am I thrilled?

2 A.M. Just got back from second visit. Nix again. Is it possible they only hang out there Mondays? I can't be sure, in which case I may have another four nights to go without results.

Sept. 29. That was very nearly my last word in this journal. Don't know how or why I'm still alive. Going to S. last night, was all but slaughtered in T.'s Row by blasted Jehu at the wheel of a black saloon, who circled once round the fountain before coming at me, neck or nothing. No clear recollection of what happened or how I saved myself, but came out of it with no broken bones, though I pretty well made a dint in the pavement. The foul bus went too fast for me to tell what make it was, and the fellow who came out of a house close by and helped me up didn't know either. Dusty, grazed, unpresentable, split sleeve and torn sock, decided nevertheless to go on to S. He wasn't there when I got in. First time I haven't found him waiting. Came in a few minutes later. *Much* concerned. Anxious to know if I'd got number and make of car. Told him, no, my own number was so nearly up I hadn't paid attention to anybody else's. Sally went unappreciated, because his idiomatic English is deficient. Persuaded me to wash my hands and face, pressed iodine and arnica on me and, better still, a good stiff drink. Convinced myself as I went over it to S. that it was no accident. It looked like a staged hit-and-run. Possibly the swine had fiendish notions of a little joke. Anyway Colney Hatch is his proper home.

General stiffness and bruises and pelting rain after supper kept me in last night. Ought not to weaken so soon, but another idea is germinating which may quicken the scent. I shall go again tonight, though.

Winkle called before tea when I was at the dentist's and Auntie shopping. Left word with V. that he'd got the *Physick* for me in Charing Cross Road with a bundle of other stuff for himself. Parcel will be at Juniper this evening if I care to call. I don't. Morning will do.

Evening post brought a card from Bel. He will be in town tomorrow till Sunday night, and would I care to have supper with him and do a show afterwards. Don't answer if yes. Shall I? Could be fun, and need not interfere with what I plan for Saturday night.

Sept. 30. Thought my luck could hardly last. V. heard the basement door early this morning and came down to the kitchen to have it out. Can't let her in on it, but she'll stand by me.

Again nobody at the house in H. St. These solo vigils ought to be deadening, but they're not. Brain very active if pins and needles elsewhere. The thing gets tighter hold of me every day. Am full of ideas about C. and Co.'s activities. I plump for espionage or gaming (faro or the wheel) with odds on the spies, because the other involves more people and is not so workable in a house known to be empty. Besides, spying could be carried on under cover of C.'s ostensibly innocent work.

Funny about that car Thursday night. It dashed off the way it had come after cruising slowly into the square and round the fountain. And there's no exit from Mulberry F. other than entry, so why come in at all?

Called at Juniper this morning and collected Barrough. Nice copy in old calf. 1652. £3 15s. Sounds salty to me, but Dad don't think so when he's set on a book. Winkle was unusually amiable and flattered at my admiration of his window, which is really O.K. Said it reminded me of Mickleham on the North Downs. Waited for him to bring up my Narrow Escape the other evening, but he said nowt. Supposed V. didn't mention it yesterday. (Turned out she hadn't thought of it when he was there.) I'm glad, as I've now my own ideas about that show and don't intend to share them.

Tried to do a spot of work on my German this afternoon. Mind wasn't on it, because busy with my plan for tonight—after I leave Bel. Am not going to freeze in H. St. this time, but shall go to that speakeasy in Old Compton Street where C. was said to hang out so much. Benny left off going after the police took names in May. Before my time. All I know is hearsay, but maybe somebody there can give me a line on C. I hanker after a bit of sleuthing anyway. Perhaps C. himself will be there.

Later. Supper with Bel at seven-thirty at the Gentilhomme in Greek Street. Resisted a violent temptation then and there to take a look at the club only a stone's throw away. Bel has a perfectly foul cold, so show's off. He was willing to try it, but I said no. He's practically lost his voice and yaps like a sick crow. Suits me, as I'd like some time to myself before going back to Soho. 10:30 now with Aunt M. already gone to bed and me yawning my head off after three or four nights on the slates. Shall get my second wind soon.

Got in a neat one tonight by suggesting that Bel collected his germs chasing around town these nippy evenings. But he won't be drawn. The beggar turns frosty directly you bring up his weekly jaunts.

Looked over my German again before pretending to go to bed. Hopeless mess. All avian portraits of C.! Sunday ought to be fairly quiet. Must scrap it and begin again or S. will turn nasty.

(N.B. If it should ever be necessary for anyone else to read this diary I hope they'll have the percipience to spot the cleverest thing in it. I mean my double references to one of the characters. I congratulate myself on that piece of disguise.)

Oct. 1. Too fagged to write much, though couldn't stay long at club last night without rousing suspicion.

Rather exciting sort of place, but not at first glance. Shabby outside, not unlike a warehouse, which it probably was. Ultra smart in, shaded lights, blue and silver furnishings, rather bored people—everything in undertones. Too discreet to be true. Very smart Turks in scarlet fezzes sold chocolates. They looked as slick and burnished as the travel agency posters. Cabaret was tame and virtuous, drinks good, music not so hot. There was a spot of seemly dancing. The floor wasn't at all crowded. By the time I got there a few of the couples were a bit screwed, but nothing riotous. But I couldn't help feeling there was an undercurrent of something different from the air of ennui on the surface. Why? Because (a) besides two muscular toughs at the door there's another chucker-out with a pug's head and shoulders behind a curtain near the bar entrance, who emerges now and again like a hideous jack-in-the-box. Why, since the place *looks* fit to bring Aunt M. to? (b) People keep disappearing through said curtain *and not reappearing.* (c) If the place is only all it looks not even Benny, much less C., would have fagged coming here more than once.

Spotted only one girl I know, and her only slightly. Hardboiled friend of Anna's, dance instructress, I think. She and escort made a blasé couple. Exchanged weary smiles, after which I joined her. Had to reintroduce self; then brought up C. She shrugged and said she hadn't seen him there some time. Looked a bit vicious, I thought, but maybe only natural look. Asked what was behind curtain. She said, "Look and see." So I did. The first thing was the chucker, the second a small extension of the bar proper which lies to left of it. Nothing out of the way about it except the look the bruiser gave me and fact the place was empty. Why, since I followed half a minute after another fellow? Only other exit is main bar. I strolled through and he wasn't there. Directly I'd done it felt it was a blunder not to have stopped for a drink at little bar. When I got back to dance floor via main bar the pug was this side the curtain eyeing me. Came away soon after, as I want another night here and overzeal at first won't do.

While I remember it, C.'s car is *not* a black saloon. But begging, borrowing or stealing is not beyond him.

Oct. 3. C. tried to kill me at S. Square this afternoon where I went to meet Mother. She wasn't there. I was far too early and hadn't been on platform 5 minutes before I saw C. near exit. Too many people about just then for me to keep him in sight. When I moved down that way to speak to him he'd vanished. Had to wait 20 minutes longer but didn't see him again though I was vigilant all the time. When right train came in at last hanging about (as well as that glimpse of C.) had so got on my nerves that I moved forward without bothering to look round me any more. There was a small squash behind. All at once, when everybody was rubbernecking the train, I got a vicious punch in back that sent me sprawling toward the platform drop. Having only one decent hand to clutch with, was nearly over the edge. I wasn't really hurt, the squawks at the back were the most unnerving. Large stout dame grabbed me, and one or two others lingered, but there was a concerted rush past, and C. could have got away by simple trick of boarding train.

This thing is getting past writing about. It's too much in my brain now. I can't look at it from the outside any longer. When that happens you don't talk or write the things. Difficult to explain, but they get too *possessive* to get off one's chest.

Later. I did *not* tell C. I was meeting Mother today. I was at station much too soon. So was he. If he'd known which train I was meeting he'd have been on time and not risked recognition by hanging around so long beforehand. It means he simply tailed me there this afternoon. So tabs he's keeping are pretty close.

Queer that Mother didn't come.

Oct. 4. I know who was with C. in the house in H. St. I know. I *know. I* know. And *does* it make you feel good, A.M.? You've got the whip hand of C.C. who tried to smash you in a car and throw you under a train. C. who . . . (*rest of sentence obliterated.*) You know. And you can tell what you know when you like. But there's more to get first.

Sat through newsreel twice. There's no mistake. Coming out of cinema, a mad impulse sent me to nearest call box to ring up C., but he wasn't at either place. Put a call through after tea at kiosk in King's Road where I rang him before. Got him this time. Said, "Friend again. How's that founder of Wenborough Hospital?" Didn't wait for answer. Hurried home to those newspapers in shed.

Aunt M. very upset about yesterday still, and inclined to read all sorts of nasty things now into that car business. Without prompting from me. I don't want her to get inquisitive.

Oct. 5. Birthday. Feel thoroughly elated (but not on that account!). Celebrated by sorting my papers. Shall give them a proper rake over and take cuttings. Can see at once date coincides, but know nothing about the bloke and shall have to dig it out to find what he and C. are up to. No job I could enjoy more.

Must post book to Dad. Thought Mother would be taking it back.

Aunt M. thinks of going to Braintree weekend after this. Suggests I have a change, too, and come along.

Remembered today I rang up C. in my own voice yesterday. Oh well. He doesn't seem to have doubted.

Oct. 9. Too seedy to bother about diary. Ill since Thursday night. All my strength has gone into stopping Aunt M. from fetching doctor. Doc in this case means police. I don't want them yet. This is my show. I can beat C. to it. He tried to poison me with chocolates I was blithering ass enough to eat. Auntie's got it in her head the Nordics are at the bottom of it all. Am rather glad she's on that tack. Whatever happens she mustn't think it's C.

Letter from Dad with cash. Says he forgot to post postcard about Gertrude going to Derby instead of here. Kept it in his pocket as usual. So fate took a hand at S. Sq.

Auntie very anxious now I should cut out of town and go with her. Too busy to argue, so suppose I will.

Oct. 10. Feel rather chirpy again, only sick about the days and nights I've missed on the job.

Letter from S. Asked Aunt M. to ring him yesterday to explain why I was giving my coaching a miss. *Again* much concerned. He was told gastritis.

Went round to pay Winkle for the Barrough. While we jawed found myself making one of my eternal clay birds and sticking it on the counter. He looked at it quite blankly, however.

Oct. 11. A pretty awful idea came to me last night. About the other fellow. Suppose he hasn't cleared off in the way I think? Suppose . . . (*Rest scribbled out.*) I'm frightened. Am definitely not going to Essex Friday. Told Aunt M. so. I must not lose time out of London now. Besides, I want to go to the St. Crispin lunch Saturday. Bel and Winkle will be there. Three heads may be better than one. Aunt M. says impossible I stay here alone. Don't mind where I am. Important thing is not to let C., figuratively speaking, out of my sight.

Oct. 12. Aunt M. very sick at me not going away with her tomorrow. Insists on shutting shop and parking me elsewhere. Pell and daughter will take me in! No matter. The only thing now is to stay put in town. Can't drive that home to Auntie without skating dangerously near mention of C. She must not suspect. I think she finds O.C. lunch plausible enough reason for my change of front, though such sudden keenness is puzzling! That, too, I can't explain to her.

Interesting tutorial this evening. How I like watching people's reactions. S. *very* troubled. Says chocolates should be analyzed, *und so weiter, nicht wahr!* I smile and accept it all meekly. Bring out one of my clay birds and stick him on table. Evokes no response from S. He has a prize poker face.

Suppose C. already suspects Aunt M. of knowing everything? I must hurry.

Oct. 13. Eleven A.M. Moving in to Mrs. Pell's after tea, which I'll have at station when I see Aunt M. off. My diary stays here. Suitcase lock faulty, and Mrs. P. the original Pandora. I shall wait till Monday to make a proper week-end entry. Anyway, time and inclination for writing goes the more action one takes.

Visited club again last night. C. wasn't there. Had a drink in the small bar. Saw nothing suspicious except pug's dreary sentry go which cramped my style of snooping.

Oct. 14. I write this in peculiar circumstances. The sixteenth was to date my next notes, but found I couldn't contain myself till then, especially with such an easy way at hand to get hold of my diary.

I am in the study at home. It's gone nine o'clock, and I've the freedom of an empty house. Am not enjoying it overmuch. How damned noisy silence is.

My double ruse should have thrown C. off my track tonight. Told everyone I was going round to S. And I came in the back way over the wall. This was both possible and expedient. Possible, because yesterday before leaving I slipped the basement key in my pocket, a mechanical action nowadays when the house is locked up, but I let it stay. I'm glad of it. If there was the remote chance C. started to tail me when I left Alma Square tonight and is keeping an eye on Mulberry Fountain, it's a front door entry he would spot. Also, the Beatons in their front room could hear me come in that way. What with taxi and doubling round these streets I ought to have thrown dust in all their eyes.

I wish the house wasn't so beastly still. Silence paralyses thought and movement.

Have had a strange and terribly exciting day. Told Philip and Wynkerrell my story, as much of it as I ever intended telling. I have talked with C. Saw him this evening, in between coming here and the end of the Bel-Winkle powwow in V. St. It was the most curiously oblique conversation, dominated by mutual fear. I couldn't help enjoying it, even to the edge of a rather horrible hysteria. There's a prick of doubt, I know, in his mind that I *am* the fellow with nose to the trail. He was fishing for certainty. After three goes at murder! "Better sure than sorry" was never C.'s motto till he was sorry. But after all, he's only those public phone calls to point to me. And if he doubts, it's a tribute to the way I've handled him. Had to admire skill with which he tried to draw me out without giving himself away. But I was giving nothing either.

It's hard to sort one's thoughts without other people by. Does everybody alone *hear* an empty house at night? I keep breaking off to listen—to what?

Bel and Winkle advise police. It will come to that. But not yet. How desperately C. pounced on the one point I meant him to clutch. The woman at . . .

Here the diary ended abruptly in a wavering scratch the pen had scored deeply across the page.

Only the margin, above and below the final entry, had something still to say. It was crowded with tiny sketches of the spotted crake. Here and there the nib had dug into the paper.

CHAPTER XXIII: THE BIRD

Who would give a bird the lie, though he cry "cuckoo" never so?
A MIDSUMMER NIGHT'S DREAM.

"FUNNY," SAID PHILIP BELTANE, blinking earnestly in a shaft of dazzling autumn sunshine that streamed through the ward window on to his bed, "but I haven't got it right yet. Saturday, is it? Then it was . . ."

"Wednesday you were knocked out. Yes. Now is this all right?"

Pardoe read over the statement he had just taken down. He read slowly and carefully, for Beltane's recovery from the gas was marked less, it seemed, by forgetfulness than by preoccupation with the trivial and irrelevant.

Beltane nodded. "That's it. Afraid I've left it to you to straighten the muddles. I'm still at the stage when telling things sets me rambling off the proper track. But you've got the sequence right. It was two telephone calls I put through after you went away. One before tea and one after. The first, of course, was to Wynkerrell to find out if he knew the bird. You'd said you hadn't yet asked him if he could identify it. So, seeing he was more often in Archy's company than I, it occurred to me he'd have seen the things or heard Archy talk about them. I gave him a ring, describing as best I could and quoting you. But he knew, of course, no more than the rest of us." He frowned heavily, the old bewilderment clouding his face. "It was after tea I thought of the library. I was prepared for a long hunt with nothing at the end of it—for I had to search the indexes in the ornithological section for no bird's name, but the name of a person."

"I knew that," Pardoe agreed. "If we accepted the fact that you didn't recognize the bird, then your remarks about a crake when you were ill could only mean that you'd arrived at it by looking up the name of somebody known to you."

"Yes. It seemed a hopeless job on the face of it. But—I found it quickly."

"And that's when you should have given us a call."

"I know. I know." Beltane rolled his head uneasily on the pillow. "But don't you see? My first thought, I admit, on finding that his was a local name for the spotted crake was—that I'd got Archy's murderer. And I was horrified and scared stiff. My second was, what proof had I of anything of the sort? Archy could have been drawing these birds because the subject of them was his friend and ally in whatever game he had on hand. I didn't know then the kind of thing Archy had said about the sketches to the maid. I felt I *had* to give the

180

crake the benefit of the doubt, a chance to explain—oh, anything you like that wasn't delivering him straight over to the police. So when I rang his number I tried to convince myself I wasn't necessarily ringing a murderer."

"And there was nothing in his manner over the telephone to increase your suspicions?"

"Not a thing. Only, as I remember it, a long silence after I'd told him of my discovery. But that, of course, didn't strike me as unnatural since he'd just heard for the first time what his name meant. Then he said he could easily explain by letting me in on something he'd hoped to keep to himself for a bit longer. He put over the superb bluff that I'd forced his hand, and that if I'd run up to town to see him there would be something at Rossetti Terrace that would solve the puzzle."

"That was the first you knew of Speyer's interest in birds?"

"Oh yes."

"But he didn't want you that night?"

"No. He said he'd be free Wednesday afternoon. Meantime I was to do nothing for fear of queering the pitch, and incidentally Scotland Yard's pitch too, and generally letting the cat out of the bag."

"He bound you to secrecy about going up to town?"

"Yes. I was to come between half-past four and five and say nothing about it. Well, I had to mention it to Franklin so's to arrange for my prep to be taken. But I hoped I'd left an impression of vagueness as to the time the appointment was . . . And then—I never had a chance to keep it."

"Because the day following your bombshell had given him an idea. He would take the train to you instead, the same train that got us down to Witley. He'd wait on the road or in the lane for your car to pick him up. There'd be some pretext—"

"There was. The book I'd dug the spotted crake from. Said he hadn't rung me about it because it might not be removable from the library, in which case I couldn't have brought it to London. He wanted a look at it, then to return to town with me in the car."

"His idea was probably to improve on the original plan of dealing with you in London. There suspicion would be brought close home. But between Witley and the city there are plenty of quiet byroads where a murderer might do his work with less immediate danger to himself. If he waylaid you on the road after you left school it would be easy to pretend that there wasn't time after all to go back for the book."

"That would be it," Beltane said. "But why did he come to the school, then?"

"This was the way of it, let's say. He didn't dare take his ticket to Witley— that's one thing we know, thanks to an observant ticket collector at Banklow— because he'd certainly be remembered at so small a place and connected with Rowan House. So he got out at Banklow; then waited for a bus which he left before it reached Witley. That procedure fits the times patly. Then he'd make his way on foot across the fields and round the back way to the school. He'd given himself far too much time so's not to miss you, and when he reached the lane incautiously drew nearer and nearer until he actually had the garage in view. That's easy as soon as you've passed the turn. Then he had the luck— for him—to catch sight of you preparing to bring the car out."

Beltane looked earnestly at the inspector. "That means he modified his plan for the second time then and there?"

"Yes. There's a curious parallel there to Mitfold's murder—premeditation followed by improvisation at the last. You were alone in the garage, nobody about, everywhere dead still and quiet and screened from sight of the school. He couldn't resist the temptation."

"I'm vague as to what happened, but I know he wasn't more than a few minutes in the garage. We were to go back to the library first and look up the bird again. Then something hit me."

"A spanner. It was flung on the seat of the Head's Bentley. Your back was turned?"

"I was fiddling with the old bus. I don't remember anything more."

Pardoe nodded. "It wouldn't take him more than a minute or two to start your engine, close the doors, and nip quietly off on Mr. Haldane's cycle so as to speed up the most risky part of his return journey. Then the meadows again and a bus, or walk, into Banklow."

After a silence Beltane said: "It's beastly. Murders and things—one never believes they belong to one's own world however much one talks about them." He added as Pardoe rose to go: "You've got the particulars I gave you about the book? Old Franco's librarian—he'll see you get it."

"And Beltane's weekend visits to town were on account of his mother. For the past two years she's been an inmate of a private nursing home for mental diseases in Highgate. He spends the prescribed hours of every Sunday afternoon with her, and as that's his main purpose in running up to London he never leaves Witley earlier than Saturday. Only his natural reticence on the subject ever provoked curiosity."

Pardoe was in the commissioner's room at New Scotland Yard. With them was Mr. Norris, the assistant commissioner who had witnessed the exhumation of Humphrey Vick's body.

Sir John Barty bent on Pardoe the slow, attentive gaze that nothing was quick enough to get by, then transferred it to the little heap of books the inspector had brought in with him and laid on the table. One of them was a thick notebook in stiff red covers, familiar to Pardoe and Salt, another *The Complete Works of William Shakespeare* and the third, almost wholly hidden by its companions, a small, slender book of a lightish-brown color.

"Reticence, yes," the commissioner said thoughtfully. "The case has been marked by it all through, from Humphrey Vick's failure to denounce his blackmailer to young Mitfold's extraordinary withholding of information."

"And still more extraordinary ambiguity in his diary," added Mr. Norris dolefully. "Those dual references, where he refers to the murderer by his familiar name and then as C. on the self-same page—C., as I understand you to say, being Crake—why, a clever counsel would pull the thing to rags on that account alone and get a stolid, look-before-you-leap British jury so damned muddled they'd feel in duty bound to reject the thing as evidence."

"Agreed, sir," Pardoe rejoined. "But the prosecution won't be basing its charges on the diary. The diary is again and again confirmation of independent evidence. There's Philip Beltane's testimony—the initial charge is the attempt to murder him—corroborated by the Banklow station officials and the traceable phone calls. There's the evidence of the proprietor of the 'Pied Monkey' in Old Compton Street, who recognizes the American photographs of Humphrey Vick as those of the man who regularly attended the club throughout the spring to play *chemin-de-fer* in its cellars, and less frequently in the summer, and was known to associate with the spotted crake. There's—"

He broke off as he noticed the commissioner had something to say.

"Oh, nothing much," Sir John remarked. "I was about to ask if that was the only entry and exit to the gambling rooms discovered in last night's raid?"

"The one behind the smaller bar, sir? No, there's a second in the spieler itself, a door leading to a perfectly innocent wine cellar and thence up steps to a narrow alley—a mere thread of a place sneaking between the 'Pied Monkey' and a block of warehouses and offices. The place is a warren. But that way's an exit only, for the small hours. The club's been watched since Wednesday night, after our chance visit to the Juniper, and the alley departures duly noted. The way in, of course, was invariably by that smart contrivance at the back of the bar worked only by the foot of the barman, a trap door to the cellar steps behind a curtain that apparently concealed nothing but an alcove. Nobody was admitted who hadn't exchanged the password with the chucker-out."

The A.C. wore an anxious look that had become his habitual expression since his experience at Hammer Street.

"You're not expecting difficulty over the arrest, Pardoe?"

"There's none anticipated, sir. We've a man watching each place. Salt and Low are fetching him in any time now, on the Witley charge, as I said. That's good enough to start with."

"And the other fellow?"

"That should be easy once we've got the crake."

The commissioner broke in. "You were reviewing the evidence for the murders?"

"Vick's first, sir. Apart from knowing, as we now do, that the 'Pied Monkey' was the blackmailer's happy hunting ground—getting other victims' evidence will be a slow job, but it's coming in—there are the checks Vick drew to self, amounts which fairly coincide with irregular cash payments made by the crake in to his own account. Some of the money he kept in hand and spent as he went along—but the paid-in sums throughout the summer invariably occur *after* the dates Vick's checks were drawn. What's more, the money that passed through his hands is altogether incompatible with what we know to have been the decline in his own ostensible source of income. And as soon as he'd found a more lucrative one in blackmail he didn't really care how badly the other went to pieces."

"A mistake," said Sir John with severe detachment. "A tidy craftsman would have gone on attending assiduously to his job whether or not it had ceased to be profitable."

"There wasn't much he fell down over, sir," Pardoe said ruefully. "We'll allow him that. But it made me think—glaring neglect contrasting so sharply with a flow of 'easy money' from somewhere that set people talking. No murderer can afford to provoke speculation about the most trivial of his affairs, and the getting of one's living isn't trivial."

He added: "So, though far from sure, I had the right man in mind early. After that other things fitted. Our Mulberry Fountain murderer had to be a man familiar with the run of the house—he went straight to Archy's room in the dark for the rope. Then, he had to know Archy's birthday. Wynkerrell could answer both requirements."

"So could Speyer," was the A.C.'s shrewd comment.

"I know, sir. And he was under suspicion too. His case demanded especially unprejudiced consideration at a time like this. And it seemed to me that if Speyer was our man, Mitfold's behavior the night of the twenty-fifth needed a lot of explaining."

"You're suggesting," said Sir John, "that he wouldn't have gone on to the tutorial?"

"Well, no—not exactly that, sir. I think perhaps he might have gone on to Rossetti Terrace, if only to confirm his suspicions by Speyer's absence. What seems absolutely redundant to me is the phone call next morning, recorded in the diary. Since he actually talked about his mistake to Speyer that night he was prepared for the professor to know the identity of the intruder to the empty house. Therefore an anonymous call next day is a stupid move, because pointless. But that phone call is the *only* intimation Wynkerrell ever gets about the Hammer Street episode."

"It's a good point," Sir John observed. "So was the interpretation you put upon Mitfold's remark that his aunt knew nothing of the attempts on his life."

"It was the crux of the problem, don't you think, sir? And Wynkerrell inadvertently gave it the importance I attached to it as early as last Monday. He reminded me of it as I was parting from him at the shop door—it was much on his mind, of course, because he wanted to reassure himself that what he was really convinced of was true: that Miss Leaf didn't know. If Archy had lied to him and had actually confided in his aunt, then the game was up, for it would never have occurred to him that his own name had after all been with-held from her. Then when I went straight from the Juniper to the meeting and interview with Miss Leaf and found she knew more than anybody else of the murderer's methods, I had to ask myself why Archy Mitfold had told an apparently superfluous lie."

"Which he confined to two people."

"Yes. I went to Witley on Tuesday where Beltane told me the same story. Nobody else suggested Miss Leaf's ignorance of the affair. So why should Mitfold have emphasized it on Saturday when he was being so frank with his friends? There was only one answer—an answer to which the diary gives admirable support—he feared for his aunt's safety if he told the truth. Obvi-ously, she too would be marked down by the murderer if she were known to share his knowledge."

"This frankness with Beltane and Wynkerrell," Mr. Norris put in, "within limits, one ought to add, I suppose?"

"Yes sir. In the first place, on Beltane's own testimony. He has said how impressed he was with the idea that Archy was keeping something up his sleeve. Of course he was—something far more sinister than the innocent Beltane suspected. He was keeping up there the name of his would-be mur-derer and, incidentally, the whole of the Hammer Street episode."

"Is it quite clear why he ever told the incomplete story to those two?"

"We can see why now, sir. In a sense it was a sprat to catch a mackerel. There was the very good chance of the murderer, in the presence of a wit-ness, letting slip something that would betray him. That he didn't is no reflec-tion on Mitfold's judgment, but only further proof of Wynkerrell's cool nerves. And the Old Boys' reunion was a fine opportunity to get the three of them together without apparent design."

The commissioner agreed. "I note that Beltane recalls one or two occa-sions that afternoon when Wynkerrell skilfully turned the conversation."

"Oh yes. At the point, for instance, where they were discussing the Sloane Square episode, he seized on the bit about the woman close behind Mitfold with the implication that she was responsible for the attack. The diary breaks off at just that point. Then again, it seems he was anxious to avoid a serious discussion of the motive for attempting to kill Mitfold. In the end when Beltane insisted on returning to it Wynkerrell jumped to his feet and hustled Archy away.

"It was after that that he had to strike quickly. The question of calling us in had been mooted and, though repudiated by Mitfold, was definitely on the cards. Wynkerrell had been obliged to throw in his weight with Beltane and urge Archy to do so, and he dared not act on the assumption that Archy wouldn't."

"His alibi for the Saturday night isn't finally broken, eh?"

"Pretty well cracked, sir," Pardoe said cheerfully. "We guarantee it won't

survive the arrest this afternoon of Mr. Leofric Williams on the blackmail
charge. He's a weak joint in the harness. Some policeman's providence it
must have been made Salt and me too early for the pictures on Wednesday and
took us round to the Juniper and a back view of Wynkerrell's partner. As soon
as I'd addressed him incorrectly I saw it wasn't Wynkerrell. Then something
clicked in my memory—that moving backward to look at the bookshop window. Mrs. James reported the little run Wynkerrell had taken backward to the
door when she was going on at him to tune down—a most unnatural perfor-
mance in the circumstances, but not if he was intent on keeping his face
hidden. You'll remember he never spoke at all, only whistled derisively at her
sister. And what simpler to complete the impression of Wynkerrell than to be
in Wynkerrell's flat at night, wearing Wynkerrell's slippers and Wynkerrell's
familiar dressing gown?"

They agreed, though the A.C. felt bound to point out that if, as seemed
evident, Mitfold's murderer had been unprepared at the last for committing
the deed at Mulberry Fountain, it was something of a puzzle how he had
arranged the alibi with Williams' help.

Pardoe frankly admitted it. "If we'd inferred that he planned to kill him at
that place, at that hour, by that method, Williams' part in it would be easily
explained. But every other factor in the murder points to its being done on the
spur of the moment. Therefore our only alternative is that he held some sort of
communication with Williams after visiting the Eaton Terrace library—he went
there right enough—and spotting the light in Miss Leaf's house when he was
sneaking round Mulberry Fountain on his way back. The telephone seems the
answer to that."

"You know, Pardoe," Sir John Barty interrupted with a twinkle, "I'm giving
only half my mind to your present discourse. The other half's on Norris'
roving eye. He can't persuade it to keep off those books you've tantalizingly
dumped under our noses. Don't keep us guessing any longer—we're both
childish on the subject."

Pardoe and the A.C. laughed.

"Well, most of their revelations you've already seen in the report, sir. I
really brought them in because with regard to Shakespeare the report does no
more than quote Mitfold's own brief references made in the diary. As one of
the two is unfamiliar I thought a look at the line itself would be interesting. As
for the smallest book, *that* contains, as you know already, the secret of the
whole affair."

He picked up the diary, turning its leaves, and smiled at a sudden recollection.

"A hint I threw out as to why Mitfold left this at home and had to return
there to write it up, unintentionally gave Salt the notion that the guilty parties
were at Alma Square. But their guilt seems to have been Paul Pry's, no more.
. . . Well, sir, here it is."

He turned the book round to the commissioner and put his finger on the open page. Norris bent over it too.

"The entry for September 25, the crucial day in the Vick- Mitfold affair. In the morning Mitfold visits the Juniper. Wynkerrell has the window out and is redressing it in the style Salt and I noticed at our first call. Mitfold—there were plenty others like him—wondered how a living was squeezed out of that lethargic business. He asks him how he got his bread-and-butter. And Wynkerrell replies with the words of Macduff's son to his mother when she inquires how he'll live, his father being gone, 'As birds do, Mother'—at which Archy laughs immoderately. Why? Because Wynkerrell was quite unconscious of the aptness of his answer. He didn't know he was the spotted crake."

"And then Mitfold gave him a *Titus Andronicus* line he didn't recognize?"

"Here it is, sir," Pardoe said, picking up the Shakespeare and turning to the end of the second scene in Act IV, 'I'll make you feed on berries and on roots'—of small importance, one might have said from our point of view, but for the fact that Mitfold accompanied the remark by a gesture illustrating it. We know that Wynkerrell had decorated his window that morning with an imitation branch of the juniper tree, a handsome, showy affair that reminded Archy on a later visit of Juniper Hill on the North Downs. The berries were little compressed balls of suede or a similar substance wired on the bough, and when Salt and I called on Monday we saw that some of them had dropped off and were scattered on the floor of the window. It was one of those berries I found at the edge of the linoleum in Hammer Street, a second in the grave. Wynkerrell probably recovered a few from the floor of the shop and slipped them in a pocket. Two fell out in the house in Hammer Street, the one at the top of the stairs perhaps when he took out his handkerchief or something like that."

"And here," said the commissioner, drawing out the third book from beneath the diary and handing it to Pardoe, "is, I presume, our bird himself."

Norris read the title, *British Nesting Birds*, and looked at the picture on the front cover, a tangled hedgerow with a bird hovering above its nest and a weasel streaking along a bough. As Pardoe ran his fingers through the pages they caught glimpses of illustrations in color and line.

The inspector turned up the index. "Beltane made one or two bad shots in the nature section in the library, then found him first go in this little book. It's by Percival Westell, and treats comprehensively of every bird that nests in Britain. See— 'Wynkerrell,' and the reference to page 28. When you look for him there you've got 'Crake, spotted,' and below a list of the bird's local names—they're half the charm of the book—of which 'Wynkerrell' occurs at the end. Something interesting there besides—you'll notice the first of the nicknames given for this crake is 'Lacky Mo.' Now, Beltane told me that in their schooldays Archy called Wynkerrell that for a whole term, nobody knew why. The other kids said he meant Ikey Mo. So that Beltane, without either of us knowing it, had already told me who the crake was."

"Just so. It's been a case in which people with the knowledge either didn't know they had it or refused to part with it in time."

"When Speyer took his mysterious walk past the house in Hammer Street on Thursday morning," said the A.C., "are we really to infer he knew the police had an eye on the place and was simply putting across a bad joke at considerable risk to himself?"

"Not at all," Pardoe said. "I had a talk with the professor this morning before going in to Banklow. He did the perfectly natural thing—after we'd left him got to work on the subject of the empty house and the hammer drawing, and arrived at the same conclusion as we did. When Salt saw him go by the place the reason he didn't stop or linger was for fear of drawing attention to himself."

There was a knock at the door. To the commissioner's "Come in," Salt entered, breathing heavily and squeezing the fingers of his right hand with his left.

"We've pulled 'em in, sir," he broke out hoarsely, and filled his lungs afresh.

"Both?"

"Yes sir. The shop's been locked since the middle of the morning, but under observation since Wynkerrell left it for Grail Street in case either of 'em went back. Williams never showed up at all, but we kept our man at his York Terrace digs, who tipped us 'e hadn't been out since brekfus' when he bought a *Daily Call* that's splashed the diary find across the front page an' left Beltane out of it——"

"Good egg," said the A.C. "That's your work, eh, Inspector?"

"The idea was, sir," Pardoe said, "that while we didn't want 'em to hear Beltane's condition was no longer critical, it would be a good thing if they could know the police had unearthed Mitfold's diary—no hint at the contents, of course. Give 'em a jolt. When jolts are delivered other things usually follow."

"They did," said Salt with grim excitement. "Williams was packing 'is bag when we nabbed 'em. He crumpled up like a bust eggshell—excuse me, sir. King's Evidence will be his little game if I know me man."

"What have you done to your hand?" the commissioner asked.

"Burnt it, sir. Nothing much more than a smart, though. We took Wynkerrell in his flat in Grail Street. He was in the bedroom. Took it quiet enough, or seemed to, and said nothing incriminating. We didn't fetch the bracelets out. He asked if he could go into the sitting room an' ring up a fellow who was coming round on book business in an hour's time. Said no, 'e couldn't telephone, but Superintendent Low should do it if he'd give 'em the number. So we all went into the front room where there was a nice coal fire an' Wynkerrell moved toward the phone on his desk makin' believe to look up the number, the super with 'im, an' all in a jiffy dragged out a drawer and made a snatch at what was inside. It was a gun—a Colt. I guess we was to be put to bye-bye an' there'd be p'raps one for hisself after. The super pitched into 'im sideways an' nearly bowled 'im over while I grabbed the gun. Beckett come running in from the hall, an' blimey, if Wynkerrell hadn't lunged at the table with the super 'anging onto 'im an' swept off a dozen sheets of writing paper an' flung 'em on the fire. Then between 'em the superintendent an' Beckett got the bracelets on 'im while I was doin' me second snatch." Salt shook his head. "He knew what 'e was about, though, an' it blazed up into a fine howdy-do in two ticks. I saved this much, sir—an' some blackened pieces as are not readable we brought in too."

He drew from his pocket an official envelope in which had been placed the folded pieces of charred paper.

Pardoe put out his hands and received tenderly all that remained legible of Tony Wynkerrell's confession.

FRAGMENT

. . . watching each bolt hole. If they're waiting for me to give Luff Williams a call and putting off the arrest till they've tapped it, their luck's out. I'm not such an oaf. I hope Williams isn't either, for all he took the mealy mouthed Yard fellow for one of our pay-up mugs. I mean to take another way out . . .

. . . not have it recorded that it was my own stupidity tripped me at last. It wasn't. The gun in the drawer for me, and this to establish that damned bad luck and not my carelessness or official acumen pricked the bubble. I don't even blame myself for ignoring Mitfold's inquisitiveness as a kid, and that lust for hoarding the results of it. How could I have foreseen that his upbringing in Westmorland and interest in its blasted birds was a potential danger to me? Or that my choice of 8 Hammer Street because it was close to Carlyle Square was to be my undoing through Speyer's moving house only a couple of weeks after my decision was taken? Or that Mitfold kept a diary and . . .

. . . old mobsters can't afford to babble in their cups, or get an itch for the spielers, or lead a double life. That tickles my sense of humor—the wicked Humphrey's escape to the bondage of a gentleman and then the periodic revulsion of feeling and yearning to escape from it for an hour or two. Not permanently. Like the rest of us he wanted to eat his cake and have it. The fool. What easy game he was. *Sir* Sampson Vick. He dared not let it go. Come to think of it, I suppose it was a step up from the Backer's service and the attentions of the G-men. Funny—in the risible sense, I mean—to think I bled him for months not on the threat of publicly dropping hints of his identity, but only of telling his wife . . .

. . . that killing him was imperative. It went against the grain because his death meant a substantial reduction of income for me. But he wasn't the only one paying for his pleasures. He'd screwed his courage to the sticking place, and if he was going to shoot his mouth about the way the world owes me a living, he'd put heart into the small fry. I would rather go this way than get seven years in . . .

. . . and thought Vick was trying to pull a trick on me about the door opening, or I would have killed him elsewhere and not that night . . . with the crowbar while he was looking up the stairs at Williams coming down. A nice economy of instrument. I hadn't bargained for so much blood. It seems as if we spent half the night washing it out. But, disposal of the body being the first imperative, we had let it lie too long . . .

. . . and though the elimination of Mitfold and, ultimately, Beltane was forced upon me, let it be noted I felt no repugnance whatever in carrying either out. The lack of motivation of the murderers in *Rope* has always appeared to me admirable. To paraphrase an old cry, murder (where possible) should be for art's sake. None of mine were. That, however, was my misfortune, not my fault. I could so willingly at a less urgent time have tried my hand on an artistic one on either the pestering Mitfold or the intolerably pi Beltane. Instead of that I was outrageously hustled, especially over Beltane. I wanted it to be taken for suicide. That's why I didn't hit as hard as I . . .

. . . was wasp poison I got the week in July I holidayed in the New Forest. It is expedient to keep such things in hand, and introducing it to the chocolates and inserting a greeting card sent to me on my own birthday was as much child's play as . . .

. . . How could the fool think he had hoodwinked me with that absurdly gruff voice on the telephone? I knew Mitfold's methods, I knew where Speyer had been living for a week, it was a Monday and infernally dark, and a little deductive work did the rest. I adopted his pseudonym, "A Friend," and tacked it onto those letters I sent. They were of small account, as it happened, but they amused me and served to introduce Humphrey into Sampson's case. A polish here and there appeals . . .

. . . but had satisfied myself he really was at the Pells and if, as I supposed, his aunt was genuinely absent, here was the opportunity I had never dared hope for. "A far, far better thing" than my plan to examine the outside of the premises while the family was away with the idea of bringing off a fourth, and successful, attempt on him. There was at least the very good chance I should need an alibi for the next hour or so. Williams has a key to this place. I've no secrets here, and it's an arrangement that has had its conveniences. I rang him up from a call box in Hospital Road and gave concise instructions, omitting Mitfold's name and my own whereabouts. The simple thing was to tell him to do what I was going to do myself that night, listen in to the radio play. It was then nine-forty. I . . .

. . . turned out the electric fire as well as the light. I had seen the gleam, so might others. I preferred for him to be discovered later. I didn't care whether it was taken for suicide or not, as in any case Beltane's testimony to the conversation of the afternoon would be dug out and would point to murder. It wasn't pleasant, nothing hugger-mugger is, first talking to him, then killing him because I *dared* not put it off any longer after what he said. How ironical, too, that he didn't know positively that Vick was dead and I responsible, and that, with murder in my mind, my first blow after all should be struck in self-defense when his nerves had got the better of him and he hit out. The fender did the rest. And all the time that ghostly light was still showing. Luckily the blind alley must have been pretty well deserted, but I didn't feel I'd pulled it off till I switched off the lights and waited a little before leaving by the basement door with the key I took from Mitfold. Even then, finding the bolt of the tradesman's gate squeaked . . .

. . . one regret is I shall never know what Mitfold wrote in his diary . . .

. . . I maintain the Vick murder was neat, and could have been watertight. It was only a string of devilish bad luck . . .

The commissioner nodded gravely as the last scorched sheet crumbled a little in Pardoe's hand.

"They all think so. Queer, eh? Even this one toes the line with the rest of them."

"More closely than the rest, I fancy," said the A.C. "Gad, the egotism—and gloating. The—the appetite for it all."

"And the overweening desire to tell the world," said Sir John Barty, "even to the extent of frustrating his own schemes, lest it fail to credit him with enough. He *could* have perfected these murders, if circumstances hadn't forced the pace. Too bad if we overlooked it. Well, all to the good from our point of view. Judging by the amount burnt, he must have detailed minutely his preliminary dealings with Vick as well as each attempt on young Mitfold. But there's enough as it stands. . . . What are you thinking about, Inspector?"

Pardoe relaxed. "Did I look vindictive? I was remembering what he said to me to excuse a flippancy he meant to exhibit—'I didn't come upon him dead as you did.' "

THE END

About the Rue Morgue Press

"Rue Morgue Press is the old-mystery lover's best friend, reprinting high quality books from the 1930s and '40s."
—*Ellery Queen's Mystery Magazine*

Since 1997, the Rue Morgue Press has reprinted scores of traditional mysteries, the kind of books that were the hallmark of the Golden Age of detective fiction. Authors reprinted or to be reprinted by the Rue Morgue include Dorothy Bowers, Joanna Cannan, Glyn Carr, Torrey Chanslor, Clyde B. Clason, Joan Coggin, Manning Coles, Lucy Cores, Frances Crane, Norbert Davis, Elizabeth Dean, Constance & Gwenyth Little, Marlys Millhiser, James Norman, Stuart Palmer, Craig Rice, Kelley Roos, Charlotte Murray Russell, Maureen Sarsfield, and Juanita Sheridan.

If you enjoyed *Deed Without a Name*, ask your bookseller about its two predecessors, *Postscript to Poison* (0-915230-77-1, $14.95) and *Shadows Before* (0-915230-81-X, $14.95). The Rue Morgue Press intends to publish all five of Bowers' books. For information on The Rue Morgue Press, turn the page.

To suggest titles or to receive a catalog of Rue Morgue Press books write P.O. Box 4119, Boulder, CO 80306, telephone 800-699-6214, or check out our website, www.ruemorguepress.com, which lists complete descriptions of all of our titles, along with lengthy biographies of our writers.